Diana Palmer is legendary for her
unforgettable tales about those long, lean,
oh-so-lovable Long, Tall Texans

THE HEART-STOPPINGLY HANDSOME MEN OF JACOBSVILLE, TEXAS

Diana PALMER

Long, Tall TEXANS

EMMETT, REGAN & BURKE

V™ *Silhouette® Books*

Published by Silhouette Books
America's Publisher of Contemporary Romance

SILHOUETTE BOOKS

LONG, TALL TEXANS

Copyright © 2001 by Harlequin Books S.A.

ISBN 0-373-48428-3

The publisher acknowledges the copyright holder of the individual works as follows:

EMMETT
Copyright © 1993 by Diana Palmer

REGAN'S PRIDE
Copyright © 1994 by Diana Palmer

THAT BURKE MAN
Copyright © 1995 by Diana Palmer

This edition published by arrangement with Harlequin Books S.A.

® and TM are trademarks of Harlequin Books S.A., used under license. Trademarks indicated with ® are registered in the United States Patent and Trademark Office, the Canadian Trade Marks Office and in other countries.

Visit Silhouette at www.eHarlequin.com

Printed in U.S.A.

CONTENTS

Dear Reader,

I hope you enjoy the rereleases of these Long, Tall Texan books. After *That Burke Man* was published, my wonderful editors at Silhouette Books sent me the original painting that was on the cover. I have it, framed, on the wall beside my desk, and I still think it's one of the most beautiful ones I've ever had. Todd Burke was a fun subject, because he, like many of my heroes, was not what he appeared to be on the surface. I do enjoy a surprise. I hope you do, too, if you haven't read this book before.

Regan's Pride was demanding and hard work, because it had a dark subplot and some explosive emotional scenes. Some characters are hard to let go of after the book is finished. Ted and Coreen really were.

Emmett...ah, Emmett! If you don't know it by now, I love kids. I have only one of my own, but I'd have loved a houseful. These three tigers of Emmett's were a hoot, even for me. James would come into the office from time to time to find out why I was splitting my sides laughing. I don't know where these scenes come from, because they're a surprise to me even while I'm writing them, but I enjoyed this book more than just about anything that came before it.

Thanks so much for your support and kindness over the years. I really enjoy your letters—even if it does seem to take forever to get an answer from me!

Love,

Diana Palmer

EMMETT

For Peggy in North Carolina, with much love!

Chapter 1

The office was in chaos. Melody Cartman eyed the window ledge with keen speculation and wondered if standing out there might get her a few minutes' reprieve. She glanced toward her newly married third cousin, Logan Deverell, and his beaming wife, Kit, and decided that she couldn't spoil their honeymoon.

"You'll cope," Kit promised in a whisper. "Just tell everyone he'll be back in touch with them next week and that Tom Walker is handling all his accounts until he returns."

"Has he told Mr. Walker that?" Melody asked, acutely aware of Mr. Walker's temper. Tom had started out in New York City, but circumstances had brought him to Houston. Texas, he'd once said, reminded him a little of his native South Dakota. Melody had often wondered if he'd been brought up by a mountain lion there, because on occasion he could give a pretty good imitation of one.

"Honest." Kit put her hand over her heart. "I swear Logan spoke to him first this time. I heard him with my own ears.''

''That's all right then. Honestly he seemed like such a nice man when I first met him. But I took him that client of Mr. Deverell's and found him involved in giving another client the bum's rush out the door. Our client and the other client both ran for it, and I was left to face the music. He never used a bad word or the same word twice, but I was three inches shorter when I escaped from his office.''

''Logan is your third cousin. Can't you call him Logan?''

Melody glanced toward the big, dark man on the telephone in his office. ''Not without a head start,'' she said finally.

''Anyway, he didn't volunteer Tom without mentioning it to him this time, so you won't get your ears burned. Think you can handle everything for a week?''

''If I can't cope by now, I'll never be able to,'' Melody said, and her brave smile made her look almost pretty. She was a tall woman, very country-looking in some ways, with freckles and a softly rounded face that was framed by long, blond-streaked light brown hair. Her eyes were brown, with tiny flecks of gold in them. If she took the time, she could look very attractive, Kit thought. But Melody wore jumpers with long-sleeved blouses, or tailored suits, and always in colors that were much better suited to the coloring of someone with dark hair and an equally dark complexion.

''You'd like Tom if you got to know him,'' Kit told her. ''He knocked that man out the door for some pretty blatant sexual harassment of his secretary. He's only bad tempered when he needs to be, and he's all alone except for a married sister back home and a nephew. He doesn't even go out with women.''

''I can see why…!''

''Not nice,'' Kit chided. ''He's a good-looking, intelligent man, and he's rich.''

''I can think of at least one ax murderer with the same

description. I read about him in there.'' She gestured toward one of the supermarket tabloids.

Kit's eyes fell to the tabloid on Melody's desk, its cover carrying color photos of a particularly gruesome murder. ''Do you actually read this stuff?'' Kit asked with a grimace. ''These photos are terrible!''

''I thought you were a detective,'' Melody said. ''Aren't detectives supposed to be used to stuff like that?''

Kit smiled sheepishly. ''Well, I don't detect *those* sort of cases.''

''I don't blame you. Actually I didn't buy it for the grisly pictures. I bought it for this nifty reducing diet. Doesn't it look interesting? You don't give up any foods, you simply cut down and cut out sweets.''

''You aren't fat, Melody,'' the other woman pointed out.

''No, I'm just big. I do wish I were slender and willowy,'' she said wistfully.

''There isn't a thing wrong with the way you are.''

''That's what you think! Actually I—''

A sudden commotion in the hall cut her off. She and Kit turned just as Emmett Deverell and his three children walked in. The kids were wearing costumes left over from their Thanksgiving Day play last month—Indian costumes. These were pretty authentic and she wouldn't really put it past the trio to barbecue somebody over hot coals.

Guy, the eldest, stood beside his father and glared at Melody. But Amy and Polk, the younger kids, made a beeline for their favorite person in the office.

''Hi, Kit!'' they said in unison. ''Hello, Melody. Can we sit and watch TV with you for a while?''

''Please?'' Amy ventured, looking up at Melody with eyes that were the same shade of green as her father's. ''We'll be ever so good. Emmett has to get our airplane tickets and Polk and I don't want to go to the airport. We got to be in the parade in the rodeo!''

"You all look very nice," Melody told them.

Guy ignored her.

Polk had already turned on the TV and was staring at the screen. "Aw, gee, Big Bird isn't on right now, Amy," he said miserably.

Melody glanced at the kids, noticing again how much they all favored their father. Guy came closest. He was tall, too, with a lean face and dark hair. Amy looked a lot like her mother, Adell, except for those green eyes. All the kids had them.

The last time Emmett had been in the office, he'd savaged Melody. The San Antonio rancher hated her and made no secret of the fact. He didn't approve of her working for Logan, who was a relative of his as well, but by blood, not marriage, as Melody was. Melody had had several days to remember and burn over his attitude. She was through being intimidated by him. He might be almost a generation older than she was, but he wasn't going to walk on her feelings anymore.

"Amy and Polk want to stay with you while I go to the airport," Emmett said icily. He didn't mention leaving Guy, because Guy disliked Melody as much as Emmett did.

Melody cocked an eyebrow, and tried to stay calm. She was melting with fear inside, but she wasn't going to let him know it. "Am I being asked?" she replied formally.

Emmett's pale green eyes glittered at her. "Yes, if you want the whole ten yards."

"In that case, Amy and Polk are welcome to watch TV while you're gone," she said, triumphant with her small victory.

Emmett didn't like the challenge in her dark eyes, or that tiny smirk. If those kids hadn't been giving him hell all morning, he wouldn't even be here. He was surly with bad temper.

"You won't help them run away or anything?" he asked,

with a sarcastic, pointed reference to her part in his ex-wife Adell's sudden departure with Melody's brother, Randy.

He wasn't going to do that to her, she promised herself. She wasn't going to let him play on her conscience. Her eyes settled on the tabloid and it triggered a memory; something Kit had elaborated on since her return from Emmett's house in San Antonio. She smiled sweetly and picked up the tabloid. "Have you seen the latest on that ax murder, Mr. Deverell?" she asked, and stuck the gory front page under his arrogant nose.

He turned green instantly. "Damn you...!" He choked before his mad dash to the rest room.

Melody and Polk and Amy and Kit chuckled helplessly. Guy glared at them and walked out to find his father.

"He has a stomach of glass," Melody pronounced, recalling Kit's revelations about how easily Emmett could be made ill with even talk of gory things. Amazing, for a rancher who was also something of a rodeo star. It was one of many paradoxes about Emmett that would have fascinated a less prejudiced woman. She took the paper and stuck it into her purse. She could use it as a talisman against future attack by Emmett. "Make yourselves comfortable, kids," she told Amy and Polk.

"That was a dirty trick," Kit laughed.

"He deserved it. Nasty, arrogant beast," she muttered, glaring at the door into the hall as if he were hiding there waiting to pounce. "If he can't take it, he shouldn't dish it out."

Kit was trying not to laugh too hard. Logan joined them, affectionately slipping an arm around his wife. "If we can't dish what out?"

"Melody made Emmett sick," Amy volunteered. "Look what's on educational television, Melody! It's 'Reading Rainbow'!"

"Good, good," Melody said absently.

"How did you make Emmett sick?" Logan asked curiously.

"Never mind. We women have to have our secret weapons, especially when it comes to people like your cousin Emmett," Kit told him. "Melody, I've given you a number where we can be reached if you need to contact us."

"I'll only use it if there's an emergency," Melody promised.

Kit smiled at her. "I know that."

"And don't let Tom give you fits," Logan told her. "He's not a bad man. It was my fault. I should have told him he was being volunteered to handle my clients that afternoon, but I was in a rush to get married."

"I remember." Melody chuckled. "It's okay. I'll manage."

"If you can't, you might turn those kids loose on him," Logan suggested.

"Don't give her any ideas. We have to leave, right now," Kit said mirthfully, tugging at her husband's arm. "Take care, Melody."

"Yes, and don't let my cousin walk on you," Logan added. "You're my secretary, not his paid baby-sitter. Keep that in mind."

"I will."

"So long."

They walked out the door just as a pale, subdued Emmett was coming back in with Guy at his heels.

"That wasn't fair," Guy said angrily, glaring at Melody.

"You kids did it to him," she pointed out. "Kit told me all about it."

"We're family. You're not!"

"Yes, she is," Amy argued. "She's our aunt. Isn't that right, Emmett?"

He looked even worse. "I'll be back for Amy and Polk about three o'clock," he said without answering the question.

"But isn't she our aunt?" Amy persisted.

"She's our stepaunt," Polk told her.

"Oh." She was satisfied and went back to watching TV. "Do take care of Emmett, Guy, and don't let him get run over by any buses."

"I don't need taking care of," Emmett muttered. "But she might," he added with a glare at Melody.

"Watch it," Logan advised sotto voce. "She slipped that tabloid into her purse."

"Turncoat!" Kit gasped, hitting her husband's shoulder.

"We men have to stick together," Logan told her, chuckling. "In today's world, there's nothing more endangered than a male. Any day now, the women's lib movement will start passing out hit lists and organizing death squads to wipe out men."

"Wouldn't surprise me." Emmett sighed. "The way it looks, we're evolving into an Amazon society where men will be used to procreate the species and then efficiently be put to death."

Melody eyed Emmett. "What an interesting idea."

"Shame on you!" Kit chuckled. "Honestly, the radicals just get all the publicity. Most women's libbers just want a fair shake—equal pay and equal rights. What's so terrible about that?"

"And there are men who are just as prejudiced against women." Logan drew Kit close. "Haven't you ever heard of the battle of the sexes? It's been around since time began. It's just getting better press."

"I suppose so." Melody sighed. "Maybe men aren't endangered after all."

"Thank you," Emmett said tersely. "I'm glad to know that I won't have to stand guard at my front door to ward off women death squads."

"Oh, I wouldn't go that far," Melody advised.

"Wouldn't you?" Emmett muttered. "And I thought you were a little shrinking violet."

"More like a Venus flytrap, actually," she replied brightly. "I thought you were going to the airport to get tickets *home?*"

"Notice how much enthusiasm she put into that question?" Logan asked with pure relish. "And you said women wouldn't leave you alone. This must be refreshing for you."

Emmett didn't look refreshed. He looked as if he might explode momentarily. "Let's go, Guy. Have a nice honeymoon, you two," he added to Logan and Kit. "I don't think much of marriage, but good luck anyway."

"Our mama ran off and left him," Amy volunteered. "Emmett doesn't want to marry anybody."

"But he must," Polk said with a serious frown. "Isn't he always bringing those real glittery, pretty ladies home?"

"Don't be silly," Guy said urbanely. "Those are good-time girls. You don't marry them."

"What's a good-time girl?" Amy asked.

"Just the same as a good-time boy, only shorter," Melody said with icy delight, and she smiled at Emmett.

He went two shades darker.

"Time to go," Kit said quickly. "Emmett, can we give you a lift? We're going straight to the airport."

"Yes," Logan said, taking his tall cousin's muscular arm in a big hand. "Come along, Guy. See you in a week, Melody. If you have any problems, call me. And if you could check on Tansy in the hospital, I'd appreciate it. Chris is watching out for her, but you can't have too many observers where my mother is concerned."

"Certainly I will," Melody agreed. "I don't have much to do in the evenings, anyway."

"I didn't think there would be a man that brave," Emmett agreed.

Melody reached for her purse. Emmett spared her a glance

that promised retribution before he made a quick exit with the others.

The chaos began to calm with Logan's exit. The telephones rang for an hour or two. After that, there were only a few calls and two clients who came in person to ask about their investments. Melody had the figures. It was only a matter of pulling them up—her boss had given her permission before he left—and showing them to the visitors.

The kids were amazingly good. They watched educational programming without a peep, except to ask for change for the soft drink machine. Melody gave it to them and then listened worriedly for sounds of the machine being mugged. Fortunately there was no such noise, and she settled down to the first peace she'd had all day.

She managed to clear her desk of work before Emmett showed up, late, to pick up the kids.

"Aw, do we have to go?" Polk groaned. "Mr. Rogers is coming on!"

"Yes, we have to go. We're leaving for home in the morning, thank God. Only one more event to go tonight—bareback bronc riding."

"Isn't that one of the most dangerous events?" Melody asked.

His eyebrows arched under the wide-brimmed Stetson he hadn't bothered to remove from his dark hair. "Any rodeo event is dangerous if a contestant is stupid or careless. I'm neither."

She knew that already. He was something of a legend in rodeo. He wouldn't be aware that she'd followed his career. She was a rodeo fan, but Emmett's attitude toward her had kept her silent about her interest in the sport.

"Thank you for letting us stay with you, Melody," Amy said, smiling up at her.

Melody smiled back. She liked the little girl very much.

She was open and warm and loving, despite her mischievous nature.

Emmett saw that smile and felt it all the way to his toes. He couldn't have imagined even a minute before that a smile could change a plain face and make it radiate beauty. But he saw the reality of it in Melody's soft features. Involuntarily his eyes fell to her body. She was what a kind man would call voluptuous, her form and shape perfectly proportioned but just a tad past slender. Adell had been bacon-thin. Melody was her exact opposite.

It irritated him that he should notice Melody in that way. She was nothing to him except a turncoat. She and her brother had disrupted and destroyed his life. Not only his, but his children's as well. He could easily have hated her for that.

"I said, let's go," he told the children.

"Okay." Polk sighed.

"I'll wait in the hall," Guy murmured. He avoided even looking at Melody.

"Guy hates you," Amy told her with blunt honesty. "But I think you're wonderful."

"I think you're wonderful, too," Melody replied.

Amy grinned and walked up to her father. "We can go now, Emmett. Can I write to my friend Melody?"

"We'll talk about it," Emmett said noncommittally. "Thanks for watching them," he said as an afterthought.

"Oh, it was my pleasu…re!" She tripped over a tomahawk that someone had left lying on the floor and ended up on her back. Guy picked up the weapon and the kids, and Emmett, made a circle around her prone body. She glared up at them, trying not to think how a sacrificial victim in an Indian encampment might have felt. In those Indian costumes, the kids looked eerie.

"Whose tomahawk?" Emmett asked as he reached down and pulled Melody up with a minimum of strain. His hand made hers tingle. She wondered if he'd felt the excitement of the contact, too, because he certainly let go of her fast.

"It's mine, Emmett," Amy said, sighing. She looked up at him, pushing back her pigtails, and her green eyes were resigned. "Go ahead and hit me. I didn't mean to make Melody hurt herself, though. I like her."

"I know you didn't mean it," Melody said, and smiled. "It's okay, nothing dented."

"Next time, be more careful where you put that thing," Emmett muttered.

"That's right, Amy," Melody said, nodding. "Between your father's ears would be a good place."

He glared at her. "You didn't hear that, Amy. Let's go, kids."

He herded the children out the door and closed it. Melody sat by herself with no ringing phones, no blaring television, no laughing children. Her life and the office were suddenly empty.

She closed up precisely at 5:00 p.m. and went by the grocery store to get enough for the weekend, which was just beginning. Thanksgiving Day had been quiet and lonely. She'd had a turkey breast, but she and Alistair had finished it off for supper the night before. So she bought ground beef for hamburgers and a small beef roast and vegetables to make stew and, later, soup. She lived on a budget, which meant that she bypassed steak and frozen eclairs. She would have loved to indulge her taste for both. Maybe someday, she thought wistfully...

She fed Alistair, her big marmalade tabby, and then made herself a light supper. She ate it with little enthusiasm. Then she curled up with Alistair on the sofa to watch a movie on television. During the last scene, a very interesting standoff between a murderer and the police, the telephone started ringing. She grimaced, hating the interruption. If she answered it, she'd surely miss the end of the movie she'd been watching for two hours. She ignored it at first. The only people who ever telephoned her were people who were selling things. But whoever was calling wouldn't give up. It stopped, briefly, only to start ringing insistently again. This time she was afraid not to answer it. It might be Kit or Logan or Tansy or even her brother.

She picked up the receiver. "Hello?"

"Is this Miss Melody Cartman?" a crisp, professional voice asked.

"Yes."

"I'm Nurse Willoughby. We have a Mr. Emmett Deverell here at city general hospital with a massive concussion. He's only just regained consciousness. He gave us your name and asked us to call and have you pick up his children at the Mellenger Hotel."

Melody stood frozen in place. The only thing that registered was that Emmett was hurt and she'd become a babysitter. She could hardly say no or argue. Concussions were terribly dangerous.

"The children are…where?"

"At the Mellenger Hotel. Room three hundred and something. He's very foggy at the moment and in a great deal of pain."

"He will be all right?" Melody asked, hating herself for being concerned.

"We hope so," came the crisp reply.

"Tell him that I'll look after the children," she said.

"Very well."

The phone went dead before she could ask another question. She stared around her like someone in a trance. Where in the world was she going to put three renegade children, one of whom hated her? And how long was she going to have them?

For one insane moment, she thought about calling Adell

and Randy, but she dismissed that idea at once. Emmett would never forgive her. At the moment, he deserved a little consideration, she supposed.

She got her coat and took a cab to the hotel. It was very late to be driving around Houston, and her little car was unreliable in wet weather. Houston was notorious for flooding, and the rain was coming down steadily now.

She asked at the desk for Emmett's room number, quickly explaining the circumstances to a sympathetic desk clerk after giving Emmett's condition and the hospital's number, so that management could check her story if they felt the need to. In fact, they did, and she didn't blame them. These days, one simply couldn't turn over three children to a total stranger who might or might not intend them harm.

When she got to the hotel room, there were muffled sounds from within. Melody, who knew the kids all too well, knocked briefly but firmly on the door.

There was a sudden silence, followed by a scuffle and a wail. The door flew open and a matronly lady with frazzled hair almost fell on Melody with relief.

"Are you their mother?" the elderly woman asked. "I'm Mrs. Johnson. Here they are, safe and sound, my fee will be added to the hotel bill. You *are* their mother?"

"Well, no," she began.

"Oh, my God!"

"I'm to take charge of them," Melody added, because it looked as if the woman might be preparing to have a heart attack on the spot.

A wavery smile replaced the horror on the woman's lined face. "Then I'll just be off. Good night!"

"Chicken," Amy muttered, peering around Melody to watch the woman's incredibly fast retreat.

"What have you three been up to?" Melody asked, glaring at them.

"Nothing at all, Melody, dear," Amy said sweetly, and grinned.

"She just wasn't used to kids, I guess," Polk added. He grinned, too.

Behind them there were the remains of two foam-filled pillows and what appeared to be the ropes that closed the heavy curtains.

"We had a pillow fight," Amy explained.

"And then we went skiing in the bathroom," Polk said.

Melody could barely see the bathroom. The door was ajar and the floor seemed to be soaked. She was beginning to understand her predecessor's agile retreat. Days and days...of this. She wouldn't have an apartment left! And all because she felt sorry for a man who had to be her worst enemy.

"Why are you here?" Guy asked belligerently. "Where's Dad?"

That brought her back to her original purpose for being there. Emmett's accident.

She sat down on the sofa, tossing her purse beside her, while she struggled to find the right words to tell them.

"Something's happened," Guy said when he saw her face. He stiffened. "What?"

Even at such a young age, he was already showing signs of great inner strength, of ability to cope with whatever life threw at him. Amy and Polk looked suddenly vulnerable, but not Guy.

"Your father has a brain concussion," Melody told them. "He's conscious now, but in a lot of pain. He'll have to stay in the hospital for a day or so. Meanwhile, he wants you to come home with me."

"He hates you," Guy said coldly. "Why would he want us to stay with you?"

"Because I'm all you've got," Melody replied. "Unless you'd rather I called the juvenile authorities...?"

Guy's massive self-confidence failed. He shrugged and turned away.

Amy climbed onto Melody's lap and clung. "Our daddy will be all right, won't he?" she asked tearfully.

"Of course he will," Melody assured her, gathering her close. "He's very tough. It will take more than a concussion to keep him down."

"Yes, it will," Polk said. He turned away because his lower lip was trembling.

"Let's get your things together and go," Melody said. "Have you had something to eat?"

"We had pizza and chocolate sundaes."

Melody could imagine that the elderly lady in charge of them had agreed with any menu that would keep them quiet. But she'd have to get some decent food into them. That would give her something to work toward. Meanwhile, she found herself actually worrying about Emmett. The first thing she was going to do when they got to the apartment was phone the hospital and get an update. Surely Emmett was indestructible, wasn't he?

She looked at the children and felt a surge of pity for them. She knew how it felt to be alone. When their parents had died, Randy had worked at two jobs to support them, while Melody was still in school. She'd carried her share of the load, but it had been lonely for both of them. She hoped these children wouldn't have the same ordeal to face that she and Randy had.

Chapter 2

The nurse on duty in Emmett's ward told Melody that Emmett would have to be confined for at least two days. He was barely conscious, but they were cautiously optimistic about his condition.

Melody was assured that she and the children would be allowed to see him the next day, during visiting hours. In the meantime, she scoured her apartment to find enough blankets and pillows for three sleepy children. She put two of them in her bed, and one of them on a cot that had belonged to Randy when he was a boy. She slept on her own pullout sofa bed, and was delighted to find that it wasn't terribly uncomfortable.

It was fortunate that she had the weekend to look after the children. Having to juggle them, along with her job, would have been a real headache. She'd have coped. But how?

They had a change of clothing. *Getting* them to change, though, was the trick.

"This isn't dirty—" Guy indicated a shirt limp and dingy and smelly from long wear "—and I won't change it."

"I'm all right, too," Polk said, grinning at her.

"We're fine, Melody," Amy agreed. She patted the woman's hand in a most patronizing way. "Now, you just get dressed yourself and don't worry about us, all right?"

Melody counted to ten. "We're going to see your father," she said calmly. "Don't you want him to think you look nice?"

"Oh, Emmett never notices unless we go naked, Melody," Amy assured her.

"And sometimes not even then," Polk said with a chuckle. "Dad's very absentminded when he's rodeoing."

"He sure doesn't seem to notice what the three of you get up to," she said quietly.

"We like our dad just the way he is," Guy said belligerently. "Nobody bad-mouths our dad."

"I wasn't bad-mouthing him," Melody said through her teeth. "Can we just go to the hospital now?"

"Sure," Guy said, folding his thin arms over his chest. "But I'm not changing clothes."

She threw up her hands. "Oh, all right," she muttered. "Have it your way. But if your clothes set off the sprinkler system, I'm climbing into a broom closet so nobody will know who brought you."

At the hospital, Melody herded them off the elevator and down the hall to the nurses' station.

"Look at all the gadgets." Polk whistled, peering over the counter at the computers. "Wouldn't I love to play with that!"

"Bite your tongue," Melody said under her breath. She smiled at an approaching nurse. "I'm Melody Cartman. You have an Emmett Deverell on this floor with a concussion…?"

A loud roar, followed by, "You're not putting that damned thing under me!" caught their attention.

"Indeed we do," the nurse told Melody. "Are you a concerned relative anxious to transfer him to another hospital?" she added hopefully.

"I'm afraid not," Melody said. "These are his children and they want to see him very much."

"Do you have him tied up in one of those white things?" Amy asked.

"No," the nurse said with a wistful sigh. She turned. "Come on, I'll take you down to his room. Perhaps a diversion will improve his mood."

"I really wouldn't count on it," Melody replied.

"I was afraid you were going to say that. Here we are."

"Dad!" Guy exclaimed, running to his father as a practical nurse laid down a trail of fire getting out the door. "How are you?"

Emmett stared at his eldest blankly. His pale green eyes were bloodshot. His dark hair was disheveled. There was a huge bump on his forehead with stitches and red antiseptic lacing it. He was wearing a white patterned hospital gown and looking as if he'd like to eat half the staff raw.

"It's almost noon," he informed Melody. "Where in hell have you been? Get me out of here!"

"Don't worry, Dad, we'll spring you," Guy promised, with a wary glance toward the nurse.

"You can't leave today, Mr. Deverell," the young nurse said apologetically. "Dr. Miller said that you must stay for at least forty-eight hours. You've had a very severe concussion. You can't go walking around the streets like that. It's very dangerous."

Emmett glared at her. "I hate it here!"

The nurse looked as if she might bite through her tongue trying not to reply in kind. She forced a smile. "I'm sure you do. But you can't leave yet. I'll leave you to visit with your family. I'm sure you're glad to see your wife and children."

"She's not the hell my wife!" Emmett raged. "I'd rather marry a pit viper!"

''I assure you that the feeling is mutual,'' Melody said to the nurse.

The woman leaned close on her way out the door. ''Dr. Miller escaped. When he comes back, I'll beg on my knees for sedation for Mr. Deverell. I swear.''

''God bless you,'' Melody said fervently.

''What are you mumbling about?'' Emmett demanded when the nurse left. ''And why haven't these kids changed clothes? They smell of pizza and dirt!''

''They wouldn't change,'' she said defensively.

''You're bigger than they are,'' he pointed out. ''Make them.''

She glanced at the kids and shook her head. ''Not me, mister. I know when I'm outnumbered. I'm not going to end my days tied to a post imitating barbecue.''

''They don't burn people at the stake,'' he said with exaggerated patience. ''That was just gossip about that lady motorist they kidnapped.''

''That's right,'' Polk said. ''Gossip.''

''Anyway, she got loose before she was very singed.'' Amy sighed.

Melody gave Emmett a speaking look. It was totally wasted.

''Are you really okay?'' Guy asked his father. He, of the three children, was the most worried. He was the oldest. He understood better than they did how serious his father's injury could have been.

''I'm okay,'' Emmett said. His voice was different when he spoke to the children; it was softer, more tender. He smiled at Guy and Melody couldn't remember ever being on the receiving end of such a smile. ''How about you kids?''

''We're fine,'' Amy told him. ''Melody has a very nice apartment, Emmett. We like it there.''

''She has a cat,'' Polk added. ''He's a big orange tabby named Alistair.''

''Alistair?'' Emmett mused.

''He was a very ordinary-looking cat,'' Melody said defensively. ''The least he deserved was a nice name.''

He leaned back against his pillows and closed his eyes. "Saints deliver us."

"I don't think the saints like you very much, Mr. Deverell, on present evidence," she couldn't resist saying.

One bloodshot pale green eye opened. "The saints didn't do this to me. It was a horse. A very nasty-tempered horse whose only purpose in life is to maim poor stupid cowboys who are dim enough to get on him. I let myself get distracted and I came off like a loose hat."

She smiled gently at the description. "I'm sure the horse is crying his eyes out with guilt."

The smile changed her. He liked what he saw. She was vulnerable when her eyes twinkled like that. He opened the other eye, too, and for one long moment they just looked at each other. Melody felt warning bells go off in her head.

"When can you come home, Emmett?" Amy asked, her big eyes on her father.

He blinked and looked down at her. "Two days they said," he replied. "God, I'm sorry about this!" He glanced toward Melody. "I had no right to involve you in my problems."

That sounded like a wholesale apology. Perhaps the head injury had erased his memory so that he'd forgotten her part in Adell's escape.

"I don't mind watching the children for you," she said hesitantly. She pushed back her hair with a nervous hand. "They're no trouble."

"Of course not, they were asleep all night," he replied. "Don't let them out of your sight."

"Aw, Dad," Polk grumbled. "We'll be good."

"Sure we will," Guy said. He glanced at Melody irritably. "If we have to."

"It's only for a day or two," Emmett said. He was feeling foggier by the minute. "I'll reimburse you, of course," he told Melody. He touched his head with an unsteady hand. "God, my head hurts!"

"I guess it does," Melody said gently. She moved closer to the bed, concerned. "Shall I call the nurse?"

"They won't give me anything until the doctor authorizes it, and he's in hiding," he said. His eyes closed. "Can't say I blame him. I was pretty unhappy about being here."

"I noticed."

He managed a weak chuckle. "If Logan had been at home, you wouldn't be landed with those kids...."

He was asleep.

"Is he going to be okay?" Amy asked. She was chewing her lower lip, looking very young and worried.

Melody smoothed back her hair. "Yes, he'll be fine," she assured the girl. "Come on. We'll go home and I'll make lunch for all of you."

"I want a hot dog," Polk said. "So does Amy."

"I hate hot dogs," Guy replied. "I don't want to stay with you. I'll stay here with Dad."

"You aren't allowed to," Melody pointed out.

He took an angry breath.

"I don't like it any more than you do," she murmured. "But we're stuck with each other. We'd better go."

They followed her out, reluctantly. She stopped long enough to assure the nurse at the desk that she'd bring the kids back the next day to visit their father. She was concerned enough to ask if it was natural for Emmett to go to sleep, and was told that the doctor would check to make sure he was all right.

Guy's dislike of Melody extended to her apartment, her cat, her furniture and especially her cooking.

"I won't eat that," he said forcefully when she put hot dogs and buns and condiments on the table. "I'll starve first."

She knew that it would give him the upper hand if she stooped to arguing with him, so she didn't. "Suit yourself. But we'll have ice cream for dessert and you won't. It's a house rule that you don't get dessert if you don't eat the main course.''

"I hate ice cream," he said triumphantly.

"No, he doesn't," Amy said sadly. "He just doesn't like you. He thinks you took our mom away. She won't even write to us or talk to us on the telephone."

"That's right," Guy said angrily. "It's all because of you! Because of your stupid brother!"

He got up, knocking over his chair, and stomped off into the bathroom, slamming the door behind him.

Melody took a bite of her own hot dog, but it tasted like so much cardboard. It was going to be a long two days.

She didn't know how true her prediction was going to be. Guy sulked for the rest of the day, while she and the other two children watched television and played Monopoly on the kitchen table. While they were going past Go for the tenth time, Guy opened the apartment door and deliberately let Alistair out....

Melody didn't discover that her cat was missing until she started to put his food into his dish.

She looked around, frowning. "Alistair?" she called. The big cat was nowhere in sight. He couldn't have gone out the window. The apartment was on the fourth story and there was no balcony. She searched the apartment, including under the bed, but she couldn't find him.

"Have any of you seen my cat?" she asked.

"Not me," Amy murmured. She was watching cartoons with Polk.

"Me, neither," he said absently.

Guy was staring out the window. He jerked his head, which she assumed meant he hadn't seen the cat.

But he looked odd. She frowned. Alistair had been curled up on the couch just before Guy had stormed off into the bathroom. She hadn't seen the cat since. But surely the boy wouldn't have done something so heartless as to let the cat out. Surely he wouldn't!

Melody had found Alistair in an alley on her way home from work late one rainy afternoon last year. He'd had a string tied around his neck and was choking. She'd freed him and taken him home. He was flea-infested and pitifully thin, but a trip to the veterinarian and some healthful food had transformed him. He'd been Melody's friend and companion and confidant ever since.

Tears stung her eyes as she searched again, her voice sounding frantic as she called her pet's name with increasing urgency.

Amy got up from the carpet and followed her, frowning. "Can't you find your cat?"

"No," Melody said, her voice raspy. She brushed at a tear on her face.

"Oh, Melody, don't cry!" Amy said. She hugged her. "It will be all right! We'll find him! Polk, Guy," she called sharply. "Come on. Help us hunt for Melody's cat! She can't find him anywhere!"

"Sure," Polk said. "We'll help."

They scoured the apartment. Guy looked, too, but his cheeks were flushed and he wouldn't meet Melody's eyes.

In desperation, Melody went to the two apartments nearby to ask her neighbors if they'd seen her cat, but no one had noticed him. There was an elevator and a staircase, but there was a door that led to the stairwell and surely it would be closed...

All the same, she checked, and was disturbed to find that the stairwell door was propped open while workmen carried materials to an apartment down the hall that was being renovated.

Leaving the children in the apartment, she rushed down the steps looking for Alistair. She called and called, but there was no answer, and he was nowhere to be found.

* * *

Defeated, Melody went back to the apartment. Her expression was so morose that the children knew without asking that she hadn't found the cat.

"I'm sorry," Amy said. "I guess you love him a lot, huh?"

"He's all I have," Melody said without looking up. The pain in her voice was almost tangible. "All I...*had*."

Guy turned up the television and sat down very close to the screen. He didn't say a word.

Melody cried herself to sleep that night. Randy had Adell, but Melody had no other family. Alistair was the only real family she had left. She was so sick at heart that she didn't know how she was going to stand it. Dismal images of Alistair being run over or chased by dogs and children made her miserable.

She got up early and fixed bacon and eggs before she called the children. They were unnaturally quiet, too, and ate very little. Melody was preoccupied all through the meal. When it was over, she went outside to search some more. But Alistair was nowhere to be found.

Later, she took the kids to the hospital to see Emmett. He was sitting up in a chair looking impatient.

"Get me the hell out of here," he said immediately. "I'm leaving whether they like it or not!"

He seemed to mean it. He was fully dressed, in the jeans and shirt and boots he'd been wearing when they'd taken him to the hospital. The shirt was bloodstained but wearable. He looked pale, even if he sounded in charge of himself.

"What did the doctor say?"

"He said I could go if I insisted, and I'm insisting," Emmett said. "I'll take the kids and go back to the hotel."

Melody went closer to him, clutching her purse. "Mr. Deverell, don't you realize what a risk you'd be taking? If you won't think of yourself, do think of the kids. What will they do if anything happens to you?"

"I won't stay here!" he muttered. "They keep trying to bathe me!"

She managed a faint smile even through her misery. "It's for your own good."

"I'm leaving," he said, his flinty pale green eyes glaring straight into her dark ones.

She sighed. "Well, you can come back with us for today," she said firmly. "I can't let you stagger around Houston alone. My boss would never forgive me."

"Think so?" He narrowed one eye. "I don't need help."

"Yes, you do. One more night won't kill me, I suppose," she added.

"Her cat ran away," Amy said. "She's very sad."

Emmett scowled. "Alistair? How could he run away? Don't you live in an apartment building?"

"Yes. I... He must have gotten out the door," she said, staring down at her feet. "The stairwell door was open, where the workmen were going in and out of the building."

sorry," he said shortly. He glanced at the kids. Amy and Polk seemed very sympathetic, but Guy was surlier than ever and his lower lip was prominent. Emmett's eyes narrowed.

e you checked yourself out?" Melody asked, changing the subject to keep from bursting into tears.

"Yes." He got to his feet, a little unsteadily.

"I'll help you, Dad," Guy said. He propped up his father's side. He wouldn't look at Melody.

"Did you drive or take a cab?" he asked her.

"I drove."

"What do you drive?"

"A Volkswagen," she told him.

He groaned. She smiled for the first time that day. As tall as he was, fitting him inside her small car, even in the front seat, was going to be an interesting experience.

And it was. He had to bring his knees up almost to his chin. Polk and Amy laughed at the picture he made.

"Poor Emmett," Amy said. "You don't fit very well."

"First you shove gory pictures under my nose. Then you stuff me into a tin can with wheels," Emmett began with a meaningful glance in Melody's direction.

''Don't insult my beautiful little car. It isn't the car's fault that you're too tall,'' she reminded him as she started her car. ''And you were horrible to me. I was only getting even.''

''I am not too tall.''

''I hope you aren't going to collapse,'' she said worriedly when he leaned his head back against the seat. ''I live on the fourth floor.''

''I'm all right. I'm just groggy.''

''I hope so,'' she murmured. She put the car in gear and reversed it.

Guy helped him into the elevator and upstairs. Amy and Polk got on the other side, and between them, they maneuvered him into Melody's apartment and onto her sofa.

The sleeping arrangements were going to be interesting, she thought. She could put Emmett and the boys in her bedroom and she and Amy could share the sleeper sofa. It wasn't ideal, but it would be adequate. What wouldn't was managing some pajamas for Emmett.

''I don't wear pajamas,'' he muttered. ''You aren't going to be in the bedroom, so it won't concern you,'' he added with a glittery green stare.

She turned away to keep him from seeing the color in her cheeks. ''All right. I'll see about getting something together for sandwiches.''

At least, he wasn't picky about what he ate. That was a mixed blessing. Perhaps it was the concussion, making him so agreeable.

''This isn't bad,'' he murmured when he'd finished off two egg salad sandwiches.

''Thank you,'' she replied.

''I hate eggs,'' Guy remarked, but he was still eating his sandwich as he said it. He didn't look at Melody.

''And me,'' Melody added for him. He looked up, surprised, and her steady gaze told him that she knew exactly how her cat had managed to get out the door and lost.

He flushed and put down the rest of his sandwich. "I'm not hungry." He got up and went into the living room with Amy and Polk, who were eating on TV tables.

Emmett ran a big hand through his dark hair. "I'm sorry about your cat," he said.

"So am I." She got up and cleared away the dishes. "There's coffee if you'd like some."

"I would. Black."

"I'll bet you don't eat catsup on steak, either," she murmured.

He smiled at her as she put a mug of steaming coffee beside his hand. "Smart girl."

"Why do you ride in rodeos?" she asked when she was sitting down.

The question surprised him. He leaned back in his chair fingering the hot mug, and considered it. "I always have," he began.

"It must be hard on the children, having you away from home so much," she continued. "Even if your housekeeper does look after them."

"They're resourceful," he said noncommittally.

"They're ruined," she returned. "And you know it. Especially Guy."

His eyes narrowed as they met hers. "They're my kids," he said quietly. "And how I raise them is none of your business."

"They're my nephews and niece," she pointed out.

His face went taut under its dark tan. "Don't bring that up."

"Why do you have to keep hiding from it?" she asked miserably. "Randy's my brother. I love him. But he couldn't have taken Adell if she hadn't wanted to go with him...!"

"My God, don't you think I know that?" he asked with bridled fury.

She saw the pain in his face, in his eyes, and she understood. "But, it wasn't because something was lacking in you,'' she said softly, trying to make him understand. ''It was because she found something in Randy that she needed. Don't you see, it wasn't your fault!''

His whole body clenched. He grimaced and lifted the cup, burning his lips as he forced coffee between them. ''It's none of your business,'' he said gruffly. ''Let it alone.''

She wanted to pursue the subject, but it wouldn't be wise. She let it go.

''There's a little ice cream,'' she told him.

He shook his head. ''I don't like sweets.''

Just like Guy, but she didn't say it. Guy hated her. He hated her enough to let her cat out the door and into the street. Her eyes closed on a wave of pain. It was just as well she wasn't mooning over Emmett, because she was certain that Guy wouldn't let that situation develop.

''You should be in bed,'' she told Emmett after a tense minute.

''Yes,'' he agreed without heat and then stood up slowly. ''Tomorrow I'll take the kids back to the hotel, and we'll get a flight out to San Antonio. We'll all be out of your hair.''

She didn't argue. There was nothing to say.

Chapter 3

Earlier in the day, Melody had telephoned the nearest veterinarian's office and animal shelter, hoping that Alistair might turn up there. But the veterinarian's receptionist hadn't heard of any lost cats, and there was only a new part-time girl at the animal shelter who wasn't very knowledgeable about recent acquisitions. In fact, she'd confided, they'd had a fire the week before, and everything was mixed up. The lady who usually ran the shelter was in the hospital, having suffered smoke inhalation trying to get the animals out. She was very sorry, but she didn't know which cats were new acquisitions and which were old ones.

Melody was sorry about the fire, but she was even more worried about her cat. She went out into the hall one last time to call Alistair, in vain because he didn't appear. She just had to accept that he was gone. It wasn't easy. It was going to be similar to losing a member of her family, and part of her blamed Guy for that. He might hate her, but why had he taken out that hatred on her cat. Alistair had done nothing to hurt him.

Melody slept fitfully, and not only because she was worried about Alistair. The couch was comfortable, as a rule, but Amy was a restless sleeper and it was hard to dodge little flailing arms and legs and not wake up.

Just before daylight, she gave up. She covered the sleeping child, her eyes tender on the little oval face with its light brown hair and straight nose so reminiscent of Adell. Amy's eyes, though, were her father's. All the kids had green eyes, every single one. Adell's were blue, and her hair was light brown. Amy was the one who most resembled her mother, despite her tomboy ways and the temper that matched her father's. That physical resemblance to her mother must have been very painful to Emmett when Adell first left him. Guy seemed to be his favorite, and it wasn't surprising. Guy looked and acted the most like him. Polk was just himself, bespectacled and slight, with no real distinguishing feature except his brain. He seemed to be far and away the brains of the bunch.

She pulled on her quilted robe, her long hair disheveled from sleep, and went slowly into the bathroom, yawning as she opened the door.

Emmett's dark eyebrows levered up when she stopped dead and turned scarlet.

"Sorry!" she gasped, jerking the door back shut.

She went into the living room and sat down in a chair, very quickly. It was disconcerting to find a naked man stepping out of her shower, even if he did have a body that would grace a centerfold in any women's magazine.

He came out a minute later with a towel wrapped around his lean hips. He had an athlete's body, wide shouldered and narrow hipped, and his legs were incredible, Melody thought. She stared at him pie-eyed, trying to act sophisticated when she was just short of star-struck.

"I'm sorry," he said. "I didn't think to lock the door. I

assumed this was a little early for you to be up, and I needed a shower.''

"Of course."

He frowned as he stared down at her. She was doing her best not to look at him, and her cheeks were flaming. He was an experienced man, and he'd been married. He understood without words why she was reacting so violently to what she'd seen.

"It's all right," he said gently, and he smiled at her. "There's nothing to be embarrassed about."

She swallowed. "Right. Would you like some breakfast?"

"Anything will suit me. I'll get dressed."

She nodded, but she didn't look as he strode back into the bedroom and gently closed the door.

She got up and went to the kitchen, surprised to find that her hands shook when she got the pans out and began to put bacon into one.

Emmett came back while she was breaking eggs into a bowl. He was wearing jeans and a white T-shirt, which stretched over his powerful muscles. He wasn't wearing shoes. He looked rakish and appealing. She pretended not to notice; her memory was giving her enough trouble.

Melody wasn't dressed because she'd forgotten to get her clothes out of the bedroom the night before. That had been an unfortunate oversight, because he was staring quite openly at her in the long green gown and matching quilted robe that fit much too well and showed an alarming amount of bare skin in the deep V neckline. She wasn't wearing makeup, but her blond-streaked brown hair and freckled pale skin gave her enough color to make her interesting to a man.

Emmett realized that she must not know that, because she kept fiddling with her hair after she'd set the eggs aside and started to heat a pan to cook them in.

"Where are the plates?" he asked. He didn't want to add to her discomfort by staring.

"They're up in the cabinet, there—" she gestured "—and so are the cups and saucers. But you don't have to…"

"I'm domesticated," he said gently. "I always was, even before I married." The words, once spoken, dispelled his good mood. He went about setting the table and didn't speak again until he was finished.

Melody had scrambled eggs and taken up the bacon while the biscuits were baking. She took them out of the oven, surprised to see that they weren't overcooked. People in the kitchen made her nervous—Emmett, especially.

"You couldn't get to your clothes, could you?" he mused. "I should have reminded you last night."

It was an intimate conversation. Having a man in her apartment at all was intimate, and after having met him in the altogether in the bathroom, Melody was more nervous than ever.

"That's all right, I'll dress when the boys get up. You could call them…?"

"Not yet," he replied. "I want to talk to you."

"About what?"

He motioned her into a chair and then sat down across from her, his big, lean hands dangling between his knees as he studied her. "About what you said last night. I've been thinking about it. Did Adell tell you that it was loving Randy, not hating me, that broke up our marriage?"

Melody clasped her hands in her lap and stared at them. "She said that she married you because you were kind and gentle and obviously cared about her so much," she told him, because only honesty would do. "When she met Randy, at the service station where she had her car worked on and bought gas, she tried to pretend it wasn't happening, that she wasn't falling in love. But she was too weak to stop it. I'm not excusing what she did, Emmett," she said when he looked haunted. "There should have been a kinder way. And I should have said no when Randy asked me to help them get away. But nothing will change what happened. She really does love him. There's no way to get around that.''

''I see.''

He looked grim. She hated the wounded expression on his lean face.

''Emmett,'' she said gently, ''you have to believe it wasn't because of you personally. She fell in love, really in love. The biggest mistake she made was marrying you when she didn't love you properly.''

''Do you know what that is?'' he asked with a bitter smile. ''Loving 'properly'?''

''Well, not really,'' she said. ''I haven't ever been in love.'' That was true enough. She'd had crushes on movie stars, and once she'd had a crush on a boy back in San Antonio. But that had been a very lukewarm relationship and the boy had gone crazy over a cheerleader who was more willing in the back seat of his car than Melody had been.

''Why?'' he asked curiously.

She sighed. ''You must have noticed that I'm oversized and not very attractive,'' she said with a wistful smile.

He frowned. ''Aren't you? Who says?''

Color came and went in her cheeks. ''Well, no one, but I…''

It disturbed him that he'd said such a thing to her, when she'd been the enemy since Randy had spirited Adell away. ''Have the kids given you any trouble?''

''Just Guy,'' she replied after a minute. ''He doesn't like me.''

''He doesn't like anybody except me,'' he said easily. ''He's the most insecure of the three.''

She nodded. ''Amy and Polk are very sweet.''

''Adell spoiled them. She favored Guy, although he took it the best of the three when she left. I think he loved her, but he never talks about her.''

''He's a very private person, isn't he? Divorce must be

hard on everyone," she replied. "My parents loved each other for thirty years—until they died. There was never any question of them getting a divorce or separating. They were happy. So were we. It was a blow when we lost them. Randy wound up being part brother and part parent to me. I was still in school."

"That explains why you were so close, I suppose." He cocked his head and studied her. "How did they die?"

"In a freak accident," she said sadly. "My mother was in very bad health—a semi-invalid. She had what Dad thought was a light heart attack. He got her into the car and was speeding, trying to get her to the hospital. He lost control in a curve and wrecked the car. They both died." She averted her eyes. "There was an oil slick on the road that he didn't see, and a light rain…just enough to bring the oil to the surface. Randy and I blamed ourselves for not insisting that Dad call an ambulance instead of trying to drive her to the emergency room himself. To this day I hate rain."

"I'm sorry," he said kindly. "I lost my parents several years apart, but it was pretty rough just the same. Especially my mother." He was silent for a moment. "She killed herself. Dad had only been dead six months when she was diagnosed with leukemia. She refused treatment, went home and took a handful of barbiturates that they'd given her for pain. I was in my last few weeks of college before graduation. I hadn't started until I was nineteen, so I was late getting out. It was pretty rough, passing my finals after the funeral," he added with a rough laugh.

"I can only imagine," she said sympathetically.

"I'd already been running the ranch and going to school as a commuting student. That's where I met Adell, at college. She was sympathetic and I was so torn up inside. I just wanted to get married and have kids and not be alone anymore." He shrugged. "I thought marriage would ease the pain. It didn't. Nobody cares like your parents do. When they die, you're alone. Except, maybe, if you've got kids," he added thoughtfully, and realized that he hadn't really paid enough attention to his own kids. He frowned. He'd avoided them since Adell left. Rodeo and ranch work had pretty much replaced parenting with him. He wondered why he hadn't noticed it until he got hit in the head.

"Do you have brothers or sisters?" Melody asked unexpectedly. She hadn't ever had occasion to question his background. Now, suddenly, she was curious about it.

"No," he said. "I had a sister, they said, but she died a few weeks after she was born. There was just me. My dad was a rodeo star. He taught me everything I know."

"He must have been good at it."

"So am I, when I'm not distracted. There was a little commotion before my ride. I wasn't paying attention and it was almost fatal."

"The kids would have missed you."

"Maybe Guy would have, although he's pretty solitary most of the time," he replied. His eyes narrowed. "Amy and Polk seem very happy to stay with anybody."

So the truce was over. She stared at him. "They probably were half starved for a little of the attention you give rodeoing," she returned abruptly. "You seem to spend your life avoiding your own children."

"You're outspoken," he said angrily.

"So are you."

His green eyes narrowed. "Not very worldly, though."

She wouldn't blush, she wouldn't blush, she wouldn't...!

"The eggs are getting cold," she reminded him.

The color in her face was noticeable now, but she was a trooper. He admired her attempt at subterfuge, even as he felt himself tensing with faint pleasure at her naiveté. Her obvious innocence excited him. "I have to make a living," he said, feeling oddly defensive. "Rodeo is what I do best, and it's profitable."

"Your cousin mentioned that the ranch is profitable, too."

"Only if it gets a boost in lean times from other capital, and times are pretty lean right now," he said shortly. "It's the kids' legacy. I can't afford to lose it."

"Yes, but there are other ways of making money besides rodeo. You must know a lot about how to manage cattle and horses and accounts."

"I do. But I like working for myself."

She stared pointedly at his head. "Yes, I can see how successful you are at it. Head not hurting this morning?"

"I haven't taken a fall that bad before," he muttered.

"You're getting older, though."

"Older! My God, I'm only in my thirties!"

"Emmett, you're so loud!" Amy protested sleepily from deep in her blankets.

"Sorry, honey," he said automatically. His green eyes narrowed and glittered on Melody. "I can ride as well as I ever did!"

"Am I arguing?" she asked in mock surprise.

He got up from his chair and towered over her. "Nobody tells me what to do."

"I wasn't," she replied pleasantly. "But when those kids reach their teens, do you really think anyone's going to be able to manage them? And what if something happens to you? What will become of them?"

She was asking questions he didn't like. He'd already started to ask them himself. He didn't like that, either. He went off toward the bedroom to call the boys and didn't say another word.

Melody worried at her own forwardness in mentioning such things to him. It was none of her business, but she was fond of Amy and Polk. Guy was a trial, but he was intelligent and he had grit. They were good kids. If Emmett woke up in time to take proper care of them, they'd be good adults. But they were heading for trouble without supervision.

* * *

Emmett came back wearing a checked shirt and black boots. Being fully dressed made him feel better armored to talk to Miss Bossy in the kitchen.

"They're getting up," he muttered, sitting.

"I'll warm everything when they get in here." She busied herself washing the dishes and cleaning the sink until the boys came out of her room, dressed. Then she escaped into the bedroom and closed the door. Emmett's stare had been provokingly intimate. She'd felt undressed in front of those knowing eyes and she wondered why he had suddenly become so disturbing to her.

Seeing him without his clothes had kindled something unfamiliar in her. She'd never been curious about men that way, even if she did daydream about love and marriage. But Emmett's powerful shoulders and hair-roughened chest and flat stomach and long, muscular legs, along with his blatant masculinity, stuck in her mind like a vivid oil painting that she couldn't cover up. He hadn't even had a white streak across his hips. That was oddly sensual. If he sunbathed, he must do it as he slept: without anything on. He looked very much like one of those marble statues she'd seen photographs of, but he was even more thrilling to look at. She reproached herself for that thought.

She looked at the rumpled bed where Emmett had lain with the boys and her pulse raced. Tonight she'd be sleeping where his body had rested. She wondered if she'd ever sleep again.

After she was dressed, she went to the kitchen and warmed the food before she put it on the table. The kids all ate hungrily, even Guy, although he wouldn't look at Melody. He was just as sullen and uncommunicative as ever.

But now, Melody was avoiding looking at him, too. Guy noticed her resentment and was surprised that it bothered him. He was guilty about the cat as well. It had been an ugly cat, all scarred and big and orange, but it had purred when he petted it. His conscience stung him.

He had to remember that Melody was responsible for his mother's departure. He'd loved his mother. She'd gone away, so it had to be because of him. He'd given her a hard time, just as he'd been giving Melody one. He'd been much more caring about his father since his mother left, because he knew it was his fault that she'd run away with that Randy Cartman. If he'd been a better boy, a nicer boy, his mother would have stayed. Maybe if he could keep his father single, his mother would come back.

Blissfully unaware of his son's mistaken reasoning, Emmett smiled at the boy. He was a bit curious about Guy's behavior. The boy and Melody were restrained with each other. Melody's eyes were accusing, and Guy's were guilt-ridden. It wasn't a big jump from that observation to the subject of the cat.

He could ask Guy about it, but it would be better to let the boy bring it up himself, when they were away from here. If it was true that Guy really had let the cat out...

He was sorry that he'd spent so much time avoiding his children. Adell's betrayal wasn't their fault. If Adell genuinely loved Randy, and had left only because of that, no one was to blame for what had happened. Least of all the kids.

Emmett felt better about himself, and them. He had a lot of omissions to make up for, and he didn't know where to start.

The kids finished breakfast and went to watch television. Emmett insisted on helping Melody clean up.

He dried while she washed and rinsed. "Tell me about the cat," he said.

Her face stiffened.

"Come on." He prodded gently.

She sighed heavily. "I found him last year in an alley," she said finally. "He had a string tied around his neck. He was thick with parasites, and half starved. It took him a long time to learn to trust me. I thought he never would.'' She washed the same plate twice. ''We've been together ever since. I'll miss him.''

''He may still turn up,'' he told her.

She shook her head sadly. ''It isn't likely. There are so many streets...''

''If he was a street cat when you got him, he's street smart. Don't give up on him yet.''

She smiled, but she didn't reply.

''What you said about the kids,'' he began, glancing toward the living room to make sure they weren't listening. ''I guess maybe I've been negligent with them. I thought they were adjusting to my being away so much. But this concussion has made me apprehensive.'' He stared at her quietly. ''Adell isn't likely to be able to handle all three of them with a stepfather, even if she wouldn't mind visitation rights. They'd be split up, with no place to go.''

''Adell loves them, you know she does,'' she replied.

''She gave up when I refused to let her see them. I never would have given up.''

''Adell isn't you,'' she reminded him. ''She isn't really a fighter.''

''That's probably why she said yes when I proposed to her,'' he said angrily. ''I was overbearing, because I wanted her so much. If I'd given her a choice, she'd probably have turned me down.''

''You have three fine children to show for your marriage,'' she said softly.

He looked down into her quiet dark eyes and something stirred deep inside his heart. He began to smile. ''You've been a surprise,'' he said absently.

''So have you,'' she replied.

He noticed that she'd thrown away a box of cat food. ''Did you mean to do that?'' he asked, lifting it.

She grimaced. "Well, he's gone, isn't he?" she asked huskily.

She turned to put away the plates and he moved, but she caught her foot on a chair leg and tripped.

He caught her easily, his reflexes honed by years of ranch work. His lean hands on her waist kindled exquisite little ripples on her skin. She looked up into his eyes and her gaze hung there, curious, a little surprised by the strength of the need she felt to be held close against him and comforted.

He seemed to understand that need in her eyes, because he reacted to it immediately. Taking the clean colorful plastic plates from her hand in a silence broken only by the blaring television, he set them on the table. Then he pulled her quite roughly into his arms.

She shivered with feeling. Never, she thought, never like this! She was frightened, but she didn't pull away. She let him hold her, closed her eyes and delighted in the security she felt for this brief moment. It made the ache in her heart subside. His shirt smelled of pleasant detergent and cologne, and it felt wonderful to be held so closely to his warm strength.

"The cat will show up," he said at her ear, his voice deep, soothing. "Don't lose heart."

She had to force herself to draw away from him. It was embarrassing to allow herself to be comforted. She was used to bearing things bravely.

She managed a wan smile. "Thanks," she said huskily.

He nodded. He picked up the plates and handed them back to her. "I'll get the kids packed," he said.

He moved out of the kitchen. He was disturbed and vaguely aroused. He didn't want to think about how his feelings had changed since his concussion. That could wait until he was more lucid and out of Melody's very disturbing presence.

Guy had noticed the embrace and he remarked on it when Emmett joined the children in the living room.

"Losing the cat upset her," Emmett said, and that explanation seemed to satisfy Guy. At the same time, the boy's face went a little paler.

Later, Emmett promised himself, he was going to have to talk to Guy about that cat. He had some suspicions that he sincerely hoped were wrong.

He and Guy weren't close, although they got along well enough. But lately the boy was standoffish and seemed to not want affection from anyone. He bossed the other two around and when he wasn't doing that, he spent his time by himself. He didn't ask for anything, least of all attention. But as Emmett pondered that, he began to wonder if Guy's solitary leanings weren't because he was afraid to get attached. He'd lost his mother, whom he adored, to a stranger. Perhaps he was afraid of losing Emmett, too.

Emmett could have told him that people don't stop loving their children, whether or not they're divorced. He'd done his kids an injustice, probably, by not letting Adell near them. He began to rethink his entire position, and he didn't like what he saw. He'd been punishing everyone for Adell's defection. Perhaps he'd been punishing himself as well. Melody had said some things that disturbed him. That might not be bad. It was time he came to grips with the past, and his kids. Fate had given him a second chance. He couldn't afford to waste it.

Chapter 4

It only took her reluctant houseguests a few minutes to pack and be ready to leave.

"You could stay another day if you need to," Melody told Emmett and her dark eyes were worried. "Concussions can be dangerous."

"Indeed they can," he said. "But the headache is gone and I'm not feeling disoriented anymore. Believe me, I don't take chances. I'm all right. I'd never take the kids with me if I wasn't sure."

"If you're sure then," she said.

"Besides," he added ruefully, "we've given you enough trouble. Thank you for taking care of those kids for me. And for your hospitality." He opened his wallet and put two twenty-dollar bills on the table. "For groceries," he said.

"They didn't eat forty dollars worth of food," she returned angrily.

"The baby-sitter cost that much for two hours, much less two days," he said, putting his wallet away. "I won't argue.

I don't want to be under any obligation to you. In my place, you'd feel exactly the same," he added with a smile when she started to protest again.

She *would* have felt the same way, she had to admit. Reluctantly, she gave in. "All right. Thank you," she said stiffly. "I hope you'll be all right," she added. She couldn't quite hide her worry for him.

Her concern touched him. "I will. I've got the world's hardest head." He guided the kids out the door. "We'll get a cab," he added when she offered to drive them.

"I'll miss you, Melody," Amy said sadly. She hugged Melody warmly. "Can't you come with us?"

"I've got a job," Melody said simply. She smiled and kissed the little girl's forehead. "But I'll miss you, too. You could write me, if your dad doesn't mind."

"Me, too?" Polk asked.

She smiled. "You, too."

He beamed. Guy didn't say a word. He stuck his hands into the pockets of his jeans and trailed after Amy and Polk.

"I'll say goodbye, then," Emmett said quietly. He searched Melody's eyes, feeling oddly disconcerted at the thought of not seeing her again. He scowled, his expression steady and intent, and a jolt of pure pleasure seared through him as he let his gaze fall slowly to her mouth. It was silky and soft looking, and he wondered how it would feel to smooth her body against his and kiss her blind.

He dragged his gaze away. He must still be concussed, he decided, to be considering that! Any such thoughts were a road to disaster. She, of all women, was off-limits. He would never forget Adell and Randy. The past would destroy any thought of a relationship with Melody.

"Goodbye," he said stiffly, and followed the kids into the elevator. Guy looked over his shoulder, and there was something in his eyes that mingled strangely with the hostility. He looked as if he were about to say something, but Emmett's gentle hand on his shoulder guided him out the door.

The apartment was quiet and lonely with everyone gone. Melody got her clothes ready for work the next day, but she did it without any real interest. With a sinking heart, she washed Alistair's bowls and put them out of sight. Tears stung her eyes at the thought of never seeing him again. She'd never dreamed that a child could be so vindictive.

Back at the hotel, Guy was totally uncommunicative until that night. After Amy and Polk went to bed, he sat down on the couch next to his father.

"Something's bothering you," Emmett remarked quietly.

Guy shrugged. "Yeah."

"Want to tell me about it?"

The boy leaned forward, resting his elbows on his knees in a position that Emmett often assumed.

"I let Melody's cat out."

Emmett's head lifted. He wasn't really surprised. He'd suspected this because of Guy's behavior. "That was cruel," he replied, "after she was kind enough to take care of all three of you. The cat was special to her. Like Barney is to you," he added, mentioning the mongrel pup that Guy was fond of back home. "Try to think how you'd feel if someone let Barney out in the streets…"

Guy burst into tears. It was the first time in memory that Emmett had seen that happen. Even when his mother left, Guy hadn't cried.

Awkwardly Emmett pulled the boy against him and patted his back. He wasn't too good at being a parent most of the time. The kids made him uncomfortable with their woes and antics, which was really why he spent so much time away from home. Now he wondered if he'd been needed more than he realized. The kids hadn't had anyone to talk to about their mother in two years, or anybody to lean on. He'd assumed that they hadn't needed that. But they were only children. Why hadn't he realized how young they really were?

"Why did you let the cat out?" Emmett asked Guy gently.

"Because I hate her! She helped Mom leave!" Guy choked. "She's nothing but a troublemaking witch!" He looked up, a little uncertainly. "You called her that!" he added defensively, because his father didn't look pleased about what he'd said.

Emmett groaned. "Yes, I did, but it was because I was hurting. Nobody made your mother leave. She went away because she never really loved me." It was painful to say that, but now that it was out, it didn't hurt so much. "She did fall in love, but with another man, and she couldn't live without him. That's not your fault or mine or Melody's. It's just life."

Guy sniffed, and pulled away, wiping his tears on the back of his hand. "Melody cried all night. I heard her. I thought it would serve her right, because of Mom. But it made me feel awful."

"It made her feel pretty awful, too."

"I know." He looked up at his father. "What'll I do?"

Emmett thought for a minute. "Go to bed. I've got an idea. We'll talk some more tomorrow."

"We're going home, aren't we?"

"Yes. Tomorrow afternoon. But first, in the morning, I want to make a few phone calls."

He made eight phone calls before he got the information he wanted. His head had stopped throbbing and he felt much better. Leaving the kids with a baby-sitter—not the elderly one of two nights ago—he went downstairs and hailed a cab.

Melody was just hanging up the telephone when she heard the outer office door open. She looked up with a smile ready for the client coming in. But it wasn't a client; it was Emmett.

And under his arm was a big, straggly-looking orange tabby cat.

"Alistair!"

She scrambled up from the desk, tears of joy streaming down her face. "Alistair! Oh, Alistair…!"

She took the cat from Emmett and kissed Alistair and hugged him and petted him and stroked him in such delight that Emmett felt even worse than he had when Guy told him what he'd done. Seeing Melody vulnerable like this touched him. It was as shocking as it had been to see Guy in tears.

"Where did you find him?" she choked, big-eyed.

He touched her cheek gently. "At the local pound," he said. He didn't add that the shelter had been in a state of chaos and the cat had inadvertently been scheduled for premature termination. That wouldn't do at all. "I suppose you know that it was Guy who let him out."

"I know," she said.

"It's my fault more than his," he murmured reluctantly. "I've blamed everyone for Adell, especially you. I couldn't stand to admit that she left because of me, because she didn't love me. I stayed away too much. The kids and the loneliness killed our marriage."

"Not the kids," she replied, clutching Alistair. "Adell loves the children. She'd love to have them visit, but…" She paused.

"But I wouldn't let her near them. That's right," he agreed tersely. "I hated her, too. Her, and your brother and you. Everybody."

"You were hurt," she said softly, her eyes searching his. "We all understood. Even Adell."

His jaw went taut. He took a deep breath and looked over her head. "We're flying out this afternoon. I have to go."

"Thank you for my cat," she said sincerely. In a fever of gratitude and without thinking of the consequences, she reached up and touched her soft lips fervently to his chin.

Shocked at the look it produced on his lean, dark face, and not a little by her own behavior, she drew back at once.

He looked down at her curiously, stunned. When she began to step away, his lean hand caught her shoulder and stopped the slow movement.

"No," he said hesitantly, searching her soft, dark eyes while his heart began to race in his chest. "Not yet, Melody."

While she was getting her breath, he let his gaze drop abruptly to her soft, parted mouth and his big hand moved up to her chin, gently cupping it as he tilted her face up.

His thumb moved hesitantly over her full lower lip. "I've…wondered," he whispered as his head began to lower. "Haven't you?"

She didn't get the chance to reply. His mouth slowly closed on hers with tender, confident mastery. It was firm, and hard, and a little rough. She let her eyes close and stopped breathing. She'd been kissed, but just the touch of a man's lips had never been quite so vivid. It had to be because of the antagonism they'd felt for each other, she thought dizzily.

But her knees were going weak and her heartbeat went wild when she felt his teeth gently nip her lower lip. She heard his breathing change even as his head lifted a fraction of an inch.

"Open it," he said roughly, his hand sliding into the thick hair at her nape. "Open your mouth…!"

His lips crushed into hers with sudden violence, hunger making him less considerate of her needs and more aware of his own. With a rough groan, he made her lips part to admit his, and his tongue probed insistently between them.

Shocked, her gasp gave him what he wanted—access to her mouth. He made a satisfied sound in his throat and penetrated the soft, warm darkness past her lips with slow thrusts.

She gasped and clutched at him as waves of physical pleasure buffeted her untried body. Her mouth pushed upward, to meet his ardor headlong. And Alistair chose that instant to insist physically on being put down, his claws digging into her arm.

She pulled away from Emmett, breathless and puzzled by

the violence in his eyes. His hand let go of her hair. She looked away while she put the battle-scarred old tomcat on his feet and dazedly watched him leap into her chair and begin to bathe himself with magnificent abandon.

She took steadying breaths and slowly looked at Emmett. He seemed as shaken as she felt. Her dark eyes stared up into his turbulent green ones with mute curiosity.

The delight he felt was far too disturbing. He could get in over his head here with no trouble at all. The chemistry was there, just as he'd known it was somewhere in the back of his mind. He was sorry about that. Of all the women he'd ever wanted, Melody was the first one that he absolutely could not have.

He forced himself to breathe normally, to pretend that it was natural for him to feel this aroused from a casual kiss. He had to force back the impulse to drag her against him.

He laughed a little angrily. "I'm glad the cat turned up," he said when he wanted to ask how she felt, if her body was throbbing as madly as his own was. He had to keep his head, talk normally. "Thanks for the hospitality."

"That's all right." She could barely speak. She cleared her throat. "Thank you for finding my cat. He…he really is all I have."

His throat felt tight. He had to stop looking at her mouth. His broad shoulders squared. "Guy's sorry for what he did. I'll make sure he doesn't do it again."

"You won't…be mean to him?"

He cocked an eyebrow. "I don't have a bullwhip."

She flushed. "Sorry," she said sheepishly.

He managed a short laugh. "I don't beat my kids. Can't you tell?"

She smiled at him, her lips still tingling with pleasure from the hunger of his mouth.

He smiled back. She looked delectable when she smiled. He wanted her. *No!* He couldn't afford to think like that.

"Well…goodbye."

"Goodbye," he said. He hesitated for an instant. She made

him want things he'd forgotten he needed. There had been women, but this one touched him in ways no one else ever had. He wanted to tell her that, but he didn't dare. There was no future in a relationship between them. Surely she knew, too, that it had been an impulse, a mad moment that was better forgotten by both of them.

With a tip of his broad-brimmed hat, he turned abruptly and left without looking back.

Melody stroked her cat with a hand that trembled. "Oh, Alistair." She sighed, cuddling him. "I've missed you so much!"

Alistair butted his head against her and purred. She laughed, imagining that he was telling her he'd missed her, too. She murmured a small prayer of thanks and carried him into the bathroom. He'd have to stay there until it was time to go home. Perhaps she could find him part of a sandwich and a saucer of milk later to keep him happy.

Emmett was set upon the minute he walked into the hotel room.

"Did you find him?" Guy asked impatiently.

Emmett put off telling him long enough to make him sweat. Object lessons stayed in the mind. "Yes, I found him," he said, and watched the young face lose its pallor. "No thanks to you," he added firmly. "He was scheduled to be put down."

"I'm sorry," Guy said tightly. He was trying not to hope for too much. Last night, his father had been approachable for the first time in memory. It had felt good to be cared about. But now Emmett seemed distant again, and Guy was feeling the transition all too much.

Emmett turned away. He didn't see the wounded look on the young face, or the hope that slowly drained out of it. "You got a second chance. Most people don't. Remember how it felt. That way you won't be tempted to do such a cruel thing again."

"You hate her," Guy muttered. "You said you did," he added defensively.

"I know." Emmett hesitated. "I'll try to explain that one day," he told his son, and somewhere in the back of his mind he was remembering the incredible softness of Melody's innocent mouth under his lips.

He paid the baby-sitter, packed the suitcases and took his kids home. Maybe when he was back in familiar surroundings, he could put Melody out of his thoughts.

Melody checked on Tansy Deverell Sunday evening. Tansy had been discharged from the hospital and had been moved to Logan's house where she had a private nurse until Kit and Logan got back so that she wouldn't be in the house alone. Spending the evening with the elderly lady took her mind off her own problems.

"I saw Emmett before they released him," Tansy mused with twinkling eyes when she was in a comfortable bed at Logan's house. "Two nurses threatened to resign, I believe?"

"I heard it was three, and the doctor." Melody chuckled. "Isn't he something? And those kids...!"

"Those kids would settle down if Guy would," Tansy replied. "He's the ringleader. He leads and the other two follow. Guy's said the least about his mother leaving them, but I think it hit him the hardest—almost as hard as it hit Emmett. They both blame themselves, when it was no one's fault."

"I told Emmett that," Melody remarked. "He actually listened. I don't know if he believed me or not, but he was...well, less volatile after that."

"Emmett's always been explosive," the elderly woman recalled. "He was high-strung and forceful when he was younger, a real hell-raiser. Adell was sheltered and shy. He just walked right over her. He was devastated when his mother committed suicide and he wanted a wife and a family right then. He picked Adell and rushed her to the altar. She never should have married him. He was the exact opposite of the kind of man she needed. She didn't want a fistful of children right away, but Emmett gave her no real choice. He's lived to regret his rashness. I'm sorry for the way things turned out for him. He's a sad, lonely man.''

"And a very bitter one," Melody added. "He hated me."

"Past tense?" Tansy fished gently.

"I don't know. He was very different when he left," she replied, frowning in confusion.

"I hope he'll go home and rethink his life after this," Tansy said. "He had a close call that could have ended tragically. The kids deserve a better shake than they're getting. If he doesn't wake up pretty soon, he'll never be able to control them when they get older.''

"I think he knows that."

"Then let's both hope he'll do something about it. They're sweet kids."

Melody only nodded. She didn't want to go into any details about why she could have cheerfully excluded Guy from that description.

"It's great to be back." Kit sighed when she stopped by the office Monday morning with a weary-looking Logan. "You really need a vacation from a vacation. We had so much fun!" She stared after Logan, who'd gone into his office to take a telephone call.

Melody stared at her grimly. "I'm glad *you* did," she said, emphasizing the "you." "Emmett landed himself in the hospital with a concussion over the weekend. *Guess* who got to look after those kids."

"Oh, Lord," Kit said on a moan. "You poor thing!"

"I kept reminding myself that they're my nieces and nephews," Melody remarked. "But it was a very long weekend." She didn't mention Alistair's adventure or Guy's part in it.

"I'm really sorry. If we'd been in town, all of us could have split them up."

"I shudder to think of the consequences," Melody mused.

"I can see them now, trying to get to each other through downtown Houston at two in the morning."

"Hmm. You might have a point there." She glanced at her watch. "I have to get to work, or I may not have a job. Have a nice day," she called, pausing to blow a kiss at her husband through the open door of his office.

Melody wondered at the obviously loving relationship the married couple had, and felt a faint envy. Probably she'd never know anything like that. Emmett had kissed her, but it had been passionate, not loving. She permitted herself to dream for just a moment about how it would have felt to be loved half to death. Then the phone rang and saved her from any more malingering.

During the time Logan and Kit had been away, Melody hadn't been forced to call on Tom Walker. That was a blessing. He strolled into the office later on the day Logan came back, a little curious, because he'd expected to have someone to advise in Logan's absence.

"I suppose I had you buffaloed?" he mused in a deep voice with a very faint crisp northwestern accent, his dark eyes twinkling as they met Melody's. "That was just bad timing before, when Logan left town. I'd already had a hell of a day. You caught the overflow. I'm sorry if I've put you off financial advisors for life." There was a faint query in his scrutiny.

"You haven't," Melody said, and smiled back. "But we really didn't have anyone with an emergency this time. Aren't you glad?"

"I guess so," he said wearily. "It's been a long week. How was the honeymoon?" he asked Logan, who joined them in the outer office.

"Nothing like it. Get married and find out for yourself," he said, chuckling as he shook Tom's hand.

The older man's face closed up. "Marriage is not for me," he said quietly. "I'm not suited for it. Besides, when would I have time for a wife?" he added with a mocking smile. "I work eighteen hours out of every twenty-four. In my spare time, I sleep.''

"That will get old one day," Logan told him. He was obviously thinking about Kit and his heart was in his face. "Time can pass you by if you don't pay attention."

Tom turned away. "I've got a client due. I just wanted to stop by and welcome you back. I'll be in touch."

"Don't forget, we're having dinner with the Rowena Marshal people next Saturday at the Sheraton."

"How could I forget? Ms. Marshal herself phoned to remind me," he said with a nip in his tone. "*After* expressing outrage that her business partner had dared to approach us about changing their investments without her knowledge. If you recall, I was against taking their account in the first place. It's been nothing short of a headache. They should have used one firm, not split their investments between two. I tried to tell them that, too. Ms. Marshal wouldn't listen."

"*Mrs.* Marshal," Logan corrected.

"Are you sure? When would she find time for a husband and family?" Tom muttered. "That cosmetic company seems to keep her as occupied as investments keep me."

"She and her husband are divorced," Logan replied. "Or so I hear."

Tom didn't say a word, but one eyebrow went up. "Am I surprised? How could a mere man compete with the power and prestige of owning one of the Fortune 500 companies?"

"I'm sure there's more to it than that," Logan replied.

Tom shrugged. "There usually is. Well, we'll see what they want to do after we talk to them. If you want the account, you can have it with my blessing. Tell her that, would you?"

Logan chuckled. "What have I ever done to you?"

Tom shook his head. "See you."

Logan watched him leave with narrow, curious dark eyes. Tom was a real puzzle even to the people who knew him best. He had a feeling his friend and the lovely Mrs. Marshal were going to strike sparks off each other from the very beginning.

He turned to Melody, who was sorting files. "Anything that can't wait until tomorrow?" he mused.

"Why, no, sir," she said with a mischievous smile. "In fact, I think I can now run the office all by myself, advise clients on the best investments, speak to civic organizations…"

"I can call Emmett and tell him you miss having him and the kids at your apartment, and that you'd like him to come back," he suggested.

She stuck both arms up in the air over her head.

He chuckled and left to pick up Kit at her office.

Emmett was wondering if his age was beginning to affect him. He was noticing things about his kids that had escaped him for months. They didn't take regular baths. They didn't have new clothes. They didn't do their homework. They played really nasty jokes on people around the ranch.

"You haven't noticed much, have you?" the housekeeper, Tally Ray remarked dryly. "I've done my best, but as they keep reminding me, I don't have any real authority to order them around."

"We'll see about that," he began irritably.

"Why don't *you* see about that? Because I'm retiring. Here's my notice. I didn't mind doing housework, but I draw the line at being a part-time mother to three kids. I want to enjoy my golden years, if you please."

"But you've been here forever!" he protested.

"And that's why I'm leaving." She patted him on the shoulder. "One week is all you get, by the way. I hope you can find somebody stupid enough to replace me."

Emmett felt the world coming down on his shoulders. *Now* what was he going to do?

He phoned Tansy, supposedly to check on her progress, but really to get some much-needed advice.

"You're playing with fire, you know," Tansy told him. "Living on the edge is only for people with no real responsibilities. Those kids need you."

"So does the ranch. How can I keep it without additional capital?"

"Get a job that doesn't have the risks of rodeo."

"Where?" he asked belligerently.

"Take down this number."

She gave it to him and he jotted it down with a pencil. "What is it?"

"It's Ted Regan's number," she replied. "He still needs somebody to manage his ranch in Jacobsville while he's in Europe. It won't be a permanent job, but it would keep you going until you decide what else you'd like to do with your life."

"Jacobsville."

"That's right. It's a small town, but close enough to Houston that you could bring the kids to see me. You'd have time to spend with them. You'd have a second chance, Emmett."

He could use one, but he didn't want to admit it. "That's an idea." He didn't add that it was going to get him closer to Melody than San Antonio was. He didn't know why it exhilarated him to think of being close enough to see her when he liked, but it did.

"Call Ted and talk to him," Tansy suggested.

"I suppose it wouldn't hurt."

It didn't. Ted Regan knew Emmett's reputation in rodeo and he didn't need to ask for credentials or qualifications. He offered Emmett the job on the spot, at a regular salary that was twice what he was pulling down on the rodeo circuit.

"Besides, it may turn into a full-time job," Ted continued in his deep, Texas drawl. "My present manager just quit. I don't know if I can spread myself thin enough to manage the ranch and keep up with my purebred business. I'm buying and selling cattle like hotcakes. I haven't got time for the day-to-day routine of ranching."

That was what worried Emmett. If he left his own ranch, he'd have to let Whit manage it for him. Whit was good, but could he hold it together?

"We'll have to talk about that later, but I will think about the offer," Emmett promised. "And thanks, I'll take the job."

"I'm glad," Ted replied. "I know you'll do it right." He gave Emmett a date to report and concluded the fine points of the agreement.

When he hung up, Emmett called the kids together and sat down with them.

"We're going to move to Jacobsville and I'm going to manage a ranch there," he began.

Guy glared at his father with pale, angry eyes in a face as lean and strong as Emmett's. "Well, I'm not moving to Jacobsville," he said curtly. "I like it here."

Amy took her cue from her eldest brother, whose pale eyes dared her to go against him. "Me, too," Amy said quickly, although not as belligerently. "I'm not going, either, Emmett!"

Emmett looked at Polk. Polk didn't say a word. He just looked at the other two, grinned and nodded.

Chapter 5

Only a week ago, Emmett might have lost his temper and said some unpleasant things to the kids. But he'd mellowed just a little since his concussion. He was sure he could handle the children's mutiny. He smiled smugly. It was just a matter of outsmarting them.

"There are horses there," he remarked. "Lots of horses. You could each have one of your own."

"We live on a ranch, Emmett," Amy reminded him. "We already have a horse each."

"There's the Astrodome in Houston," he added.

"There's the Alamo here," Guy said.

"And the place where they film all the movies, outside town," Polk added.

"All our friends are here," Amy wailed.

He was losing ground. He began to lose some self-confidence. "You can make new friends," he told them. "There are lots of kids in Jacobsville."

"We don't want new friends." Amy began to cry.

"Oh, stop that!" Emmett groaned. He glared at all three of them. "Listen, don't you want us to be a family?" he asked.

Amy stopped crying. Her eyes were red but they lifted bravely. "A family?" she echoed.

"Yes, a family!" He pushed back his unruly dark hair from his broad forehead. "I haven't been much of a father since your mother left us," he confessed curtly. "I want us to spend more time together. I want to be able to stay at home with you. If I take this job, I won't be away all the time at rodeos. I'll be home at night, all the time, and on weekends. We can do things together."

Guy stared at him warily. "You mean, things like going to movies and goofy golf and baseball games? Things like that?" he said slowly, hardly able to believe that his father actually might want to spend any time with them. That wasn't the impression he'd been giving since their mother had left.

"Yes," Emmett said. "And if you had problems that you needed to talk to me about, I'd be there."

"What about Mrs. Ray?"

"She's resigning," Emmett said sadly. "She says she's reached the age where she needs peace and quiet and flowers to grow. So we'd have to replace her even if we stay here."

Guy and Amy and Polk exchanged resigned glances. They didn't want the risk of a housekeeper they couldn't control. There was always that one chance in a million that their father might come up with someone they couldn't frighten or intimidate.

"Melody could stay with us, couldn't she?" Amy asked suddenly.

"Sure!" Polk agreed, beaming.

Guy's complexion went pale. He muttered something under his breath and got up and went to the window to stare out it. He knew for certain that Melody wouldn't want him around, even if she did like the other two. She'd never forgive him for what he'd done to her cat. Besides, he reminded himself forcibly, he didn't like her. It was her fault that he didn't have a mother anymore.

Emmett found the suggestion warming, if impractical. He'd done a lot of thinking about Melody himself. "Melody has a job," Emmett said. It surprised him that the kids found it so easy to picture Melody as part of their lives. It surprised him even more that he did, too.

"Jacobsville isn't very big, is it?" Guy asked without looking at his father. "There's not much to do there, I guess."

"You're old enough to start learning how to manage a ranch," Emmett told him. "You can come around with me and learn the ropes."

Guy's usually taciturn face brightened. He turned. "I could?"

"Yes." Emmett's eyes narrowed. "I'll have to turn things over to you one day," he added. "You might as well know one end of a rope from the other when the time comes."

Guy felt as if he'd been offered a new start with his father. It was a good feeling. Guy looked at his siblings. "I'll go," he said, his expression warning them that they'd better agree.

Amy and Polk stood close together. "I guess it would be nice to have you at home all the time, Emmett," Amy said softly. "It would be 'specially nice if you didn't have to ride any more mean horses."

"We don't want you to die, Dad," Polk agreed solemnly. "You're sort of all we've got."

Emmett's lean face hardened. "Maybe you're sort of all I've got, too. Ever think of it like that?"

Guy looked uncomfortable and Polk just smiled. But Amy slid onto his lap and hugged him. She looked up with soft, loving eyes. "I'm glad you're our daddy, Emmett," she said.

At that moment, so was he. Very, very glad.

* * *

It couldn't last, of course, all that peace and affection. They moved to Jacobsville and they hadn't been in the big sprawling ranch house two hours when the cook started screaming bloody murder and ran out of the house with her apron over her head.

"What's the matter?" Emmett called.

"There's a snake in the sink! There's a snake in the sink!"

"Oh, for God's sake, woman, what kind of snake is it?" Emmett grumbled absently, more concerned about the books he'd been going over than this gray-haired woman's hysterics over some small reptile.

"It's twenty feet long!"

"This is Texas," Emmett explained patiently. "There aren't any twenty-foot-long snakes here. You're thinking of boa constrictors and pythons. They come from the jungle."

"Hey, Dad, look what we found in the barn!" Guy called, grinning.

He came out with a *huge* black-and-white striped snake. It wasn't twenty feet long, but it was at least six.

"Aaaaahhhhhhhhh!" the cook screamed and started running again.

"Go put it back in the barn," Emmett told them.

"But it's just a king snake," Polk protested.

"And he's very friendly, Emmett," Amy agreed.

"Put it back in the barn or she'll never come back. I'll have to cook and we'll starve," he explained, gesturing toward the figure growing smaller in the distance. He scowled. "As it is, I'll have to run her to ground in the truck. Never saw anyone run that fast!"

"Spoilsport," Guy muttered. He petted the snake, which didn't seem to mind being handled in the least. "Come on, Teddy. It's back to the corn bin for you, I guess. I had hoped we could let him sleep with us. In case there were any mice inside," he said, justifying his reply.

Emmett could see the woman's face if she started to make up a bed and found the snake with its head on the pillow.

"Better not," he replied. "I'll load my pistol. If you see a mouse, I'll shoot it for you."

"The snake's a better bet, the way you shoot," Guy drawled.

Emmett glowered at him, but the boy just grinned. He and the other kids took the snake out to the barn. Half a mile down the road, Emmett caught up with the cook and part-time housekeeper, Mrs. Jenson. After swearing that the kids would never do any such thing again, he coaxed her into coming back and finishing those delicious salmon croquettes she'd started to make.

It was a hard adjustment, being home all the time. Emmett discovered that fatherhood wasn't something he could take for granted anymore. He had to work at it. All the problems the children had at school—problems that poor Mrs. Ray had handled before—were now dumped squarely in his lap.

Polk had a terrible time with fractions, and refused to do them at all in school. Amy had attitude problems and fought with her classmates. Guy was belligerent with his teachers and wouldn't mind, spending hours and hours at in-school suspension. All these problems with teachers erupted in Emmett's face, now that he had sole charge of the children.

"Why can't you kids just go to school and get educated like other children do?" he asked. He had notes from three angry teachers in his hand, and he was waving them at the children while they watched television and pretended to listen.

"It's not my fault I can't do fractions. The teacher says I'm not mathematical," Polk said with a proud smile.

"And I have a bad attitude, on account of I don't have a mommy and my daddy is never home and I need discipline and attention," Amy said smartly.

That stung. Emmett brushed it off and tried to pretend he hadn't heard it. "What's your excuse?" Emmett asked Guy.

Guy shrugged. "Beats me. Mrs. Bartley seems to have trouble relating to me or something."

Emmett's eyes narrowed. "That wouldn't have anything to do with the mouse you stuck in her purse before lunch yesterday?"

"Awww, Dad, it was only a little mouse!"

"You have to stop that sort of thing," Emmett said firmly. "We need a little more discipline around here, I can see that right now."

"You bet, Emmett," Amy agreed readily. She propped her hands under her chin and stared at him. "He's right, isn't he, guys?" she asked her brothers.

"It isn't our fault that the educational system is in chaos," Polk reported. "We're just the innocent victims of bureaucracy."

Guy nodded. "That's right."

Emmett sat down and crossed his long legs. "Victims or not, I'll thank you to start minding your manners at school. Or I might just forget to pay the electric bill. How would you watch television then?" he concluded smugly.

Amy sighed. "Well, Emmett, I guess we'd just have to watch it by candlelight."

Melody had put the children and Emmett forcibly out of her mind several times over the weeks that followed. Christmas came and went. She exchanged cards and presents with Randy and Adell, but it was still a lonely time.

It disturbed her that she kept staring at dark-haired men because they looked a little like Emmett. Remembering how he'd kissed her before he went back to San Antonio didn't help her nerves, either. She seemed to walk around in a perpetual state of nervousness, jumping when people came into the office.

"You are a case," Kit said, shaking her head when Melody leaped back from the filing cabinet as she came into the office after work.

"Nerves," Melody agreed. "I have nerves. It comes from mollycoddling nervous investors all day. It's a wonder I haven't shaken my desk apart."

"Work is all it is, hmm?" Kit asked.

"Of course," Melody replied.

The dark-haired woman only smiled. "Have you heard that Emmett and the kids moved to Jacobsville?"

Melody stopped filing and stared at her. "They did?"

"Emmett's accident must have made him do some hard thinking about his life. He phoned Logan last night and said he's given up rodeo to manage Ted Regan's cattle ranch in Jacobsville."

"Has he sold his own ranch?"

"He hired a manager. I suppose he'll make more than enough to keep his own place going until the economy gets a bit better. Meanwhile, he's having plenty of time with his kids."

"They all need that," Melody replied. "Guy especially."

"You don't like Guy, do you?"

"I don't really dislike him. But he hates me. He can't forget that I helped his mother leave. I can't say I blame him. Divorce is hard on little children."

"It's hard on any kind of children, even big ones," Kit replied. "Why don't you go home? I'll take over here until Logan's ready to leave."

"How nice of you!"

"Well, not really. I enjoy spending time with my husband. Since we both work at different jobs now, every second is precious."

Melody envied her that happiness, but she didn't mind an early night. She said so.

"You're doing a terrific job here," Kit said before she left. "We both appreciate you."

Melody grinned. "You're only saying that because I don't wear blouses cut to my knees or have a breathy voice."

"That, too." Kit chuckled.

Melody waved and went back to her lonely apartment. A telephone call from her brother shocked her speechless.

"You never phone me," she reminded Randy. "I even had to call you at Christmas. Is something wrong?"

"You know me pretty well, don't you? It's not that anything is wrong. It's just that…we have a sort of awkward situation," he began slowly.

"Randy?" she persisted.

There was an audible sigh. "I don't know how to tell you, and you can't tell anyone…especially not Logan or Tansy. Not yet."

"Why not?"

"Because if it gets back to Emmett, I don't know what we'll do!"

She was getting worried. "Randy, what is it?" she said proddingly.

"Well, it's like this. Adell's pregnant."

Melody remembered belatedly congratulating her brother, but the news was a complication that wasn't going to make things easier for Emmett and the kids. A new child in a mixed family always brought turmoil. It was a shame, too, when Emmett and the kids had just gotten settled into a new life in Jacobsville.

On the other hand, she was going to be an aunt again, and a real one this time, because Randy was her own blood. It would be his first child. She couldn't be sad about that. But she hurt for Emmett. It wasn't going to be easy for him to learn that his ex-wife was pregnant by the man who'd taken her from him. It was going to cause all sorts of problems.

* * *

Emmett stopped outside Logan's office and hesitated. He hadn't wanted to come here, but Melody was playing on his senses. He'd missed her. Christmas, even with the kids, had been oddly lonely for him this year. There was a hollow place inside him that a casual date couldn't fill any longer. He'd brooded over what do about it, and he'd finally come to the conclusion that he needed to see Melody again, to make sure he wasn't overreacting to her.

He'd looked for days for an excuse to show up here. He'd finally found one, in the guise of letting Logan invest some money for him. But he hadn't telephoned first. He wanted to know if Melody was as attracted to him as he was to her. The element of surprise was going to tell him that.

He opened the door and walked in. She was typing at the computer. She didn't see him at first, not until he closed the door and the sound distracted her.

She looked up with her usual welcoming smile for clients, but it fell short when she saw the man in the gray suit and Stetson standing just inside the door.

"Emmett!" she said involuntarily.

The light in her eyes couldn't lie. Emmett smiled, because she was glad to see him and it showed. He liked the way she looked in that figure-hugging beige dress, with her long hair in a neat French braid and her dark eyes warm in her freckled face.

"Hello," he replied. He moved close to the desk, feeling his body throb, his heart race as he drank in the sight and scent of her from scant inches away. His voice dropped an octave involuntarily in reaction. "You look well."

"I am. I'm fine. How about you?" she asked worriedly.

"No more problems. I have a hard head," he replied. His eyes slid over her face and down to the mouth he'd possessed briefly so long ago. It made him hungry to remember how eager and willing she'd been.

"Emmett!"

The exclamation came from Logan, who'd walked out with a letter to find his cousin standing over his flustered secretary.

"Hello, Logan," Emmett said, extending a hand.

"You look prosperous," Logan murmured with a smile. "What brings you to Houston?"

"I needed some advice. I was about to make an appointment…"

"No need for that. I'm not busy right now. Come on in." He handed the letter to Melody and tried not to notice that her hands were trembling. Emmett obviously had a powerful effect on her.

"I wanted to see you about some investments," Emmett said when they were sitting in Logan's office.

"Imagine that," Logan said thoughtfully. "You said you didn't trust the stock market."

"I've changed," the other man replied doggedly.

"Indeed you have. How is it, being a full-time father?"

Emmett tossed his hat onto a nearby chair. "It's hell," he said flatly. "I get all the hassles now. I never realized how much trouble three little kids could be. In fact, they're never *out* of trouble."

"Now that you're home at night, that will change, I imagine," came the droll reply. "You've spent a lot of time avoiding them."

"You know why."

Logan nodded. "Yes, I do. Are you finding your way out of the pit, Emmett?" he asked kindly.

Emmett ran a lean hand through his thick, dark hair. "Maybe. I don't know. A lot of things have changed since I had the fall. Maybe I was looking at it all the wrong way."

"Divorce isn't easy on anyone," Logan said quietly. "It would kill me if Kit left me, for any reason. I don't know if I could take it if it was for another man."

"That's how I felt. I thought I loved Adell," he said heavily. "I really did. But now I'm not sure it wasn't just hurt pride."

"Having her run out in the middle of the night with the other man involved couldn't have helped."

"It didn't. I guess maybe I understand why she did it now, though. She isn't a fighter," he added, echoing the words Melody had spoken. "She probably figured I'd play on her sympathy and talk her out of it if I had the chance." He smiled faintly. "That's what would have happened. She never could stand up to me in a fight." He leaned back. "It's all water under the bridge. I have to go on living. So does she. I want to make some provisions for the kids, in case anything happens to me. That's really why I'm here. I've got a little spare cash and I want to put it where it can grow."

Logan considered it for a moment, his eyes narrowed. "All right. I've got a few ideas. How long are you going to be in town?"

"Until tomorrow," came the surprising answer. "Mrs. Jenson is living in, so that she can watch the kids while I'm away. I…have a few other things to do while I'm in town."

"Where can I reach you?"

Emmett gave him the number at his hotel. "Until six," he said. "I may have plans for the evening."

"Oh," Logan said with a chuckle. "Confinement getting to you, is it? I gather the plans have something to do with a woman."

"Well, yes."

"From what I remember, the kids would make any sort of relationship impossible. I haven't forgotten that they were trying to take off the door of the bathroom when Kit and I were in there, at your ranch."

Emmett grinned at the darkly accusing stare. "So they did. Good thing the screwdriver was too big, wasn't it?"

Logan gave in to laughter. Emmett was as incorrigible as his kids.

He showed the other man out, but Emmett seemed strangely reluctant to leave. Perhaps he wanted to tell Melody something about the children, Logan decided, so he said his goodbyes and went back into his office.

Melody was typing nonsense into the computer, because Emmett's stare made her too nervous to function.

"Is there something you needed to ask me?" she said finally, dark eyes lifting to his.

"Yes," he said with a husky laugh. "What are you doing for dinner?"

Doing for dinner. *Doing for dinner.* The words passed through her mind with very little effect. She stared at him blankly. The telephone rang loudly and she jumped, fumbling the receiver all over the desk before she finally got it to her ear and gave the correct response.

"I'll put you through to Mr. Deverell," she said breathlessly, and buzzed Logan to give the caller's identity.

When she put the receiver back down, she was still very visibly shaken.

Emmett had his Stetson by the brim and he was watching her with a half-amused look that glittered in his green eyes. "Looking for excuses not to go?" he asked softly.

"Oh, no!" she replied huskily. "But why?"

"Why not?"

Her pulse started to run away. She wanted to refuse. She should. But somehow she couldn't. "I…what time?" she asked.

"Six."

"This isn't a good idea, you know," she said. "I'm still Randy's sister, and the past hasn't changed. Not at all."

He moved closer to the desk and his lean hand toyed with a notepad on its paper-littered surface. His pale green eyes searched her dark ones quietly. "That's true. Maybe I've changed. I enjoy your company. I want to take you out for a meal. That's all," he added flatly. "You won't have to fight me off over dessert and coffee."

She laughed nervously. "That was the last thought in my mind."

He didn't believe that. But she relaxed, and he felt glad that he'd said it. He didn't want to make her uneasy. She'd been too much on his mind lately and he wanted to find a way to purge her from it. Perhaps closer acquaintance would solve the problem for him. Often women who seemed nice weren't, and they couldn't keep up the act when a man took the time to get to know them.

Melody was relieved by his blunt statement. There had been a time or two when she had found herself having to talk her way out of a difficult situation.

"I'll see you at six, then," he said.

He stuck the Stetson back on his head and went to the door. He paused there and turned. "I'm rabidly old-fashioned in one respect. I like dresses."

She grinned impishly. "Yes, but how do you *look* in a dress?" she asked curiously.

His pale eyes splintered with good humor. "Wear what you damned well please, then," he mused. "See you later."

Melody owned one nice dress. It was black with a silvery draped bodice and spaghetti straps. It flattered her full-figured body without making her sexiness blatant. She coiled her hair around the top of her head and wore more makeup than usual. The final touch was high heels. Most men she dated were her height or shorter. But Emmett was very tall, and she could get away with wearing high heels when she went out with him. She liked the way she felt when she was dressed up; very feminine and sensuous.

Now, she wondered, why should she think of herself as

sensuous? She had to douse that thought before Emmett read it in her face. She didn't want any complications.

He was prompt. The doorbell sounded exactly at six. She opened the door and there he was, very elegant in dark slacks and a white dinner jacket with a red carnation in the buttonhole of his lapel. The stark white contrasted handsomely with his lean, dark face and dark hair. He had on a cream-colored Stetson to set off the elegance.

"You look very nice," she said huskily.

"Stole my line," he mused, grinning at her. "Ready to go?"

"I'll just get my wrap and my purse."

She draped a black mantilla over her shoulders and picked up her small black crepe purse. She checked to make sure Alistair had water and cat food. He was curled up on the couch asleep, so she didn't disturb him.

Emmett waited while she locked the door before he took her hand in his and led her along the corridor.

If someone had told her that holding hands could be a powerful aphrodisiac she might have laughed, but with Emmett, it was. His lean, strong hand curled into her fingers with confident possession. Beside him she felt protected and unexpectedly feminine. She couldn't remember ever feeling that way with another date.

He saw her expression as he led her into the empty elevator and pushed the Down button. He'd let go of her hand to do that. Now he leaned elegantly against the rail inside the elevator as it started to move and just watched her, registering the conflicting emotions that washed over her face.

The tension between them was chaotic. She could barely breathe as she met his eyes and felt her knees go weak.

"You look lovely," he said, his voice deep, his eyes faintly glittery. "Black provides a backdrop for all the color in your hair and your face." His eyes fell to her draped bodice and lingered there, making her feel shivery all over.

"How do you like Jacobsville, you and the children?" she asked quickly, hoping to distract him.

"What? Oh, so far, so good. It's no picnic, but I think we're all getting the hang of it. It's going to be the best thing that ever happened to the children," he added quietly. "I honestly didn't realize how much out of hand they'd gotten."

He looked broody for a minute, and Melody wondered if there wasn't more to it than that. But before she could voice her opinions, the elevator door opened and they were on their way out.

He stopped, taking her hand back in his and holding it warmly while he searched her eyes. "I like it better like this. Don't you?" he asked softly, and he didn't smile. His eyes dropped to her mouth. "For now," he added, very gently.

Chapter 6

The cool air on her face felt good as they left the apartment house and walked down the street. Melody was still vibrating from the heady experience of being on a date with Emmett. He, on the other hand, seemed perfectly nonchalant. Her heart was racing like a mad thing while they walked, hand in hand.

He led her to the car and unlocked it, but when he partially opened her door, he stood still, so that she couldn't get past him. She was so close that she could smell his tangy cologne, feel the warm strength of his body. It made her react in an unexpected way, and she moved back against the car a little self-consciously.

"You're nervous of me. Why?" he asked.

She twisted her bag in her hands and laughed. "I'm not, really." She shrugged. "It's just that it's been a long time since I've been out for the evening."

He tilted her face up to his quiet eyes. His thumb smoothed against her chin and her full lower lip, making sensation after sensation wash over her. She wasn't fooling him. He read quite accurately her helpless physical response to him. Whatever else she was, she wasn't experienced. That was unique to a man who deliberately chose women for their sophistication and disinterest in involvement. Melody was different.

"That's the only reason?" he said, probing softly.

She couldn't hide her expression quickly enough. "Well… maybe not the only one," she said demurely.

He smiled with pure delight. He bent and his lips brushed gently across her wide forehead. She smelled of soap and skin cream and floral cologne. The mingled scents appealed to his senses. "There's nothing to worry about," he said quietly. "Nothing at all." He moved away from her then, still good-natured. "I hope you like a smorgasbord of choices. This restaurant has international fare."

The change from tenderness to companionship was unsettling, but Melody managed the shift. "I love international fare," she said.

He opened the car door the rest of the way and helped her inside. All the way to the restaurant, the most intimate thing he discussed was the stock market and the state of the economy. By the time they disembarked, Melody could have been forgiven for thinking she'd dreamed that gentle kiss in the parking lot.

It wasn't a terribly ritzy place to eat. The food was very good and moderately priced, but Melody didn't have to worry if her clothes were good enough to wear to it. The thought made her smile.

Emmett cocked an eyebrow. "Private thoughts?"

"I was just glad that I'm properly dressed for this place, without being underdressed," she confessed on a laugh. "I don't have the wardrobe for those French restaurants where they don't even bother to put the prices on the menus."

He chuckled. "I've eaten in a couple of those," he replied.

"I never felt very comfortable in them, though. My idea of a good lunch is a McDonald's hamburger."

"Good old Scottish cooking," she mused, tongue-in-cheek.

He laughed with her as he sampled his rare steak. "You're remarkably good-humored."

"Oh, I like laughter," she told him. "Life is too short to go around with a long face complaining about everything."

He studied her over a bite of nicely browned steak. "You manage to work for my cousin without complaints?"

"Well...not many," she said. "And he's my cousin, too, you know."

His eyes grew somber and they fell to his plate. "So he **is**."

"You look so remote." She hesitated. "Oh, I see. You **were** thinking that Adell was related to him by marriage, and **she**'s still related to him because she's married to Randy—" She broke off, flushing.

He put down his fork. His appetite had gone. He'd thought he was getting over Adell's defection, but apparently the wounds were still open.

"I'm sorry," she said with a grimace. "I've ruined it all by bringing them up, haven't I?" She laid down her own fork. "It won't work, Emmett," she said suddenly, without stopping to choose her words. "There are too many scars for us to be able to get along. You're never going to be able to forget about Randy and Adell." That was true—and he didn't even know what she did, either, about Adell being pregnant. She felt guilty.

He lifted his eyes to her face. It made him angry that she'd assumed that he was romantically interested in her. It made him more angry that he'd actually been thinking along those lines until she'd dragged Randy and Adell into the conversation.

He lashed out in frustration. "Aren't you taking too much

for granted? My God, this was only a dinner invitation, not a proposal of marriage!'' he said angrily. His eyes calmed. ''Or is that what you thought I might be considering by asking you out?'' He smiled at her embarrassment without humor. ''Do I really seem the sort of man who can't wait to get married a second time?''

She had to force down the hopes she'd been nursing since his invitation to this meal. He obviously had cold feet about any relationship between them, and he was hiding it in sarcasm. She knew that as surely as if he'd told her so.

''Of course not,'' she lied. ''That isn't what I was thinking at all. I only meant that taking me out isn't a good idea.''

''For once, we agree on something.'' He lifted his coffee cup to his firm lips, averting his gaze. He must have been out of his mind to have come up to Houston in the first place. Asking Melody out had been another temporary mental aberration. He had enough trouble already without rushing out to search for more.

''Are you finished?'' he asked when he'd drained his cup.

She was glad she hadn't wanted dessert. He seemed to be in a flaming rush to leave. She was eager to oblige him. The evening had been an unmitigated disaster!

He drove her back to her apartment in a furious silence, without even tuning in a song on the radio to break the tension. Melody didn't feel any more inclined toward conversation than he seemed to.

She rode up in the elevator beside him without looking to the side. He paused at her door, sighing angrily.

''Thank you for an interesting evening,'' she said tightly.

''It was gratitude for keeping the kids,'' he said, his words as clipped as her own. ''That's all. It was a belated thank-you for kindnesses rendered.''

''And accepted in the same vein,'' she said. ''No complications wanted.''

"That's right, and you remember it," he said through his teeth. "You're the last damned complication I need right now!"

"Did I offer to be one?" she asked, aghast.

"Whether you did or not is beside the point! I've got kids who can't get along with anyone because they don't get any love at home. Their father doesn't give a damn about them and their mother ran away with your damned brother!"

The anger she'd felt was suddenly gone as she saw through the furious words to the hurt beneath it. He was wounded. She wondered if he knew how obvious it was, and decided that he didn't. Her dark eyes lost their glare and became gentle. She reached out with unexpected bravery and took one of his big, lean hands in hers.

"Come inside and have some coffee, Emmett," she said gently. "You can tell me all about it."

He must be daft. He kept telling himself he was as he let her lead him like a lamb into the softly lit kitchen.

He perched himself on her tallest stool and watched broodingly while she filled the coffeemaker and turned it on.

She sat down at the counter next to him, her mantilla and purse deposited on the kitchen table until she had time to move them.

"What's wrong with the children?" she asked.

He sighed heavily. "Polk won't try to do his math. Guy can't get along with his teacher. Amy can't get along with anybody, and her teacher sends me this damned note that says she doesn't get enough attention at home."

"And you're doing the best you can, only nobody knows it but you, and those words hurt."

He lifted narrowed, wounded eyes to hers. "Yes, it hurts," he said flatly. "I've done my best to provide for them. All I've had since Adell walked out is a housekeeper. Now, I'm trying to put things right, but I can't do it overnight!"

She smoothed her fingers gently over the backs of his

strong, lean hands. "Why don't you write Amy's teacher a note and tell her that," she suggested. "Teachers don't read minds, you know. They have to be told about problems. They're people, too, just like you and me. They can make allowances, when they know the situation."

He relaxed. His tall, broad-shouldered form seemed to slump. "I'm tired," he said. "It's a shock. New surroundings, new people, a new job with more responsibilities than I've had in years and the kids on top of it. I guess I got snarled up in it all."

"It's perfectly understandable. Don't the kids like it better, having you home?"

"I don't know. Guy's still standoffish. I've tried to get him interested in things around the ranch, but he's shying away from me. He's not adjusting very well to school, because the teacher wants him to mind and he won't. He can't seem to conform, and his temper is his worst enemy. Amy and Polk aren't much better, but at least I can handle them when they're not driving school officials batty."

"Better them than you?" she teased.

He chuckled reluctantly. "Not really. I'll have to bone up on fractions and spend some time with Polk. Maybe I just haven't found the right tack with Guy yet. He likes ranching, but we don't have much in common outside it."

"Emmett, hasn't it occurred to you that these problems could be nothing more than pleas for attention?" she asked. "Randy and I used to get into all sorts of trouble when Dad got too wrapped up in Mother's illness to notice us. It's a child's nature to want to be loved, to have proof of that love."

"Not only a child's, Melody," he said unexpectedly. His eyes searched hers from much too close. "Even adults can go off the deep end when no one gives a damn about them."

"You know the kids love you."

"I know." His chest rose and fell heavily and his eyes

grew intimate, holding hers for much longer than necessary, making her own pulse race.

"The, uh, the coffee's ready, I think," she said. Her voice sounded husky, even shaky. She dragged her eyes away from his and went to get the coffee.

She took down cups and saucers from the cabinet, and while she got the coffee service together, Emmett moved around the living room, restless and unsettled. His eyes searched out the books in her bookcase, the framed prints on the wall. He seemed to be noticing everything, taking inventory of her likes and dislikes.

He was thumbing through a volume of poetry when she put the coffee things on the dining-room table.

He put the book down and joined her at the table. She put cream and sugar into hers. He left his own black.

"I've got some cookies around here somewhere," she offered.

"No need. I don't have much of a sweet tooth," he said. He stared into his coffee. "How did you know?"

"Know what?"

He looked up with a rueful smile. "That I needed to talk about the kids."

"You picked a fight for no reason," she murmured dryly. "I used to have a friend in school who did the same thing. She never said what was bothering her. She picked fights until I made her tell me." She fingered the rim of her coffee cup. "Or maybe you didn't exactly pick a fight for no reason," she added sadly. "You aren't over Randy and Adell, really."

He moved restlessly in the chair. "It's going to take time."

Her eyes lifted to his. He didn't know that Adell was pregnant. How was she going to tell him? How could she tell him?

He saw that curious expression and scowled. "There's

something," he said slowly. "Something you're holding back. What is it?"

She averted her gaze to the coffee cup. "Nothing."

"Now you sound like one of the kids." He moved her coffee cup out of her reach and caught her hand in his over the small table. "Out with it. You made me talk when I didn't want to. It's your turn."

"Emmett…"

He nodded reassuringly. "Come on."

She winced. Her big, dark eyes were full of sadness, sorrow. "Adell…is pregnant."

He didn't react at all for a minute. He let go of her hand and sat back in his chair. He let out a long, rough breath. "Well."

"You'd have found out sooner or later. I didn't want to have to be the one to tell you."

He looked at her. "You didn't? Why?" he asked, letting the shock of what he'd learned pass over him for the moment.

"You resent me enough already because of my brother," she said miserably.

His eyes searched her wan, sad face. "Do I?" he wondered aloud. It didn't feel like hatred. No, not at all.

He drained his coffee cup, and she took it, and hers, into the kitchen. She felt terrible. Working helped sometimes, so she busied herself loading the dishwasher. There wasn't much, but she'd saved last night's pots and pans to make a load. Behind her, she felt Emmett's eyes and could only imagine the torment he must be feeling. She wanted to console him, but she didn't know how.

After a minute, Emmett got up and poised himself against the kitchen counter to watch her work. He didn't want to think about Adell being pregnant by her new husband. He wasn't going to let himself do that now. Later would be time enough.

Melody was graceful for such a tall woman, he thought

reluctantly, watching her hands as she put the dishes into the dishwasher.

She noticed the look she was getting. It made her tingle. He'd long since taken off his dinner jacket and tie and Stetson. His long-sleeved, pristine white shirt was partially unbuttoned and the sleeves were rolled up. He looked elegant and rakish, and Melody was surprised that he seemed to find her so interesting. He'd been married, and she knew very well that women still chased him. He had more experience than any man she'd ever dated. It made her nervous to remember how vulnerable she was with him, how easily he could overrule her and take anything he wanted. She hoped her unease didn't show too much.

"You're efficient," he remarked.

She smiled. "Oh, I'm very domestic. I had to learn early. My mother was an invalid for years before she and Dad died. Randy and I would have starved if I hadn't been able to cook."

His face closed up at the mention of his ex-wife's new husband.

Melody put detergent into the dishwasher and started it running. Her eyes flicked to Emmett and away. "Yes, I know, you hate my brother as much as you hate me."

His green eyes were completely without hostility for once as he studied her. The black dress she was wearing suited her fair complexion. Its fit emphasized her full breasts and hips and small waist, and the milky-white softness of her shoulders with their scattering of freckles. He liked what he saw when he looked at her, even if it was against his better judgment.

"I don't hate you," he said quietly.

"Pull the other one, Emmett."

She'd turned and was starting out the door when he moved with surprising speed and blocked her way. "I like the way you say my name. Say it again."

His arm was across the doorway, almost touching the tips of her breasts. She tensed at the sensual threat of it. "This isn't wise," she said seriously, meeting his green eyes levelly.

One eye narrowed. His gaze on her face was intent, curious. "Isn't it? Maybe not. We're years apart—almost a generation. Funny, I always thought you were older. I don't know why. You seem very mature for a woman just barely out of her teens."

"I had to grow up fast. May I get by, please?"

He could see her breathing quicken. "Why are you afraid of me?"

Her eyes darted up and down again. Her cheeks colored. "Am I?"

He reached out and caught her by the waist. He tugged, pulling her slowly to him, so that her mouth was poised just under his.

"Maybe intimidated is a better choice of words," he murmured. His hands slid up her rib cage with slow sensuality, making her flinch at the sudden pleasure of their touch. "I know a hell of a lot more than you do about this, don't I, little one?" His breath was warm on her parted lips. "Is that what's wrong?"

"Yes," she whispered breathlessly.

He looked at her mouth instead of her eyes. It trembled, pink and soft like some pastel flower, waiting to be touched. She was so young, he thought. She really was off-limits to a man his age.

But even as he thought it, his lips moved the scant inches necessary to bring them right down over her whispered gasp, and took possession of that petal-pink mouth.

She grasped his shirtfront and stiffened in surprise.

"Shh," he whispered against her lips while he worked with sensuous mastery at parting them. "You're safe. You're perfectly safe. There won't be anything to regret. Relax for me.''

She'd been kissed. She'd been kissed plenty of times, and even by him! There was certainly no reason why Emmett's mouth should be so different from any other man's.

But, it was. Her whole body felt as if it contracted while Emmett's warm, strong arms enveloped her and his tongue slowly, tenderly impaled her mouth as it had once before. She stiffened again as the throbbing pleasure began to make her feel unwanted, unwelcome sensations. She fought them.

He felt the resistance, as slight as it was, and lifted his dark head.

"You're still holding back from me," he said, his voice tender if a little unsteady. "I'm not going to hurt you."

"It makes me feel funny," she replied dizzily.

His nose brushed lazily against hers. "Where?"

"In my stomach..."

"Good," he whispered. His lips eased back down and brushed hers apart, teasing it to make her mouth follow his in a sensual daze. His hands slid to her hips and contracted in a strangely arousing rhythm, pulling and pushing, brushing her legs against his.

She shivered. He felt that and lifted his head to search her wide, curious eyes.

"You're so young," he said quietly. He took a slow, steadying breath. "And so responsive that I'm likely to take advantage of it."

Desire had her in its grip. She wasn't afraid. She was hungry. "How?" she asked in a breathless whisper, and her eyes clung to his hard mouth as she spoke. "What will you do to me?"

His fingers eased up her rib cage and came to rest against the soft swell of her breasts. He nibbled at her mouth. One lean hand slowly cupped her and began to caress her with tender mastery. She started to stiffen until the dark delight of it made her go boneless in his embrace. She could have resisted his desire, but not her own. He was years beyond her in experience, and she reacted with helpless curiosity and need.

He nibbled tenderly at her lower lip. "I know. It's forbidden territory, isn't it?" he whispered into her parting lips. "Nice girls don't let men do this. Except that they do, Melody," he breathed as he drew her even closer. "This is part and parcel of being human." His thumb drew suddenly, tenderly, across her taut nipple, a fiery touch that caused her whole body to clench. Her nails bit into him and she gasped. "If I hurt you, I want to know it," he whispered. "Because it's only meant to arouse, not to bruise."

She shivered, but she didn't back away. She felt as if she had pulses where she'd never suspected, throbbing and hot. "It didn't hurt, Emmett," she admitted huskily, although she was too shy to look at him. She closed her eyes and hid them against his shirtfront. "Do it again."

He hadn't expected this kind of honesty, or as much co-operation. It ate at his control. His hand swallowed her, making magic on her body. She gave in without a sound, and he felt ten feet taller. He paused just long enough to unfasten his shirt halfway down his chest and drag her hand inside it, against the damp tangle of hair over the warm, hard muscles.

The feel of his body like that made her pulse throb. "You're hairy," she whispered.

"I'm like this all over," he whispered roughly. His hand moved down to her hips. The other one joined it. He pulled her into the blatant arousal of his body and held her there firmly but gently. "It's all right. Be still," he said when she tried unsuccessfully to pull away. He searched her face, finding shy curiosity there. "Have you never felt a man's body in full arousal before?"

"No," she managed to say, embarrassed.

"There's a first time for everything," he said softly, lowering his head. "I need oblivion and you need teaching. Think of it as a…reciprocal exchange."

"It isn't a good idea," she said unsteadily.

"I know. But it will be sweet."

And it was. The sweetest kind of exchange, savagely tender and violently arousing.

Her nails thrust gently into the hair at the back of his head while he kissed her and slowly caressed her breasts with hands that held a faint tremor at the license they were being given so generously.

In turn, she was learning about his body, enjoying the feel of the thick mat of hair over warm, firm muscles. She smoothed her hands sensually up and down his chest with delight while he taught her the intricacies of openmouthed kissing. By the time he began to brush against her rhythmically with his hips, she was whimpering with the same desire that was riding him. But it couldn't go on. He was fast reaching the point of no return, and seducing her was impossible.

She felt swollen from head to toe, throbbing, when he finally lifted his head to look into her misty, half-closed eyes. He was more aroused than he could remember being in recent years. His body throbbed painfully with the need for release.

He pushed her hips away from his and took her face in his hands before he kissed her again, with growing tenderness.

She started to move closer, but he caught her by the waist and kept her away.

Her eyes asked the question that her swollen lips wouldn't form.

"Does the term 'playing with fire' ring any chimes?" he asked with forced, husky laughter.

"I don't care," she said unsteadily. Her face colored, but she didn't look away. "I like the way you feel."

His face tautened. "I like the way you feel, too, but a few minutes of feverish sex isn't going to improve our situation. And I did promise you that there would be nothing to regret.'' He forced himself to let her go and move away. He lit a cigarette. He hardly smoked these days, but he needed something to steady his nerves.

''A few minutes of feverish sex?'' she said with a feeble attempt at humor as she leaned back against the counter and stared at him from a face that held lingering traces of desire.

He glanced at her and laughed, too. ''Yes, well, it may be crude, but it was all I could think of at the time. I had to save you from yourself. Not to mention, from me.'' His eyes were bold on her breasts, assessing their taut peaks before his gaze lifted again to her flushed, excited face. ''You're a quick study.''

''Is that what I am?''

''That, and alarmingly innocent, for all your response just now,'' he added, the laughter leaving his eyes, to be replaced with quiet introspection. ''Why are you still a virgin, Melody?''

She didn't bother to deny it. She knew all too well from what Kit had told her that he was definitely no novice. Women apparently fell over themselves trying to climb into bed with him. ''I'm oversized and old-fashioned and plain, didn't you notice?'' she asked, stung by the question.

''Don't take offense,'' he said quietly. ''It wasn't a sarcastic question. If you want to know the truth,'' he added, his voice going sensual and soft, and his green eyes glittery, as he looked at her, ''it excites me to the point of madness.''

She drew a slow breath. ''That's a new observation,'' she replied. ''Most people think I'm crazy or fanatically careful. The truth is that nobody ever put on enough pressure to make me careless.''

''Until now?'' he asked gently.

She started to deny it, but that was pointless. He knew. She saw it in his eyes.

''Until now,'' she echoed.

He lifted the cigarette to his lips and blew out a faint cloud of smoke. Half angrily, he turned on the faucet and held the barely touched cigarette under it, extinguishing it. He tossed the finished remains into the trash can and stood staring down at it.

"I used to smoke a pack a day. I've lost my enthusiasm for it. Addiction is unwise." He turned and stared at her intently. "Any kind of addiction."

"Smoking is bad for you. I never even tried it."

"Good for you." He took the almost full package out of his pocket and dropped that into the trash can, too. "I have to go."

She didn't want that. She felt a sudden, acute sense of loss that was puzzling.

She moved out of the kitchen and preceded him to the front door. But when she would have opened it, his big, lean hand flattened on its surface and prevented her.

"What are you doing Sunday?" he asked abruptly, and against his better judgment.

Chapter 7

Melody felt the floor giving way under her feet, and realized that it was because her heart was beating so fast. For a minute she thought he might be joking. But he didn't look as if he were, and there was a new softness in his green eyes.

"Why?" Her voice sounded like a croak.

He'd buttoned his shirt and put his dinner jacket back on. He finished with his tie and picked up his Stetson before he answered her. "I want you to spend the day with us so that I can show you the ranch," he said quietly. "Amy and Polk have talked about you since we left here. They actually asked if you couldn't come and look after them when our housekeeper quit in San Antonio," he added with a smile. "They think you're great."

"I think they're great, too." She hesitated. "I'd love to. But Guy wouldn't like it."

"I know," he said easily. "Guy's been distrustful of everyone since his mother left." He grimaced, remembering what she'd told him about Adell. "I wouldn't dare tell him

she's pregnant—him or the other kids. Not until I have time
to prepare them.''

"They'll adjust," she said softly. "It's amazing what people, even little people, can do when they have to."

"I guess so." He searched her dark eyes for a long time
and laughed softly. "I hated you that night you helped Adell
meet Randy at the airport to leave me," he recalled. "I said
some terrible things to you. I guess I scared you pretty good,
too, when I went after Randy." He shifted restlessly. "I'm
sorry."

The belated apology was unexpected, as was the invitation
to Jacobsville.

"People in pain lash out," she said simply. "I understood."

"All the same, you backed away from me when I first
came to town with the kids."

"Self-protection," she mused. "Survival instinct."

"Yes, well I notice that it's done a nosedive tonight," he
murmured, letting his eyes fall to the wrinkled black fabric
of her bodice that his exploring hands had disturbed.

She cleared her throat. "What time Sunday?"

"I'll pick you up about ten. Or do you go to church?"

"I do, usually. But I'll play hooky Sunday. I could drive
down," she added.

"I hate the idea of having you on the roads alone," he
said. "It's a good long drive from Jacobsville to Houston."

She smiled. He was being protective. She didn't mind one
bit. It was nice to be cared about, to have someone worry
about her welfare. These days, that was unusual.

"Okay," she said gently.

His chest rose and fell heavily. He smiled back at her.
"Can you ride?"

"A little."

"Play checkers?"

She blew on her nails and buffed them on her sleeve. "World champion class," she informed him.

He lifted an eyebrow. "Well, we'll see about that!"

She grinned. "Okay." Her eyes narrowed. "You'll be sure you take matches and ropes away from those kids before I get there?"

"I'll confiscate everything incendiary," he swore, hand over his heart. "Also sharp objects, blunt instruments and listening devices."

"They sound like a renegade branch of the CIA."

He leaned close. "They are. Juvenile division."

She laughed delightedly. "They're good kids, Emmett," she said. "All three of them."

"Guy was honestly sorry about the cat," he said with emphasis. "He's never done cruel things. Mischievous, yes, but they always drew the line at deliberately hurting people. He learned something from it."

"I'm glad."

"Sunday, then?"

She nodded. Her eyes sketched his face with soft hunger. He returned the look, but he didn't touch her again. It was a wrench, because he wanted to. The feel of her body in his hands had made him weak-kneed. His eyes slowly dragged over her and he felt himself going taut. He had to get out of here before he did something stupid.

"I have to go. Good night," he said softly.

"Good night."

He opened the door and turned, silhouetted in the hall light. "Wear jeans and boots," he cautioned. "If we go riding, it's safer."

"I'll remember."

He winked at her, producing an odd jerky sensation in the region of her heart. Then he tipped his Stetson down over his thick, dark hair and walked away, whistling to himself.

Melody closed the door reluctantly. She could have stood

watching him all the way to the elevator with the greatest pleasure.

Amy and Polk had been looking forward to Melody's visit all week. When she drove up with Emmett, they opened her car door and ran into her arms, laughing and talking together. Guy didn't move off the porch. He stood there, a little belligerent, with his hands tight in his jeans pockets, glaring.

Melody noticed him there, and thought how like his father he looked. It wounded her that she and Guy were enemies. It was going to make any relationship she tried to form with Emmett impossible. Emmett probably knew it, too, she thought. But perhaps friendship was all he had in mind. Then she remembered the way he'd kissed her and what he'd said about her innocence. No. Friendship wouldn't be all of it.

Fielding Amy and Polk, Emmett opened the door for all of them. Mrs. Jenson, looking harassed, stayed just long enough to meet Melody and then beat a hasty retreat to the kitchen.

"What did you do, try to tie her to the television?" Emmett asked his angelic brood.

"Not at all, Emmett," Amy assured him, smiling up at them. "Melody, how do you like our new house?"

"It's very nice, Amy," Melody replied. "Hello, Guy," she added coolly.

Guy only shrugged and didn't look at her.

He pretended to be watching television intently while Polk and Amy showed Melody all their treasures and school papers. Just as if she was already their mother, he thought bitterly. Well, he wasn't going to show her anything of his! Melody hated him, and he certainly hated her. She wasn't *his* mother. She wasn't ever going to be!

He glanced at her from his pale eyes, and his mind began working. It wasn't certain yet. He had time. He had to remember that, and not panic because his father had brought her down to the ranch. He could get her right out of his father's life if he just kept his head. The one thing he couldn't afford to do was let things get serious between them. His mother would come back one day. She'd get tired of her new husband and come home, and they'd all be a family again. Guy was sure of it. He just had to stop his father from getting involved with any other woman until that happened. And he would, too.

Melody was blissfully unaware of Guy's plotting, and frankly glad when he wandered off later to play with his dog, Barney.

"We can go riding after lunch, if you like," Emmett said, smiling at her while Amy and Polk turned their attention back to a nature special on television.

"I'd like that."

"Come on. I'll show you my horses." He held out his hand. She put hers into it, tingling at the contact. He looked good, she thought, in jeans and a blue-checked shirt and boots. He was tall and lean and she loved looking at him, touching him.

He was doing some looking of his own. She was wearing yellow jeans and a matching yellow knit sweater that suited her fair complexion. She walked just in front of him toward the front porch and his eyes narrowed on the fit of those jeans. He had to do some quick mental exercises to stop the physical reaction his interest provoked.

"It's beautiful here," she said, gazing lovingly around at the long, bare horizon and the white-fenced acreage thick with red-coated cattle. There were live oak and pecan trees all around the house, along with pines and thick glossy-leaved bushes.

"I guess it is. I miss my own place." He stuck his hands into his pockets and stared out at the barn. "I guess this place will be lush and green when spring comes. Right now, it looks a bit barren. And there's no mesquite," he muttered.

"Don't tell me you miss the thorns on the mesquite," she teased.

The light in her face made him hungry for things he didn't realize he wanted. He took his hands out of his pockets and captured one of her hands in his. "Come on and see the horses."

"Okay!"

He smiled and led her out to the barn. A small calf was resting in a stall by himself. Emmett explained that the calf's mother had died and he was malnourished before he'd been found. They were feeding him up before they went through the process of trying to pair him with a foster mother.

Down the aisle from the calf in a separate section of the huge barn, he had several saddle horses and a stud Appaloosa stallion in separate quarters. The stallion wasn't kept with the other horses. Emmett explained that it was because he was too volatile.

"I love Apps," he said wistfully, gazing at the big animal, which was mostly splashy red and with white spots. "They're beautiful, but they have unpredictable qualities."

"Just like people," she teased.

He glanced down at her from under the wide brim of his gray working hat. "Just like people," he agreed. He let his eyes run down her body boldly. "You bother me in tight jeans. I didn't know you were going to look so sexy."

She laughed self-consciously. "Well, I never," she murmured.

"I know you've never," he murmured dryly. "That's another thing that excites me."

"You'll turn my head if you aren't careful," she said, trying to lighten the atmosphere.

"I'm tired of being careful." He drew up a booted foot and rested it on the lowest rung of a gate. "In between work and more work, you're all I think about lately," he said matter-of-factly, watching her with glittery green eyes. "I don't look at other women. I haven't slept with anyone since long before I got thrown off that bronc.''

She was almost afraid to ask, but she had to know. "Because of...me?"

He nodded slowly. "Because of you." He sighed heavily. "Melody, you're barely twenty. It's a hell of a jump from your age to mine, and I've got a built-in family. I can't seduce you because my conscience won't let me. I can't stay away from you because you're obsessing me. Know that old saying about being caught between a rock and a hard place? I don't have any trouble understanding it these days."

She met his eyes steadily. "You want to sleep with me."

He frowned lightly, his expression whimsical. "I hadn't thought about *sleeping,* exactly," he said meaningfully. He scowled and his eyes narrowed thoughtfully. "On the other hand, I wouldn't mind holding you all night in my arms. I haven't wanted to do that since I was courting Adell." He pushed his hat back from his forehead, and his level stare didn't waver. "In fact, to be brutally frank, what I wanted to do with Adell was pretty limited. It's...different with you."

That was nice. She began to smile. She felt a delicious kindling of joy deep inside herself. He had to care a little, for there to be a difference. She wanted him, too, but it was much more than a physical need. The thought of lying close in his arms all night gave her a warm, comforting sort of pleasure.

"You don't wear pajamas," she said absently.

His eyebrows went up.

She flushed, remembering how he looked without clothes. "Sorry! I guess my mind was wandering."

"Oh? Where was it wandering?"

She traced the grain of the wood on the gate. "I was thinking about sleeping with you," she said quietly. "I haven't been held in a long time. Not...by anyone who cared about me."

"Neither have I."

She glanced at him. "Oh?" she said with a cold, speaking look, because she'd heard about the rodeo groupies of the past year.

His broad shoulders lifted and fell. "Being held in a sexual frenzy isn't the same." He scowled. "And I think there has to be more to a marriage than good sex. That's new for me. Adell and I had nothing in common except desire and a love of children."

"That's pretty important, isn't it?" she asked.

"Yes. But common interests, mutual respect—those things make a relationship last." He smiled wistfully, studying her. "Funny, I could never talk to Adell the way I can to you. She liked sex, but she was ice-cold in the daylight, as if it embarrassed her that she had physical needs."

"I think a lot of women are like that," she said.

He tilted her chin up. "Are you going to be?" he asked, smiling indulgently. "Will you want the lights out the first time?"

She considered that. "I haven't let anybody see me without my clothes, except my doctor," she said. "I think it will be embarrassing, and I'll be self-conscious, because I'm big and a little overweight..."

He touched her mouth with a lean forefinger. He wasn't smiling. "You aren't overweight or oversized. You look like a woman should," he said. "I don't know why you think men should go lusting after skin and bones. There are exceptions, but most of us like a well-rounded figure with big breasts."

She flushed, but he wouldn't let her look away.

"Don't be embarrassed," he said gently. "There's nothing wrong with you. Nothing at all."

"Thanks," she said huskily. It was unusual to feel smaller than an Amazon. She smiled at him. Her eyes turned toward the doors of the barn, toward the outside, which was sunlit and peaceful. "It must be nice to live on a ranch," she said with unconscious wistfulness. "I know it's hard work, but you're so far away from technology."

He laughed uproariously.

"What's so funny?"

"Wait until you see the main-frame computer in my office," he mused dryly. "Not to mention the state-of-the-art jet printer, the fax machine, the color hand scanner, the photocopier and the modem."

She stared at him blankly.

"I have to buy and sell cattle, keep up with sales reports, tally information about the herds and the cross-breeding program. I'm in constant contact with breeders and buyers, the National Cattlemen's Association, the Texas branch of it, not to mention veterinarians and state officials—"

"But you raise cattle, don't you?" she faltered.

"Raising cattle is big business these days, honey," he said, the endearment, which he never used, coming so naturally with her that he hardly noticed he'd said it.

She noticed, though. Her face colored and her eyes brightened.

He touched her hair, fingering its thick, elegant length in the French plait. He wondered how it would feel to run his fingers through its thick, loosened strands at night. She didn't usually wear it down. "Honey," he repeated. "It's an endearment that suits you. Your hair looks like wildflower honey in spots, all golden and glowing in the sunlight, Melody."

As he spoke, he moved closer and his head began to bend. He brushed his mouth over hers until he coaxed it to open. Then he kissed her with piercing hunger, with possession.

Seconds later, she was riveted to every inch of him, held so close that she could feel him in an intimacy they'd only shared once before.

"God!" He ground out the single word, and his hand

slipped under her yellow knit sweater to raid her soft femininity. He kissed her hungrily for a long few seconds and then lifted his head to look into her dazed eyes while his hand felt for the catch to her bra and snapped it with practiced efficiency.

He glanced around them to make sure they weren't being observed. Then, while he watched her, his hand moved up to softly caress her bare breast. He felt it swell, felt its tip go hard and hot in his damp palm.

"Your breasts are very full," he whispered huskily. "I love touching them like this."

"Emmett," she protested weakly, and hid her face against his chest.

She was shy, but not at all inhibited or coquettish. He loved that honesty. His lean hand covered her completely, and he searched for her mouth until he found it.

She felt hot all over. Shaky. Throbbing with a kind of fever. She moaned faintly.

"Yes," he said roughly. "It isn't enough, is it?"

His hands went to the hem of the sweater and abruptly pushed it up, along with her loose bra. Then he stood and stared at her with an expression she'd never seen on a man's face before. She blushed, because certainly no man had ever looked at her bare breasts before.

"Baby," he said unsteadily, "you are a walking, blushing work of art!"

He made her feel beautiful. She watched him watching her and couldn't manage to feel any embarrassment. His eyes were explicit and very, very flattering.

His hands shook as he forced himself to pull the fabric down. He couldn't be sure those kids weren't hiding out somewhere nearby and he could lose his head much too easily if he did what he wanted to.

Her misty eyes asked a question.

He avoided meeting them while he reached behind her and refastened the bra under the cover of her sweater.

"I don't have a lot of control with you," he confessed quietly. "I don't want to push my luck and spoil things."

"You only looked at me," she whispered.

"That wasn't all I wanted to do, though," he said bluntly. He met her eyes. "I wanted to put my mouth on your breasts and taste you with my tongue and my teeth. And if I'd done that, I'd have taken you standing up, right here."

She stared at him blankly. "You would…bite me?" she asked uncertainly.

He laughed at her expression. "Not like that, for God's sake! I'd nibble you." He shook his head, because she so obviously didn't understand. "Melody, you're incredible. Just incredible. Have you done anything with a man beyond kissing him?"

She glowered at him. "Does it matter?"

"Yes, it does. I don't want to scare you."

"Did I act scared?" she asked, big-eyed.

He smiled, delighted. "No."

"I'm not afraid of you. I'm a little intimidated because I've never felt anything so overpowering before. But I enjoy having you touch me." She lowered her eyes to his broad chest. "I…would like to make love to you, Emmett."

He didn't say anything. After a minute, she was horrified that she'd gone too far, said too much, been too blatant.

She started to turn away, but he caught her softly rounded chin and turned her face back to his.

"I want that, too," he said tautly. "And that complicates things royally. I have three children. You might have noticed…?"

"They're pretty hard to miss," she agreed.

"And then there's the very obvious fact of your virginity." He brushed at his jeans. "Listen, I know it isn't modern or sophisticated, but I was raised to think of innocence as something too special to make an entertainment of. Do you understand? My parents always said that a decent man didn't make a plaything of an innocent woman, not when there were so many around who knew the score and weren't looking for marriage. But if a man seduced a virgin, he married her and made her the mother of his children. I'm afraid I still feel that way. I don't sleep with women who aren't experienced. Not ever.''

''I see.'' She shivered a little, wrapping her arms around her chest. He was telling her that they had no future. She'd hoped. How she'd hoped! But she had to retain as much of her pride as she could. She forced a smile. ''Well, no harm done. Do you think we could have some coffee?''

He felt her pain as if it had been his own. Amazing, he thought, that she cared so much that his words could wound her. He discovered that he couldn't bear to hurt her.

He pulled her into his arms and held her, feeling her stiff posture. He knew what to do about that. His hand slid sensuously down to her hips and moved her against him in a slow, sweet rotation.

She tried to move away, but he wouldn't let her.

''This hasn't happened with anyone since I first found you working in Logan's office,'' he whispered at her ear. ''Do you feel how capable I am right now? I don't even have to work up to wanting you. I touch you, and I can take you. You'd have to be a man to appreciate how sweet that immediate response is.''

''You just got through saying...''

''That I don't sleep with virgins,'' he finished for her. He smiled against her forehead. ''That's right. Why don't you rip my shirt open and kiss me to death? You could push me down in the aisle here and ravish me, if you liked.''

''Emmett,'' she said uncertainly, lifting her face to his.

''I'll get something to use the first few months,'' he said

matter-of-factly, "so that you have plenty of time to decide whether or not you want to let me make you pregnant."

She stopped breathing. Her eyes went wide and shocked, and her heart began beating against her rib cage. "Wh... what?"

"Three is probably too many already," he murmured. "And the world is certainly overpopulated. But I would love to give you a baby," he whispered. "I may not be the best father around, and I've got a lot to learn, but I love kids. We could have just one together, with honey-brown hair," he added thoughtfully, studying her. "That would be unique. Wouldn't you like to touch me?" he added huskily, dragging her hand to his chest. "I'd like it."

"Emmett, I can't get pregnant!"

"Yes, you can," he said. "It's easy. All we have to do is not use anything when we make love." He lifted his head and frowned down at her. "Didn't you take health classes in school?"

"That's not what I meant! I can't go around getting pregnant!"

"You can if you're married," he reminded her.

"I'm not married!"

"You will be." He bent his head and kissed her, slowly and with a deepening hunger. "I can't wait long, either," he said unsteadily. "Some men can go for months without sex, but I can't. I have to have it. I've abstained since just before Kit and Logan got married, when I first realized that I wanted you. But it's been a long, dry spell, Melody." He moaned against her mouth. His hands became insistent. "Very long."

She melted into him. It wasn't a conscious decision, but she wanted him so badly that she couldn't manage any reasons to tell him she wouldn't marry him. The kids, the consequences, all took a back seat to his throbbing need and her desperation to satisfy it.

"I'll marry you," she said huskily. "I'm probably crazy,

and I know you are, and I don't know how I'll manage being
a mother to three kids when one of them hates me. But I
guess I'll cope, if you're actually proposing and not kidding
around."

He lifted his head and searched her eyes. His hands on her
hips were firm and bold. He ground her belly into his in
blatant need. "Does it feel like I'm joking?" he asked unsteadily.

"No."

He brushed her lips with his and whispered something so
explicit that she flushed and buried her face in his hot throat.

"Shocked that I can talk to you that way?" he asked
roughly. "I'll make you like it, though. I'll make you like
what I was talking about, too."

She pressed closer. Her legs trembled. "I know that," she
breathed.

His head lifted. He searched her eyes. "Once you agree,
there won't be any going back."

"No."

"Okay, then. We'll go and tell the kids."

"Not yet," she pleaded. "Not for at least a week or two.
I want you to be sure, Emmett."

"I already am," he said quietly. It was quick, maybe too
quick, but he didn't have a thought of hesitating. What he
knew about her was more than enough. They'd have a good
life together. He cared for her and he knew it was mutual.

"For the children," she hedged. "Let's give them a little
time. Just a little, to get used to seeing us together, and doing
things with them, before we hit them with it."

He groaned. "How much do you think I can stand?"

She smiled gently. "I'll be very careful not to make it any
worse for you than it is."

He sighed roughly. "All right. But just a week or two."

She nodded. "That's fine."

Chapter 8

Melody went through the next two weeks in a kind of daze. She'd never felt as close to anyone as she felt toward Emmett and Amy and Polk. They went riding and to movies and ball games. They went to rodeos. They watched new releases on the VCR at her apartment and on his at the ranch. All the while, they grew closer as they talked about themselves and their hopes and dreams.

There was nothing physical. Emmett was restrained to the point of madness, only kissing her lightly when he took her home. He never deepened the kisses or touched her or made suggestive remarks. Except for the way he looked at her now, they might have been nothing more than friends.

The one sadness Melody had was that Guy was more withdrawn than ever, and she couldn't help but think he was plotting against them. Amy and Polk had looked worried a time or two, as if they had something on their minds. Melody was tempted to try to pry it out of them, but there was never an opportunity.

Guy did find one way to irritate her. He found every photograph he had of his mother and put them all in plain view. He talked about Adell at every opportunity. Behind the irritating behavior was fear, but it didn't help Melody to know it. Guy had become her enemy, and she didn't know how to deal with him.

"You aren't giving Melody a chance, are you?" Emmett asked Guy late one evening after he'd taken Melody home and Amy and Polk had gone to bed.

Guy didn't look at him. "I thought you still loved my mother."

He frowned. "What?"

Guy shifted on the chair. "You were real mad when she went away, but you used to talk about her all the time. I know you miss her. So do we." He looked up at his father. "Why don't you tell her you want her to come back? She might. Maybe she doesn't like her husband. Maybe she'd like a reason to come back!"

Emmett couldn't tell him about Adell's pregnancy. It would be the last straw for the boy right now. He grimaced. He hadn't known that Guy was nursing such futile hopes. No wonder he was resentful of Melody and upset about her being around all the time.

"Son," he began slowly, "you have to understand that sometimes even people who care about each other can't live together."

"But you and my mother did," Guy returned. "You were happy, I know you were!"

That was desperation. Guy was growing up so fast, Emmett wasn't sure how to handle it. All that rodeoing, when his kids had needed him and he'd turned away from them, was coming back to haunt him now.

"Your mother wasn't happy with me," Emmett said quietly. "That's the root of the whole matter. She loves Randy," he added, gritting his teeth as he made the grudging admission. "There is no chance, whatsoever, that she'll ever divorce him and come back to us. You have to accept that."

"No!" Guy stood up. "She's my mother! She didn't want to go, you made her! You were never home!"

Emmett tightened the rein on his temper. "That's true," he said quietly. "Maybe my actions helped her make the decision. But the fact is, if she'd loved me, she'd never have left me. You don't run away from people you love."

Guy's lower lip trembled. "She didn't love me?"

"Not you! Me!"

Guy averted his eyes. "I don't like Melody. Does she have to keep coming around here?" he said, changing the subject.

"I'm going to marry her."

Guy looked horrified. He gaped at his father. "You can't! You can't do that! What about Mom?"

"Your mother is married," he said flatly. "I'm sure she still loves you and Amy and Polk, but she won't be coming back. You're going to have to take it like a man and learn to live with it. Life isn't a cartoon or a movie. Things don't always work out to a happy ending."

"I don't want Melody here!" Guy said harshly. "She's not going to be my mother!"

Emmett felt exasperated. Arguing was getting him nowhere. He stood up abruptly. "I'll marry whom I please," he said flatly. "If you don't like it, that's tough. But you'd better not give her any trouble," he added with quiet menace. "If her cat disappears again, or anything happens to her that upsets her, I'll hold you responsible."

Guy flushed, averting his head. The cat haunted him. He couldn't tell his father how sick he'd been when he knew Alistair might have died because of him.

"I won't bother her stupid cat," he said shortly.

Emmett sighed wearily. "The other kids love her," he said. "She's kind and gentle and if you'd give her half a chance, she'd care about you, too. But you're the original tough guy, aren't you?'' his father asked. ''You're Mr. Cool. Nobody is going to get close to you. Not even me.''

Guy averted his eyes.

''I've done everything I can think of to reach you,'' Emmett continued. ''Including involving you in the routine of running a ranch, but you're too busy or there's a television program on or you have to play with Barney.''

''You're only doing it because *she* isn't around,'' Guy said icily. ''You'd rather be with her than me.''

Emmett smiled half amusedly. ''When you're a few years older, the reason will become perfectly obvious to you.''

Guy flushed. ''I know about girls. There's this one at school, but she thinks I'm ugly and stupid. She said so, in front of her girlfriends. I hate girls!'' He stuck his hands into his jeans and glared at his father. ''Especially Melody!''

Emmett could only barely remember being eleven years old and hating girls. He smiled faintly. ''Well, I'm marrying her whether you like it or not,'' he said pleasantly.

Guy turned and stormed off into his room and slammed the door. Emmett lifted an eyebrow. Parenting, he decided, was not a job for the weakhearted. He was going to have to find some way to get to that boy, while there was still time.

The next weekend, Emmett and Melody made a formal announcement to Amy and Polk. They knew. Guy had told already them, and they were unusually reserved, glancing at their older brother uncertainly.

''Will you live with us, Melody?'' Amy asked.

''Yes,'' Melody said quietly. ''I hope we'll be good friends. I don't have a family, you know,'' she added without looking at them. ''Only my brother.''

''Yeah, her brother who stole our mother!'' Guy burst out. ''Well, I don't want you here…!''

''Go to your room,'' Emmett said. His voice was low and

very quiet, but the look in his eyes made Guy obey without another word.

"Guy said you'll be mean to us," Amy told Melody worriedly. "He said you were only pretending to be nice until you hooked Emmett."

Melody went down on her knees in front of the little girl and studied the green eyes in the softly tanned thin face framed by pigtails.

"Amy, do you know how you feel with different people? I mean, you feel happy around some, and nervous and unhappy around others?"

Amy frowned. "I guess so."

"Well, sometimes when we don't know people very well, we have to trust our feelings about them. I can't promise you that I'll never be angry, that I'll never lose my temper, that I'll never hurt your feelings. I'm just a person, and I'm not perfect. But I'll love you a lot, if you'll let me," she added with a smile. "All of you. I know I'll never be your real mother, but I can be your friend and you can be mine."

Amy seemed to accept that, and to relax. She smiled. "Polk and I think you're the greatest. Guy just doesn't want you around because he thinks Emmett and our mother will get married again someday." She grimaced. "But they won't."

Melody wondered at the wisdom in that small voice. Amy was something of a conundrum. At times she seemed much older than her eight years.

"Do you love Emmett?" Amy asked out of the blue.

Melody blushed, embarrassed.

"Yes. Do you?" Polk seconded, joining Amy, his eyes large under the spectacles as he smiled at her.

Emmett pursed his lips, and his eyes twinkled. "That's it, kids, make her tell you!"

Melody glared at him. "You can be quiet."

"I want to know," he persisted. He chuckled softly. "Never mind, then. I'll find out for myself, later."

That went right over Amy's and Polk's heads, thank goodness. They began to talk about school and soon afterward, supper was put on the table. Guy's was taken to his room by an irritable Mrs. Jenson, because he refused to come out.

The boy's behavior was the one regret in Melody's mind when Emmett left the kids with Mrs. Jenson and drove her back to Houston.

"He isn't going to accept it," she said, when they were in her apartment and the door was closed. She looked up at Emmett worriedly. "I can't come between you and your son...Emmett!"

He'd lifted her off the floor in midspeech and carried her without a word into the dark bedroom. He laid her gently on the coverlet and slid onto it beside her. When she tried to speak, his mouth covered her protesting lips. Seconds later, she couldn't speak at all.

Guy and his attitude were forgotten in the slow, tender moments that followed. Emmett eased her out of her dress and slip so gently that she hardly noticed, and his warm mouth moved slowly over every inch of her, kindling unmanageable sensations that quickly made her writhe and moan.

Her eyes grew accustomed to the semidarkness, so that when he removed her bra, she could see his eyes glitter as he looked at her.

"Sometimes I think I dreamed you," he said huskily. Then his head bent, and what he'd once described to her began to happen all at once. His warm mouth nibbled tenderly at her taut nipples before it moved hungrily over the swollen softness around them. He held her and caressed her to the point of madness, and when his hands invaded the most intimate part of her, she was helpless, enslaved.

He whirled her body against the length of his and enveloped her while he kissed her mouth into submission. The abrasion of his jeans and shirt against her unclothed skin was as exciting as the mouth that was tutoring her own.

She clung to him when he lifted his head. He was breathing roughly and his chest was shaking with the beat of his heart. Against her stomach, she could feel the hard, impatient maleness of him.

"Emmett?" she whispered unsteadily.

"Do you want me?" he asked in a harsh, husky tone.

"Oh, yes," she said honestly.

"All of me, right now?"

"Yes!"

He sat up, and it was an effort. His hand shot out and the room exploded in light.

For a shocked instant, Melody lay on the coverlet disoriented. Then she saw him looking at her body, at the soft pink nudity that her thin white briefs did nothing to disguise, at the taut, swollen evidence of her desire. She went scarlet and began to lift her hands to her breasts to hide them.

He shook his head, and his hands caught hers. "You're mine," he said quietly. "We're engaged. That gives me the right to look at you like this. In fact, it gives me a few other rights that I'm damned tempted to exercise." His hot gaze fell to her stomach and lower, to her long, elegant legs. His hand followed his eyes, and she gasped and moved restlessly, helplessly, on the coverlet.

He eased down, his face somber, almost stern, as his fingers trespassed gently past the elastic band. He touched her and she fought him, wincing.

"Easy," he said gently. "It isn't supposed to hurt."

"It…does!"

He bent and brushed his lips tenderly against her wild eyes, her cheeks, her trembling mouth. "You're frightened. There's no need. None at all. When it happens, it will be as easy as falling into water, as easy as breathing. Your body is soft and elastic here," he whispered. "It will absorb mine, like a glove absorbing a hand."

The analogy made her shiver. He kissed her flickering eyelids, tracing her long lashes with his tongue. "I don't want you to be afraid of me. I promise that I won't hurt you, in any way."

She looked at him worriedly, her eyes big and uncertain.

He nodded. "I suppose I knew all along that it would take more than words." He reached over and turned off the lamp before he slid alongside her again. "It will be easier for you in the dark, won't it?" he whispered.

She didn't understand what he meant until it began. The soft, stroking motion kindled explosive feelings in her untried body. She tried to fight them at first, but the tide of pleasure he induced was as overwhelming as life itself. She gave in to it, gloried in it, wept and writhed and moaned in an anguish of hot, building tension that finally splintered into the most incredible surge of pleasure she'd ever imagined in her wildest dreams.

He gathered her close and held her trembling body, fighting his own demons even as he banished hers. His lips smoothed over her hot face, tenderly calming her.

"That, magnified," he whispered at her ear, "is what I'm going to give you on our wedding night."

She clung to him, dazed. "I never dreamed…!"

"You're more than I ever hoped for," he said quietly, cradling her in his arms. "You don't tease or play games, do you? And you're not ashamed to feel what I can give you, or to admit that you do feel it."

She touched his lean cheek and felt the muscles taut in it. "I like to think I'll be able to give it back, when I know how," she murmured shyly.

He kissed her with aching tenderness. "You will," he said quietly. "Lovemaking should be mutual. I won't ever take my pleasure at your expense."

He was a surprisingly considerate man. She had a fleeting glimpse of him as a lover, and her body moved unconsciously on the coverlet.

"I want you, too, very badly," he said, feeling and understanding the movement. "But we'll wait until after we're married. I don't want a tarnished memory of our first loving. Hors d'oeuvres, on the other hand," he murmured wickedly, "are perfectly permissible."

He bent and nuzzled his mouth over her breast, feeling her instant response, hearing her urgent cry.

It couldn't last. He was too hungry for her, and the risk grew by the minute. Finally he groaned and got to his feet, shivering a little with the effort.

"I'd better go home while I still can," he mused wryly. "Don't get up. And try not to faint. I'm going to turn on the light."

She would have protested at the beginning, but it didn't matter now. He knew her almost as well as a lover.

The light came on and she lay there, letting him look at her. The briefs he'd stripped from her were tossed onto the foot of the bed. There was nothing between her and his narrow, hungry green eyes.

"I hope you don't believe in divorce," he said in a faintly strangled tone. "Because you'd have to change your name and move to the jungle to escape me."

She stretched deliberately, glorying in the growing tautness of his lean, fit body. She could imagine how it was going to feel grinding into hers, and her lips parted on a rush of breath.

"That goes double for you," she whispered. "You'll belong to me, too, when we're married."

"It's more than desire for you, isn't it?" he asked quietly. "Yes."

He searched her eyes. "For me, too, Melody," he replied. "It's more than enough to start with. I'll arrange the ceremony for next Saturday."

"All right."

"I'll make sure I've got what we need to keep you from getting pregnant right away," he added.

"I can see the doctor and get him to put me on the pill," she began.

He sat down on the bed beside her, his eyes troubled. He drew the cover over her prone body with a rueful, reluctant smile. "Too much temptation can kill even a strong man," he said dryly. The smile faded. "Listen, I know the pill is pretty foolproof, and everybody says it's safe. But I feel uncomfortable about letting you take chances with your health."

"If I don't take the pill... Well, I've heard that some men don't like using what they have to use," she said hesitantly.

He touched her face tenderly. "Well, I'm not *some* men," he replied honestly, "And I believe pregnancy shouldn't be an accident."

"I know." She traced his hand where it lay on the cover beside her head. "The kids will need time, too, to get used to me before we start creating new complications."

"In the meanwhile, I can take care of it."

"If you're that worried about the pill, you can come with me and talk to the doctor yourself," she said. "There are other ways."

"How do you feel about it?" he asked.

She flushed and averted her eyes.

He turned her face back. "It's too serious an issue to evade because of modesty. How do you feel about it?"

She searched his hard face. "I'm not afraid to take the pill. I don't think it's so risky. And I want to be...very, very close to you when we love each other," she said huskily. "As close as we can get when we fit together."

His face went ruddy. He actually shivered.

"Oh, Emmett, I want you...!" She drew him down and kissed him with helpless urgency, feeling him throw off the covers as he levered himself over her. His knee urged her legs apart and he slid between them, shaking as he pushed down, letting her feel him in total intimacy.

He groaned harshly, his body stilling suddenly as the danger of the situation cut through his desire for her.

Her body was new to pleasure and hungry for it. He understood her headlong rush toward it, but he had to protect her from a danger she still didn't understand.

"Lie still. Lord, baby, please...!"

His hands forced her a few inches away from his tormented body. She moaned, but he persisted. "Melody, it hurts me." He ground out the words.

She lay still, curious. Her big eyes found the pallor of his face even as she felt him tremble.

"Hurts?" she asked uncertainly.

He dragged her hand up against him. "Here," he said huskily. "It hurts like hell. You've got to stop moving against me. All right?"

"Yes." But she didn't move her hand, even when his withdrew. She moved back a little and looked down with open curiosity.

He saw her expression and sighed heavily. "All right. Here."

He rolled over onto his back and lay there, stoically letting her look and touch and experience him. He shivered a little, but her touch soothed more than it wounded.

She drew away almost at once, embarrassed by her own boldness, and smiled at him.

He threw the coverlet at her. She understood without words, wrapping herself up in it to remove the threat with a wicked smile on her face.

"Witch," he accused.

"You liked it," she said right back.

He stretched, winced and put his hands under his head while he studied her. His body began to relax, but slowly.

"When you're through having anatomy lessons, I'll leave," he said pointedly.

Her eyebrows lifted. "You call this an anatomy lesson?" she asked with a mock surprise. "When I'm totally nude and you're lying there with all your clothes on?"

"I'm modest," he informed her.

She pursed her lips and stared at his jeans. "Take them off. I dare you."

He laughed with pure delight. "No! Damn it, woman, have you no shame?"

"Shame is for people who don't want to have sex with other people." She leaned closer, fanning the coverlet between her breasts. "I'm famished!" she whispered with a mock leer.

He chuckled at her uninhibited display. "Come here, you torment."

He pulled her down and kissed her, but with slow, sweet tenderness, not passion. "I adore you," he whispered. "And I take it back about the jungle. If you ever want to get away from me, it had better be Mars."

"I'll keep that in mind." She kissed him back. "I really don't mind taking the pill."

He nodded. "It's your body. It has to be your decision." He smiled ruefully. "Having just discovered you, I don't want to risk losing you."

That made her feel warm all over. "You won't," she said softly. She pushed back his thick, dark hair. "Can I love you?"

He threw his arms out to either side and closed his eyes. "Go ahead."

She hit him. "You know what I mean."

He searched her face for a long moment. "You're serious."

"Yes." She traced his chin and then his mouth as her eyes levered back up to hold his.

He smoothed his hands over her shoulders, under the coverlet, savoring her magnolia-petal skin. "Love is important to a woman, isn't it?" he asked with faint cynicism.

"It's important to most men, too," she said softly. Her eyes were warm and steady, without deceit. "I'm going to love you anyway. I just thought it would be polite to ask. But if you're going to be difficult about it, just pretend you don't notice that I'm crazy about you."

He sighed and smiled. "It would be pretty difficult to miss. Even your breasts blush when I look at you."

"They do not...Emmett!"

She made a grab for the cover, but it was too late. "See?" he asked, nodding toward the faint ruddy color below her collarbone. But the smile faded almost at once. He touched her reverently. "You are so incredibly lovely," he whispered, almost choking on the emotion he felt. He closed his eyes and dragged himself off the bed. "I have to go. Now. Immediately. Without delay."

She had to fight back a smile at his desperate look. She pulled the cover back around her and got up, looking so smug that he glowered at her.

"Proud of yourself?" he muttered, blatantly aroused and with no way to hide it from the new wisdom in her twinkling brown eyes.

She glanced down and back up. "Yep," she said, grinning.

He laughed defeatedly, shaking his head. "I'm out of here."

"Until Saturday," she reminded him pertly as she walked with him to the door. "After that, you're mine!"

"And you're mine," he returned. He caught the doorknob and glanced down at her with quiet introspection, taking in her flushed face, her swollen mouth, her joy-filled eyes. His soul seemed to clench at the pleasure it gave him to want her.

She saw that tension and understood it. "I won't ever hurt

you," she said suddenly, dead serious. "But I'll love you until it hurts. If you really don't want that, you'd better say so now. Once I've lived with you, I honestly don't know if I can let go…"

He pressed his fingers against her lips. "You won't have to," he said quietly. "Love doesn't come with money-back guarantees. It's a risk. We'll take it together."

"All right."

He sighed gently, and he smiled at her. "Sleep well."

"No, I won't," she said.

"Neither will I." His eyes darkened. "I do want you so desperately," he said huskily, emotion throbbing in his voice.

"Then stay with me," she invited quietly.

"I want to," he said fervently. "But we'll do things properly. Not for our sakes, but for the children's. A white wedding may be old-fashioned in this unstructured society, but I want one for us."

She smiled at him. "So do I. But I'd do anything for you."

Incredible, the burst of inner light he felt at the words. He smiled, a little dazedly as he let it ripple through him. "Anything?" he murmured.

She studied him. "Well, almost anything. I wouldn't kiss a snake or eat a chocolate covered ant for you."

He bent and kissed her quickly. "Okay. No kissing snakes and eating ants. Now good night!"

"Good night."

He winked at her and went out the door. She locked it behind him. On second thought, she mused privately, if it wasn't a venomous snake, and she could keep her eyes closed while she kissed it…

Emmett had just finished arranging the small service when Guy came into his office, his hands in his back pockets, looking repentant but still belligerent.

"Well?" Emmett asked curtly.

Guy's thin shoulders rose and fell. "I'm sorry," he said stiffly.

"For what?"

"What I said. The way I acted." Guy stared at the floor. "My mom really won't come back?"

"No."

He took a slow, audible breath before he glanced at his father. "But she didn't go away because of me?"

"Of course not," Emmett said. "She loves all you kids. If you want to know, I wouldn't let her near you after she left," he confessed heavily. "I was wrong, too. Dead wrong. If you want to see her, talk to her, it's all right."

Guy didn't say anything for a minute. "Melody hates me, doesn't she?"

"No. It isn't in her nature to hate people," Emmett said quietly. "But you haven't gone out of your way to endear yourself to her, either."

"Yeah. She won't forget about the cat, I guess."

"If you meet her halfway, it won't matter at all," Emmett said. "You have to compromise. I'm a hell of a bad teacher, in that respect, but I'm learning. We'll both have to learn."

"Okay. I'll try."

Emmett smiled. "And you might reconsider getting used to the business side of ranch work," he added.

Guy shrugged. "I guess I could." He glanced warily at his father. Emmett looked pretty different lately. He looked happy.

"Things going better at school, are they?"

"Since I beat up Buddy Haskell, they're going great," Guy said simply.

"You what?"

"He made a remark about smelly ranchers who walk around all day in cow...well, in manure." Guy corrected himself, grinning. "He said you smelled like that, so I pasted him one. The teacher was too busy talking to the other teachers to even notice." He chuckled. "He told her he walked into a door."

Emmett looked skyward. "Now, listen, here…"

"Homework to do," Guy said quickly. "Have to get on it, right now. I'm helping Polk with fractions." He frowned. "Isn't it amazing that he can do multiplication in his head but he can't add a fourth and a half?"

"He'll be a rocket scientist one day," Emmett replied.

"God help us if he can't do fractions by then," Guy mused. He left his father sitting there and went to get his books.

Emmett felt a glimmer of hope that Guy would change his attitude. If Guy came around, it would be clear sailing for sure. Except that Adell was pregnant, and he should have told the boy. Well, there was no need, and plenty of time for him to find it out. Plenty of time, now.

Chapter 9

The wedding was held at the local Methodist church. Ted Regan came down for it, and so did Tansy, Logan and Kit Deverell. Amy was flower girl and Polk carried the rings on a pillow. Guy sat stiffly on the pew reserved for family, having declined belligerently at any sort of participation in the wedding.

Despite the talk he'd had with his father, he'd still hoped that his mother might come along at the last minute and stop the service, say that she was wrong, that she loved his father and wanted to marry him again. But it didn't happen. Nobody wanted him, he thought suddenly. His mother had run away and never even phoned or written, and now his dad wanted somebody's company besides his. He glanced at his brother and sister, so radiant at the thought of their new stepmother. He'd have to make the most of it. He was sorry that he'd made things so hard for Melody. He hoped that his dad was right, and she didn't have a vengeful nature.

As he watched, Emmett spoke the words, put the ring on

Melody's finger and lifted her short veil. He looked at her for a long, long time before he finally bent and kissed her. It was the gentlest kiss she'd ever had from him, one of respect and affection and delight. She gave it back in the same way, brimming with joy.

After the service, Ted Regan stopped long enough to congratulate them. Having heard him called "old man Regan," Melody's first glimpse of him was a surprise. He wasn't old, but he did have prematurely silver hair, a great shock of it, combed to one side. He had pale blue eyes and a long, lean, very tanned face. He reminded her of the actor, Randolph Scott, an impression that was emphasized when he spoke in a slow Texas drawl.

"Can't say I've ever wanted to marry anybody," Ted mused, "but I guess it's all right for some people. Best of luck. Don't even think about going back to San Antonio," he added as he shook Emmett's hand and his blue eyes glittered like cold steel. "I'll hunt you down and drag you back here at the end of a rope if you even try. You've accomplished more in a month than any other foreman I've hired accomplished in a year. I'll even give you a half interest in the place if that's what it takes to keep you."

Emmett felt a foot taller. Marrying Melody was delight enough, but praise from tight-lipped Ted Regan was something of a rarity and accepted with pride.

"Thanks," Emmett told the other man, who was as tall and fit as he was himself, despite the fact that Ted was almost forty years old. "I like my job a lot. I can't think of anything that would make me quit at the moment." He frowned. "Maybe if a cow fell in the well..."

"I don't think you could stuff a calf down that wellhead," Ted reminded him. "Unless it was cooked and ground up."

"Point taken. I'll stay for a spell."

"Good." He clamped his white Stetson back on his head and tilted it at a rakish angle. "I'm off to Colorado for the national cattlemen's meeting. More damned politics than horses in the industry these days." He walked off, shaking his head.

"He's never married? Really?" Melody asked her new husband as she watched the tall man walk away.

"They say there isn't a woman in south Texas brave enough," Emmett said under his breath. "He's very pleasant in company, but he can scorch leather when he's upset. We've got two old cowboys who hide in the barn every time he stops by to check the books!"

"You don't," she implored.

He chuckled, drawing her against his side as they moved lazily toward the car where the kids were waiting. "Oh, Ted and I get along pretty well. Peas in a pod, you know." He glanced at her mischievously. "Or didn't you know that I can scorch leather, too, on occasion?"

She leaned closer. "I'll settle for having you scorch me tonight," she whispered.

He drew in a breath. "Lady, that kind of talk will get you ravished on the hood of the car," he said with an uncomfortable look. "Shame on you, saying such things to a man, and near a church, too!"

"No better place for it," she said gently. "We're married. With my body, I thee worship...?" She wiggled her hand with the plain gold band she'd asked for on her third finger under his nose.

"Shameless," he repeated.

"Yes. And tonight you'll be on your knees giving thanks that I am," she said smugly.

He glanced at her. "You'll be the one on your knees, begging for mercy."

She grinned at him. "Promise?" She wiggled her eyebrows.

He laughed out loud and hugged her. Probably she was bluffing, but he didn't mind at all. He'd never been so happy in all his life. Except for Guy's attitude, he amended, watching the boy's faintly reticent stare as they approached him.

Guy's face set in familiar lines, unsmiling and resentful, and Emmett lost his temper at that look, not realizing that Guy was nervous and intimidated because he wanted to congratulate them but was uncertain of the reaction he was going to get from Melody.

Emmett wasn't about to let the boy put a damper on Melody's wedding day. Best way to avoid trouble was with a good strong offensive, he thought. "Put a sock in it," he told Guy when he opened his mouth to speak. "Or you can go and pay a visit to that military school we've talked about."

Melody was shocked at the threat and the expression it produced on Guy's face.

She started to protest, but Emmett stopped her.

"I've given you more rope than you've earned," he told Guy coldly. "I won't plead with you anymore. Melody is my wife. If you can't accept that, a good private school is the best answer. I enjoyed it. You might, too."

Guy's pallor was obvious. He swallowed. "I don't want to go away to school," he said heavily.

"That's your only other option," Emmett said.

Guy's head lifted with what pride he could manage. "I'm ready to go home when you are." He glanced at Melody and away. "Congratulations," he said in a ghostly tone, and turned to get into the back seat with an excited Amy and Polk.

Melody's heart ached for his wounded pride. "Oh, Emmett...!" she moaned.

He averted his gaze from her pleading eyes. "Some boys take a firm hand," he said curtly. "I've been too lenient with all three of them, and they've gone wild. It's never pleasant to get the upper hand back once you've lost it." He looked at her. "I won't hurt the boy. I won't send him away unless I have to. But you must see that allowing him to persecute you and dictate to me is impossible. He's only eleven years old.''

"I know. But…''

He bent and kissed her gently. "It will take time. We both knew that from the beginning. Stop trying to gulp down the future. We haven't begun.''

"All right. I'll try.''

She wasn't going to give up, though. She'd wait until he was less tense and then approach him about Guy. She really couldn't let him send the boy away before she'd even tried to make friends with him. It was Guy's home as well as Emmett's and hers. The look on the boy's face haunted her.

They took the kids home and a beaming Mrs. Jenson congratulated them while Melody changed into a simple gray dress for travel. They were going to have a three-day honeymoon down in Cancún. The kids were bitterly disappointed that they couldn't go, but Melody promised Amy and Polk that they'd go as a family very soon. Amy had remarked that she guessed newly married people did need a *little* time alone. A remark that sent Emmett into gales of laughter.

Guy didn't speak to his father. Melody stopped just in front of him as Emmett was saying goodbye to the other kids.

"He won't do it" was all she said. She smiled. "It will be all right, you know.''

Guy was shocked. He couldn't even speak. He hadn't expected her to say anything to him after the way he'd treated her. Now he needed to talk, and he couldn't.

It was too late, anyway. She was gone, with his father.

"They look nice together, don't you think?" Amy asked with a sigh. She glared at Guy. "You're going to get it when Emmett gets back. You were awful at their wedding.''

"I'm not going to get it, but you are if you don't watch your mouth," Guy said, daring her.

"Will you two stop fighting? Look, Alistair likes to play

with a string!'' Polk called, dangling a string while the cat played with it.

The big tabby was staying at the ranch, and Mrs. Jenson had ironclad orders not to let him out. Guy went to stand by Polk and Amy while he watched the cat. He hoped Alistair had a forgiving nature, as well as Melody, or things could get real hectic here.

Cancún was a vision. The colors of the sea and the blistering white of the beach, the modern Mexican architecture with exaggerated Mayan motifs made a potpourri of images that Melody found fascinating. She'd been to Mexico before, but never to this particular part of it. Despite the crowd of tourists, she drank in the atmosphere with delight.

Emmett looked good in white swimming trunks. She admired his long, tanned legs with covetous eyes, not to mention his broad, hair-matted chest and arms and flat stomach. He was delicious, and a lot of other women seemed to think so, because they kept walking by with their flabby, white-skinned husbands, staring unashamedly at him.

''One more time, lady, and I'm going to leap up and crown you with my tanning lotion,'' Melody muttered under her breath.

''What was that?'' Emmett asked without opening his eyes.

''That skinny brunette. She keeps walking by, leering at you.''

''My, my, are you *jealous?*'' he teased.

She stared at him without blinking. ''Why don't you go back to the room with me and find out?''

His heart began to beat wildly. ''We've only been here an hour or so. I thought you might be too tired,'' he said gently.

She shook her head very slowly. Her long hair was loosened, blowing softly in the ocean breeze. She searched his green eyes. ''I want you,'' she whispered.

His body reacted sharply and he laughed with self-conscious delight. "Damn it, woman...!"

"Recite multiplication tables," she whispered with a gleeful smile.

He glared at her. "You'd better have packed something that prevents multiplication, because I forgot to."

"I did." She'd decided on the pill, despite his objections, because she felt it was the safest way to prevent a child until they were ready. She stood up, holding out her hand. "I've waited twenty years," she murmured dryly. "I do hope you're going to be worth it."

He got to his feet, his pale eyes shimmering with a kind of knowledge that made her blush. "Honey, I can guarantee it."

He took her hand and they went back to the room in a tense, delicious silence.

She went straight into his arms the minute the door closed, determined not to admit that she was nervous of him this way. It was broad daylight, but waiting until tonight would have inhibited both of them. Besides, she thought as she lifted her face to look at him, she loved him. It would be all right, as long as he didn't compare her with any of his past lovers. She hoped that she was going to be enough for him, because despite her bravado, she felt vaguely inadequate.

But that fear was quickly forgotten when he bent to kiss her, and the heat of his body and the skill of his mouth and hands turned her nervous response into sensual fever.

He eased her onto the bed and very efficiently moved everything out of his way, so that her nude body was cradled to his in the slow preliminary to their first loving.

"Shh," he whispered when she began to writhe and pull at him. "Not so fast, little one. Don't gulp it. Sip it. Slow down."

"It aches," she whispered unsteadily as his mouth teased and tormented hers. "I ache all over."

"So do I," he said on soft, unsteady laughter. "But we're building to one hell of an explosion, and it's too soon for you, despite what you think. No, don't touch me like that, not yet," he said softly, stilling her hand. "This is all for you. My turn will come later, when I've satisfied you to the tips of your pretty pink toes. Kiss me, sweetheart."

He coaxed her mouth back up to his and his hands moved again, tasting her body as his mouth tasted her lips, and then settled hungrily on her breasts and her soft, flat stomach, experiencing, exploring her, making her crazy for his possession.

"I can't…bear it…!" She whimpered finally, anguish in her wide, haunted eyes. "Oh, please…!"

"All right," he whispered tenderly, moving over her. "Gently, little one," he breathed. "Gently, gently."

He held her firmly, his face above hers, his muscular body cording as he positioned her and began to move down. He was afraid of hurting her, even as it excited him beyond bearing to be her first lover. But she didn't flinch, didn't fight. She lay there, shivering, her eyes open and fixed with pain and wonder on his taut face as he invaded the sweet, warm softness of her innocence and was slowly, painstakingly engulfed by it.

She flinched and he grimaced, stilling until she relaxed again. He could barely breathe. "Is it bad?" he managed to ask.

"It was. It's not now." She closed her eyes and willed her body to accept him. And it did, abruptly, and generously. She let out a long sigh of relief.

He moved as close as he could then, fighting a hellish surge of tense pleasure that begged for relief.

"It doesn't hurt anymore," she whispered shyly. Imagine, talking to a man while you were doing this!

"That's what you think," he groaned.

"Oh, Emmett," she breathed. She lifted to him, watching him shiver. She liked his reaction. She felt suddenly confident, all woman. She lifted again. He protested, but he didn't try to stop her. His face clenched and he breathed roughly. She loved him. It was going to be so beautiful.

"Witch!" he groaned.

"Do you like it?" she teased, moving sensually.

"I'll show you how much I like it," he breathed with a smiling threat. He whipped over onto his side, taking her with him. His strong, lean hands caught her hips and he laughed with something savage, untamed, in his pale eyes as he slid one long leg between both of hers and began to rock her in that deep intimacy.

She gasped as pleasure began to sting her body with bursts of throbbing heat.

"Did you think you could match me so quickly?" he whispered with passionate tenderness as he teased her mouth with his. And all the while, his hands pulled and pushed and teased while he invaded her trembling innocence. He watched her face the whole time, enjoying the stunned wonder of her dark eyes. "How does this feel?" he whispered.

She cried out at the shock of pleasure that came with the movement. Her hands caught at his powerful arms, but the great waves of sensation kept coming, faster and faster, his whole body an instrument of pleasure as he held her and quickly deepened his possession, laughing like a devil as he drove her down into the fires of fulfillment and watched her body splinter into ecstasy against the hard whip of his passion.

Only when she began to cry out in a hoarse, sobbing oblivion did he allow himself the delight of joining her in that lofty plane of mindless joy.

The explosions of pleasure surged through him like tidal waves, lifting, slamming into him, burning him in feverish delight. He called her name, again and again, clutching her to him as he gave in to satiation.

It wasn't like other times, other women. He shivered, but he couldn't stop. His lean hands pulled her into him, over him, and he moved helplessly under her soft, warm body, coaxing her mouth down to cover his as he began the rhythm all over again.

She hadn't imagined what it would be like. He was inexhaustible, incoherent in his passion, but the skill and mastery were beyond her dreams. He raised her to levels she couldn't have pictured, gave her endless ecstasy, made her alternately wanton and exhausted as the day turned finally to night.

When she was too tired to turn her head to kiss him, she fell into a deep, dreamless sleep.

A sweet smell and the feel of light disturbed her. Light shone into her eyes. She put up a hand and felt the warmth of sunlight filtering in through the venetian blinds.

She opened her eyes. Emmett was holding a warm pastry under her nose, letting her smell it.

"Hungry?" he asked softly, smiling at her.

He was fully dressed and she was wearing a sheer blue nightgown. She didn't remember putting it on, but she must have. She smiled back at him. "Starved. Oh!"

She moved and grimaced. He chuckled wickedly, because he knew why she'd grimaced.

"Are you sore?" he asked with mock sympathy.

"Yes, I'm sore," she murmured, blushing. "I hope your back is broken…"

He kissed her gently, stemming the words. "You're the best lover I've ever had," he whispered.

"But I couldn't be," she protested. "I didn't know anything."

"Yes, you did," he replied, kissing her eyelids shut. "You knew how to love me, and you did. It was the most beautiful, the most exquisitely fulfilling night of my life. Even Mars won't be far enough for you to run to get away from me now. I've just been farther out than that in your arms."

She sighed and snuggled closer to him. "Now I know what they meant, when they said it was like eating potato chips." She laughed delightedly. "Oh, Emmett, I like it!"

"I'm glad. So do I." He lifted his head and cocked a rueful eyebrow. "I suppose for a few days now we'll be good friends and companions."

She peered at him through her long lashes. "In health class, nobody ever said you got sore."

"That was my fault," he said, and looked guilty. "I should have stopped after the first time. I'm sorry. It had been a long time and you went to my head. But I should have had more control."

"I wasn't complaining," she said sincerely. "I loved it. I'd do it all over again if I could."

"So would I. That's the hell of it." He brushed his mouth gently against hers. "Was it worth the wait?" he asked seriously, searching her soft, dark eyes.

"Yes," she whispered. "It was worth waiting all my life for."

"For me, too," he replied tersely. "My God, I never dreamed it would feel like that with you." He touched her face gently. "Mrs. Deverell," he said as he kissed her forehead with aching tenderness. "Mrs. Melody Deverell."

She looped her arms around his neck and nuzzled her face into his warm throat. "I'm still sleepy."

Her vulnerability made him strong, made him ache with tenderness. He bent and lifted her, carrying her to the armchair. He sat down with her in his lap and put down the pastry. Then he lifted a cup of hot coffee to her lips.

She sipped it, staring at him curiously.

"What do you want to do today?" he asked quietly.

"Stay with you."

He smiled. "What else?"

"Nothing," she said. "Only that." She reached up and put her lips gently to his. "I love you so much. More than anything or anyone in all the world." She kissed him again and felt him tremble.

He put the coffee cup down and turned her against his broad, bare chest. He held her gently, undemanding, for a long time, staring across her bright head to the window. "Go to sleep," he breathed at her temple. "I'll hold you while you sleep."

She smiled drowsily and curled closer to him, resting her cheek on his shoulder.

She slept and he watched her, fascinated by the color in her face, the soft sigh of her breath against his throat, the trusting, tender posture of her body in his arms. He thought that he'd never been so happy in all his life.

But with that feeling came a quiet regret that their first intimacy had been so turbulent. She'd given in to him, loved him, responded completely to his fierce ardor. He should have given her tenderness instead of raw passion. It was just that it had been so long and he'd wanted her so desperately. He couldn't hold back.

Now, looking down at her sleeping face, he felt an aching need to cradle her against him in bed and show her the most exquisite kind of tenderness.

Next time, he promised himself. The thing was, she wouldn't be capable of intimacy for several days; probably not until they went home again. He grimaced. Well. Better late than never. After a minute, he closed his eyes and fell asleep himself, wrapped in her warmth and love.

When Melody and Emmett drove up at the front door of the ranch house, Guy was peering out the window. He'd worried himself sick about how he was going to keep Emmett from shipping him off to a military school. He didn't know how he was going to cope with so many changes at once.

He was no longer part of his own family. Now he was going to be an outsider in Emmett and Melody's, an unwanted burden. Amy and Polk were ecstatic. They would accept Melody and love her and be loved by her. He wasn't sure that he could fit in. She might still be pretending to care about him, until she was settled with his father. Some of his friends at school had stepparents. He'd heard some terrible stories about that. Oh, why, why, did people have to get divorced? he agonized.

Melody had hugged Amy and Polk and greeted Mrs. Jenson. She came into the house, looking for Guy. He glanced at her warily.

"How are you?" she asked.

He shrugged, painfully shy. She looked radiant. It was a contrast of some magnitude to the way he looked, and felt.

"Guy. You might at least say hello," Emmett said, interfering all too quickly, his green eyes flashing.

"Hello," Guy replied, dropping his eyes.

Melody put her fingers against Emmett's hard mouth. "Let's get our clothes changed. I want to pass out the presents," she said, before Emmett could do any more damage to her fragile relationship with Guy. "I brought stuff for all of you," she told the children. "Even Mrs. Jenson."

"Why, how sweet of you, Mrs. Deverell!" the older woman exclaimed. She hadn't anticipated liking Emmett's young wife. But the woman was not what she expected. She beamed. "I'll just fix some coffee and cake."

She went off toward the kitchen with an excited Amy and Polk, while Guy sat down on the sofa, idly stroking Alistair. The cat seemed to like him. It was forever following him around and purring. He was glad something liked him. Even Amy and Polk had been resentful and unkind since the wedding. He felt alone in the world except for this cat he'd been so cruel to in the beginning.

"I'm glad you like me, Alistair," he told the tabby.

Alistair looked up with half-closed green eyes and purred even louder.

"You can't be cruel to him," Melody told Emmett gently when they were cloistered in the master bedroom. "He'll try. I know he will, and so will I. You can't expect him to be instantly happy, Emmett. It's hard for him. Really hard."

He sighed heavily, drawing her gently to him. "I'm impatient. Too impatient sometimes." He searched her soft eyes and something alien flared in his as he touched her face. "I can't bear the thought of letting anything or anyone hurt you," he said hesitantly. He drew her close, feeling her soft response to the words as he bent to kiss her. "I can't bear to let you out of my sight…"

She kissed him back, hungry for him because even though they'd been passionate lovers that one time, they hadn't been able to make love again because it had taken such a long time for her to recover from his ardor that first day.

His tall, powerful body began to vibrate, to harden. "I want you," he choked, and his mouth became insistent.

"Tonight," she promised, smiling at him. "Oh, Emmett, tonight…!"

When they rejoined the family, several hectic minutes later, Melody was flushed and shy and Emmett was grinding his teeth. But he looked at her with wonder and delight. It got better and better, he thought. The walls were thick, but she was still a little shy. He'd have to have a radio on or something tonight. Tonight. His body began to throb and he went off into the kitchen to see about coffee.

Melody passed out presents: a set of Mexican coins and a cup and string-tied ball toy for Amy; a book on the Mayans and a few replicated artifacts for Polk, who seemed bent on being an archaeologist. And for Guy, a serape and a pocketknife with a hand-carved handle.

Guy was speechless. He'd wanted a pocketknife of his own for ages, because he loved to whittle things out of wood. He was forever borrowing his father's. Melody had noticed. Imagine that, he thought regretfully. He'd been terrible to her, but she'd gone to a lot of trouble to buy something he really wanted.

He looked up at her, shyly.

"Do you like it?" she asked, frowning. "I wasn't sure..."

"It's great!" he said slowly. "Thanks."

"Don't abuse the privilege," Emmett told him firmly. "You can't use it to carve your initials in the walls or make devices of torture to use on unsuspecting tourists."

Guy grinned. "Sure, Dad."

It was the first time he'd seen the boy smile in weeks. He glanced at Melody and nodded. She'd known, and he hadn't, the way to his son's heart. He had a lot to learn about his own children and his new wife.

Amy tugged at his sleeve. "Emmett, it was very nice of you to think of us on your honeymoon," she said, smiling radiantly at him.

"It sure was!" Polk enthused. "Look at this *atl-atl,*" he said, displaying the use of the Aztec throwing stick that looked something like an arrow on a slab of bamboo. "Ancient Aztecs used to hunt with these, did you know?"

"I know about dinosaurs and Pleistocene animals," Emmett corrected him. "My minor was paleontology, not archaeology."

"Archaeology is a branch of anthropology," Polk said authoritatively. "I'm going to study it when I get out of high school. Just think, Dad, maybe I'll be the one to find the first *Homo Erectus* remains in the United States!"

Emmett frowned. "There's no proof that *Homo Erectus* ever set foot here."

"Yet," Polk said. And grinned.

Amy tugged on Emmett's sleeve again. "Emmett?"

"Hmm?" he murmured, still distracted by Polk's question.

"Are you and Melody going to have any babies?"

Emmett stared at her. "What?"

"Babies. You know. People have sex and they get babies." She grinned. "I learned about that on television. There was this movie and it showed what people do in bed together." She frowned. "Do you and Melody have sex?"

Melody went scarlet and Emmett actually blushed.

"Shut up, Amy!" Guy muttered. "Honest to God, are you ever going to grow up? Come on, let's go outside and play with Polk's *atl-atl.*"

"It's mine! I didn't say you could play with it!" Polk raged, his glasses sparkling.

"I'll let you see my knife," Guy offered.

The smaller boy hesitated. "Well…"

Guy put an arm around Polk and led him toward the door. "Just think, Polk, I can whittle arrows for that *atl-atl.* If we set up a fort just down past the barn, we can lie in wait for that nasty-tempered old bull…"

"You shoot one arrow at that bull and I'll stop your allowance forever!" Emmett called after them.

"Aw, Dad!" Guy groaned.

"I mean it!"

Amy went with the boys, glowering at her father. "Emmett, you're not the same man since we moved down here. You never let us have fun anymore."

"Considering what you people call fun, it's a miracle I haven't had to bail all three of you out of jail!"

Amy just shook her head and went out behind the boys.

"See?" Melody told him. "Guy will come around. It will take time, that's all. He's already loosening up, didn't you notice?"

He had. Guy was much more like his old self, like the boy he'd been before Emmett ever saw Melody in Logan's office. He drew her close and kissed her softly. "All right. I give in.'' He eased her across his lap on the sofa and kissed her more thoroughly, feeling the warmth and tenderness of it right through his body.

''I love you,'' she whispered, smiling against his mouth. ''Kiss me…!''

He gathered her up and devoured her until they were both trembling. His mouth slid down to her throat and he held her, shivering. He was afraid. He'd never been so afraid. She obsessed him, delighted him, made him whole. He'd lost his father, whom he idolized. His mother had killed herself. Adell had left him. If he lost Melody…!

''Emmett!'' she protested gently, because his arms were bruising her.

He lifted his dark head and looked at her. The expression on his face, in his eyes, touched her deeply.

She reached up to press soft, tender kisses against his fearful eyes, his cheeks, his nose, his mouth until she felt him begin to relax. Then she drew back and searched his eyes.

''Emmett, I will never leave you,'' she whispered, and put her fingers over his mouth when he tried to speak. ''Never,'' she repeated, understanding what was bothering him. She put her mouth against his and held on, feeling him shiver as he gathered her against him and kissed her with quiet desperation.

She knew then that he felt something powerful for her, even if he'd never said so. She smoothed his hair and lay quietly in his arms until the brunt of his passion was spent. Then she curled against him, trustingly, and sighed.

He stared over her head toward the door, a little less horrified than he'd been. How shocking, he thought, to discover so late in life that he'd never known what love was. At least, not until now.

Chapter 10

Emmett wanted to tell Melody what he felt. He wanted to shout it to the world. But he couldn't manage it. He felt choked up with the knowledge. He looked down at her and his heart seemed to swell to the point of bursting.

"You delight me," he whispered huskily. His hand touched her hair, her cheek. "Oh, God, I'd do anything for you...!"

She drew his mouth down to hers again and kissed him tenderly.

"Coffee's on," Mrs. Jenson said with a wicked smile as she came into the room with a tray. "I suppose you newlyweds would rather live on kisses than cake, but here it is, anyway. If you need anything else, just call."

"Thanks, Mrs. Jenson," Emmett murmured.

Melody shyly climbed off Emmett's lap to sit beside him on the sofa. "Yes, indeed, it looks delicious!" she said enthusiastically.

"Could you peek out the window occasionally?" Emmett

called to Mrs. Jenson. "Just to make sure the kids aren't making shish kebab of any of old Man Regan's cattle?"

"Why do you think the curtains aren't drawn?" she asked, tongue-in-cheek. "All the same, they're a nice bunch of kids. They went down to Mark Gary's cabin yesterday with a straggly bunch of old silk flowers they found. His dog got run over in the road and they felt sorry for him. Guy even offered to give him Barney because he was so upset."

Emmett was touched. He didn't seem to know his own kids at all. "That was nice of them."

"Yes, it was. They've got a lot of heart." She twisted her apron. "Of course, there was this one little incident while you were away."

"Little?" he asked hesitantly.

She shifted. "Well, you know how they feel about that inspector who comes out here—the one who yelled at Barney and made Amy cry? The one everybody in the county hates?"

Emmett's face hardened. "I had words with him about upsetting Amy."

"You weren't here," she pointed out. "He made a remark that Guy didn't like about that big Appaloosa stallion of yours that Guy adores. Then he made a couple of remarks about you."

"What did they do?" Emmett asked with resignation.

"Nothing really vicious..."

"What did they do?" he repeated.

She grimaced. "They put a potato in his tail pipe."

"Did he take it out?"

She cleared her throat. "He was too busy at the time."

"Doing what?"

"Trying to get the snake out of his front seat."

Emmett buried his face in his hands. "Oh, my God!" he wailed. "He'll shut us down for sure!"

"I don't think so."

There was hope? He lifted his head. "Why?"

"Well, the kids had some food coloring they got out of the cabinet. They sort of colored the snake up before they put it in the cab. I don't like snakes, you know, but it was real pretty. Sort of blue and pink and yellow and green, with polka dots." She shrugged. "It seems that the gentleman went back to his office and told them he'd been shut up in his car with a blue and pink and yellow and green polka-dotted snake by three midget commandos." She wiped her hands on her apron. "I hear he's having therapy. There's this new inspector. He's real nice, and he likes snakes. We, uh, didn't let him see Guy's, of course. The food coloring will wear off, eventually."

Emmett hadn't stopped laughing when she got back to the kitchen.

Melody could hardly contain herself. She hoped that the kids never got it in for her!

Guy was nervous around his father. He hadn't forgotten the threat about military school, and there was the incident with the snake. He was sure Mrs. Jenson had mentioned it.

Because he was uncertain of his position now that Melody was in residence, he tried to keep out of everyone's way.

That night, an impatient Emmett hustled the kids to bed and turned off the television long before the news was due to come on.

He held out his hand, his eyes quiet and tender as they met Melody's.

"You look impatient, Mr. Deverell," she said demurely as he tugged her along the hall toward their bedroom.

"Impatient, desperate and a few other things. How I wish these walls were soundproof," he muttered under his breath. He closed the door and locked it before he turned on the radio by the bed to a country-western station. He looked down at Melody, who was blushing. He drew her against him and bent to brush his mouth sensuously over her own. "We're starving for each other," he whispered. "I don't want eavesdroppers, and we both get pretty vocal when we let go in bed."

"Yes." She shivered as his hands smoothed down her body. "It's been so long—!" Her voice broke.

"Eons." He lifted her onto the bed and followed her down.

Tenderness still wasn't possible, he thought as the room began to spin around them. Not yet…!

Later, when the anguish of wanting each other was spent, he aroused her again, but tenderly this time. He moved against her in a soft, sweet rhythm that was unlike anything they'd ever done together. All the while, he looked into her eyes and smoothed away her damp hair, kissed her forehead, her nose, her cheeks, her eyes. Until speech was no longer possible, he whispered broken endearments and praise.

When the spiral caught them, her body convulsed violently, despite the slow, gentle rhythm, and she began to sob under the warm crush of his mouth. The rainbow of sensation made her cry out and he was vaguely aware of the radio drowning out the sound as his muscles corded and his hips arched violently, convulsively, against her.

They were both shaking with reaction when the room came back into focus. She was crying softly, because the force of the ecstasy he'd given her had been devastating.

"I wanted to give you tenderness," he whispered with exhausted regret. "I wanted it to be soft and slow and gentle and I couldn't…!"

"But it was," she protested. She lifted up, resting her arm across his damp, throbbing chest as she looked down into his eyes. "Emmett, it was!"

"Not at the last," he said through his teeth.

"Oh. Then. Well, of course not," she murmured shyly. She smiled at him wickedly and laughed deep in her throat.

"You lose control," she whispered. "I like to watch you cry out, and know that it's because of me, because of the pleasure you get from my body."

He touched her face with wonder. "I like to watch you for the same reason. Melody," he said quietly, "I never watched before. The pleasure I gave never mattered that much before."

"I'm glad." She drew her face gently against his, wrapping him up in the sweetness of her adoration. "I'd die for you, Emmett," she whispered.

He drew her down and enveloped her hungrily. His hands in her hair were unsteady as he used them to turn her head so that he could find her mouth. His lips trembled, too, with the rage of feeling she unleashed in him.

Incredible man, she thought dizzily. So much a man...

She eased her hips over his and coaxed his body into deep intimacy, pressing soft kisses over his hair-roughened chest as she shifted over him until he groaned. He lay like a pagan sacrifice, and she sat up, feeling the power of her own femininity as he writhed and moaned beneath the slow movement of her hips.

"I love you," she whispered, increasing the pressure. "I love you, Emmett, I love you!"

His lean hands bit into her hips and he arched, crying out helplessly as she fulfilled him and, in the process, herself. In the back of her mind she was grateful for the radio. If those kids had heard... She moved again and he lost the ability to think at all.

Breakfast was uncomfortable for the whole next week.

"You sure must like country-western music a lot, Emmett," Amy muttered. "But does it have to be so loud?"

"All those wailing cowboys," Polk said with a shake of his unruly hair.

"Sounds more like rock music than country," Amy agreed.

Melody's face was scarlet. She didn't dare look at Emmett. The muffled laughter coming from the head of the table was bad enough.

"I'll try to keep the volume down," Emmett promised dryly. "It helps us sleep."

"That's right," Melody agreed.

"Bill Turner wants me to go hunting with him Saturday," Guy remarked. "We're going after squirrels."

"No," Melody said abruptly.

Guy glared at her. "I can go if I want to."

"No," she said flatly. "Emmett?"

He glanced at her and frowned. She was giving him muted signals that he didn't understand. But if she was that vehement about it, there had to be a reason.

"Dad?" Guy asked belligerently.

"Melody said no," Emmett replied. "Eat your eggs."

"She's not my mother!" Guy burst out. "She can't tell me what to do!"

"She's my wife, and the hell she can't tell you what to do! This is her house now, just as much as it's mine and Amy's and Polk's and yours!"

Guy got up from the table. "I hate her!" he raged. He turned and ran out of the house. He'd wanted to go hunting more than anything in the world. It would have been the first time he'd ever shot a rifle, ever hunted anything. He'd been sure Emmett would let him go, and now that interfering woman was telling him he couldn't and Emmett took her side against his! He hated her! He ran off into the small wooded glade past the barn and stayed there for the rest of the afternoon, refusing to budge even when Amy and Polk came to find him.

"Why didn't you want him to go?" Emmett asked Melody

after Guy and the other two had gone. "Is it the thought of shooting a squirrel that bothers you?"

"It's the thought of Bill shooting him," she replied worriedly. "Emmett, the weekend before we married, Bill was out beyond the barn with a .22 rifle shooting wildly all around the place. He wasn't even aiming at anything. I yelled at him when one of the bullets whizzed past me and he stopped."

"Why didn't you tell me?" he demanded.

"He begged me not to. He said you might fire him." She looked up at him. "He promised he wouldn't do it again, and he hasn't, but he's careless and haphazard. Would you really trust Guy's life to somebody like that?"

"No, certainly not. I'll talk to Guy later."

"Thanks." She grimaced. "I guess I'm public enemy number one again," she said miserably.

"He'll understand when I explain it. All the same," he said with a glowering look, "he's not going to talk to you like that."

"Look at you bristle." She sighed, resting her chin on her hands. "A conceited woman would think you're head over heels in love with me."

He stared at her levelly. "I *am* head over heels in love with you," he said matter-of-factly.

Her breath stopped in her throat as she met the soft sensuality of his eyes and got lost in their green depths. "You what?" she faltered.

"I love you," he repeated. "Adore you. Worship the ground you walk on." He grinned. "We could go into the bedroom and I could tell you some more. But it's broad daylight and the radio's unplugged. And Mrs. Jenson won't confuse wailing with country music," he added, tongue-in-cheek.

She blushed, laughing. "Well, you do your share of that, too. It isn't all me!"

"I know," he said shamelessly. He sighed warmly and smiled at her. "I like just looking at you with your clothes off. Being able to make love to you is a bonus."

"I used to think I was oversized and plain before you came along," she murmured.

"Not anymore, I'll wager," he murmured, staring pointedly at her breasts. "If you're oversized, long live big girls."

She laughed. "Emmett!"

He grimaced. "I have to go to work. I don't want to," he added, when he got up and paused to kiss her on his way out. "But I don't get paid for kissing you."

"Pity," she whispered. "When you do it so well!"

He chuckled. "So do you."

"Emmett?"

He paused. "Hmm?"

"I love you, too," she said solemnly.

He smiled. "You tell me that with your body, every time we love each other." He traced a line down her straight nose. "I was telling you, the same way, but you didn't realize it, did you?"

She shook her head. Her eyes blazed with feeling. "I could walk on a cloud..."

"So could I." He bent and kissed her very softly. "One day, when the sharp edge wears off the hunger, maybe I'll be able to make love to you as tenderly as I want to in my heart," he whispered. "Right now, I can't tone down the desire I feel for you. If I have any regret, it's that."

"Have I complained?" she asked softly. "I want you just as badly, Emmett. It will keep." She smiled. She beamed. "I didn't know you loved me!"

"Well, you do, now." He pulled his hat low over his eyes. "Don't let it go to your head just because I walk into fence posts staring at you like a love-struck boy."

She put her hand over her heart, one of his favorite postures, and grinned back at him. "Would I do that?"

His green eyes glittered with mischief. "We'd better find a rock station to listen to tonight," he murmured dryly.

She laughed with pure delight as he winked and went out the door. She had the world, she thought. She had the whole world. Emmett loved her! Everything was going to be perfect now.

The euphoria lasted until suppertime, when she went to feed Alistair. And she couldn't find him.

She looked through the house, in all his favorite places, but he wasn't anywhere to be seen. It was cold outside and threatening rain. Surely he wouldn't have gone out voluntarily! He hated the outdoors. He hated getting wet even more.

Then she remembered that Guy had been angry with her. The last time he'd been angry with her, he'd let Alistair out, and she almost hadn't got him back. But the boy wouldn't be that cruel again, would he?

She came back into the dining room, white in the face and obviously troubled.

"What's wrong?" Emmett asked, pausing with a bowl of mashed potatoes in his hand and an uplifted spoon over his plate.

"Alistair's missing," she said unsteadily.

She didn't look at Guy, but everyone else did.

"I didn't let him out," Guy said. He felt frightened. He hadn't been near the big cat. He liked him, now. The last thing he'd ever want to do was hurt the animal. But everybody, including his father, was giving him looks like daggers. Everybody except Melody, who couldn't seem to look at him at all.

"I didn't!" Guy repeated. "I haven't even seen him today...!"

"You were mad because Melody didn't want you to go hunting with Bill," Emmett said curtly.

"I didn't let her cat out!" Guy got to his feet. "Dad, I'm not lying! I didn't do it! Why won't you believe me?"

"Because the last time you got mad at Melody, you turned him out into the streets of Houston," Emmett said icily. "And he wound up at the city pound, where instead of being put with new arrivals to be offered for adoption, he was accidentally mixed in a bunch scheduled for immediate termination!"

Melody's gasp was audible. Emmett had never told her that. She shivered, and Guy saw it, and felt sick all over again. She looked devastated. He was sorry he'd been so angry about Bill.

He'd complained to one of the cowboys about being deprived of the hunting trip, and the cowboy had told him, tongue-in-cheek, that Bill couldn't get anybody to go with him after he'd accidentally wounded his last hunting partner. He'd added that Bill had damned near accidentally shot Melody herself a couple of weeks back, too. Guy hadn't known that. It had surprised and then pleased him that Melody had argued about letting him go. He wanted to ask her about it over supper and apologize. He'd been about to, when Melody couldn't find Alistair. And right now Guy felt in danger of becoming the entrée instead of a fellow diner.

Emmett put the mashed potatoes down. "Let's go," he said, tossing his napkin onto the table. "Everybody outside. We're going to find Alistair if it takes all night. Then," he added with a cold glare at his eldest son, "you and I are going to have a long talk about the future."

"You can't send me to military school." Guy choked. "I won't go!"

"You'll go," Emmett said, and kept walking. Melody barely heard him. She was too frightened for Alistair to notice much of what was being said. Guy had seemed so friendly, until she'd argued over that hunting trip. He was never going to accept her. He hated her. He had to, in order to put her pet at risk a second time. She was devastated.

So was Guy. He was going to be banished because of something he hadn't even done. He was going to be sent away. Military school. Demerits. Uniforms. No sister and brother to play with. No ranch.

"No," he said to himself. "No, I won't go!"

The others had gone out the door. Guy rushed to his room and got the few things he couldn't do without, including his allowance. He went back through the house, his heart pounding like mad, into his father's study. There was a small telephone journal, where important numbers were kept. His mother's number was there. He'd always wanted to use it, but he hadn't had the nerve. Now he did. He had absolutely nothing left to lose.

The phone rang and rang, and Guy watched the door nervously, chewing on his lip. He didn't want to be caught. He had to get away, but he needed a place to go. His mother was his only hope. She loved him. He knew she did, even if his father didn't.

"Hello?"

"Mom?" His voice wavered. "Mom, it's me. Guy."

"Guy!" There was excitement in her soft voice. "How are you? Does your father know you're calling me?" she added hesitantly.

"Mom, he's got a new wife," he began.

"Yes, I know. Randy's sister." She didn't even sound upset. "Melody is sweet and kind. She'll be good to you. I'm happy that your father has finally found someone he can really love, Guy…"

"But she hates me," he wailed. "She blames me for stuff I don't do. Look, can I come and live with you? They don't really want me here!"

There was a pause. "Son, you know I'd love nothing better. I really would love to have you. But, you see…I'm pregnant. And I'm having a hard time. I can't really look after you right now, having to stay in bed so much. But after the baby comes…'' she added. ''Guy? *Guy?*''

There was nothing but a dial tone on the other end of the line.

Guy stood looking at the replaced receiver. His mother was pregnant. She was going to have a baby. Not his father's baby. Randy's baby. That meant she was certainly never going to come back. She would have another family of her own, Randy's children.

Now, Guy thought numbly, he had no one at all. His father was remarried and would have other children, too. His mother didn't want him. He had nobody in the whole world.

He turned and walked out the front door. The rain was starting to come down in sheets. It was cold, and his jacket wasn't waterproof, but he really didn't care. He had nothing left to lose. His home, his secure life, his father, his mother, his family were all nothing but memories. He was unwanted and unloved.

Well, he thought with bitter sorrow, perhaps he could make it alone. He had twenty dollars in his pocket and he didn't mind hard work. There had to be someplace he could go where nobody would care about his age.

He started walking across the field toward the main highway. He didn't look back.

''Alistair!'' Melody wailed. They'd been searching for half an hour, with no success at all. The big tabby cat hadn't turned up yet.

''You won't stop me this time,'' Emmett said angrily as they paused just inside the barn. ''Guy won't be hurt by a little discipline. I'm going to enroll him in the same military school where I went when I was a boy.''

''But he was getting used to me,'' Melody said miserably.

"I know he was. I shouldn't have said anything about Bill…"

"And let him go off with the man and get killed?" He stared at her. "Melody, part of being a parent is knowing when to say no for a child's own good. You have to expect rebellion and tantrums, and not let yourself be swayed by them. Parenting is a rough job. Loving a child isn't enough. You have to prepare him to live in a hostile world."

"I guess there's more to it than I realized." She looked up at him. "Guy is so like you," she said gently. "I care about him. I don't want him to be hurt."

"Neither do I, but education isn't a punishment. I think he'll like it. I was homesick at first, but I loved it after the first two weeks. If he doesn't take to it," he added quietly, "he can come back home."

She smiled through her sadness. "You're a nice man."

"I'm a wet man," he replied. "Let's look for a few more minutes…"

"Emmett!" Amy shouted. "Emmett, he's here, he's here!"

"What?" He went into the barn, following her excited voice.

Emmett and Melody peered over into the corn crib and there, curled up on some hay, was a sleepy, purring Alistair.

"Oh, you monster!" Melody grumbled. She picked him up and cradled him close, murmuring softly to him.

"Found your cat, did you?" Larry, the eldest of the cowboys, asked with a smile. "Meant to tell you he'd got out, but we had a few head get lost and I had to go help hunt them. He ran out past me when I was talking to Ellie Jenson in the kitchen. Guess my spurs spooked him," he added ruefully. "No harm done, though, I suppose, was there? I'll be more careful next time, boss."

He tipped his hat and went to put up the tack he was carrying, water dripping off his hat.

Emmett and Melody exchanged horrified glances.

"Guy!" she whispered.

He drew in a deep breath. "Well, I guess I'll eat crow for a month," he muttered. "Come on. I might as well get it over with."

But it wasn't that easy. They went back into the house and the telephone was ringing off the hook. Mrs. Jenson had gone home an hour earlier, and Guy was apparently unwilling to pick up the receiver.

Emmett grabbed it up. "Hello?"

"Emmett! Thank God! It's Adell," she said.

Hearing her voice threw him off balance. He'd avoided talking to her for two years. Now, it was like hearing any woman's voice.

"Hello, Adell," he said pleasantly. "What can I do for you?"

"It's Guy," she said. "I've been trying to get you for a half hour. Guy called, and he sounded pretty desperate. He wanted to come and live with me, but I blurted out about the baby, and he hung up. I'm so worried. I didn't mean to tell him like that, Emmett. I didn't mean it to sound as if I didn't love him or want him...!"

"It's all a misunderstanding," Emmett said gently. "Now don't worry. He's hiding in his room and we'll get it straightened out. He'll be fine."

"I knew it would be hard for the kids when you got married again, but Melody's so sweet," she said softly. "She's just what the four of you need. The boys will worship her when they get used to her, and so will Amy."

"They already do," he said. "I've been pretty bullheaded over this, Adell. I'm sorry."

"I did it the wrong way," she confessed. "I ran when I should have stood up and been honest with you. I guess if we'd really loved each other it would have been different.

But I didn't know what love was until Randy came along.''
She hesitated. "I hope you know what I'm talking about.''

"I do now,'' he said, staring quietly at Melody. "Oh, yes,
I understand now.''

"Let me know about Guy?''

"Of course. Adell, I'm glad for you and Randy, about the
baby.''

"We're ecstatic,'' she said. "I can hardly wait. A baby
might be just the thing for the kids.''

"You can bring it down to meet them when it's born,''
he said.

"Thanks. I will. But what I meant was if you and Melody
had one of your own eventually, it would bring them closer
to her.''

He stared at Melody and flushed as the glory of fathering
her child made his knees weak.

"Emmett?'' Adell called.

"What? Oh. Yes. You can call the kids or write to them
if you want,'' he said absently. "They can come and visit,
too, when it's convenient. Or you and Randy can come down
here. Tell him I won't hit him.''

"He knows that. We both felt guilty over what he'd done
to you, for a long time. I'm glad it worked out.''

"So am I. I'll have Guy call you back.''

"That would be nice. Tell him I love him, and that I didn't
mean he wasn't welcome here.''

"I will.'' He hung up, his eyes slow and warm on Melody's face. "Adell thinks I should make you pregnant,'' he
mused.

She caught her breath. "Well!''

He moved toward her, and paused to frame her face in his
big, lean hands. "I think I should, too,'' he whispered. "Not
right away, not until we're really a family. But I'd like it
very much if we had a child together, Melody.'' He bent and
drew his lips softly over hers.

"So would I." She clung to him, giving him back the kiss. She smiled warmly. "But for now, we'd better tell Guy that he isn't going to be banished to Siberia."

"Good point."

They went to his room and knocked. There was no answer. With a rueful smile, Emmett pushed it open, but Guy wasn't there.

Emmett looked around. Some of Guy's favorite possessions were missing, including that whittling knife that Melody had given him. He looked at her with fear in his eyes.

"He's run away, hasn't he?" she asked with faint panic.

His face was grim. "I'm afraid that's just what he's done," he replied.

Chapter 11

Jacobsville seemed to be a long way from anywhere, Guy thought, huddled miserably in his jacket while rain poured down on his bare head and soaked his sneakers. He was cold and getting colder by the minute. He should have taken time to search for the raincoat he could never find, but he'd been afraid someone would try to stop him.

After a few wet minutes, he managed to flag down a family of Mexicans driving toward Houston. With his meager Spanish, painstakingly taught to him by his bilingual father, he made them understand that he was on his way to his family. They smiled and nodded and gestured him into the crowded car of smiling, welcoming faces. People, he thought, were generally pretty nice. He was pleasantly surprised. Too bad he couldn't say that for his own family. They'd probably find Melody's cat dead and nobody would speak to him for the rest of his life. It wasn't his fault, but he guessed maybe he deserved it for what he'd done in Houston.

The Mexican family stopped at Victoria to get gas, and

Guy had second thoughts about continuing on to Houston. He might as well try to find a place to stay here. Victoria was big enough that he could get lost in it.

He found a vacant lot where a small building stood with its door ajar. It was still raining. He darted into the shack and came face-to-face with a couple of men who looked as if murder might be their favorite Sunday pastime.

It took forever just to get the kids into Emmett's Bronco and strapped in. All the while, the rain was getting worse and Melody was chewing on her fingernails. They'd called the local police and a *bolo* went out over the air to law enforcement vehicles. Emmett had a CB unit and a scanner in the Bronco, and the scanner was turned on so that they'd hear immediately if Guy was spotted.

Emmett was actually able to track the boy down the highway at the end of the ranch road, until the footprints abruptly stopped.

He got back into the vehicle, his hat dripping water. "This is as far as he walked," he said tersely, turning toward Melody. "Thank God for thick mud and a light drizzling rain. I tracked him to the other side of the road. He's headed that way, toward Victoria."

He wheeled the vehicle around in the road and set off with grim determination toward the city.

"I hope to God whoever he was riding with needed gas, and that he found some decent person and not a pervert to get into the car with.

"He's a smart boy," Melody said gently, touching his arm. "He'll be all right, Emmett. I know he will." She grimaced. "Oh, it's my fault!"

"No, it's not," he said tersely. "It takes a little work to turn five people into a family. It doesn't happen overnight, you know."

"I'm learning that. All the same, Guy's more important to

me than Alistair, even if I do love the stupid cat,'' she added quietly, staring worriedly through the misty windshield.

It took forever to get into the city. Then Emmett stopped at the nearest gas station before he proceeded to the next few. They were almost at the far end of town before an attendant remembered a bareheaded boy in a leather bomber jacket and jeans and sneakers.

''He was pretty wet,'' the man said with a grin. ''Came in with a family of Mexicans, but he didn't want to go on to Houston with them. I had to explain. Kid spoke really lousy Spanish,'' he murmured sheepishly.

''Did you see which way he went?''

''No. I'm sorry, but we got busy and I didn't notice. Can't have gotten far, though. It's only been ten or fifteen minutes, and he didn't hitch another ride, I'm sure of that.''

''Thanks. Thanks a lot. Okay if I leave the Bronco here while we look for him?''

''Sure, it's okay! Just park it anywhere. I'll look out for it.''

''Much obliged.''

Emmett pulled it out of the way and parked it. He turned to the others. ''We're going to spread out and go over this area of town like tar paper. Amy, you go with Melody. Polk, with me. If you find him, sing out.''

''All right, Emmett,'' Amy said politely. ''We'll find him.''

''God, I hope so,'' he said heavily. It was already dark. The streetlights were a blessing, but any city was dangerous at night. They had to find the boy soon, or they might never find him.

They piled out of the Bronco and Emmett paused to look hard at Melody. ''Don't go anywhere you don't feel comfortable. I don't like having any of us out on these streets at night. Stay where it's lighted. If you get in trouble, scream. I'll hear you.''

She smiled up at him. "Amy and I both will," she mused.

"I can scream good, Emmett," Amy said. "Want to hear me?"

"Not just yet, thanks," he murmured, tugging a pigtail. "Get going."

Melody and Amy went down one street, Emmett another. They met a policeman cruising by, and Emmett stopped to talk to him. He explained the situation.

"We got the *bolo* on the radio," the patrolman, an elderly man, replied. "We're watching for him. He's pretty safe if he's still in this area. Hope you find him."

"So do I," Emmett said quietly. "He's got the wrong end of the stick. He thinks we don't care about him because we have to say no sometimes."

"Prisons are full of kids who never got said no to," the policeman mused. "Might tell him that."

"He'll get an earful, after he gets hugged half to death," Emmett said with a wry smile.

"That's how I raised my four. One's a lawyer now." With a twinkle in his eyes he added, "Of course, the others are respectable..."

Emmett laughed despite his fears and lifted his hand as the patrol car pulled away into the darkness.

Down the street, Melody was huddled in her coat, drawing Amy closer as the rain began to fall again. She looked and looked, and found nothing. Finally, yielding to defeat, she turned and guided Amy back toward the service station.

The shack in the empty lot had caught her eye earlier, but she hadn't paid it much mind because she was sure Guy would be trying to make some distance.

Now, she wasn't so certain.

"Let's take a look in there, just in case," she told Amy. "Stay close."

"Okay, Melody."

They moved quickly toward the shack, and as they approached it, loud voices could be heard. There was a violent thumping noise, and the ramshackle door suddenly moved and Guy came tearing out of it. His face was bleeding and his jacket was half off. A thin, dirty man was holding the half that was off, dragging at it.

"I said, I want the damned jacket!" the surly voice repeated.

"It's Guy!" Amy exclaimed.

"Yes." Melody's eyes blazed with anger. She was never so happy for her size. "Stay behind me," she called as she broke into a run.

Guy was fighting the man, but the other one had a stick and was raising it.

"You leave my son alone!" Melody yelled at them.

The men stopped suddenly and gaped at her. So did a shocked, delighted Guy. While they were gaping, she sailed right into the one who had Guy by the sleeve, performed a jump kick accompanied by a cry that would have made her instructor applaud and landed her foot squarely into the attacker's gut.

Guy barely had time for one astonished look at her threatening stance. Loosened by the man's collapse, Guy turned quickly to place a hard kick in the other man's groin before he could bring down the stick he was holding up and then planted a hard fist right into his cheek. The second man went down with a little cry of pain and landed unconscious.

"Are you all right?" Melody asked Guy, dragging him close to hug him. "Oh, you holy terror, if you *ever* do anything like this again…!" She was barely coherent, crying and mumbling, searching his face for cuts and bruises, brushing back his unruly damp hair. But the whole time she was holding him as his mother once had when he stumbled and fell, when he was hurt or afraid.

Big boys weren't supposed to like this sort of thing, of

course, much less tolerate it. And he was going to twist away from her any minute now and make some curt remark. But just for a minute or so, it wouldn't hurt to be hugged and cried over.

"How did you *do* that?" he asked, aghast.

"Oh, that. Well, I have a belt in tae kwon do. Just a brown. I never finished my training."

"*Just* a brown!" He caught his breath. "That was great! Like watching Chuck Norris or Jean Claude Van Damme," he added, naming his two idols. "Listen, could you teach me some of that?"

"You and the other kids, too," she promised. "Then next time, you'll be prepared." She grimaced as she studied him. "Listen, Alistair's fine, one of the men accidentally let him out," she said miserably, drawing back. "I'm so sorry. All of us are sorry for blaming you. For heaven's sake, you're more important than a cat, even if he was the only friend I had! Your father was frantic, and so were the rest of us!"

Guy felt strange. He sort of smiled and couldn't stop. "I'm all right." He looked down at the squirming, groaning men. "Uh, it might not be a bad idea if we leave," he suggested, taking her arm. "You and I were pretty much a match for them, but we've Amy to think about."

"You're right. I do wish I had a gun," she muttered, glaring at them.

"Can you shoot one?" Guy asked on the way down the street.

"Sure I can shoot," she said. "I've won awards."

"Really?"

"You still can't go hunting with Bill," she said curtly, glaring at him. "He'd kill you. He's not responsible with a gun. If you go hunting, I'll take you, or your father will. Or we'll all go. But I'm not shooting anything, even if I do go along, and I couldn't skin a squirrel if my life depended on it."

"We wouldn't go hunting to kill stuff," Guy said. "We'd go hunting so that we can grumble about how cold it was and how much big game got away. And so that we can sit and talk away from cars and horns and clocks."

"Oh."

He shrugged. "It would be all right if you came along, I guess. We could shoot at targets."

"I can shoot, too," Amy said. "I have a bow and arrow that Emmett made me."

"Polk can bring his *atl-atl*," Guy remarked. "We'd be the most dangerous family in the woods."

Melody laughed. She felt exhausted now. They came to the street where the service station sat on the corner, and there were Emmett and Polk coming toward them.

"Guy!" Emmett shouted.

The boy ran to him, and Emmett lifted him off the ground in a bear hug. "My God, you are something! I wish I'd hit you harder when you were a little kid!"

"I guess you should have, all right," Guy murmured, fighting tears. "I'm sorry, Dad...!"

"*I'm* sorry," Emmett corrected grimly. He put the boy down. "We're all sorry. If you had any idea how worried we were!" His green eyes began to glitter. "Son, if you ever, *ever* do anything like this to us again, I'll...I'll...!"

"He's trying to think up something bad enough to threaten you with," Melody translated, grinning at him. "It may take a while."

"Some men were beating up Guy, Emmett," Amy said excitedly. "Melody knocked one of them out, and Guy hit the other one. They're lying in the dirt back there."

"You'd better show me those men," Emmett said. The remark Amy had made about Melody went right over his head. He was incensed that anyone should hit his child. "Why were they beating on you?" Emmett asked slowly.

"They wanted my jacket," Guy said, grimacing. "I should

have had better sense than to go in there in the first place, but I was wet and miserable and I didn't think. They were tramps, I think—maybe hitchhikers.''

"Let's check this out, just in case," Emmett said, and he looked pretty dangerous, Guy thought as they walked together toward the shack. But a police car came by before they reached it. Emmett told the officer what had happened, and he was told that there had been some trouble with transients lately. He went to check, but the men were long gone. Which was just as well.

The fighting Deverells climbed back into their Bronco and went home.

A little later, with three exhausted kids tucked up in bed before they managed to rehash the exciting incident, Melody lay curled up in Emmett's hard arms, smiling with pure bliss after the most tender loving she'd ever known.

"This is what I wanted it to be on our wedding night," he said drowsily. "But I was too desperate for you." He bent and brushed his mouth lovingly over her soft lips, smiling warmly.

"When we get around to making a baby, I want it to be like it was tonight," she whispered into his warm throat. "We've never been closer than this."

"I know." He cradled her body to his and stretched lazily. "Guy's going to be Alistair's champion from now on, I imagine," he murmured.

"Friends to the end. Alistair's sleeping with him."

"He's your champion, too. You should have heard him telling Polk what you did to that tramp on his behalf." He glanced at her. "Polk told him what you said, about his being more important to you than Alistair. He's been strutting all night."

"He's a very special boy. But he's much more sensitive than he looks." She traced his thick eyebrows. "We'll have to remember that. Both of us. And no military school. If he goes, I'm going with him.''

''For protection?''

''Laugh if you like, but I'm a brown belt in tae kwon do.''

''What?''

She shrugged, smiling at his surprise. ''Didn't you wonder how I was able to drop a man that size so easily? I didn't have anything else to do on long winter nights, so I enrolled in a Korean karate class. It was very educational.''

''No wonder you didn't balk when I asked you to go with Amy to look for Guy. I worried about doing that. Men are going to feel protective about their women. It's their nature.''

''I know that. I don't mind. Just as long as you know that I'm not helpless all the time.'' She rolled over and kissed his chest, feeling his breath catch as her lips pressed through the thick hair to the hard, warm flesh beneath it. ''Of course,'' she whispered, ''there are times when I really enjoy being helpless.''

''Is this one of them?'' he murmured, coaxing her mouth closer.

''I think so.''

''Good. Let's be helpless together...''

He rolled her over and very quickly, the friendly banter turned to something much more serious and intense.

Randy and a very pregnant Adell came to visit two months later. The children accepted her condition without comment, and there were no problems.

By the time Emmett and his family drove Adell and Randy back to the airport, they were friends. Randy, who looked so much like his sister, was obviously the end of Adell's rainbow.

''Nice to see them so happy,'' Emmett remarked as he and Melody watched the other couple walk off toward the loading ramp, arms close around each other.

"Yes, isn't it?" Melody asked with a sigh. "Emmett, I'm so happy I could burst."

"So am I." He bent to kiss her, very softly. "And the kids were so good, weren't they? I could hardly believe they were the same bunch that put on their Thanksgiving Indian costumes and attacked that car of Florida tourists that got lost on the place last week. We really are going to have to start enforcing some new codes of behavior."

"Oh, maybe not," Melody said. "They've been so good today…"

"Excuse me?"

A uniformed security guard with a grim expression tapped on Emmett's shoulder.

"Yes?" Emmett asked politely.

"Someone said those might be your kids…?"

He gestured toward the concourse. Emmett noticed three things. An empty pet carrier. A screaming, running woman. Three laughing children holding equal parts of an enormous, friendly python. It looked almost identical to a Far Side® cartoon by Gary Larson that the twins had just been looking at in the book he'd bought them earlier…

Emmett didn't dare do what he felt like doing. Hysterical laughter was not going to help him. He looked at the security guard. He put his hand over his heart. "Officer," he said pleasantly, "I have never seen those kids before in my life.…"

Melody gave him a glare that was good for two headaches and a lonely night, and went running down the concourse after the children.

* * * * *

REGAN'S PRIDE

For Babs

Chapter 1

The tall, silver-haired man stood quietly apart from the rest of the mourners, his eyes narrowed and contemptuous on the slender, black-clad figure beside his sister. His cousin Barry was dead, and that woman was responsible. Not only had she tormented her husband of two years into alcoholism, but she'd allowed him to get behind the wheel of a car when he was drunk and he'd gone off a bridge to his death. And there she stood, four million dollars richer, without a single tear in her eyes. She looked completely untouchable—and Ted Regan knew that she had been, as far as her husband had been concerned.

His sister noticed his cold stare and left the widow's side to join him.

"Stop glaring at her. How can you be so unfeeling?" Sandy asked angrily. His sister had dark hair. At forty, he was fifteen years older than she, and prematurely gray. They shared the same pale blue eyes, though, and the same temper.

"Am I being unfeeling?" he asked with a careless smile, and raised his smoking cigarette to his mouth.

"You promised you were going to give that up," she reminded him.

He lifted a dark eyebrow. "I did. I only smoke when I'm under a lot of stress, and only outdoors."

"I wasn't worried about secondhand smoke. You're my brother, and I care about you," she said simply.

He smiled, and his hand touched her face briefly. "I'll try to quit. Again," he said wryly. He glanced at the widow with cold eyes. "She's a case, isn't she? I haven't seen a single tear. They were married for two years."

"Nobody knows what goes on inside a marriage, Ted," she reminded him quietly.

"I suppose not," he mused. "I've never wanted to marry anybody, but it seems to work out for a few people."

"Like the Ballengers here in Jacobsville," she agreed with a smile. "They go on forever. I envy them."

Ted wasn't going to touch that line with a pole. He drew on the cigarette, and his harsh gaze went back to the heavily veiled woman by the black limousine.

"Why the veil?" he asked coldly. "Is she afraid Barry's mother may wonder why there aren't any tears in her big blue eyes?"

"You're so cynical and harsh, Ted, it's no wonder to me that you've never married," she said with resignation. "I've heard people say that no woman in south Texas would be brave enough to take you on!"

"There's no woman in south Texas that I'd have," he countered.

"Least of all, Coreen Tarleton," she added for him, because the way he was looking at her best friend spoke volumes.

"She's even younger than you," he said curtly. "Twenty-four to my forty," he added quietly. "Years too young for me, even if I were interested. Which I am not," he added with a speaking glance.

"She isn't what you think," Sandy said.

"I'm glad you're loyal to the people you love, tidbit, but you're never going to convince me that the merry widow over there is grieving."

"You've always been unkind to her," Sandy said.

He stiffened. "She was a pest once."

Sandy didn't reply. She'd often thought that Ted had been in love for the first time in his life with Coreen, but he'd let the age difference stand between them. He was forty, but he had the physique of a man half that age, and the expensive dark suit he was wearing flattered it. He was a working millionaire. He never sat at a desk. He was slender and strong, and as handsome as the late cowboy star Randolph Scott. But he had no use for women now; not since Coreen had married.

"You're coming back to the house with us, aren't you?" Sandy asked after a minute. "They're reading the will after lunch."

"In a hurry, is she?" he asked icily.

"It was Barry's mother's idea, not hers," Sandy shot back angrily.

"No surprises there," he remarked, his blue eyes searching for Barry's small, elegant mother in her black designer suit. "Tina probably would enjoy dumping Coreen on the front lawn in her underwear."

"She does seem a little hostile."

Ted ground out the cigarette under the heel of his highly polished dress boot. "Is that a surprise?" he asked frankly. "Coreen killed her son."

"Ted!"

His blue eyes looked hard enough to cut diamond. "She never loved him," he told her. "She married him because her father had died and she had nothing, not even a house to live in. And then she spent two years teasing and taunting him and making him unhappy. He used to cry on my shoulder...."

"How? You never went near their house, except once, to visit for a few hours," she recalled. "You even refused to be best man at his wedding."

He averted his eyes. "He came to Victoria pretty often to see me," he said. "And he wasn't a stranger to a telephone. We had business dealings together. I heard all about Coreen from him," he added darkly. "She drove him to drink."

"Coreen is my friend," she responded. "Even if I believed that about her, it wouldn't matter. Friends accept the bad with the good."

He shrugged. "I wouldn't know. I don't have friends."

How well Sandy knew it, too. Ted didn't trust anyone that close, man or woman.

"You could make the gesture of giving her your condolences," she said finally.

He lifted an eyebrow. "Why should I give her sympathy when she doesn't care that her husband is dead? Besides, I don't do a damned thing for the sake of appearances."

She made a sound in her throat and went back to Coreen.

The ride back to the redbrick mansion was short. Coreen was quiet. They were almost to the front door before she looked at Sandy and spoke.

"Ted was saying something about me, wasn't he?" she asked, her voice strained. Her face was very pale in its frame of short, straight black hair and her deep blue eyes were tragic.

Sandy grimaced. "Yes."

"You don't have to soft-pedal Ted's attitude to me," came the wistful reply. "I've known Ted ever since you and I became friends in college, remember?"

"Yes, I remember," Sandy agreed.

"Ted never liked me, even before I married his cousin." She didn't mention how she knew it, or that Ted had been the catalyst who caused her to rush headlong into a marriage that she hadn't even wanted.

"Ted doesn't want commitment. He plays the field," Sandy said evasively.

"His mother really affected him, didn't she?" Coreen knew about their childhood, because Sandy had told her.

"Yes, she did. He's been a rounder most of his life because of it," she added on a sigh. "I used to think he had a case on you, before you married," she added with a swift glance. "He was violent about you. He still is. Odd, wouldn't you say?"

Coreen didn't betray her thoughts by a single expression. She'd learned to hide her feelings very well. Barry had homed in on any sign of weakness or vulnerability. She'd made the mistake once, only once, of talking about Ted, during the first weeks of her marriage to Barry. She hadn't realized until later that she'd given away her feelings for him. Barry had gotten drunk that night and hurt her badly. It had taught her to keep her deepest feelings carefully concealed.

"It will all be over soon," Sandy remarked.

"Will it?" Coreen asked quietly. Her long, elegant fingers were contracting on her black clutch bag.

"Why did Tina want the will read so quickly?" Sandy asked suddenly.

"Because she's sure that Barry left everything to her, including the house," she said quietly. "You know how opposed she was to our marriage. She'll have me out the front door by nightfall if the will did make her sole beneficiary. And I'll bet it did. It would be like Barry. Even when we were married, I had to live on a household allowance of a hundred dollars a week, and bills and groceries had to come out of that."

Her best friend stared at her. It had suddenly dawned on her that the dress Coreen was wearing wasn't a new one. In fact, it was several years out of style.

"I only have the clothes I bought before I married," Coreen said with ragged pride, avoiding her friend's eyes. "I've made do. It didn't matter."

All Sandy could think about was that Tina was wearing a new designer dress and driving a new Lincoln. "But, why? Why did he treat you that way?"

Coreen smiled sadly. "He had his reasons," she said evasively. "I don't care about the money," she added quietly. "I can type and I have the equivalent of an associate degree in sociology. I'll find a way to make a living."

"But Barry would have left you something, surely!"

She shook her head at Sandy's expression. "He hated me, didn't you know? He was used to women fawning all over him. He couldn't stand being anyone's second choice," she said enigmatically. "At least there won't be any more fear," she added with nightmarish memories in her eyes. "I'm so ashamed."

"Of what?"

"The relief I feel," she whispered, as if the car had ears. "It's over! It's finally over! I don't even care if people think I killed him." She shivered.

Sandy was curious, but she didn't pry. Coreen would tell her one day. Barry had done everything in his power to keep her from seeing Coreen. He didn't like anyone near his wife, not even another woman. At first, Sandy had thought it was obsessive love for Coreen that caused him to behave that way. But slowly it dawned on her that it was something much darker. Whatever it was, Coreen had kept to herself, despite Sandy's careful probing.

"It will be nice not to have to sneak around to have lunch with you once in a while," Sandy said.

Worried blue eyes met hers through the delicate lace veil. "You didn't tell Ted that we had to meet like that?"

"No. I haven't told Ted," was the reply. Sandy hesitated. "If you must know, Ted wouldn't let me talk about you at all."

The thin shoulders moved restlessly and the blue eyes went back to the window. "I see."

"I don't," Sandy muttered. "I don't understand him at all. And today I'm actually ashamed of the way he's acting."

"He loved Barry."

"Maybe he did, in his way, but he never tried to see your side of it. Barry wasn't the same with another man as he was with you. Barry bullied you, but most people don't try to bully Ted, if they've got any sense at all."

"Yes, I know."

The limousine stopped and the driver got out to open the door for them.

"Thanks, Henry," Coreen said gratefully.

Henry was in his fifties, an ex-military man with close-cropped gray hair and muscle. He'd been her salvation since he came to work for Barry six months ago. There had been gossip about that, and some people thought that Coreen was cuckolding her husband. Actually Henry had served a purpose that she couldn't tell anyone about.

"You're welcome, Mrs. Tarleton," Henry said gently.

Sandy went into the house with Coreen, noticing with curiosity that there seemed to be no maid, no butler, no household staff at all. In a house with eight bedrooms and bathrooms, that seemed odd.

Coreen saw the puzzled look on her friend's face. She took off her veiled hat and laid it on the hall table. "Barry fired all the staff except Henry. He tried to fire Henry, too, but I convinced him that he needed a chauffeur."

There was no reply.

Coreen turned and stared at Sandy levelly. "Do you think I'm sleeping with Henry?"

Sandy pursed her lips. "Not now that I've seen him," she replied with a twinkle in her eyes.

Coreen laughed, for the first time in days. She turned and

led the way into the living room. "Sit down and I'll make a pot of coffee."

"You will not. I'll make it. You're the one who needs to rest. Have you slept at all?"

The shorter woman's shoulders lifted and fell. She was just five foot five in her stocking feet, for all her slenderness. Sandy, three inches taller, towered over her. "The nightmares won't stop," she confessed with a small twist of her lips.

"Did the doctor give you anything to make you sleep?"

"I don't take drugs."

"A sleeping pill when someone has died violently is hardly considered a drug."

"I don't care. I don't want to be out of control." She sat down. "Are you sure you don't want me to...?"

The front door opened and closed. There hadn't been a knock, and only one person considered himself privileged enough to just walk in. Coreen refused to look up as Ted entered the living room, loosening his tie as he came. He wasn't wearing his Stetson, or even the dress boots he usually favored. He looked elegant and strange in his expensive suit.

"I was just about to make coffee," Sandy said, giving him a warning look. "Want some?"

"Sure. A couple of leftover biscuits would be nice, too. I didn't stop for breakfast."

"I'll see what I can find to fix." Sandy didn't mention that it was odd no one had offered to bring food. It was an accepted tradition in most rural areas, and this was Jacobsville, Texas. It was a very close-knit community.

Ted didn't have any inhibitions about asking embarrassing questions. He sat down in the big armchair across from the burgundy velvet-covered sofa where Coreen was sitting. "Why didn't anybody bring food?" he asked her bluntly. He smiled coldly. "Do your neighbors think you killed him, too?"

Coreen felt the nausea in the pit of her stomach. She swallowed it down and lifted cool blue eyes to his. She ignored the blatant insult. "We had no close neighbors, nor did we have any close friends. Barry didn't like people around us."

His expression tautened as he glared at her. "And you didn't like Barry around you," he said with soft venom. "He told me all about you, Coreen. Everything."

She could imagine the sort of things Barry had confided. He liked having people think she was frigid. She closed her eyes and rubbed at her forehead, where the beginnings of a headache were forming. "Don't you have a business to run?" she asked heavily. "Several businesses, in fact?"

He crossed one long leg over the other. "My favorite cousin is dead," he reminded her. "I'm here for the funeral."

"The funeral is over," she said pointedly.

"And you're four million dollars to the good. At least, until the will is read. Tina's on the way back from the cemetery."

"Urged on by you, no doubt," she said.

His eyebrows arched. "I didn't need to urge her."

The pain and torment of the past two years ate at her like acid. Her eyes were haunted. "No, of course you didn't."

She got up from the sofa, elegant in the expensive black dress that clung to her slender—too slender—body. He didn't like noticing how drawn she looked. He knew that she hadn't loved Barry; she certainly wasn't mourning him.

"Don't expect much," he said with a cold smile.

The accusation in his eyes hurt. "I didn't kill Barry," she said.

He stood up, too, slowly. "You let him get into a car and drive when he'd had five neat whiskeys." He nodded at her look of surprise. "I grew up in Jacobsville. I'm acquainted with most people who live here, and you know that Sandy and I have just moved back into the old homestead. Everybody's been talking about Barry's death. You were at a party and he wanted you to drive him home. You refused. So he went alone, and shot right off a bridge."

So that was how the gossips had twisted it. She stared at Ted without speaking. Sandy hadn't mentioned that they were coming home to Jacobsville. How was she going to survive living in the same town with Ted?

"No defense?" he challenged mockingly. "No excuses?"

"Why bother?" she returned wearily. "You wouldn't believe me."

"That's a fact." He stuck his hands into his pockets, aware of loud noises in the kitchen. Sandy, reminding him that she was still around.

Coreen folded her hands in front of her to keep them from trembling. Did he have to look at her with such cold accusation?

"Barry wrote to me two weeks ago. He said that he'd changed his will and that I was mentioned in it." He stared at her mockingly. "Didn't you know?"

She didn't. She only knew that Barry had changed the will. She knew nothing of what was in it.

"Tina's in it, too, I imagine," he continued with a smile so smug that it made her hands curl.

She was tired. Tired of the aftermath of the nightmare she'd been living, tired of his endless prodding. She pushed back her short hair with a heavy sigh. "Go away, Ted," she said miserably. "Please..."

She was dead on her feet. The ordeal had crushed her spirit. She felt tears threatening and she turned away to hide them, just as their betraying glitter began to show. She caught her toe in the rug and stumbled as she wheeled around. She gasped as she saw the floor coming up to meet her.

Incredibly he moved forward and caught her by the shoulders. He pulled her around and looked into her pale, drawn face. Then without a word, he slid his arms around her and stood holding her, gently, without passion.

"How did you manage that?" he asked, as if he thought she'd done it deliberately.

She hadn't. She was always tripping over her own feet these days. Tears stung her eyes as she stood rigidly in his hold, her heart breaking. He didn't know, couldn't know, how it had been.

"I didn't manage it," she whispered in a raw tone. "I tripped, and not because I couldn't wait to get your arms around me! I don't need anything from you!"

Her tone made him bristle with bad temper. "Not even my love?" he asked mockingly, at her ear. "You begged for it, once," he reminded her coldly.

She shivered. The memory, like most others of the past two years, wasn't that pleasant. She started to step back but his big hands flattened on her shoulder blades and held her against him. She was aware, too aware, of the clean scent of his whipcord lean body, of the rough sigh of his breath, the movement of his broad chest so close that the tips of her breasts almost touched it. Ted, she thought achingly. Ted!

Her hands were clenched against his chest, to keep them honest. She closed her eyes and ground her teeth together.

The hands on her back had become reluctantly caressing, and she felt his warm breath at the hair above her temple. He was so tall that she barely came up to his nose.

Under the warmth of his shirtfront, she could feel hard muscle and thick hair. He was offering her comfort, something she hadn't had in two long years. But he was like Barry, a strong, domineering man, and she was no longer the young woman who'd worshiped him. She knew what men were under their civilized veneer, and now she couldn't stand this close to a man without feeling threatened and afraid; Barry had made sure of it. She made a choked, involuntary sound as she felt Ted's hands contract around her upper arms. He was bruising her without even realizing it. Or did he realize it? Was he thinking of ways to punish her, ways that Barry hadn't gotten to?

Ted heard the pitiful sound she made, and the control he thought he had went into eclipse. "Oh, for God's sake," he groaned, and suddenly wrapped her up tight so that she was standing completely against him from head to toe. His tall body seemed to ripple with pleasure as he felt her against it.

Coreen shuddered. Two years ago, it would have been heaven to stand this close to Ted. But now, there were only vague memories of Ted and bitter, violent ones of Barry. Physical contact made her afraid now.

The tears came, and she stood rigidly in Ted's embrace and let them fall hotly to her cheeks as she gave in to the pain. The sobs shook her whole body. She cried for Barry, whom she never loved. She cried for herself, because Ted held her in contempt, and even if he hadn't, Barry had destroyed her as a woman. She wept until she was exhausted, drained.

Sandy stopped at the doorway, her eyes on Ted's expression as he bent over Coreen's dark head. Shocked, Sandy quickly made a noise to alert him to her presence, because she knew he wouldn't want anyone to see the look on his face in that one brief, unguarded moment.

"Coffee!" she announced brightly, and without looking directly at him.

Ted released Coreen slowly, producing a handkerchief that he pressed angrily into her trembling hands. She wouldn't look up at him. That registered, along with her rigid posture that hadn't relaxed even when she cried in his arms, and the deep ache inside him that holding her had created.

"Sit down, Corrie, and have a buttered biscuit," Sandy said as Ted moved quickly away and sat down again. "I found these wrapped up on the table."

"Mrs. Masterson came early this morning and made breakfast," Coreen recalled shakily. "I don't think I ate any."

"Tina said that she's staying at a motel," Ted remarked. He was furious at his own weakness. He hadn't meant to let it go that far.

She wiped her eyes and looked at him then. "She and I don't get along. She didn't want to stay here," she replied. "I did offer."

He averted his eyes to the cup of black coffee that Sandy handed him.

"You should take a few days to rest," Sandy told her friend. "Go down to the Caribbean or somewhere and get away from here."

"Why not?" Ted drawled, staring coldly at the widow. "You can afford it."

"Stop," Coreen said wildly, her eyes like saucers in her white face. "Stop it, can't you?"

"Ted, please!" Sandy added.

The sound of a car coming up the driveway diverted him. He got up and went to the door, refusing to look at Coreen again. His loss of control had shaken him.

"I can't stand this," Coreen whispered frantically. "He does nothing but try to get at me!"

"Barry said something to him," Sandy revealed curtly. "I don't know what. He mentioned at the cemetery that he'd seen him quite often and that Barry had told him things about you."

"Knowing Barry, he invented some of them to make himself look even more pitiful," Coreen said softly. "I was his scapegoat, his excuse for every terrible thing he did. He drank because of me, didn't you know?"

"He drank because he wanted to," Sandy corrected.

"You're the only person in Jacobsville who believes that," her friend said. She sipped her coffee, aware of voices in the hall, one deep and gentle, the other sharp and impatient.

"I thought that lawyer would be here by now," Tina Tarleton said irritably, stripping off her white gloves as she joined the women. She was resplendent in a black suit by Chanel and had on only the finest accessories to match.

"I imagine he had to go by his office and get the paper-work first," Coreen said.

Tina glared at her. "No doubt he'll be here soon. I'd start packing if I were you."

"I already have," Coreen said. "It didn't take long," she added enigmatically.

Another car came up. Sandy went to the hall window. "The lawyer," she announced, and went to open the door.

"Finally," Tina snapped. "It's about time!"

Coreen didn't reply. She was staring at the chair where Barry used to sit, remembering. Her eyes were suddenly haunted, almost afraid.

Ted glared at her from his own chair. So she felt guilty, did she? And well she should. He hoped her conscience hurt her. He hoped she never had another minute's peace.

She felt his glare and looked at him. His hands almost broke the arms of the chair he was occupying as he stared into her dead eyes with violence in his own.

The lawyer, a tall, graying gentleman, came into the room with Sandy and broke the spell. Coreen was ready to give thanks. She couldn't really understand why Ted should hate her so much over the death of a cousin he wasn't really that close to. But, then, he'd always hated her. Or at least, he'd given the appearance of hating her. He'd been hostile since that first time, two years ago, when he'd found himself forced into her company....

Chapter 2

Coreen had been friends with Sandy Regan for four years, but she was in her second year of college before she really got to know Ted Regan. She was helping her father in his feed store in Jacobsville and Ted had come in with the new foreman at his ranch to open an account.

In the past, he'd always done business with a rival feed store, but it had just gone out of business. He was forced to buy from Coreen's father, or drive to Victoria for supplies. He was courteous to Coreen, but not overly friendly. That wasn't new. From the beginning of her friendship with his sister, he'd been cool to her.

Coreen had found him fascinating from the first time she'd looked into those pale eyes, when Sandy had introduced them. Ted had given her a long, careful appraisal, and obviously found the sight of her offensive because he absented himself immediately after the introduction and thereafter maintained a careful distance whenever Coreen came out to the ranch.

Coreen wasn't hurt; she took it for granted that a sophisticated man like Ted wouldn't want to encourage her by being friendly. She'd been gangly and tomboyish in her jeans and sweatshirt and sneakers. Ted was almost a generation older, and already a millionaire. His name had been linked with some of the most beautiful and eligible women around Texas, even if his distaste for marriage was well-known.

But he noticed Coreen. Although it might have been reluctant on his part, his pale eyes followed her around the store every week while she filled his orders. But he came no closer than necessary.

As time went by, Coreen heard about him from Sandy and got to know him in a secondhand sort of way. Slowly she began to fall in love, until two years ago, he had become her whole life. He pretended not to see her interest, but it became more obvious as she fumbled and stammered when he came around the store.

It was inevitable that he would touch her from time to time as they passed paperwork back and forth, and suddenly it was like electricity between them. Once, she stood with her back to the counter and suddenly looked up into his eyes. He was standing so close that she could breathe in the very masculine scent of his cologne. He hadn't moved, hadn't blinked, and the intensity of the stare had made her knees weak. His gaze had dropped abruptly to her soft, pink mouth and her heartbeat had gone wild. She might be innocent, but even a novice could recognize the sort of desire that had flared unexpectedly in Ted's hard, lean face at that moment. It was the first time he'd ever really looked at her, she knew. It was as if, before, he'd forced himself not to notice her slender body and pretty face.

Her father's arrival had broken the spell, and Ted's expression had become one of self-contempt mingled with anger and something much more violent. He'd left the store at once.

Coreen had built dreams on that look they'd shared. As if Ted was caught in the same web, his trips to the feed store became more frequent and always, he watched her.

In her turn, she noticed that he usually came in on Wednesdays and on Saturdays, so she started dressing to the hilt on those days. Her slender, tomboyish figure could look elegant when she chose the right sort of clothes, and Ted didn't, or couldn't, hide his interest. His pale eyes followed her with visible hunger every time he came near her. The tension between them grew swiftly until one day things came to a head.

They were in the storeroom together, looking for a particular kind of bridle bit he wanted for his tack room. Coreen tripped over some coiled rope and Ted caught her easily, his reflexes honed by years of dangerous ranch work.

"Careful," he'd murmured at her forehead. "You could have pitched headfirst into those shovels."

"With my hard head, I'd never have felt it." She laughed, looking up at him. "I'm clumsy sometimes..."

The laughter had stopped when she saw his face. The lean hands holding her had brought her quite suddenly against the length of his body and secured her there. She could feel his chest move against her breasts when he breathed, and his breathing was as ragged as her own.

With a soft laugh full of self-contempt, he bent and brushed his open mouth roughly over her lips, teasing them with a skill that Coreen had never experienced. She stiffened, and he searched her eyes narrowly. Then he did it again, and this time she held her face up for him, poised like a sacrifice in his warm embrace.

"Do you know how old I am?" he asked against her mouth in a voice gone deep and gravelly with emotion.

"No."

"I'm thirty-eight," he murmured. "You're nearly twenty-two. I'm sixteen years your senior. We're almost a generation apart."

"I don't care...!" she began breathlessly.

His head lifted. "There's no future in it," he said mercilessly as he searched her face with quick, hard eyes. "You're infatuated and set on your first love affair, but it can't, it won't, be me. I'm long past the age of hand-holding and petting."

She stared at him uncomprehendingly. Her body was throbbing with emotion and she wanted nothing more than his mouth on hers.

"You aren't even listening," he chided huskily. His gaze fell to her soft mouth. "Do you know what you're inviting?" He drew her up on her tiptoes and his hard mouth closed slowly, expertly, on hers, teasing her lips apart with a steady insistent pressure that made her body feel swollen and shivery. She hesitated, frightened by it.

"No, you don't," he whispered, containing her instinctive withdrawal. "If I teach you nothing else, it's going to be that desire isn't a game."

One lean hand went to her nape, holding her head steady, and then his mouth began to torment hers in brief, rough, biting kisses. He aroused her so swiftly, so completely, that she pressed into him with a harsh whimper and clung, her legs trembling against his as her young body pleaded for relief from the torment that racked it.

She had no control, but Ted never lost his. Tempestuous seconds later, he lifted his mouth from hers slowly, inch by inch, his hands contracting around her upper arms as he eased her away from him and looked down into her shattered eyes.

She knew how she must look, with her swollen mouth still pleading for his kisses, her body trembling with the residue of what he'd aroused. She couldn't hide her reaction. But none of his showed in his face.

"Do you begin to see how dangerous it is?" he asked with unusual softness in his deep voice. "I could have you against the counter, right now. You're too shaken, too curious, to deny me, and I'm fairly human in my needs. I can see everything you feel, everything you want, in your face. You have no defense at all.''

''But you…don't you…want me?'' she stammered.

His face contorted for an instant. Then suddenly, all expression left his face. His hands contracted and one corner of his mouth pulled up. ''I want a woman,'' he said mercilessly. ''You're handy. That's all it is.''

The revelation was shattering to her ego. ''Oh. Oh, I…I see.''

''I hope so. You're very obvious lately, Coreen. You hang around the ranch waiting for me, you dress up when I come into the feed store. It's flattering, but I don't want your juvenile attention or your misplaced infatuation. I'm sorry to be so blunt, but that's how it is. You aren't the kind of woman who attracts me. You have the body and the outlook of an adolescent.''

She went scarlet. Had she been so obvious? She moved back from him, her arms crossing over her breasts. She was devastated.

His jaw tautened as he looked at her wounded expression, but he didn't recant. ''Don't take it so hard,'' he said curtly. ''You'll learn soon enough that we have to settle for what we can get in life. I'll send Billy for supplies from now on. And you'll find some excuse not to come out to the ranch to see Sandy. Won't you?''

She managed to nod. With a tight smile and threatening tears, she escaped the storeroom and somehow got through the rest of the day. Ted had paused at the front steps to look back at her, an expression of such pain on his face for an instant that she might have been forgiven for thinking he'd lied to her about his feelings. But later she decided that it must have been the sunlight reflecting off those cold blue eyes. He'd let her down hard, but if he couldn't return her feelings, maybe it was kinder in the long run.

From then on, Ted sent his foreman to buy supplies and never set foot in the feed store again. Coreen saw him occasionally on the streets of Jacobsville, the town being so small that it was impossible to avoid people forever. But she didn't look at him or speak to him. They went to the same cafeteria for lunch one day, totally by chance, and she left her coffee sitting untouched and went out the back way as he was being seated. Once she caught him watching her from across the street, his face faintly bemused, but he never came close. If he had, she'd have been gone like a shot. Perhaps he knew that. Her fragile pride had taken a hard knock.

She was eventually invited out to the ranch to visit Sandy, again, supposedly with Ted's blessing. Rather than make Sandy suspicious about her motives, she went, but first she made absolutely sure that Ted was out of town or at least away from the ranch. Sandy noticed and mentioned it, emphasizing that Ted had said it was perfectly all right for her to be there. Coreen wouldn't discuss it, no matter how much Sandy pried.

Once, after that, Ted came upon her unexpectedly at a social event. She'd gone with Sandy to a square dance to celebrate her twenty-second birthday. Neither of them had dates. Sandy hadn't mentioned that her brother had planned to go until they were already there. In the middle of a square dance, Coreen found herself passed from one partner to the other until she came face-to-face with a somber Ted. To his surprise, and everyone else's, she walked off the dance floor and went home.

Gossip ran rampant in Jacobsville after that, because it was the first time in memory that any woman had snubbed Ted Regan publicly. Her father found it curious and amusing. Sandy was devastated; but it was the last time she tried to play Cupid.

There was one social event that Coreen hadn't planned on attending, since Ted would certainly be there. Her father belonged to a gun club and Coreen had always gone with him to target practice and meetings. Ted was the club president.

Coreen had long since stopped going to the club, but when the annual dance came around, her father insisted that she attend. She didn't want to. Sandy had already told her in a puzzled way that Ted went wild every time Coreen's name was mentioned since that square dance. She probably wondered if it was something more than having Coreen snub him at the dance, but she was too polite to ask.

Ted's venomous glare when he saw her at the gun club party was unsettling. She was wearing a sequined silver dress with spaghetti straps and a low V-neckline, with silver high heels dyed to match it. Her black hair had been waist-length at the time, and it was in a complicated coiffure with tiny wisps curling around her oval face. She looked devastating and the other men in attendance paid her compliments and danced with her. Ted danced with no one. He nursed a whiskey soda on the sidelines, talked to the other men present and glared at Coreen.

He seemed angry out of all proportion to her attendance. Ted had been wearing a dinner jacket with a ruffled white shirt and diamond-and-gold cuff links, and expensive black slacks. There was a red carnation in his lapel. The unattached women fell over themselves trying to attract him, but he ignored them. And then, incredibly, Ted had taken her by the hand, without asking if she wanted to dance, and pulled her into his arms.

Her heart had beaten her breathless while they slowly circled the floor. This was more than a duty dance, because his pale blue eyes were narrowed with anger. As the lights lowered, he'd maneuvered her to the side door and out into the moonlit darkness. There, he'd all but thrown her back against the wall.

"Why did you come tonight?" he said tersely. His blue

eyes flared like matches as he stared at her in the light from
the inside.

"Not because of you," she began quickly, ready to explain
that she hadn't wanted to attend in the first place, but her
well-meaning father had insisted. He didn't know about her
crush on Ted. He wanted her to meet some eligible men.

"No?" Ted had challenged. His cold gaze had wandered
over her and his lids came down to cover the expression in
them. "You want me. Your eyes tell me so every time you
look at me. You can walk away from dances or refuse to
speak to me on the street, but you're only fooling yourself if
you think it doesn't show!"

Her dark blue eyes had glittered up at him with temper.
"You're very conceited!"

He'd paused to light a cigarette, but as his eyes swept over
her, he suddenly tossed it off the porch into the sand and
stepped forward. "It isn't conceit." He bit off the words,
jerking her into his body.

His hand caught her by the nape and held her face poised
for the downward descent of his. Her missed breath was audible.

The look in her eyes made him hesitate. Despite all her
denials, she looked as if he was offering her heaven. Her
breath came in sharp little jerks that were audible.

That excited him. His free hand went to her bodice and
spread at the top of the V-neckline against her soft, warm
skin. She gasped and as her mouth opened, his lips parted
and settled on it. Her faint, anguished moan sent him spinning right off the edge of the world.

He forgot her age and his conscience the second he felt
her soft, warm mouth tremble before it began to answer the
insistent pressure of his own. He remembered too well the
first taste he'd had of her, because his dreams had tormented
him ever since. He'd thought he was imagining the pleasure

he'd had with her, but he wasn't. The reality was just as devastating as the memory, and he couldn't help himself.

The hand behind her head contracted, bringing her mouth in to closer contact with his, and his free hand slid uninhibitedly down inside her bodice to cover one small, hard-tipped breast.

She protested, but not strongly enough to deter him. The feel of that big, warm, callused hand so intimately on her skin made her tremble with new sensations. She clung to his arms while he tasted and touched. She barely noticed the tiny strap being eased down her arm, or the slow relinquishing of her mouth, until she felt his mouth slide down her throat, over her collarbone and finally onto the warm silkiness of her breast.

She made a harsh sound and her nails bit into his arms.

"Don't cry out," he whispered at her breast. "Bite back those exciting little cries or we're going to become the evening's entertainment." His hand lifted her gently to his waiting mouth. He took the hard nipple inside and slowly, tenderly, began to suckle her.

She wept noiselessly at the ecstasy of his touch, clinging, shivering, as his mouth pleasured her. When it lifted, she hung against him, yielded, waiting, her eyes half-closed and misty with arousal. He looked at her face for one long instant before he pushed the other strap down her arm and watched the silky material fall to her waist. His hands arched her and his head bent. He hesitated just long enough to fill his eyes with the exquisite sight of her bare breasts before he took her inside his hungry mouth, and for a few brief, incandescent seconds, she flew among the stars with him.

She slumped against him when he finally managed to stop. She heard him dragging in long, ragged breaths while he lifted her bodice back into place and eased the shoulder straps up to support it. Then he held her while she shivered.

"Am I the first?" he asked roughly.

"Yes." She couldn't have lied to him. She was too weak.

The callused hands at her back contracted bruisingly for a minute. He cursed under his breath, furiously. "This is wrong. Wrong!" He bit off the words. "You're so young…!"

Her soft cheek nuzzled against his throat. "I love you," she whispered. "I love you more than my own life."

"Stop it!" He pushed her away. His eyes were frightening, glittery and dangerous. He moved back, his face rigid with controlled passion, tormented. "I don't want your love!"

She looked at him sadly, her big blue eyes soft and gentle and vulnerable. "I know," she said.

His face corded until it looked like a mask over the lean framework of his cheekbones. His fists clenched at his side. "Stay away from me, Coreen," he said huskily. "I have nothing to give you. Nothing at all."

"I know that, too," she said, her voice calm even as her legs trembled under her. At that moment, he looked capable of the worst kind of violence. "You won't believe me, but I only came tonight because my father wanted me to."

His face looked drawn, older. His eyes were like a rainy day, full of storms. "Don't build any dreams on what just happened. It was only sex," he said bluntly. "That's all it was, just a flash of sexual need that got loose for a minute. I'll never marry, and love isn't in my vocabulary."

"Because you won't let it be," she said quietly.

"Leave it alone, Coreen," he returned coldly.

She felt the chill, as she hadn't before. He was as unapproachable now as stone. The song that was playing inside suddenly caught her attention and she laughed a little nervously. "'Thanks for the Memory'." She identified it, and thought how appropriate it was.

"Don't kid yourself that this was any romantic interlude," he said with brutal honesty as he fought for breath. "You're just a kid...little more than a stick figure with two marbles for breasts. Now go away. Get out of my life and stay out!''

He'd walked off and left her out there. It was a summer night and warm. Coreen, wounded to the heart by that parting shot, had gone to her father's car and sat down in it. She hadn't gone back inside even when her father came out and asked what was wrong. A headache, she'd told him. He'd seen her leave with Ted, and he knew by the look on her face that she was hurt. He made their excuses and took her home.

Coreen had never gone to another gun club meeting or accepted another invitation from Sandy to come out to the ranch and ride horses. And on the rare occasions when Ted came into the store, she'd made herself scarce. She couldn't even meet his eyes, ashamed of her own lack of control and his biting comment about her body. For a man who thought she was too small-breasted, he certainly hadn't been reticent about touching her there, she thought. She knew so little about men, though, perhaps he meant the whole thing as a punishment. But if that had been so, why had his hands trembled?

Eventually she'd come to grips with it. She'd put Ted into a compartment of her past and locked him up, and she'd pretended that the night of the dance had never happened. Then her father had a heart attack and became an invalid. It was up to Coreen to run the business and she wasn't doing very well. That was when Barry had come into her life. Coreen and her father had been forced to put the feed store on the market and Barry had liked the prospect of owning it. He'd also liked the looks of Coreen, and suddenly made himself indispensable to her and her father. Anything they needed, he'd get them, despite her pride and protests.

He was always around, offering comfort and soft kisses to Coreen, who was upset about the doctor's prognosis, and hungry for a little kindness. Ted's behavior had killed something vulnerable in her. Barry's attention was a soothing balm to her wounds.

Ted had heard that his favorite cousin, Barry, was seeing a lot of Coreen. Ted stopped by often to see her father, and he watched her now, in an intense, disturbing way. He was gentle, almost hesitant, when he spoke to her. But Coreen had learned her lesson. She was distant and barely polite, so remote that they might have been strangers. When he came close, she moved away. That had stopped him in his tracks the first time it happened.

After that, he became cruel with her, at a time when she needed tenderness desperately. He began to taunt her about Barry, out of her father's hearing, mocking her for trying to entice his rich cousin to take care of her. Everyone knew that the feed store was about to go bankrupt because of the neglect of her sick father and his mounting medical bills.

The taunts frightened her. She knew how desperate their situation was becoming, and she daren't ask Ted for help in his present mood. Ironically his attitude pushed her further into Barry's waiting arms. Her vulnerability appealed to Barry. He took over, assuming the debts and taking the load from Coreen's shoulders.

The night her father died, Barry took charge of everything, paid all the expenses and proposed marriage to Coreen. She was confused and frightened, and when Ted came by the house to pay his respects, Barry wouldn't let him near her. Ted left in a furious mood and Barry convinced Coreen that his cousin hadn't wanted to speak to her, anyway.

Barry was beside her every minute at the funeral, keeping her away from Ted's suspicious, concerned gaze and making sure he had not a minute alone with her. The same day, he presented her with a marriage license and coaxed her into taking a blood test.

Ted left on a European business trip just after he refused

Barry's invitation to be best man at the wedding. Ted's face when Barry made the announcement was indescribable. He looked at Coreen with eyes so terrible that she trembled and dropped her own. He strode out without a word to her and got on a plane the same day. It was confirmation, if Coreen needed it, that Ted didn't care what she did with her life as long as it didn't involve him. She might as well marry Barry as anyone, she decided, since she couldn't have the one man she loved.

But she was naive about the demands of marriage, and especially about the man Barry really was behind his social mask. Coreen lived in agony after her marriage. Barry knew nothing of tenderness and he was incapable of any normal method of satisfaction in bed. He had abnormal ways of fulfillment that hurt her and his cruelty wore away her confidence and her self-esteem until she became clumsy and withdrawn. Ted didn't come near them and Sandy's invitations were ignored by Barry. He all but broke up her friendship with Sandy. Not that it wouldn't have been broken up, anyway. Ted moved to Victoria and took Sandy with him, keeping the old Regan homestead for a holiday house and turning over the management of his cattle ranch to a man named Emmett Deverell.

Barry had known how Coreen felt about Ted. Eventually Ted became the best weapon in his arsenal, his favorite way of asserting his power over Coreen by taunting her about the man who didn't want her. They'd been married just a year when Ted finally accepted Barry's invitation to visit them in Jacobsville. Coreen hadn't expected Ted to come, but he had.

By that time, Coreen was more afraid of Barry than she'd ever dreamed she could be. He was impotent and he made intimacy degrading, a disgusting ordeal that made her physically sick. When he drank, which became a regular thing after their marriage, he became even more brutal. He blamed her for his impotence, he blamed her infatuation for Ted and harped on it all the time until finally she stiffened whenever she heard Ted's name. She tried to leave him several times, but a man of such wealth had his own ways of finding her and dealing with her, and with anyone who tried to help her. In the end she gave up trying, for fear of causing a tragedy. When he turned to other women, it was almost a relief. For a long time, he left her alone and she had peace, although she wondered if he was impotent with his lovers. But he began to taunt her again, after he'd run into Ted at a business conference. And he'd invited Ted to visit them in Jacobsville.

Ted had watched her covertly during that brief visit, as if something puzzled him. She was jumpy and nervous, and when Barry asked her for anything, she almost ran to get it.

"See?" Barry had laughed. "Isn't she the perfect little homemaker? That's my girl."

Ted hadn't laughed. He'd noticed the harried, hunted expression on Coreen's face and the pitiful thinness of her body. He'd also noticed the full liquor cabinet and remarked on it, because everyone knew that it was Tina's house that Barry and Coreen were staying in, and that Tina detested liquor.

"Oh, a swallow of alcohol doesn't hurt, and Coreen likes her gin, don't you, honey?" he teased.

Coreen kept her eyes hidden. "Of course," she lied. He'd already warned her about what would happen if she didn't go along with anything he said. He'd been even more explicit about the consequences if she so much as looked longingly at Ted. He'd invited his cousin to torment Coreen, and it was working. He was in a better humor than he'd enjoyed in months.

"Get us a drink. What will you have, Ted?"

The older man declined and and he didn't stay long. Ted had never come back to visit after that. Barry met his cousin occasionally and he enjoyed telling Coreen how sorry Ted felt for him. She knew that Barry was telling him lies about her, but she was too afraid to ask what they were.

Her life had become almost meaningless. It didn't help that her earlier clumsiness had been magnified tenfold. She was forever falling into flowerpots or tripping over throw rugs. Barry made it worse by constantly calling attention to it, chiding her and calling her names. Eventually she didn't react anymore. Her self-esteem was so low that it no longer seemed important to defend herself. She tried to run away. But he always found her...

He mentioned once how his mother, Tina, had controlled him all his life. Perhaps his weakness stemmed from her dominance and the lack of a father. His drinking grew worse. There were other women, scores of them, and in between he was cruel to Coreen, in bed and out of it. He was no longer discreet with his affairs. But he was less interested in tormenting Coreen as well. Until that card came from Sandy on Coreen's birthday, the day before the tragic accident that had killed Barry. It had Ted's signature on it, too, a shocking addition, and Barry had gone crazy at the sight of it. He'd gotten drunk and that night he'd held Coreen down on the sofa with a knife at her throat and threatened to cut her up....

A sudden buzz of conversation brought Coreen back to the present. Shivering from the memory, she focused her eyes on the big oak desk where the lawyer was sitting and realized that he was almost through reading the will.

"That does it, I'm afraid," he concluded, peering over his small glasses at them. "Everything goes to his mother. The one exception is the stallion he willed to his cousin, Ted Regan. And a legacy of one hundred thousand dollars is to be left to Mrs. Barry Tarleton, under the administration of Ted Regan, to be held in trust for her until she reaches the age of twenty-five. Are there any questions?"

Ted was scowling as he looked at Coreen, but there was

no shock or surprise on her face. There was only stiff resignation and a frightening calmness.

Tina got to her feet. She glanced at Coreen coldly. "I'll give you a little while to get out of the house. Just to stem any further gossip, you understand, not out of any regard. I blame you for what happened to my son. I always will." She turned and left the room, her expression foreboding.

Coreen didn't reply. She stared at her hands in her lap. She couldn't look at Ted. She was homeless, and Ted controlled the only money she had. She could imagine that she'd have to go on her knees to him to get a new pair of stockings. She was going to have to get a job, quick.

"She could have waited until tomorrow," Sandy muttered to Ted when they were back outside, watching Tina climb into the Lincoln.

"Why did he do that?" Ted asked with open puzzlement. "For God's sake, he was worth millions! He's involved me in it, and she'll have literally nothing for another year, until she turns twenty-five! She'll even have to ask me for gas money!"

Sandy glanced at him with faint surprise at the concern he'd betrayed for Coreen. "She'll cope. She knew Barry wasn't leaving her much. She's prepared. She said it didn't matter."

"Hell, of course it matters! Someone needs to talk some sense into her! She could sue for a widow's allowance."

"I doubt that she will. Money was never one of her priorities, or didn't you know?"

He didn't reply. His eyes were narrow and introspective.

"She looks odd, did you notice?" Sandy asked worriedly. "Really odd. I hope she isn't going to do anything foolish."

"Let's go," Ted said as he got in behind the steering wheel, and he sounded bitter. "I want to talk to that lawyer before we go home."

Sandy frowned as she looked at him. She was worried, but

it wasn't about Coreen's money problems, or the will. Coreen was hopelessly clumsy since she'd married Barry. She said that she liked to skydive and go up in sailplanes, especially when she was upset, because she said it relaxed her. But she'd related tales of some of the craziest accidents Sandy had ever heard of. Sometimes she thought that Barry had programmed Coreen to be accident-prone. The few times early in their marriage that she'd seen her friend, before Barry had cut her out of Coreen's life, he'd enjoyed embarrassing Coreen about her clumsiness.

Ted didn't know about the accidents. Until the funeral, he'd walked away every time Sandy even mentioned Coreen, almost as if it hurt him to talk about her. He had the strangest attitude about her friend. He didn't care much for women, she knew, but the way he treated Coreen was intriguing. And the most curious thing had been the way he'd looked, holding Coreen in the living room earlier. The expression on his face had been one of torment, not hatred.

She was never going to understand her brother, she thought. The violence of his reaction to Coreen was completely at odds with the tenderness he'd shown her. Perhaps he did care, in some way, and simply didn't realize it.

Sandy insisted on staying with Coreen overnight, and she offered her best friend the sanctuary of the ranch until she found a place to live. Coreen refused bluntly, put off by even the thought of having to look at Ted over coffee every morning.

Coreen got her friend away the next morning, after a long and sleepless night blaming herself and remembering Ted's accusation of the day before.

"We're just getting moved in. Remember, Ted leased the place, along with the cattle farm, and we moved to Victoria about the time you married Barry. Ted's away a lot now, over at our cattle farm on the outskirts of Jacobsville, that

Emmett Deverell and his family operate for him. We're going to have thoroughbred horses at our place and some nice saddle mounts. We can go riding like we used to. Won't you come with me? I'll work it out with Ted," Sandy pleaded.

"And let Ted drive me into a nervous breakdown?" came the brittle laugh. "No, thanks. He hates me. I didn't realize how much until yesterday. He would rather it had been me than Barry, didn't you see? He thinks I'm a murderess…!"

Sandy hugged her shaken friend close. "My brother is an idiot!" she said angrily. "Listen, he's not as brutal as he seems when you get to know him, really he isn't."

"He's never been anything except cruel to me," Coreen replied, subdued. She pulled away. "Tell him to do whatever he likes with the trust, I won't need it. I can take care of myself. Be happy, Sandy. You've got a great career with that computer company, even a part interest. Make your mark in the world, and think of me once in a while. Try to remember all the good times, won't you?"

Sandy felt a chill run up her spine. Coreen had that restless look about her, all over again. There had been two bad accidents over the years because of Coreen's passion for flying and skydiving: a broken leg and two cracked ribs. Sandy had gone to see her in the hospital and Barry had been always in residence, refusing to let Coreen talk much about how the accidents had happened.

"Please be careful. You really are a little accident-prone," she began.

Coreen shivered. "Not really," she said. "Not anymore. Anyway, the people I skydive with watch out for me. I'll get better. I'm not suicidal, you know," she chided gently, and watched her friend blush. "I wouldn't kill myself over Ted's bad opinion of me. I wouldn't give him the satisfaction."

"Ted wouldn't want to see you hurt," Sandy said gently.

"Of course not," she said placatingly. "Now, go home.

You've got a life of your own, although I really appreciate having you here. I needed you.''

"Ted came voluntarily," she said pointedly. "I didn't ask him to."

Coreen's blue eyes darkened with pain. "He came to make me pay for hurting Barry," she said. "He's always found ways to make me pay, even for trying to care about him."

"You know why Ted won't let anyone close," Sandy said quietly. "Our mother was much younger than Dad. She ran away with another man when I was just a kid. Dad took it real hard. He gave Ted a vicious distrust of women, and I was the scapegoat until he died. Ted's kind to me, and he likes pretty women, but he wants no part of marriage."

"I noticed."

Sandy watched her closely. "He changed when you married. For the past two years, he's been a stranger. After he came back from that visit with you and Barry, he took off for Canada and stayed up there for a month and then he moved us to Victoria. He couldn't bear to talk about you."

"God knows why, I never did anything to him," Coreen said. "He knew Barry wanted to marry me and he thought I was after Barry's money, but he never tried to stop us."

Sandy let it drop, but not willingly. "Send me a postcard from wherever you move. I'll phone you then," she suggested. "We could meet somewhere for lunch."

Coreen's eyes were distracted. "Of course." She glanced at Sandy. "The birthday card..."

"Surprised, were you?" Sandy asked. "So was I. Ted had just talked to Barry. A day or two later, he saw a photograph of you and Barry in the Jacobsville paper he got in Victoria. He became very quiet when he saw it. You weren't smiling and you looked...fragile."

Coreen remembered the photograph. She and Barry had been at a charity banquet and he'd been drinking heavily—

much more so than usual. She'd been at the end of her rope
when the photographer caught them.

"Then Ted remembered that your birthday was upcom-
ing," Sandy continued, "and he picked out a card to send
you. For a man who hates you, he's amazingly contradictory,
isn't he?"

She wondered at Ted's motives. Had he known how jealous Barry was of him? Had he done it to cause trouble? She
couldn't bear to believe that he had. It was the card that had
provoked Barry to threaten her that last night. Had it only
been a week ago? She shivered mentally. She hugged Sandy
and watched the other woman leave. When the car was out
of sight, she picked up the telephone receiver and dialed.

"Hello, Randy?" she asked with a bright laugh. "When's
the next jump? Tomorrow? Well, count me in. No, I'm not
afraid of storms. It probably won't even be cloudy, you know
how often they miss the forecast. Besides, I need a diversion.
I'll see you out at the airfield at eight."

"Sure thing, lovely" came the teasing reply. She put the
phone down and went to make sure her borrowed skydiving
outfit was clean. She wouldn't think about getting out of the
house right now. Tomorrow afternoon would be soon enough
to start searching for an apartment and a job.

It was overcast, but not enough to deter the enthusiastic
crowd of jumpers. The jump from the plane was exhilarating,
and even the sting from the faint pull of the stitches below
her collarbone didn't detract from the pleasure of free-fall.
Coreen had always loved the feeling she got from it. Earth-
bound people would never experience the rush of adrenaline
that came from danger, the surge of emotion that rivaled the
greatest pleasure she'd ever known—an unexpected glimpse
of Ted Regan's face.

She pulled the cords to turn the parachute, looking for her
mark below. Two other skydivers were heading down below

her. But a gust of wind began to move her in a direction she didn't want to go, and when she looked up, she saw a gigantic thunderhead and a streak of lightning.

It was all she could do not to panic, and in her frantic haste to get her parachute going in the right direction, she overcontrolled it.

She was headed for a group of power lines. She'd read about ballooners who went into those electrical lines and didn't live to tell about it. She could see herself hitting them, see the sparks.

With a helpless cry as the thunder echoed around her, she jerked on the cord and moved her body, trying to force the stubborn 'chute to ignore the wind and bend to her will.

It was a losing battle, and she knew it. But she had nerve, and she wasn't going to give up until the last minute. The lightning forked past her and she closed her eyes, gritted her teeth and tried again to change direction.

The power lines were coming up. She was almost on them. She pulled her legs up with bent knees and jerked the 'chute. Her feet almost touched them, almost…but another gust of wind picked her up and moved her just a few inches, just enough to spare her landing on those innocent-looking black cables.

She let out a heavy sigh of relief. Rain had started to fall. She closed her eyes and through the thunder and lightning, she gave a prayer of thanks.

When she opened her eyes again, aware of the terrible darkness all around her as the unpredicted storm blew in, she saw what her fear had caused her to miss just minutes ago. There was a line of trees ahead, a thick conglomeration of pines and a few deciduous trees. They were right in the way. There was no cleared field, no place for her to land. She was going to go into those trees.

What if she landed in the very top of one? Would it take her weight, or would she fall to her death? And what about that huge oak? If she got caught in those leafy limbs, she could still be there when the first frost came!

The thought would have amused her once, but now she was too bent on survival to make jokes.

She didn't try to change direction. There was no use. Lightning streaked past her and hit one of the trees, smoke rising from it.

She thought that this was going to make an interesting addition to the obituary column, but at least she wouldn't go out in any dull manner.

She allowed herself one last thought, of Ted Regan's face when he read about it. She hoped that whoever planned her funeral wouldn't ruin it by letting Ted stand over her and make nasty remarks about her character.

The trees were coming closer. She could see the branches individually now, and with a sense of resignation, she let her body relax. If the fall didn't get her, the lightning probably would. She'd chosen her fate, and here it was.

It hadn't been a suicide attempt, although people would probably think so. She'd only wanted the freedom of the sky while she tried to come to grips with the rest of her life. She'd wanted to forget Ted's accusations and the cold way he'd looked at her.

What she remembered, though, was the rough, hungry clasp of his arms around her. Had he felt pity, for those few seconds when his embrace had bruised her? Or had it been a reflex action, the natural reaction of a man to having a woman in his arms? She'd never know.

She could picture his blue eyes and feel his mouth on hers, all those long years ago. She closed her own, waiting for death to come up and claim her. Her last conscious thought was that in whatever realm she progressed to, perhaps she could forget the one man she'd ever loved. And once she was gone, perhaps Ted could forgive her for everything he thought she'd done.

The impact was sudden, and surprisingly without pain. She felt the roughness of leaves and limbs and a hard, rough blow to her head. And then she felt nothing at all.

Chapter 3

Ted Regan had been sitting at his desk trying to make sense of a new prospectus. Sandy had only just gone out the door, after spending the night at the ranch. Suddenly, the front door was opened with force and his sister came running back in, red-faced and shaking.

"What is it?" he asked quickly, putting the papers aside.

"It's Corrie." She choked. Tears were running down her cheeks. "It was on the radio...she's been in a terrible accident!"

His heart stopped, started and ran away. He jerked out of his chair and took her by the arms. It wasn't pity for her that motivated him; it was the horror that made him go cold. "Is she dead?" She couldn't answer and he actually shook her. "Tell me! Is she all right?"

His white, desperate face shocked her into speech. "She was taken to the Jacobsville General emergency room." She choked out the words. "The radio said she was skydiving and fell into some trees or power lines or something. They don't know her condition."

He didn't stop to get his hat. He shepherded her out the door at a dead run.

Later, he didn't even remember the ride to the hospital. He marched straight to the desk, demanding to know how Coreen was and where she was. The woman clerk didn't try to deny him the information. She told him at once.

He walked straight into the recovery room, despite loud objections from a nurse.

Coreen was lying on a stretcher there, clad in a faded hospital gown. There were cuts and bruises all over her face and arms, and she was asleep.

"How is she?" he demanded.

The middle-aged nurse who was checking her vital signs nodded. "She'll be fine," she told him. "Dr. Burns can tell you anything you want to know. You're a relative?"

Technically he was, he supposed. If he said no, they wouldn't let him near her. "Yes," he said.

"Dr. Burns?" the nurse called to a green-gowned man outside the door. He excused himself from the doctor to whom he was speaking and came into the recovery room.

"This gentleman is a relative of Mrs. Tarleton."

Ted introduced himself and the doctor shook his hand warmly.

"I hope you know how much we all appreciate the pediatric critical care unit you funded here, Mr. Regan," the doctor said, and the nurse became flustered as she realized who their distinguished visitor was.

"It was my pleasure. How's Corrie?" he asked, nodding toward the pale woman on the bed.

"Minor concussion, a cracked rib and a burst appendix. We've repaired the damage, but someone should tell her not to skydive during thunderstorms," he said frankly. "This is her second close call in as many months. And we won't even go into the damage she sustained in the glider crash or her most recent brush with a sheet of tin..."

Ted went very still. "What glider crash?"·

Dr. Burns lifted an eyebrow. "You said you were a relative?"

"Distant," he confessed. "Her husband was buried yesterday."

"Yes, I know."

"I'm from Victoria. I've just moved back here, into my grandfather's house."

"Oh, yes, the old Regan homeplace."·

"The same," Ted continued. "I'd lost touch with Barry in the past few weeks, but we were cousins and fairly close. Funny, he never told me about any of Corrie's mishaps."

"That's surprising," the doctor said coolly, a sentiment that Ted could have seconded. He glanced down at Coreen's still form. "She's got two left feet. Her husband told me that a woman friend of Coreen's let her take up the glider and she flew it too close to the trees. Good thing it was insured. She needs to be watched. And I mean watched, until she's past this latest trauma. Then I'd strongly suggest some counseling. Nobody has so many accidents without an underlying cause. Perhaps she's running from something. Running scared."

Ted thought about that later when he and Sandy were drinking black coffee in the waiting room, waiting for them to move Corrie down into a private room. She was conscious, but barely out from under the anesthetic.

"Did you know that she'd had this sort of accident before?" Ted asked his sister.

She nodded. "I went to see her in the hospital. Or tried to. Barry didn't like it that I was there, and he wouldn't let me do more than wish her a speedy recovery. He kept everyone away from her, even then."

"Why didn't you say anything?"

"You didn't want to know, Ted," she replied honestly. "You hate Corrie. That was the last thing she said to me before I left, and there was a look in her eyes…'' She grimaced. ''She said something about my trying to remember the good times she and I had. It was an odd way of putting it, and I was afraid then that she planned to go up. She loves skydiving, but she's clumsy.''

''I only remember Coreen ever being clumsy one time before she married,'' he said curtly. ''How long has she been acting this way?''

She looked at him levelly. ''Since about a month after she married Barry…about the same time he decided that Corrie and I shouldn't spend so much time together.''

He was shocked. His white face told its own story, added to the way he was smoking. He wondered if his attitude at the funeral had driven Corrie into that airplane. Had he made her feel so much guilt that she couldn't even live with it? He hadn't really meant to, but he'd been fond of his young cousin, who'd always looked to him for advice and support, even above that of his own parents. And Coreen had let Barry drive drunk. That was the thing that haunted him. It was as if she'd condemned him to death.

''Well, I'll go over to the house in a day or so and have Henry open it up for me, so that I can get her clothes and things,'' Sandy said heavily. She finished her coffee. ''Tina will probably have the locks changed soon and Corrie will have no place to go at all. I'll take her up to the apartment in Victoria with me.…''

''We'll bring her to the ranch,'' Ted said firmly. ''We can watch her, without letting her know that we are.''

Sandy searched his face. ''You won't be cruel to her?''

His jaw tautened. ''I'll keep out of her way,'' he said, angry at the implication that he could hurt her now, when she could have been killed. His blue eyes impaled her. ''That should please her.''

He got up and moved down the corridor. Sandy stared after him with open curiosity.

* * *

Coreen was lying quietly in bed, feeling the bruises and cuts and breaks as if they were living things. The door opened and a familiar man walked in.

"Hello," she said groggily, and without smiling. "Did you come to gloat? Sorry to disappoint you, but one funeral is all you get this week."

He put his hands into his pockets and stood over her. Bravado, he concluded when he saw the faint fear in her eyes that underlaid the anger.

"How are you?" he asked.

She put a hand to her bruised forehead. "Tired," she said flatly.

"Jumping out of airplanes," he said with disgust, his eyes flaring at her. "In a damned thunderstorm! You haven't grown up at all."

Her dark blue eyes stared into his pale ones with weary resignation. "Leave me alone, Ted," she said in a drained voice. "I can't fight you right now."

He moved closer to the bed, his heart contracting at the sight of her lying there that way. "You little fool!" he said huskily. Suddenly he bent, one lean hand resting beside her head on the pillow, and his mouth covered hers so unexpectedly that she flinched.

He felt her involuntary movement and quickly lifted his lips from hers. His eyes stabbed into her own. He didn't know what he'd expected, but her rigid posture surprised him.

"That's new," he said, frowning absently.

She couldn't breathe. "Don't do that," she whispered.

"Why not?" he asked angrily. His chest rose and fell raggedly. "You wanted it once. Your eyes begged me for it every time you looked at me. But you don't feel that way now, do you? Did you know that Barry cried when he told me how frigid you were, that you wouldn't let him touch you…Corrie!"

She was crying, great tearing sobs that pulsed out of her like blood out of a wound.

"That was a low thing to say." He ground out his words. "I'm sorry. Corrie, I'm sorry, I'm sorry…" He bent, his face contorting with self-contempt, and his mouth traveled over her wan face in soft, tender kisses that sipped away the tears and the pain and the hurt, finally ending against the soft trembling of her mouth. "Corrie," he groaned as he nibbled at her lips.

She put her hand up to his face and pressed it hard against his mouth. "Don't," she pleaded.

The hand was trembling. He warmed it in his own and brought it hungrily to his mouth, palm up.

"How could you take such a risk?" he demanded huskily, lifting his mouth from her hand. She tried to pull it away, but he didn't let go of it even then, and his face was hard, like the glittery eyes that watched her without even blinking.

"You don't care if I die," she accused shakenly.

He winced. "Do you think I want you dead?" he asked roughly.

Her eyes were sad and bitter. "Don't you?" she asked on a harsh laugh. "Would you forgive me for Barry's death if I died, too?"

He drew in a harsh breath. It had become painfully clear to him that he could hurt her badly.

There was a soft knock on the door and Sandy walked in, raising her eyebrows at the sight of Ted standing by Coreen's bed, holding her hand.

"Did Ted tell you that you're coming home with me?" Sandy asked gently.

"That isn't necessary…!"

"Yes, it is," Ted said curtly. "We'll get a nurse for you."

Coreen panicked. "No!" she said. "No, I won't!"

"You will," he replied coldly. "If I have to pick you up and carry you in my arms every step of the way!"

Coreen felt the words in her heart. She averted her eyes.

He hadn't meant it personally, of course. But the phrasing touched her deeply.

"You need to get some sleep," Sandy said gently. "I'll be back later."

"*We'll* be back later," Ted corrected, his eyes daring Coreen to argue with him. He glanced at Sandy. "She's on the fifth floor, and she might try to tie a few sheets together and parachute out of here."

Sandy laughed. Coreen's eyes were so tragic that it didn't last. "It's all right," she told her friend. "You'll be fine."

"Will I?" she asked, looking at Ted with open fear.

Sandy saw the way they were staring at each other, made an excuse and left them alone.

"What is it?" Ted asked softly.

She didn't reply. She simply shook her head, confusedly.

He stood beside her, watching her eyes. "It was only a kiss," he said quietly. "I know I shouldn't have done it, but you frightened me."

She searched his lean face. "Frightened you?"

He pushed his hands deep into his pockets to keep from reaching for her. His emotions were teetering on a knife-edge. "We thought you were dying until we got here."

"I'm not suicidal," she said firmly, "regardless of what you think. I love skydiving. I only wanted to get away from the world for a little while."

"You almost got away permanently. Skydiving in a thunderstorm!"

"It wasn't raining when I went up. Haven't you ever done anything the least bit dangerous?" she asked.

"Why, yes," he replied, holding her eyes. "I kissed you," he said dryly, and walked out of the room before she could respond.

Ted lifted a rigid Coreen out of the wheelchair and carried her to the car, while Sandy held the door open. Coreen thanked the nurses and hesitantly linked her arms around Ted's neck.

"I'm heavy," she protested when he picked her up.

His face was very close to hers, so close that his eyes filled the world. "You hardly weigh anything at all," he said bitterly.

She grimaced. "That isn't what that tiny intern said when he had to heft me onto the cart."

He laughed. It was a sound that Coreen had never heard before, and her expression said so.

Her eyes were drowning him in warm, unfamiliar feelings. He shifted her a little roughly as he turned and started toward the car, still holding her eyes. "Is this how you got your claws into Barry?" he asked under his breath. "Looking at him with those soft, hungry eyes?"

She averted her face and stiffened even more in his arms. "Think what you like about me, Ted. I don't care."

"Yes, you do," he said through his teeth. "That's what makes it so damned unforgivable."

"What?"

He glared down at her. "You were married and you still lusted after me," he said harshly. "You denied your husband because of it, and he knew it. It was why he drank. It was why he died," he added, growing colder inside as the guilt ate at him. "He told me, didn't you know? Do you think I could ever forgive you for that?"

The bitterness in him was damning. She couldn't deny it now because they were within Sandy's earshot. It wouldn't have mattered regardless, because he had his own opinion and he wouldn't change it. She hadn't used him to hurt Barry, it was the other way around. But he liked his opinion of her. It reinforced his warped view of women.

He put her in the back seat, so that she could stretch out,

and she didn't say another word. She left all the conversation to him and Sandy. There wasn't much.

The bedroom they gave her was done in soft beiges and pinks, and the bed was a huge four-poster.

"The bed was Ted's once," Sandy said when she'd tucked her friend up, "but he wanted something less antiquated when we redecorated the house."

Coreen tingled all over, thinking that Ted had once slept where she was lying. It would probably be the closest she ever got to him, she thought on a silent laugh. Now he had even more reason to blame her for Barry's death. He would feel guilty that Barry was denied a happy marriage because his wife didn't want him, she wanted Ted.

"I'll go see about something for us to eat. We drove up without lunch. Are you hungry?"

"I had a little gelatin and some soup," Corrie recalled. "It was nice, but I could eat a sandwich."

"No sooner said than done."

She left and Coreen shifted the pillows behind her. She was wearing a sleeveless white cotton gown with a high neckline and a tiny blue and pink embroidered flower pattern in the bodice that drew no attention at all to her small, high breasts. She wished she had a robe, but she'd forgotten to ask Sandy to stop by the house and get one. It didn't matter. She was covered the way a Victorian spinster might be. She grimaced when she remembered the low-cut fashions she'd worn only two years before, things she could never wear again. Not now.

The door opened and Ted walked in. He'd changed into jeans and boots and an open-necked chambray shirt, and he looked rangy and dangerous.

Her eyes fell to the opening at his throat where thick hair peeked out. She'd never seen Ted without a shirt. She'd never seen Ted much at all, except in the distance.

If she was looking, so was he. His eyes had found the embroidery and he was staring at it with interest.

She jerked the sheet up to her collarbone irritably. "They're just marbles," she said without thinking.

He smiled. It was unconscious and instinctive, because she looked so angry, lying there with her poor bruised face. "Not quite," he mused.

She glared at him. "Sandy's fixing something to eat."

"I know. When she's through destroying the kitchen, I'll cook a few omelets."

"She said she was making sandwiches. Anyone can make a sandwich."

"Not without bread, and Mrs. Bird told me at breakfast that she'd made toast with the last of it. Sandy's trying to cook steaks."

"Oh, dear," she said, because she'd been threatened with Sandy's steaks several times in the past.

Ted's head lifted. He heard the muttered curses coming from the kitchen and smelled smoke. "There goes the first one."

"You might stop her," she suggested.

"Not with all those knives in there," he replied. He moved closer to the bed and sat down beside her. He held her eyes and suddenly pulled the sheet away, staying it when she tried to make a grab for it.

"Let go of it, Ted," she warned.

"What are you afraid of?" he asked with a quizzical smile. "Sandy's within shouting range."

"What are you doing?" she returned uneasily.

His lean hand pressed palm-down over her breastbone, shocking her into stillness. His hand was so big that his fingers spread halfway over one small breast. He let it rest there, waiting for her to react.

Coreen grabbed his wrist, trying to remove his hand. She was sore there, and she didn't want him to feel the stitches.

She tugged hard and then lay there gaping at him, with eyes so big they looked like blue china saucers.

He might have found that reaction very strange in a woman who'd been married for almost two years, if he hadn't known she was frigid. Her resistance to his touch after the funeral and now was beginning to eat at his curiosity. If Barry had told the truth, and Coreen had harbored a dark passion for Ted, then why was she avoiding his touch so arduously? It disturbed him somehow to know that she didn't hunger for his kisses anymore. Her actions had implications that he wasn't certain he was ready to face just yet. She hadn't been frigid two years ago....

He scowled as he finally let her lift his hand away and push it aside.

"What did you think you were doing?" she asked, flustered.

"Experimenting," he said. "For a woman who's panting lustfully after me, you're surprisingly reluctant to be touched."

"I'm not...lusting after you." She choked, averting her eyes.

"So I noticed. Then why did you hold me over Barry's head?" he asked with faint distaste.

It wasn't easy to appear calm when she was churning inside. "I didn't," she said wearily.

"No?" One lean hand was resting beside her body. He looked down at her breasts and she tugged the sheet over them. He lifted an eyebrow. "Overreacting a bit, aren't you? I haven't touched you there."

"I'm not an art exhibit," she informed him. "And you needn't say that you wouldn't buy any tickets, because I know it already! You told me why over two years ago."

His pale eyes slid over her face and up to meet her angry gaze. "In the most cruel way I could find," he agreed, and there was a hint of regret in his voice. "Did Sandy ever tell you why?"

"Yes," she said. "But I never hurt you."

"No, although you were pretty persistent for a while there." His eyes searched hers quietly. "I wanted you out of my hair."

"Congratulations. You succeeded."

His jaw tautened. "Why did you marry Barry?"

The question came like a lightning bolt. She started from the sudden shock of it. She couldn't bear to tell him the truth. She averted her eyes. "He asked me."

"And you accepted, just like that?" he asked impatiently.

"He looked after Dad when no one else bothered," she said simply. "We were down to our last dollar. He not only bought the feed store, but he also advanced us the cash to keep Dad's doctor bills paid while the paperwork was finalized. I owed him so much. Marriage seemed a very small price to pay for my father's peace of mind," she finished, without telling him the whole truth of it, that his own attitude had pushed her right into Barry's arms. If Ted had been just a little more sympathetic...but it didn't bear thinking about.

He got up from the bed abruptly and strode to the window. He rested one shoulder against the windowsill and stared out at the lush green pastures where black-coated cattle were grazing; his prize black Angus.

"Did you love him?" he asked.

She twisted the pretty edging of the sheet. "I was...fond of him, at first."

He looked at her. "Did you ever want him, even at the beginning?"

She shuddered. She wasn't quick enough to hide it.

"You wanted me," he said coldly. "I haven't forgotten the party at the gun club, even if you have. You would have given me anything that night."

"You wouldn't have taken it," she said somberly, staring at him unblinking. "You even told me why. Remember?"

He averted his gaze back to the pasture. He didn't like remembering the things he'd said to her. Absently he pulled a cigarette out of his pocket. But he only looked at it for a minute and pushed it back into the pack with a wry smile in her direction.

"I promised Sandy I'd quit," he explained.

"Imagine you doing something a mere woman wanted," she murmured.

"Sandy's my sister."

"And the only woman you like."

He turned, leaning his back against the sill. He folded his arms and crossed his long legs, surveying her with pursed lips and an odd little smile. "I could like you, if I tried," he said. He jerked away from the window. "But I'm not going to try."

"Of course not," she agreed. "What would be the point?"

He paused beside the bed. "You aren't going to be able to do much for a few weeks, in your condition," he said. "I hope you like it here, because you're staying for the duration, even if I have to tie you up."

She sat up in bed, grimacing at the pain, her blue eyes angry. "I could go home…"

"You don't have a home anymore," he said bluntly.

She lay back down, wincing at the pain. She felt broken and bruised. Her eyes closed, to shut him out. "No. I haven't, have I?" she agreed.

He hated her lack of spirit. His pale eyes lanced over her dark hair and narrowed as he saw the silver threads that meandered through it. "Why, you're going gray, Coreen," he said, surprised.

"Yes." Her eyes opened. "Your hair used to be the color of mine, didn't it?" she asked.

"Not since I turned thirty. It grayed prematurely. It's even gone gray on my chest."

"Has it? I didn't notice."

He lifted an eyebrow, because her gaze had seemed to be locked to his throat when he'd first entered the room.

"Damn, damn, damn!" echoed down the hall from the kitchen, along with a more pungent smell of smoke.

"I'd better get in there while there's some beef left in the freezer. I'll send her to keep you company while I cook."

"I can cook," she said hesitantly. "I used to do all the cooking at home, before I married."

He lifted an eyebrow. "Did you?" he asked indifferently. "I never noticed."

She averted her eyes. He couldn't have made it more plain than that, but she'd known that he never paid attention to her while Barry was courting her. She watched him leave the room with sad, resigned eyes, mourning the woman she'd been. He hadn't wanted her when she was whole. There was no chance that he'd want her now, in her damaged condition. And even if he did, she reminded herself, she had nothing left to give him.

Chapter 4

Coreen had only the one gown to wear, and none of her clothes. She wanted to remind them that she needed her things from the house she'd shared with Barry, but she was apprehensive about letting anyone go there to see the room she'd occupied. Fortunately, Ted's housekeeper, Mrs. Bird, had a daughter about Coreen's size who'd married and gone to live overseas. Mrs. Bird brought her an armload of pretty things on loan, and she told Sandy that she didn't need anything else at the moment. Things were hectic for the first few days she was in residence, anyway. Sandy had to go to work and Ted had two mares in foal. He stayed out with his horses most of the time, while a grateful Coreen was left pretty much to herself in the daytime. She didn't mind. Having Ted near her was disconcerting and made her nervous.

She sat at the window in her room every day and watched him work the horses out in the corral. He was gentle with his horses, patient and kind. Coreen wished that she'd had such kindness from him.

There was a particular horse that she favored, a thoroughbred, which was coal black with a white blaze on his forehead and white stockings on all four feet. There had been a similar horse that Sandy always loaned her when they went riding. Not that this one could be the same horse. It was much younger than the horse Sandy had let her borrow. It might be a descendant, though.

She knew that she shouldn't be spying on Ted, but it gave her such pleasure to look at him. He was long and lean and he moved with the liquid grace of a cowboy. He could spin a lariat so expertly that no horse ever escaped his noose. He could ride bareback as easily as he could ride in a saddle. His temper was quick and hot, and she'd seen him lose it once with one of his men over some equipment. She'd moved away from the open window, shivering with reaction. Barry had always yelled when he was going to hit her. It was probably just as well that Ted didn't want any part of her, she assured herself, because she was as intimidated by his temper as she was by his strength.

All the same, she couldn't keep away from the window. Her mind rolled back the terrible time in between, and she was a young woman again, in love with Ted and full of hope that he might care one day.

It was inevitable that Ted would notice her blatant interest. The silent figure by the window was drawing attention, and not only from the recipient. Ted's men had begun to rag him gently about Coreen's "calf eyes" following him around wherever he went.

Ted came by her room late on the day before Sandy was due back and paused in the doorway. "Do you want a tray in your room tonight, as usual?" he asked curtly.

She was surprised by his hostility as much as by the question. She'd had her meals on trays ever since her arrival, which was perfectly fine with her; she couldn't eat with Ted glaring across a table at her. She fumbled around for a reply.

"Sandy won't be back until tomorrow," he reminded her. "And I have a date tonight. She's an attorney from Victoria who's having supper here."

She could tell that he'd hoped to shock her. He had. She couldn't hide her reaction quickly enough to escape his pointed scrutiny. "I…wouldn't want to intrude. A tray in my room is fine," she said quickly.

He stared at her with one narrowed eye, his face cold and hard. "You need something to do with your time while you're here."

She didn't know how to take this frontal assault. She just stared at him.

"Something besides watching me out the window every time I move," he added bluntly.

She averted her face with a caught breath. "I was watching the horses, not you," she said.

"All the same, you'll be happier with something to occupy you." He didn't add that so would he, but then, he didn't have to.

Her hands, unseen, clenched on her robe. He was putting the knife in already. She'd thought that her condition might win her just enough sympathy to keep his hostility at bay. She was wrong.

"Yes," she agreed without looking up. "I would…like something to do."

He studied her down-bent head with mingled feelings, the strongest of which was guilt. She'd driven her husband to drink and ultimately caused him to die, all because she wanted a man she couldn't have and taunted her husband with him. Ted had felt the guilt like a knife in his gut ever since he'd heard about Barry's death. Coreen's presence was aggravating his self-contempt. She was a constant reminder of the pain his cousin had suffered.

He'd deliberately invited Lillian over for supper, not because he really wanted to, but because it was important to make Coreen understand that he still wasn't interested in her. He couldn't bear having his unwanted houseguest stare at him longingly through the curtains. He couldn't even avoid her while he worked, for God's sake!

"This isn't going to work out," he said aloud, his eyes narrow and cold.

"You might not believe it, but I tried to tell Sandy that," she said with a faint smile. She lifted her eyes. "I'll start looking for a place the minute I can stand up without falling."

He shifted restlessly. "I'll see if I can help you."

"Thank you," she said with the dregs of her dignity. It had taken quite a bruising already. "And nothing expensive, please. I still have to find a job."

"There may be some way to break provisions in Barry's will," he said curtly. "I'll check into it. Failing that, I'll make sure that you have a living allowance, at least."

She started to express her thanks again, but she felt like a parrot. She just nodded.

"I'll send Mrs. Bird along to see what you want to eat."

"Whatever she's cooking will be fine," she replied with stilted courtesy. "I wouldn't want to cause any more trouble than I already have."

He didn't answer her. His eyes were still cold, accusing, when he turned and went down the hall. It wasn't until he reached his own room that he remembered the devastation Coreen had faced in one week. Whether or not she loved Barry, she'd been widowed, injured, and she'd lost her home and her income. A man would have to be made of stone to feel no pity at all for such a victim of circumstances. He blamed her for too much, perhaps. She looked very fragile in that big, four-poster bed, and he didn't like the way he felt after being so savage to her.

But he put his guilt aside with his working clothes. He showered and changed into a neat pair of white slacks with a stripped designer shirt, a linen sport coat and tie. Then, without seeing Coreen again, he drove to the Jacobsville airport to meet Lillian's flight from Victoria.

Coreen was getting more and more depressed. She could hear Ted and his houseguest all the way down the hall, laughing and talking, as if they were old and good friends. Probably they were.

She didn't know how she could bear much more of Ted's reluctant hospitality. If Sandy had been here, it would have been different. She couldn't expect her best friend to give up her job just to keep Coreen company. Sandy had to travel, which meant that Coreen would be stuck here often with just Ted and Mrs. Bird for company.

Mrs. Bird had brought her a tray, grumbling about their dinner guest.

"Wants her coffee weaker and her salad with dressing on the side," Mrs. Bird harrumphed, swinging her ample figure around as she placed the tray over Coreen's lap. "Doesn't care for beef, because it has cholesterol, and dessert is out of the question."

"She must be healthy," Coreen remarked as she savored the smell of the cheese soup and freshly baked bread she'd been served.

"Skinny as a rail. They say it's going to be the new fad." She eyed Coreen critically, seeing the hollows in her cheeks. "Nothing like cheese soup and bread to fatten up little skeletons."

"I haven't had much appetite. But this is wonderful," she said with honest enjoyment, and smiled.

The housekeeper smiled back. "I made apple pie for dessert with apples I dried myself."

Coreen was impressed. "I love apple pie!"

"So I was told, and with ice cream. You'll get that, too." She grinned at Coreen and went back toward the door. "Just set that by the bed and I'll get it later, after they've gone. On their way to a play at the civic center, they said, then he has to take her back to the airport to catch a late flight.''

''Is she nice?'' Coreen asked curiously.

The older woman hesitated, her gray hair stringy from long hours in the kitchen.

''Well, I suppose she is, in her own way. She's stylish and real smart, and she and Ted have known each other for a long time. Expected them to get married once, she was that crazy about him. But Ted doesn't want to get married. Broke her heart. They're friends still, but don't you think she wouldn't jump at the chance to marry him.''

''I guess he can be nice when he likes,'' Coreen said without committing herself. She started eating her soup.

''Nice to some,'' Mrs. Bird said, faintly puzzled. ''Well, I'll leave you to it.''

''Thank you.''

''No trouble. It's a pleasure to see people enjoy their food.''

Coreen finished her lonely meal and put the tray aside. She wished she had something to read, but there wasn't even a magazine, much less television or a radio. She felt cut off from the world in the pretty antique bedroom.

The laughter from the other room grated on her nerves. She tried to imagine Ted laughing with her, wanting her company, enjoying conversation like that. He only ever seemed to scowl when he was with her. Lillian must be special to him. She didn't want to be jealous. She had no right. He laughed again, and Coreen felt the hot sting of tears.

Her blurred vision cleared on the face of the clock. It was only seven o'clock. She hoped that she could go to sleep, to block out the sound of Ted's pleasure in the other woman. She turned off her light and closed her eyes with bitter resignation. Incredibly she slept the night through.

* * *

The next day, she didn't watch out the window while Ted worked his horses. She put on a pair of too-large jeans and an equally large T-shirt with a Texas logo on it and curled up in a chair to read the paper she'd begged from Mrs. Bird.

The news was depressing. She glanced at the comics page, and finally settled on the word puzzle. It kept her mind busy, so that she wouldn't remember that Ted wanted her out of his house. She was still too wobbly and sore to do much. An employer was going to expect more than she was capable of giving just yet. She hoped Sandy would come home today. Her friend would help her escape from this prison Ted had made for her. He hadn't told her to stay in her room, but he'd made it very obvious that he didn't want her around him.

It was after lunch when she heard a car drive up. Minutes later, a smiling Sandy came into the room and fell onto the bed in an exaggerated pose.

"I'm tired!" she groaned, smiling at Coreen. "I thought I'd never get that new computer system put together for our client. But I did. Now I can take a day off and spend some time with you. How's it been going?"

"Just fine," Coreen said blithely. "Could you help me find an apartment?"

Sandy's expression was comical. "I gather that Ted's been at it again?" she muttered.

"We've had this discussion before," Coreen said quietly. "You know how he feels about me, about having me here. He's accused me of leering at him again, and maybe I have. God help me, I can't seem to stop…" She bit her lip. "Only, it isn't leering and it isn't lust. You can't know how it was with Barry," she added, her eyes wide and tragic. "If you did, you'd realize how incredible it is that I can even look at a man without shuddering!"

Sandy sat up, brushing her hair out of her eyes. "Maybe if you talked to Ted…"

"Why?" Coreen asked solemnly. "He doesn't want to know anything about my marriage, or about me. He's made it very clear that I'm here on sufferance and that he isn't interested in me."

"Mrs. Bird mentioned that Lillian came to supper last night," the other woman murmured. "Did you get to meet her?"

Coreen shook her head.

Sandy sighed angrily. "He can't help the way he is. I'm sorry, Corrie. I'm very sorry that I finagled you into this corner. I had hoped…well, that's not important now. Do you want out?"

"Yes, please" came the immediate reply.

"Okay. We can both move up to Victoria, into my old apartment. I never have gotten around to leasing it, so it's still empty. It's plenty big enough for both of us, and you won't have my brother to contend with."

"But your job…"

"I work at our branch office in Victoria as well as the headquarter office in Houston," Sandy reminded her.

"I don't want to impose," Coreen said firmly.

"You're my best friend. How could you impose?"

"I'll need my things from the house," she said hesitantly. "I hate to ask, but could you…?"

"Of course I can go get them for you."

"Henry has a key. He's still living in the chauffeur's quarters, I'm sure, because Tina will need him to take care of the place until she moves in. My clothes will be in the closet, in the second bedroom on the right upstairs. There isn't much in the drawers, and I'd already packed up my own books and tapes, and the few things mother gave me."

"I'll run down there this afternoon, if you like."

"Thank you, Sandy."

"What are friends for? Now you stop worrying! By next

week, we'll be in Victoria and all these bad memories will
be just that.''

Sandy went to get them some coffee and cake, which they
ate with relish. Ted came in just after Sandy had gone to
change her clothes and get some suitcases to pack Coreen's
dresses in.

Coreen was still sitting in the armchair by the window.
She flushed when he looked at her. ''I was talking to Sandy,
not leering at you out the window,'' she said with faint de-
fensiveness.

His pale eyes narrowed. ''It's a hell of a pity you didn't
spend some of that misplaced longing on poor Barry,'' he
said mockingly.

Her features grew very still. ''He had women,'' she said.

''No wonder, if he had a wife who wouldn't let him touch
her,'' he returned. His face held such distaste that she
squirmed in her chair. ''You tormented him and then you let
him get in a car when he'd been drinking,'' he said curtly.
''I won't ever forget, or forgive, that. You ended up with
nothing and that's all you deserved. My God, the very sight
of you sickens me!'' he added roughly, and the contempt in
his eyes hurt her for an instant before he turned away and
continued on down the hall.

She didn't move until he was out of sight. The pain went
even too deep for tears. She thought of how it was going to
be for another week, before she and Sandy left for Victoria,
knowing exactly how Ted felt about her, what he thought,
and having to face his scorn day after endless day. She
couldn't take it. She couldn't take any more. She was going
to have to get away now.

If she waited until Sandy left to pick up her clothes, Ted
would probably leave shortly thereafter. Then she could get
a cab to the depot and a bus to Houston. She had just enough
money for a flight. There was surely a YWCA in Houston,

where she could stay. Even that would be infinitely better than here, with Ted tormenting her in reprisal for his cousin's death. If she'd been stronger, she'd have fought him tooth and nail. But she hadn't the heart for any more fighting right now. She only hoped she had enough strength to get out of here.

Sandy, unaware of Ted's visit, popped her head in the door. "I'm going. Ted said that he'll drive me over to your house. I'll be back in a couple of hours. Bye!"

Coreen had wanted to catch her eye and tell her she was leaving, but Sandy was already on her way out the front door. She heard her call something to Mrs. Bird. Two car doors slammed and an engine revved up.

Thirty harrowing minutes later, she said a hesitant goodbye to Mrs. Bird, asking first if she could have the loan of the clothes she was wearing, with a pair of Sandy's shoes, just until she could get her own.

"But I thought Sandy and Ted were going over to the house to get your things," Mrs. Bird said, puzzled.

"I'm meeting them there," Coreen lied glibly. "I just remembered some things I need that they won't know about."

"But, dear, you're just not in any shape to be trying to do something like this!"

"I'm doing just fine," Coreen assured her with a gentle smile. "Thank you so much for your kindness. I won't ever forget you."

Mrs. Bird was frowning now. "You should wait. Let me call over at your house and make sure they're there."

"It won't matter, honestly, I'll be fine." She heard the horn and smiled her relief. "There's the taxi I called. Now don't worry, all right?"

Mrs. Bird grimaced. "You're so pale."

"I'm a trooper. I'll be fine." She clutched her purse closer.

It was all she had left of her own right now, all her worldly possessions. "I'll be in touch."

"You're coming back, aren't you?"

"I may stay at the house," she lied. "I'll see what they think," she added deliberately. "Okay?"

Mrs. Bird relaxed. "Okay. Be careful, now."

"Oh, I will. I will. Goodbye."

Coreen made her way outside very slowly, grimacing as her bruised ribs protested the movement. She was weak and not as steady on her feet as she would have liked, but she made it to the cab with as much haste as possible. Her heart was going like a jackhammer and she was tense with nerves. She couldn't bear the thought that she might be stopped at the last minute. She got in, waving at Mrs. Bird, and gave him her destination. As she rode away, she sighed with relief. She was free at last. There would be no more torment. Barry was gone and soon she'd be away from Ted. Then maybe she could have some peace again.

Ted and Sandy had found Henry, the chauffeur, in his small apartment when they got to the house to get Coreen's things. Henry had the keys. He unlocked the front door and showed them up to her room, his whole mood somber.

"Poor kid," he said as they opened her closet and stopped dead at the sight that met their eyes. "He kept her poor for two years, hounded her and harassed her, brought her back every time she tried to run away. I hated working for him, but I couldn't leave her here to cope with it by herself."

Ted's eyes flashed dangerously as he turned from his shocked contemplation of the three dresses in the huge closet to stare angrily at the older man.

"My cousin had millions of dollars," he began.

Henry nodded. "Yes, sir, he did, and he bought himself the best clothes and the best cars and the best women in Houston," he added, not backing down an inch from the threatening set of Ted's lithe body. "But all Coreen got was the back of his hand and the edge of his tongue. He cut her bad that last night he slept here, the night before the party. I had to drive her to the doctor and lie about how she got that way, with him barely sober and standing right there beside her and swearing she fell on a sheet of tin. I never saw so much blood…"

Ted and Sandy had both gone very still.

"He cut her? With what?" Ted demanded, his expression one of angry disbelief.

"With a knife, Mr. Regan," Henry said. "He had her down in the living room on the couch when I came in to see if he needed anything before I went to bed. He was cursing her, and threatening to kill her. I thought I'd talked some sense into him, but he kept cursing her about some birthday card she'd got and accused her of being unfaithful," he added, frowning curiously at the expression that washed over Ted's face. "He cut her before I could get to him. She screamed and the blood went everywhere. That seemed to bring him to his senses. We took her to the doctor and got her sewed up, then he went back out again. We didn't see him all of the next day—not until he came home to take her to that party with him."

Ted sat down in a chair. "It was over a birthday card?"

"Yes, sir. Seemed to make him crazy. He used to hit her sometimes. She never talked about it, but I could see the bruises. I'm glad he's dead," he added icily. "He was a brute, and I don't care if he was your cousin, he got what he deserved. He was going to bring her back here that night and start on her again. He'd probably have killed her, but I wouldn't let her leave the party with him. He'd already dismissed me when he dragged her out front, and he was threatening her again. Nobody heard but the three of us. The gossip was just that she let him drive drunk." Henry's dark eyes narrowed. "She didn't do anything except save herself from being cut worse than she already had been, or maybe killed. In the mood he was in, drinking like he was, he could have done anything to her."

"You're lying," Ted said through his teeth. His face had gone pasty.

He turned to Sandy, aware that Ted wasn't being responsive. "You get her to show you the stitches, Miss Regan," Henry returned, talking to her. "It was a bad cut. The doctor thinks she's just clumsy, because of all those things that happened to her. Mr. Barry is what happened to her," he added. "She never crashed in any glider…he knocked her down a flight of stairs!"

Ted's indrawn breath was audible. He put his head in his hands and Sandy ushered Henry out of the room, thanking him for his help. Ted hadn't moved when she got back and closed the door.

She didn't say a word. He looked as if his conscience was killing him already.

"Did you know?" he asked finally, raising a tortured face to hers.

"No," she replied heavily. "I believed what she told me, just as you did. Barry wouldn't let me see her at all. We had to meet for lunch secretly, and she never talked about her marriage. Nobody knew. Except Henry, apparently."

Ted got to his feet. "She can't know what we've found out," he said slowly.

"Of course not."

He glanced at her. "There's more than this, I imagine," he said with the beginning of horror in his eyes.

She only nodded.

He turned, his heart stilled in his chest as he remembered what he'd said to Coreen just before he and Sandy had come over here. He probably couldn't undo the damage he'd done. He'd spent too much time hurting Coreen.

Sandy was staring at him and he hadn't been aware of her question. "What?" he murmured absently.

"I said, what are we going to do about Corrie?"

"For now," he said with a heavy sigh, "let's just get her stuff packed and get out of here."

Chapter 5

Ted carried the bags into the house. Only one of them had been needed to hold Coreen's pitiful few things. The others they'd carried were empty. It was only just beginning to sink in that Coreen had been the victim, not his cousin. Barry had lied to him from the very beginning, and because of those lies, he'd been cruel to Coreen. It was unbearable to remember it. Poor little thing, broken and bruised and terrified, and all she'd had from him was more humiliation and blame. He'd given her nothing else, in all the time he'd known her.

Mrs. Bird had gone home by the time they'd arrived. She left supper in the kitchen and a note saying that Coreen had promised to be in touch.

Ted read it twice, but it still hadn't quite made sense when a tight-lipped Sandy came back into the kitchen. "Her room is empty," she said. "She's gone."

"*Gone?*" He exploded. "My God, she could barely walk! Where could she have gone?"

"I have no idea," Sandy said miserably, dropping into a

chair. "She doesn't have a relative in the world. And it's a big world, too. She has the borrowed clothes on her back and she has less than a hundred dollars in her purse. Her credit cards won't do her any good. I'm sure Tina has canceled them all by now."

Ted muttered under his breath, ramming his hands deep into his pockets. "Any guesses?"

"I'll phone Mrs. Bird. She might have said something before she left. Failing that, I'll start telephoning cab companies. What I can't understand is why she left so suddenly," she said, shaking her head as she picked up the telephone receiver and began to press numbered buttons. "I'd already promised her that we'd move up to my apartment in Victoria next week."

"When did you talk about that?" he demanded suddenly.

"Just before you came in... Hello, Mrs. Bird? Yes, do you know where Coreen went? You don't? Then do you know what cab company...yes, I know the one. Thanks. No, it's all right, we'll find her, don't worry."

She hung up and started thumbing through the telephone directory, while Ted stared at the floor and cursed himself.

He knew there would be no hope of finding her before dark. He only hoped she had enough money to stay at a decent hotel, with doors that would lock. He refused to let Sandy go with him while he searched. It was his fault that she'd run away. Now he had to persuade her to come back. It wasn't going to be easy.

Coreen was sitting quietly in the common room of the YWCA when he arrived. She looked tired and sick, and a woman who looked as if she might be a social worker was sitting with her, taking notes on a clipboard.

Ted felt his whole body tensing when he got close enough to hear what was being said.

"...unlikely that we can place you until you're in better

physical condition, Mrs. Tarleton, but in the meanwhile we can work on finding accommodation for you. Now…''

''She has accommodation already,'' Ted said quietly.

Coreen's head turned and her eyes mirrored her horror. She went deathly pale and gripped the arms of the chair for dear life as Ted came closer, tall and elegant in his gray suit and matching Stetson and boots. The only splash of color was in the conservative stripe of his white shirt and the paisley tie he wore with it. He looked very rich.

''Do you know this man, Coreen?'' the social worker asked suspiciously.

''He's my best friend's brother,'' Coreen managed to say. ''And he needn't have come here. I can take care of myself.''

''She has a cracked rib and some deep lacerations from a skydiving accident,'' Ted told the older woman quietly. ''She's been staying with us while she got better. There's been a misunderstanding.''

The older woman's eyes narrowed. ''Considering the condition Mrs. Tarleton arrived here in, I should think that is an understatement Mr.…?''

''Regan,'' he said shortly. ''Ted Regan.''

It was a name that was known in south Texas. The woman's arrogance retreated. ''I see.''

''No, you don't. But we'll see that Coreen is properly cared for. She was recently widowed.''

''A misfortune,'' the woman said. And before Ted could agree, her eyes hardened and she added, ''Because after speaking with another social worker in Jacobsville this morning, I should have enjoyed bringing her late husband before a grand jury.''

Ted didn't respond as Coreen had expected him to, in ready defense of his cousin. He didn't reply at all. She had protested that telephone call, but the social worker had been adamant about getting to the truth. In the end, Coreen was too shell-shocked to refuse her answers.

"Where are your things, Coreen?" he asked, and his tone wasn't one she recognized.

Her frantic eyes met those of the social worker. "I don't have to go, do I?" she asked in a hoarse whisper.

Ted's face contorted before he got it under control. His hand went deep into his pocket and clenched there. "It's all right," he said, controlling the urge to pick her up and run for it. "I'm going to be away on business. Sandy will be all alone at the house. She'd enjoy having you keep her company."

She had so few options. She was tired and hurting more than ever from her physical wounds with all the exertion she'd been forced to make. The emotional wounds were even worse. She looked up at Ted with a tortured expression.

"You'll never have cause to run away again, Coreen," he said huskily, his features rigid. "I swear you won't!"

She didn't trust him. It was in her eyes. She averted them to the social worker, and saw the indecision there. The woman would fight for her if she could. But Ted Regan was powerful, much more formidable than Barry had ever been.

It was the past all over again. Money and power, taking charge, taking control, taking over. She couldn't run. She had no energy left.

"I'll go back," she said in a defeated tone.

"Your things?"

She gestured at the small, thin bag. "This is all I have."

His expression fascinated the social worker, who thought she'd seen them all.

"You will take care of her?" the older woman asked with a last, faint worry.

He nodded. He didn't trust his voice to speak. Coreen stood up, but when he offered his hand, she moved out of reach. Her eyes didn't quite make it to his face as she turned to thank the social worker before she moved toward the door.

His car, a sleek Jaguar, was sitting right outside the door.

He helped her into the passenger seat and went around to get in beside her, stowing his Stetson upside-down on the hat carrier above the visor.

Coreen's hands clenched over the legs of her loose, borrowed jeans. She stared at them, noticing idly that her small, thin wedding band was still on her ring finger. Barry had given her that one piece of jewelry; no other. She didn't know why she was still wearing it, after all this time.

Ted noticed her tension. "I'm sorry," he said curtly.

She looked out the windshield, unmoving, unmoved. "Sandy shouldn't have made you come."

"Sandy doesn't make me do anything," he said quietly. "I apologize for the things I said to you, Coreen."

She didn't understand his change of heart, and she didn't trust it. She didn't answer.

He knew that it was going to be difficult. He hadn't realized that all his apologies were going to be futile as well. She wouldn't even look at him.

He started the car and drove them quickly and efficiently back to Jacobsville.

Mrs. Bird had lunch ready by the time they arrived, but Coreen was too worn-out to eat any. Refusing Ted's help, she let Sandy ease her down the hall and back into bed again. Mrs. Bird came in right behind her, fussing and coaxing until she got her to eat a sandwich. But she'd barely swallowed it down when the long, uncertain hours caught up with her. She closed her eyes and went to sleep.

Ted looked up as Sandy joined him in the living room. "How is she?" he asked.

"Sleeping. Poor little thing, she's worn-out. Why did she do it?" she added. "Did she tell you?"

With a set expression, he moved to his desk and picked up the telephone. "I'm going to fly up to Kansas and check on a stallion I'm thinking of buying."

Sandy was beginning to get a picture she didn't like. "You said something to her, didn't you?" she began.

"It's ancient history now," he replied. "She's safe from me. I won't hurt her anymore."

"So you think she's finally paid enough for the privilege of loving you? How kind of you," Sandy returned angrily.

His fingers trembled a little on the telephone face. "She doesn't love me," he replied coolly. "She was infatuated. That's all it was."

"You're sure?"

"If she'd loved me, she wouldn't have married my cousin, much less have stayed with him for two years," he said.

"As I remember, you were singularly unkind to her while her father was dying, Ted," Sandy reminded him as she got up from the sofa. "Barry pretended to be kind and gentle and offered her comfort, something you never did."

His face contorted as he stared sightlessly out the window. "Don't you think I know?" he growled.

She frowned, waiting. But he got the number he'd dialed, and business replaced torment in his deep voice.

Coreen didn't wake up until Ted had gone. Sandy sat with her for the rest of the day, and the one thing they didn't talk about in the hours that followed was Sandy's brother.

True to his word, Ted stayed away until he could put off his return no longer. Coreen got stronger by the day, and she was moving around with alacrity by the time Ted walked in the door one sunny afternoon.

She was laughing at something Sandy had said, her blue eyes full of humor, her elfin face smiling, aglow with pleasure. But she heard his step and turned her head, and all of it, every bit of it, went out of her like dying light. Ted felt suddenly empty. He'd dreamed over and over again of coming back and having Coreen's face light up when he walked in the door. It had once, years ago, for so brief a time. But it wasn't joy that claimed her features now. It was pain.

He couldn't bear to see it. He put his case down and greeted Sandy with what he thought was normal composure before he glanced at their houseguest.

"Hello, Coreen," he said with careful indifference.

"Ted." She didn't move, as if he had her in his sights and might fire at any minute. In the old jeans and ribbed knit top she was wearing, every thin line of her body was visible. Defensively, her arms folded over her breasts.

He forced his eyes away from her.

"Did you find your stallion before you went on to the cattleman's conference in Los Angeles?" Sandy asked pleasantly.

"Not really," he returned. He sat down and crossed his long legs. "I wasn't looking too hard."

"Lillian phoned twice while you were away," Sandy continued. "She said it was urgent."

"I'll call her later. How are you feeling, Coreen?"

"Much better, thanks," she replied. Her eyes sought his warily. "If you'd rather I left…"

"I wouldn't," he said curtly. His pale eyes sought hers and tried to hold them, but Coreen wasn't taking any more chances. She averted her own gaze to Sandy and smiled at her.

"Then I'll leave you two to talk," she said. She got to her feet, ignoring Ted's quiet protest that there was no need to absent herself. She walked out of the living room and back down the hall to the bedroom they'd given her.

"Well, what else did you expect?" Sandy asked when she heard the muffled curse leave his lips as he stood by the window. "She's had nothing but pain from men."

Ted reached for a cigarette and almost had it lit when Sandy took it from between his lips and tossed it into the fireplace.

"Stop that," she told him. "I'm tired of watching people try to kill themselves."

He glared at her. "You're not my keeper."

"You need one," she said shortly, her whole posture challenging. "Why don't you go and return Lillian's call? She's crazy about you, and old enough not to make you feel so guilty."

The innuendo didn't get past him. "Maybe I'll do that," he said, turning from the window. "Haven't you got something to do?"

"I had a date, but I broke it," she said. "I can't leave Coreen alone with you."

His eyes flashed dangerously in a face gone suddenly pale.

"Don't start rattling at me, you old snake," she returned. "I trust you, but she doesn't. I don't guess you've even noticed that she's afraid of you."

He stood very still. "What?"

"She's afraid of you, Ted," she repeated. "Good grief, don't you ever *look?*"

He let out a rough breath between his teeth and ran an angry hand around the back of his neck. "She never was before," he said defensively.

"That's right," she said. "Before she was married, she never once thought that a man would be physically cruel to her."

He rammed his hands into his pockets. "Damned little toad," he said huskily. "I pitied him, and there he was, feeding me lies about her to keep me angry, to keep me away so that I wouldn't know what he was doing to her!"

"Would you have cared?" Sandy challenged with a mocking laugh. "You're the last person on earth Coreen would look to for help!"

His broad chest rose and fell heavily as he struggled with memories that hurt him. "Then, or now?" he asked.

"What's the difference?" she replied. "You don't have to worry about her watching you anymore, by the way. She won't go near the window in her room, even to open it."

He made a sound under his breath and left the room, staring straight ahead with eyes that didn't even see.

Coreen had wandered outside on shaky legs to watch the horses. Ted was gone. She'd made sure before she'd ever left the house.

The jeans she was wearing were her own, the single pair she had. She wore sneakers and a loose top over it. It was overcast, with threatening weather, and she wondered if it would rain. The parched fields looked as if they could use some rain.

She paused at the stable door and frowned because she heard voices in the back, down the clean straw-aisle that ran widely from one open door to the other.

When Ted came out into the aisle, she turned quickly and started back toward the house.

"Coreen!"

His voice stopped her. She turned, her deep blue eyes wide and wary as they met his pale ones under the brim of his Stetson.

He was wearing working clothes, stained jeans with chaps and a patterned Western-cut shirt. His face was grim and he looked out of humor—as usual.

"I didn't know you were out here," she began defensively, coloring as he stared down at her.

"Oh, I know that," he said bitterly. "You leave rooms when I walk into them, you stay in your bedroom until I leave in the mornings, you won't even come out on the damned porch if you think I'm within a mile of my own house!"

Her lips parted on a shaky breath and she backed away from him.

"No...!" He bit down hard on his anger and took a deep breath. "Here, now, it's all right," he said, forcing himself to talk softly. "I'm not going to hurt you, Coreen," he added quizzically when her rigid posture showed no sign of relaxing.

She folded her arms over her breasts and just watched him, her whole stance wary, apprehensive.

He took off his Stetson and wiped his sweaty forehead on his sleeve. "Do you remember Amarillo, the horse Sandy used to let you borrow? He sired a foal by Merry Midnight. She's a two-year-old filly. We call her Topper. Want to see her?"

She softened toward him. She loved the horses. "Yes," she said after a minute.

He held out a hand. "Come on, then."

She moved toward him, but her arms stayed where they were.

He pretended not to notice that she wouldn't touch him. It was her feelings that mattered right now, not his own. He led her into the stable and out the back, to the back of the stable where the beautiful black horse with the white blaze and stockings stood in her big, clean stall grazing on fresh corn in a trough.

"Hello, Topper," he said to the horse. "Hello, girl."

He opened the corral door and motioned for Coreen to follow him. He smoothed his hand over the velvet nose and turned the horse's head so that Coreen could stroke her.

"Why, she's soft," she exclaimed.

"Like velvet, isn't she?" he mused, liking the way her eyes lit up with pleasure. He hadn't seen them that way in a long, long time.

"Why is she called Topper?"

He shrugged. "No particular reason. It seemed to fit. She's a two-year-old, and we hope she's going to make a thoroughbred racer. I've got a trainer coming soon to start working with her."

"A racer," she echoed. "You mean, like in the Kentucky Derby?"

"That's what we're hoping for next year," he confessed.

"Well, she's certainly beautiful enough," she had to admit.

He watched her stroke the horse's mane and ears. Topper paid her very little attention. She was intent on her breakfast.

A sudden clap of thunder made Topper jump. Coreen made a similar movement, gasping at the unexpected noise.

"Looks as if we may be in for a spring shower," he remarked, looking toward the sudden darkness outside the stable.

"Or a tornado," she added nervously.

"Oh, I don't think so," he said to reassure her. They moved out of the stall and he snapped the lock shut again before he strode to the back of the stable and looked out.

The sky was very dark, with blue-black clouds just over the horizon. Lightning flashed and a rumble of thunder followed it. "Beautiful, isn't it?" he remarked as he noticed her out of the corner of his eye. "Nature, in all her splendor."

"Violence," she corrected, shivering. Her eyes were apprehensive as she watched the lightning fork. "I hate loud noises."

He leaned against the wall and watched her curiously, his eyes intent on her wan face. "Loud noises, like a raised voice?" he asked gently.

She didn't look at him. "Something like that."

He moved away from the wall, and her eyes swept to encompass him, the same fear in them as the storm produced.

"Is it only loud noises, or is it men who come too close as well?" he queried.

She put up a defensive hand when he took another step toward her.

He saw her body tense. His pale eyes narrowed. Outside, the wind was growing bolder as the storm clouds darkened.

"Storms increase the number of negative ions in the atmosphere. Scientists say that we feel better when that happens,'' he remarked.

"Do they?'' she murmured.

He drew in a slow, steady breath. "Coreen, I know about your marriage.''

She laughed coldly. "Do you?''

"Harry told us. Everything.''

The pseudosmile left her lips. She searched his eyes, looking for the truth. He hid his feelings very well. Nothing, nothing showed there.

"And you believed him?'' she said after a shocked minute. "How amazing.''

He grimaced. "Yes. I suppose that's how I thought you'd take it.''

She averted her eyes to the storm and stiffened again when a violent thunderclap shook the ground. Rain was peppering down, splattering in the dust just outside the door. It would be impossible to get to the house now without getting wet. She couldn't run this time.

"Nothing's changed,'' she said. "Nothing at all.''

He tossed his Stetson to one side and propped a boot on a bale of hay while they watched the rain come down. "We need that,'' he remarked. "We've just started planting hay.''

"Have you?''

He started to reach for a cigarette to calm his nerves when he realized that Sandy had taken his last pack out of his shirt pocket. He laughed softly.

Coreen glanced at him.

"Sandy's stolen my smokes,'' he explained lazily. "She thinks cigarettes will kill me. She can't talk me into stopping, so she's gone militant.''

"Oh.''

He raised an eyebrow and smiled amusedly. "Don't you have any two-syllable words in your vocabulary?''

He was trying to be kind. She understood that, but she

didn't want any more trouble than she already had. She stared toward the house, hating the rain that imprisoned her here with Ted.

He saw her impatience to leave and it angered him out of all proportion.

"Damn it!" he burst out.

Her face jerked toward his. Her eyes were enormous, frightened.

"Oh, for God's sake," he groaned. "I've never hit a woman in my life! I lose my temper from time to time. I'm impatient and when things upset me, I say so. That doesn't mean I'm going to hurt you, honey!"

The endearment went through her as if it were electricity. He'd never once used an endearment when they spoke. She'd never even heard him use them to Sandy. Her eyes dropped, embarrassed.

He looked at her openly, curious, astonished at her reaction to what had been an involuntary slip of the tongue.

He moved a step closer, slowly, so that he wouldn't alarm her. She looked up, but she didn't back away. He stopped an arm's length from her, because that was when she tensed. His pale eyes wandered over her face and from the distance, he could see the deep hollows in it, the shadows under her eyes.

"You don't sleep at all, do you?" he asked gently.

"There's been so much," she faltered. "You can't imagine—"

"I think I can," he interrupted bluntly. "Coreen, I think some therapy would be a good idea. You must have realized that a warped relationship can damage you emotionally."

"I'm not ready for that now," she said evenly. "I'm tired and I hurt all over. I just want to rest and not have to think about things that disturb me." She drew in a long, weary breath. Her hand went to her short hair and toyed with a strand of it beside her flushed cheek. "I know you don't want me here, Ted. Why won't you let me go to Victoria and stay with Sandy?''

His jutting chin raised and one eye narrowed. ''Who says I won't?''

''Sandy. She said you kept finding excuses why we can't use the apartment.''

''They're not excuses,'' he said. ''They're reasons. Good reasons.''

Her thin shoulders rose and fell impotently.

''You'd be alone during the day, when Sandy's working,'' he explained quietly. ''At least I'm somewhere nearby when she's gone, or Mrs. Bird is.''

''You aren't responsible for me.''

''Yes, I am,'' he said. ''I'm responsible for the trust Barry left you. That makes you my concern.''

''Oh, I don't want the money,'' she said wearily, turning away. ''Money was never why I married him!''

''The money is yours,'' he argued. ''And you'll take it, all right.''

Her head came up. For an instant he thought he'd found the spark he'd been looking for, a way to bring her out of her shell and back into the world. But the spark died even as he watched.

''I don't feel like fighting,'' she said. ''When I'm back on my feet, I'll find a job and a place to stay. Then I'll be out of your hair for good.''

That was what he was afraid of. He wanted to talk to her, to explain how he felt, but the rain began to fall more slowly, and the instant it lessened to a sprinkle Coreen was out of the stable and on her way to the house as if pack dogs were nipping at her heels.

Chapter 6

"He's so restless lately, have you noticed?" Sandy asked Coreen one afternoon when Ted was working on a truck with two of his men. "I've never heard him use language like that within earshot of the house."

The language was audible, all right. Coreen peeked out the window toward the metal building where the ranch vehicles were kept. One of the men with Ted had thrown down a wrench and he was stomping off in disgust.

"Hawkins, get back here or get another job!" Ted yelled after him.

"I'll get another job, then!" came the angry reply. "Can't be worse than this!"

"Coward!" the third man called after him gleefully.

"Do you want to go with him, Charlie?" Ted asked with a dangerous smile.

Charlie picked up the dropped wrench and offered it to the greasy man bending over the engine of the truck.

Coreen was shivering. Angry voices still made her uneasy,

and Ted was much more volatile than she'd ever realized. At home, without any social restraints on his temper, it seemed to be terrible.

"How do you stand it?" Coreen asked Sandy nervously, as they set the table.

Sandy stopped what she was doing and turned to her friend, hardly aware of a cessation of the noise outside. "He isn't like Barry," she said softly. "He isn't a violent man. It takes a lot to make him fight, and he doesn't hit women. He's just upset because he's been unkind to you, and that's why he's being impossible to live with. He's sorry about the way he's treated you and too proud to apologize for it."

"He's very loud," Coreen muttered.

"He's a marshmallow inside" came the musing reply. "What you see isn't the real man. Ted hides what he feels under that prickly exterior. It keeps people from finding out how vulnerable he really is."

"In a pig's eye," Coreen retorted. "He's steel right through."

Sandy put a plate down a little noisily. "But you don't hate him," she added, her voice as clear as a bell in the room.

Coreen flushed. She started to argue, aware of Sandy's level stare and a tiny flicker of diverted attention that was quickly concealed.

"Do you?" she persisted.

"No," Coreen confessed, her eyes lowered. "But it might have been easier for me if I had, once. Barry made my life so miserable. You can't imagine what it's like to have someone taunt you with feelings you can't help, to hold another man's rejection over your head for years, reminding you over and over again that you weren't worth loving. He was so jealous of Ted…insanely jealous, even though he didn't really want me himself. He couldn't stand it when he found out how I felt about Ted. I think he would have killed me, that last night…"

A faint sound from behind her brought her head around. Ted had been standing in the open doorway. His face was hard and drawn, oddly pale.

"Well, get an earful, Ted," Coreen muttered with the first show of spirit yet. An open sack of flour sat on the table beside her and she accidentally knocked it with her elbow, jumping to catch it before it fell. Even then she fumbled and had to clutch it to her.

"Miss Graceful," Ted drawled without thinking.

To Coreen, it was the last straw. She could see the sudden recognition, the regret, in Ted's face as he remembered too late what Harry had told them about Barry taunting her with her clumsiness. But her self-control was gone. It was one taunt too many.

She didn't even think. She wheeled and threw the bag of flour at him without a single hesitation.

The bag was made of paper and it broke immediately. Ted's shocked expression was coated in a white layer of flour, like the whole front of him. It mingled with the grease to give him a vaguely mottled look.

"Tarred and feathered," Sandy remarked pleasantly and suddenly broke into gales of laughter.

Ted glared at her and then Coreen, who was as shocked by her own actions as Ted seemed to be.

Coreen saw the flash of anger in his pale eyes and the color that overlaid his cheekbones as he stared at her. She felt sick all over, remembering how Barry had reacted if she showed any spirit at all. She felt her knees shaking as she stared up at Ted, waiting for the explosion, waiting for him to hit her.

That expression in her eyes stopped Ted's anger cold. He calmed down at once. "For a woman who hates violence," he remarked through floury lips, "you have an absolutely *amazing* lack of restraint."

With a rueful smile, he turned and left a white trail behind him on his way out of the kitchen.

"And let that be a lesson to you!" Sandy yelled after him. "Never make a woman mad when she's cooking!"

The cowboy who was helping him must have been standing on the front porch, because there was a cry of dismay followed by such howling laughter that muttered curses echoed from the hall.

Coreen was devastated by what she'd done. She was even more devastated by the fact that Ted hadn't retaliated. It was such a relief that she started crying. Sandy hugged her, fighting her own amusement. "Now, now, he won't die from a coating of flour. Listen, Coreen, listen, if he doesn't get it all off, we can toss him in the pan and fry him up nice and toasty. He's already covered with grease and now he's properly battered…"

Coreen felt the tears turn to laughter at the thought of a crispy Ted lying on a big platter.

Ted was cleaned up when he came to supper. He glared at both women, but he didn't say a word about what had happened.

Coreen ate with a little more appetite than she'd had. She and Barry had rarely eaten together, except when they were first married. And that had only been so that he could torment her about Ted.

When they progressed to dessert, Ted picked up his second cup of coffee and walked out of the room without a word.

"He's in a snit," Sandy remarked. "But he'll regret leaving that cake behind. Why don't you take it to him and make up?"

"I don't want to make up."

"Yes, you do." Sandy smiled at her. "Go on. It won't hurt."

"That's what you think. You knew he was standing there, didn't you?"

Sandy flushed. "I only wanted him to know that you didn't hate him. I thought it might help. I'm sorry."

Coreen didn't answer. She got up and took the dish of cake to the room Ted used as a study. The door wasn't closed. He was sitting behind his big oak desk staring blankly at the opposite wall with his coffee cup perched on one big hand.

"Didn't you want any cake?" Coreen asked hesitantly.

He leaned back in the chair, still with the coffee cup in his hand, and stared at her. "Sandy sent you, didn't she?" He laughed when her expression gave her away. "I didn't think you'd come of your own accord."

She moved into the room, ignoring the sarcastic remark, and put his cake on the desk.

"I didn't mean to say what I did," he said quietly. "I know that you aren't normally a clumsy woman. It was a slip of the tongue that I regretted the minute I made it."

"And I overreacted," she confessed. She traced the grain of the wood on his desk. "I'm sorry, too." She glanced up. "You didn't try to hit me."

His face went rigid. "I don't have to beat up a woman to feel like a man."

"It's nice to know for sure, though."

He could understand how she might feel that way. He didn't like thinking about it. He sipped his coffee and put the cup on the desk, watching her with a faint smile. "I don't suppose you might like to kiss and make up?" he asked unexpectedly.

Her shocked eyes met his.

"Oh, nothing heavy," he clarified. His eyes were watchful, but teasing and oddly tender. "It would do you good, to be kissed in a way that wouldn't hurt you or scar you."

"I don't ever want to be that close to a man again," she said miserably.

"Sure you feel that way, now," he returned, his voice still soft. "But it isn't natural to let it continue. It would be a pity to waste those maternal instincts you used to have. Do you remember when Mary Gibbs brought her baby into your father's store, Coreen?" he added wistfully, as if the memory was one he cherished. "You'd stand there and hold that little boy, and your face would glow."

"But, you never saw me..." she began.

His eyes lifted to hers. "I never stopped seeing you," he replied bluntly. "I watched you all the time, even when you didn't know I was around. My God, honey, you still don't understand, do you?"

She shook her head.

"I'm forty years old," he said softly. "You're barely twenty-four."

She just looked at him. It still didn't register, and her eyes told him so.

He let out a rough sigh. "I'm sixteen years older than you are," he said heavily. "You don't realize, you can't realize, what a burden that age difference would become."

Her eyes slid over his lean, tanned face. "I'm nothing to you," she said simply. "So what difference does it make? I don't hate you, but I don't love you, either. You made sure of that. You're safe, Ted," she added without expression. "I'll never be a threat to you, or any other man, ever again."

She turned and started out of the room. She hadn't even heard him move when she saw his arm slide past her and push the office door shut with a hard snap.

Too nervous to turn, she hesitated. He had her by both shoulders all at once, and the next minute, she was standing with her back to the door and a furious Ted towering over her.

"Which doesn't mean that I'm not a threat to you," he

replied with glittery pale blue eyes. "I'm so damned tired of being noble…!"

He bent and moved his mouth square over hers with an economy of motion that left her no time to anticipate it.

She gasped under the warm, hard crush of his lips and her hands went automatically to his shirtfront to push.

He lifted his mouth just enough to allow speech, but when he spoke, his lips were still touching hers. "I'm not going to hurt you," he said tenderly. "Not in any way at all. I'm not even going to hold you. Try not to fight me, sweetheart. Just this once, let me kiss you."

It would be fatal. She knew it. But the sweet pressure of his mouth on hers was nectar. It had been years, and she'd loved him so much. Their time had already passed, but this tiny space of seconds was like a reminder of what could have been.

She didn't fight. Her lips brushed against his in a slow, gentle glide that became, eventually, insistent and deep. But he didn't hold her or imprison her. Only their lips touched, for seconds that seemed endless.

When he finally lifted his head, she was breathless.

His pale eyes searched hers solemnly. "That's how it could have been," he said huskily. "And even that is just the beginning."

She managed to shake off her languor and shook her head. "Don't torment me, Ted," she whispered bitterly.

He scowled. "Torment you?"

"I can't go through it again," she whispered, wincing. "He tormented me with you. He told me what you said when you came to visit us," she added, looking up with anguished eyes. "That you'd only played with me before I married him, that you'd never wanted me anyway, because I was so thin and boyish, that I wasn't woman enough…"

His eyes closed. "Coreen…"

She pulled away from him and opened the door.

"It wasn't true," he said roughly.

She looked at him over her shoulder. "But, it was," she said sadly. "You told me so yourself, that night at the dance."

"I lied," he said bitingly.

She smiled sadly. "It's all right, Ted. It was all a long time ago. But don't...don't try to make me care for you again. We both know that you have...new interests, now."

She was gone before he made the connection. Lillian. She thought he was involved with Lillian. He could have cursed himself for bringing the woman here in the first place. He'd fouled up everything. Coreen wouldn't let him near her. She'd believed Barry. She thought Ted was only playing. For a minute, he felt total despair. There had to be a way, some way, to show her that things were different now. He just didn't know how.

As it turned out, Topper was the bait that lured Coreen out of the house. She enjoyed watching the trainer work the young filly on the track out behind the house. While she watched Topper, Ted watched her.

She was blooming here, with no one to hurt her or torment her. Day by day, her complexion turned rosy and she began to smile. Her blue eyes lit like fireflies and she began to gain a little weight as well.

She was standing on the lower rail of the track, watching Topper run, when she felt Ted behind her. She didn't have to turn and look. She knew when he was close by. It was like intuition.

"The sun's hot," he said, lifting her down by the waist. "Don't stay out here too long."

"Oh, Ted, don't fuss, I'm having...oh!"

When she turned, the bandage around his arm shocked her speechless. It was bloody, but he looked amused at her horror.

"Bull gored me, that's all," he mused. "Nothing to worry about."

Her hands trembled as she touched the bandage. "It hasn't even stopped bleeding! Come on." He didn't budge. She caught him by his good arm, her face contorted with worry. "Ted, come on! Please!"

He let her drag him into the house through the back door that led into the kitchen. She held his arm over the sink and unwrapped the makeshift bandage. There was too much blood even to see the damage, and thank goodness she wasn't squeamish.

She bathed the wound very gently, and then held pressure over it, wincing at the pain she must be causing him. But after two minutes, the bleeding hadn't stopped.

She looked up into his eyes worriedly. "It's cut a vein," she said. "It won't stop bleeding. You have to go to the doctor!"

He smiled gently at her. "Coreen, I've been gored before," he began. "I know what to do."

Her jaw set. "I'm taking you to the doctor, Ted, you might as well stop arguing because I'll call an ambulance if you don't."

He opened his mouth to argue, but the paleness of her complexion and the wild look in her eyes stopped him. It touched him deeply that she was that concerned. And he liked the new show of spirit. She'd been subdued for so long now that he'd despaired of her strength ever returning.

"All right, Corrie," he said, using the familiar nickname for the first time since she'd been here.

She didn't notice. She was terrified that he was going to bleed to death. If only Sandy or Mrs. Bird was here! She had no one to help her.

Ted dug out his truck keys and handed them to her. "Can you handle it? It's a long bed."

"Yes, I can drive," she muttered, herding him toward the

big red-and-white truck. "And I won't back it into a barn or a ditch."

He chuckled. "Okay."

For a man who was bleeding to death, he certainly was cheerful! She got him into the truck and climbed in under the wheel, demanding the name and address of his doctor.

She didn't falter all the way to town. Her eyes kept shifting worriedly to the soaked towel around his forearm, but he was amazingly unconcerned. Just as well, she thought; she was frightened enough for both of them.

At the doctor's office, she led him inside and gave his name to the receptionist, who knew Ted and smothered a grin at the sight of him being led around by this small, determined woman.

But when she noticed the way he was bleeding, she called the nurse and got them right into an examination room. Dr. Lou Blakely came in, wearing a white coat and a grin on her pretty face.

"You're Dr. Lou Blakely?" Coreen asked.

The willowy blond woman chuckled as she began to examine Ted's wound. "Lou is short for Louise," she explained. "What happened to you, Ted?"

"A bad-tempered bull. She wouldn't rest until she dragged me here," he muttered good-naturedly, nodding toward Coreen.

"She did the right thing," Lou said, frowning. "You'll need stitches. How about your tetanus booster?"

"Current," he said. "Barely."

"You'll need another. Betty!" she called to her nurse. "Bring some sutures and iodine and a tetanus hypodermic, will you, while I check on Mr. Bailey in room three?"

"Right away" came the reply.

"I'll be back in a minute," Lou promised, stepping down the hall.

"You can wait outside if you'd rather not watch," Ted

told Coreen, who was sitting stiffly in a chair by the examination table.

She looked up, her face almost tragic. Tears rolled down her cheeks. "If you want me to…"

He let out a sharp breath. "Corrie!" He held out his good hand and she took it. Her lower lip trembled. "Oh, honey!" he whispered huskily, his eyes glittery with feeling. "Honey, don't cry! I'm all right!"

"It's bleeding so," she whispered brokenly.

He pulled her head to his chest and pressed it there, overcome by tenderness. Tears in her eyes affected him violently. His hand contracted in her hair. "I'm all right!" he said huskily.

Lou and the nurse entered together and Coreen had to let go of Ted while they worked.

Lou smiled at Coreen. "He's tougher than he looks. Honest."

Coreen nodded, not trusting her voice.

They finished, finally, and Coreen went out with the nurse, Betty, while Lou gave the tetanus booster to Ted.

"How long have you been married?" Betty asked, oblivious to the fact that Coreen was wearing Barry's wedding band, not Ted's.

"Oh, I, uh…"

"Not long enough," Ted replied, sliding an arm around her shoulders. "Come on, baby, I'll take you home. Thanks, Betty."

"Sure thing, Mr. Regan."

"You let her think we were married," Coreen protested when they reached the truck.

"Betty's new here. And explanations take too long." He paused at the passenger door and looked down at her with quiet, soft eyes. "You're still wearing his wedding band. Why?"

She twisted it on her finger. "I thought if I took it off,

you'd think it was one more black mark against me,'' she said with resignation.

He caught her hand and wrenched the ring off, glaring at it. He dropped it in the sand and ground it under his heel, staring into Coreen's shocked eyes.

"But..."

He bent and put his mouth over hers in a brief, hard kiss. "Drive me home."

He got into the truck and closed the door. She hesitated, looking down at where the ring had been. But she didn't try to pick it up. Whatever had been, her marriage was a thing of the past. She had to put it out of sight, like the wedding ring that signified it. Was that what Ted had meant with the gesture?

She drove the truck back to the ranch, silent and thoughtful.

When Sandy returned from work, she was astonished at Ted's refusal to see a doctor without prodding.

"You idiot," she fumed at him over supper. "I try to save you from lung cancer by hiding your cigarettes and here you go trying to get tetanus! Thank goodness Corrie was here!"

He was watching Coreen. "Yes," he agreed. "Thank goodness she was."

Sandy put down her fork and sipped her hot tea. "Ted, have you checked on the apartment for me?" she asked.

He lowered his eyes to his plate and toyed with a bit of steak. "I haven't had time, Sandy. I'll get around to it in a day or so."

Sandy glanced toward Coreen and rolled her eyes.

"You know very well that Corrie doesn't need to be on her own all day while you work," Ted said surprisingly. "At least she's properly looked after here."

"I'm much better," Coreen protested. "I don't hurt nearly as much when I move around, and I'm not dizzy."

"You're still in a state of shock, though," he replied. "You've been through a lot. Too much," he added shortly.

"He's right," Sandy agreed. "You aren't really unhappy here, are you Corrie?"

There was a hesitation. Coreen glanced shyly at Ted. "I like watching the trainer with Topper," she confessed. "If I move to Victoria, I'd miss that."

They both smiled. "You'll stay, then," Ted said.

"Yes, thank you, for now. But I should be able to get a job soon," Coreen added slowly. "And find a place of my own."

Ted put down his fork and glared at her. "What's wrong with staying here?"

"But I can't," she told him. "Ted, I'm not part of the family, I'm a financial burden you've assumed until I reach twenty-five. You don't have to..."

"Oh, hell, I know I don't have to," he muttered. "Have you thought about what you're qualified to do? And how much strength it's going to require, working an eight-hour day? And what it will cost, even in Jacobsville, to rent rooms?"

She'd tried not to think about her situation. It showed in her face.

"It's a big house," he coaxed. "Sandy and I are all alone here. You're company for her, the best friend she has."

"But..."

"Corrie, just get well," he said gently. "You've got an allowance from the legacy that will more than take care of your odds and ends until you're completely well. Don't think about tomorrow. There's plenty of time for that."

"Listen to him, will you?" Sandy said, smiling. "Honestly, I'll go crazy if you leave now."

"If I'm not in the way," she faltered.

Everyone knew that meant "yes." Ted started eating again, and his smile betrayed just a little smugness.

* * *

The trainer was an elderly man who'd worked with thoroughbreds all his life. He had a son named Barney who came to visit on weekends, and who noticed Coreen very quickly. He was a sweet-natured man, not terribly educated, but kind. She warmed to Barney quickly and began to spend time with him when he came on the weekends to visit his father.

The problem began when Ted started spending more time at home and noticed the amount of contact Coreen was having with his trainer's closest relation. He didn't like it, and he stopped it. Coreen missed Barney and asked his father why he hadn't come back.

He told her that Ted had arranged a nice job for his son, and that Barney was over the moon about it. But Coreen wondered if it had been a benevolent gesture on Ted's part or something more. It didn't occur to her that he might be jealous; she simply saw it as one more way he'd found to get at her.

She had to know, so she went looking for him that same morning. She found him in his office, talking on the telephone. She started to back out, but he gestured impatiently for her to come in.

He was giving somebody hell over the telephone. He finished with a curt demand and hung up before the person at the other end of the line had time for any outcry.

''Well?'' he demanded, and the leftover anger in his pale eyes made her stand very still.

Chapter 7

Ted saw her apprehension and forced himself to calm down. He leaned back in his swivel chair with his hands behind his head and stared at her patiently. "What can I do for you?" he asked.

She hesitated. "Barney's Dad said that you found him a job in Victoria."

He nodded slowly, and began to look more unapproachable. His silver hair caught the light and glittered like metal. "So?"

She didn't know how to answer that. She wanted to ask if he'd sent Barney away deliberately because she was spending so much time with him, but that might sound as if she were accusing him of being jealous. Heaven knew, she didn't think that was the reason!

"Go ahead," he invited.

Her eyebrows arched. "Go ahead and do what?"

"Ask me if I did it to keep him away from here."

She folded her hands in front of her. "Did you?" she asked.

His pale eyes in one glance took in her body in its pale pink short-sleeved knit top and close-fitting jeans. She was gaining a little weight, and she looked pretty. "What?" he murmured absently, distracted.

"I asked if you sent Barney away because he was spending so much time with me."

His eyes narrowed and grew cold as they levered back up to meet hers. "As a matter of fact, I did."

Her lips parted on a expelled breath. "Oh. I see."

"Do you?" he replied. He leaned forward suddenly and got to his feet. "You might remember that I hired his father, not him."

"You don't have to justify yourself," she said in a subdued tone as she turned away. Bitter memories intruded on the present, and her voice was almost absent as she murmured, "Anything that I like has to go, doesn't it, even people? Barry once had a dog shot because I stroked it—"

She was stopped in midsentence by the steely lean hand that caught her arm and spun her around. She gasped at the suddenness of the action. Nor did he let her go when he had her standing stock-still.

"I didn't have the damned man shot, I got him a good job," he said through his teeth, and his pale eyes were flashing dangerously at her. "I do nothing to deliberately hurt you! Stop tarring me with the same brush you used on my cousin."

His anger was intimidating. He was like a summer storm in anger, all flashing fury. But she remembered when she'd thrown the flour at him and he hadn't retaliated. He could control his temper. Barry had never tried.

His other hand caught her by the waist, lightly, and held her when she would have pulled back. His gaze was curious now, speculative.

"Sandy says you're afraid of me," he asked bluntly. "Are you?"

She lowered her eyes to his chest, and she watched its regular rise and fall. "You're…volatile."

"I've always been volatile," he returned. "Hot tempers run in my family. But I've told you before that I don't attack women."

"I know that. Not even when you're drowned in flour," she added with a faint smile.

He tilted her face up to his, and she expected to find humor in his eyes. But she didn't. He was solemn, searching her wan face with intent curiosity.

"You were telling Sandy that Barry taunted you with me…"

She pushed at him. "Please, don't!"

"No, Coreen, I'm not trying to embarrass you," he said gently. He stilled her uncoordinated movements. "Listen, he was playing both ends against the middle. He told me that I was the reason you couldn't bear for him to touch you."

"That wasn't true." She couldn't look at him. "I never felt anything with him, physically, except fear and pain. It had nothing to do with you."

"It made me feel guilty all the same," he returned abruptly. "When Barry was young, he was my shadow. He always seemed to look on me as a father figure after his own father died."

"He envied you," she replied. "You were everything he wanted to be, and never could. He…said once that he wanted me because he thought you did. It was like a contest for him, taking something you prized away from you." She laughed bitterly. "Funny, isn't it? He married me and then found out that you didn't want me at all."

"And made you pay for it?"

She shivered. "I don't want to talk about it, Ted."

He drew in an angry breath, staring over her head toward the wall. Her comment about the dog Barry had ordered shot gave him even more unwanted insight into what her married life had been like. He hated what he was seeing.

"It's all over now," she said after a minute. His nearness was disturbing to her. She drew back from him and he let her go, but his eyes still held her, filled with turmoil, with emotions she couldn't read.

"Did Sandy ever tell you about our father and mother?" he asked hesitantly.

She nodded. "Many times."

He ran a lean hand through his silver hair. "The age difference between them destroyed their marriage. Eventually he couldn't keep up with her in the social whirl she liked. She started going out alone, left him behind. It was inevitable that she'd fall in love with someone closer to her own age and leave him, but he couldn't see it. He grieved all his life for her, and Sandy and I paid for that. He blamed us because she left him. He said that if it hadn't been for him wanting kids, she'd still be with him."

She winced at his tone, and her heart ached for the little boy he once was. It must have hurt him terribly to overhear such things. "Oh, Ted, if it hadn't been you and Sandy it would have been some other excuse. She couldn't have loved him enough, don't you see? If she had, she'd have been home with him, not going to parties! She wouldn't have wanted to go anywhere without him!"

He turned and looked at her, his eyes narrow and assessive. "Is that your definition of a happy marriage? Two people who are inseparable?"

"Two people with common interests," she corrected, "who love each other but are kind to each other and want the same things from life." She shrugged helplessly. "Barry wanted bright lights and alcohol and beautiful companions. He liked people with his same sort of intolerance for differences and his pleasure-oriented attitude toward life. I don't like social occasions at all. I like being outdoors and I love animals." She folded her arms over her breasts. "He wouldn't even let me have a goldfish in the house."

He felt as if he'd never known one single thing about her as she said that. She liked the outdoors, liked animals…of course she did; she'd spent plenty of time at the ranch before she married Barry. She loved horses and riding and she'd never been one for parties. Why hadn't he noticed? She even liked skeet shooting, or she had before he'd made it impossible for her to go to the gun club with her father.

His tormented look puzzled her. She studied him curiously.

"I never knew you," he said slowly.

"You never wanted to," she replied flatly. She sighed and turned away. "And what does it matter now, anyway, Ted?"

She had her hand on the doorknob when he spoke.

"If Barney's company means that much to you, I'll withdraw the job offer," he said bitterly.

She didn't look back. "No, it's…he's very happy, his father said. He was just being friendly, Ted, that's all. You and Sandy have been very kind to me. It's just that…" How could she tell him that she was alone too much, that she needed someone to talk to? Sandy had to work and so did he. Besides, it would sound as if she was begging him to keep her company. "Never mind."

"Are you lonely, Coreen?" he asked softly.

Her hand tightened on the doorknob. She drew in a slow breath. "Aren't most people?" she asked in a haunted tone. She opened the door and went out.

Coreen was surprised to find Ted at the table the next morning when she went to eat breakfast. Sandy had said that she'd have to leave very early for an appointment in Houston, and Coreen had given herself the luxury of sleeping late. It was after ten when she dressed in jeans and a floppy knit blouse and went in search of toast and coffee.

She stopped in the doorway, staring at Ted.

"Sleepyhead," he chided kindly. "Sit down and eat."

"It's after ten," she commented.

"Oh, I had something to do this morning," he said mysteriously. He poured her a cup of coffee and put it at her place, pushing the milk and sugar toward her. "Nibble on something and then I've got a surprise for you."

Her eyes widened. "For me?"

He nodded. His pale eyes twinkled. "No, I'm not going to tell you yet. Eat up."

She hadn't had many pleasant surprises. She ate a piece of toast and drank her coffee, all the while watching Ted intently for any giveaway expression. It wasn't like him to give presents, except to Sandy.

"Through?" he commented when she dabbed at her unvarnished lips. "Okay. Come on."

He led her through the kitchen, calling a greeting to Mrs. Bird on the way through. They went out to the stable and she looked up at him curiously as he stopped at the first stall and opened it to let her in.

Curled up on a soft cloth in the stall was a baby collie. Coreen could hardly breathe as she looked at it.

She went down on her knees beside the little thing. It opened its eyes and made tiny whimpering sounds. She gathered it up in her arms and cuddled it, laughing when it licked her chin. Tears of joy and gratitude and surprise rolled soundlessly down her cheeks.

Ted knelt beside her. "He's a beaut, isn't he? He's already been to the vet for his shots and checkup. He's purebred, too, you'll have to name him…Corrie!" he exclaimed when he saw the tears, shocked speechless.

"Thank you." She choked out the words, smiling up at him. "Oh, thank you, Ted, he's the most beautiful… thing…!" Impulsively she reached up to pull his face down and she kissed him enthusiastically on his hard mouth.

Then, embarrassed, she pulled back at once and turned her

attention to the puppy. "I'll call him Shep," she whispered huskily. "Isn't he gorgeous?"

Ted was silent. His pale eyes were riveted to her bent head and he was scowling. He wondered if she even realized what she'd done. The impulse that had led him in search of the puppy made him feel good. It was the first spark of pleasure he'd seen her betray since she'd been here.

"Well, I can see that I won't get another sensible word out of you today. I've got to go to work." He got up.

Coreen stood up, too, clutching her puppy. "Why?" she asked breathlessly.

He touched her mouth with his forefinger. "Maybe I like seeing you happy."

"Thank you. I'll take ever such good care of him."

He smiled. "Sure you will." He withdrew his hand and left her to it.

Sandy was fascinated by the puppy. She was more fascinated by the fact that Ted had bought it for Coreen.

"He's never wanted animals around, except for the horses and the cattle dogs he uses on the beef property," Sandy explained. "He'd have let me have pets, if I'd wanted to, but he's never been much of an animal lover—well, except for the horses," she repeated. She frowned. "Curious, isn't it, that he'd buy you a dog."

"I don't understand it, either," Coreen confessed. "But isn't he a beautiful dog?"

"Indeed he is. My, my, isn't my brother a mass of contradictions." She sighed.

Coreen and the puppy were inseparable after that. He followed her on her walks and laid in the corner while she helped Mrs. Bird in the kitchen. She bathed him and combed him, careful not to hurt him where he'd had his shots from the vet. She doted on him, and vice versa.

When she went to ask Ted about some paperwork Sandy

had mentioned he needed help with, Shep came trotting along at her heels.

"My God, the terrible twins," Ted drawled when they walked into his study, but he was smiling when he said it.

"Isn't he cute?" She chuckled. The puppy had already made a world of difference in her. His vulnerability brought out all her protective instincts, as Sandy had already related.

"I hear you're fighting his battles already," he mentioned.

She flushed. "Well, it was a vicious big dog. I couldn't let him hurt Shep."

"What was it you threw at him?" he asked. "A handful of eggs, wasn't it?"

She flushed even more and then glared at him. "Well, they scared him off, didn't they?"

"And I didn't get my chocolate cake for dessert because they were the last eggs Mrs. Bird had, and she didn't have a way to get to the store to buy more," he added.

"Oh, Ted, I'm sorry! I didn't know!"

He laughed at her expression. "I can live without chocolate cake for one more day. You threw flour at me and eggs at the invading dog—I guess it'll be milk cartons you'll be heaving next." He pursed his lips. "Talk about mixing up cake the hard way…!"

"Stop making nasty remarks about me or I'll sic Shep on you," she threatened.

The puppy waddled over to him and began licking his outstretched hand. He gave her a speaking glance.

She glared harder. "Traitor," she told Shep.

"Little things like me," he commented, and his face softened as he looked at the dog.

"Haven't you ever wanted children?" she asked without thinking.

His eyes came up and met hers and then suddenly dropped to her waistline and lingered there for so long that she felt hot all over. Her lips parted. Her body responded to that look in ways she hadn't dreamed it could. She stared at him breathlessly while his hot gaze levered back up to her mouth and then to her shocked eyes.

"Are you reading my mind already?" he asked tautly when he saw her expression.

She couldn't find an answer that wouldn't incriminate her. He got up from the chair, slowly, holding her gaze as he walked carefully around the puppy and stopped just in front of her, so close that she could feel the heat of his body and the soft whip of his breath on her temple.

"I've never let myself want a child," he said roughly. "Do you know why?"

She barely had the strength to shake her head.

"Because people would mistake me for its grandfather. I'm feeling my years a bit, Corrie. I wouldn't be able to do all the things children like doing with their parents. By the time a child of mine was ready for college, I'd be almost ready for Social Security."

Her blue eyes sought his and searched his lean, dark face. "You're so handsome," she said involuntarily. "It would…be a pity not to have a child of your own."

His heartbeat went wild. He'd never felt such desire for a woman. He reached out and touched her throat, where a pulse shuddered just under the skin.

"Thinking about children excites you," he commented roughly. "Did you want one of your own?"

"Not with him," she said, her voice unsteady. "I made sure that I couldn't."

His hand stilled at her throat. "What do you mean, you made sure?" he demanded.

There was a note to his voice, an urgency, that was disturbing. She searched his worried eyes. "I mean, I took something to prevent a child," she said.

He let out a breath that he hadn't realized he was holding. "You didn't have surgery?"

"Oh, no," she said. His eyes disturbed her. "Why would it bother you to think that I couldn't have a child?" she blurted out, and then stood still with horror at what she'd asked so blatantly.

If she'd shocked herself, it seemed that she'd shocked him even more. He stared at her blankly for a moment. Then he scowled and searched her eyes until she flushed.

"I don't know," he said honestly. He moved closer, bringing his hands up to frame her oval face. They were faintly callused hands, warm and strong against her skin.

Her fascinated eyes fell to his mouth and she remembered how it had felt the morning he gave her Shep, when she'd kissed him so uninhibitedly.

His hands tilted her head just a little, and one thumb eased up to her lower lip, teasing it to part from her top one.

"Keep your eyes open while I kiss you," he said huskily, bending slowly toward her. "I want you to know who I am, every minute!"

As if she could forget, she thought with faint hysteria. His hard mouth parted against hers, his lips easing down on hers with a slow, sensuous pressure.

She stiffened and her hands went to his shirt, but he didn't stop.

His hand came up to stroke her cheek, toy with her mouth while his lips explored it. And all the while he watched her watching him, seeing her pupils begin to dilate when his body shifted against her, dragging her breasts against his broad chest.

His free hand slid down her back to the base of her spine and gathered her sinuously against him, so that she felt his jean-clad thigh push between her own legs in an intimacy that was new and exciting.

He lifted his head to look at her. His breathing was as unsteady as her own, and there was nothing calm in his eyes now. He traced her cheek and the outline of her mouth. At the same time, his muscular leg moved farther between hers and his hand pressed her closer in a new and disturbing intimacy. She could feel the insistent pressure of him against the inside of her thigh. It was the first time since she'd first met him that he'd ever allowed her to feel his body in complete arousal.

She started to pull back instinctively, but he moved so that he was perched against the edge of his desk. He drew her in between his legs and held her there by both hips, deliberately moving her to make her aware of what he was feeling.

She blushed and her eyes couldn't get higher than his chin.

"Look at me, Corrie," he said huskily.

She had to drag her eyes up, and they were shy, apprehensive, excited all at once.

His lips parted on a slowly released breath, and his hands lifted her slightly into an even more intimate position. He caught his breath sharply at the sensations it brought and his teeth clenched. He held her there firmly, groaning softly with pleasure at her involuntary movement.

"Ted...!" she protested in a feverish whisper.

"I'd like to make you feel the kind of pleasure it gives me to hold you like this, Corrie," he said, staring into her eyes. He smiled gently. "Embarrassed?"

"I've never done this with you," she faltered.

"No," he agreed. His eyes fell to her soft knit blouse and lingered where her nipples pressed visibly against the cloth.

She knew what he was looking for. Her own body was her worst enemy, but she couldn't hide it from him.

One long leg came around her legs at the knee, holding her, while his hand slid under the knit top. He caught her eyes and slowly lifted his hand under the hem until it reached the thin garment that was no barrier to his touch. He traced the nipple with his forefinger and thumb and felt her whole body jerk.

"Is this where he cut you?" he asked very quietly.

She swallowed. "No. It's...the other one," she whispered.

"I'll be very careful with you," he promised softly. "Don't be frightened."

He reached around behind her and unfastened the catch. Seconds later, his hand pressed tenderly against her bareness and she gasped at the sensations he drew from her body so effortlessly.

His hands slid up her rib cage, taking the fabric with them, and when she caught them, he only shook his head and kept going.

The impact of his eyes on her bare flesh made her very still. He studied the long, thin scar with the tracks of removed stitches still visible, and his jaw tautened. Then his attention turned to her other breast and lingered there for a long moment on the perfection of it, the firm, creamy softness with its hard, dusky tip.

When she saw his head bend, she was too hypnotized to register what it meant. Then his mouth opened on her unblemished breast and began to suckle her. She stiffened and clutched at him, making a tiny cry in her throat.

He drew back at once to see whether passion or fear had produced that choked sound.

"Am I hurting you?" he asked softly.

She bit her lower lip, hesitating as she tried to decide between the truth and a lie.

But he knew. A warm light darkened his pale eyes. "Don't be embarrassed," he said softly. "I'm enjoying it, too. You're so soft, Corrie. It's like rubbing my lips over a rose petal."

He bent again, and this time she had no resistance left. She gave in to him without a protest, moaning softly as he suckled her until she trembled, totally given over to the delicious sensations he was creating.

She felt him lift her, turn her, so that she was suddenly lying back on the desk among the papers and pens. His mouth was insistent, demanding, and she felt his hand on her inner thigh, parting her legs. He lowered his hips against hers. The blatant feel of him in intimacy, even through two layers of denim, was explosive. She cried out and lifted helplessly upward, straining against him, while one lean hand snaked under her and pulled her into him with a quick, hard rhythm.

Her nails dug into his shoulders and she shivered, moaning so hungrily that his mouth left her breast to grind into her own and silence her. She shivered again, her hands urgent, clinging, pulling, in a delirium of anguished hunger.

He was as far gone as she was, totally without restraint. Ignoring the clutter of the desk, he pressed her down into it with the weight of his body and drove against her with a harsh, blind groan of pleasure.

She hadn't realized what could happen, even when two people were fully clothed. She bit his lower lip ardently, tugged at his thick silver hair, moved under him with wanton little jerks until the pleasure made her shake all over. She wept because it wasn't enough, and there was no possibility of getting any closer to him.

He realized belatedly how far they were going. His breath left him in a rough explosion, and for an instant his hands were cruel as he fought for control.

"Help me," he whispered into her open, ardent mouth. "Help me, Corrie. Lie still, honey, please...!"

She sobbed brokenly under his mouth while he soothed and gentled her until passion slowly gave way to exhaustion and her body stopped shivering.

Finally her eyes opened. The ceiling was above her and she felt paper clips under her shoulders and what felt like a pencil against her jean-clad hip. Seconds later, Ted's pale, hard face lifted and his turbulent pale blue eyes looked into hers.

She felt as shocked as he looked, and a lot more embarrassed.

"Easy now," he said softly. "It's all right." He lifted himself away from her and moved off the side of the huge desk, his eyes on the disorder they'd created. Half his paperwork was scattered all over the floor and there were tears in some of the rest.

He was amazed to find her that responsive after what she'd been through. She might have found her husband repulsive, but she was as helpless in Ted's arms now as she'd been the first time he'd ever kissed her. The knowledge of it, and the involuntary pride, filled his face as he watched her fumble under her floppy shirt with the catches to her brassiere.

She saw that expression and didn't understand it. Her hands finished closing the fastening and dropped to her sides. She stared at him, finding her own curiosity magnified in his eyes. He looked sexy, she thought, with his mouth faintly swollen from the long contact with hers, and his silver hair falling roguishly onto his forehead.

She searched for Shep, who'd given up on her and gone to sleep on the floor in the corner. "Some watchdog you are," she muttered at the sleeping puppy.

"I don't think he was convinced that you wanted to be rescued," Ted murmured.

She flushed, touching her shirt absently, wincing as her hand came into contact with the cut.

He scowled, understanding immediately. "I was too rough, wasn't I? I'm sorry. I realize that it must still be pretty sore."

"It's all right," she said. Her shy gaze dropped to his broad chest. "You didn't hurt me. There's something I'd like to ask you."

"Go ahead."

Her teeth nibbled at her lower lip. She could still taste him on it. "Is it only that good in the beginning?" She lifted her head, frowning worriedly as she met his curious eyes. "I mean, before people actually have se…when they get really intimate," she amended quickly.

Chapter 8

He didn't look shocked, she thought. In fact, he was smiling. "No. It feels like that all the time, all the way," he said gently. "Especially when two people want each other so desperately."

"Oh." She squared her shoulders. "I've been lonely," she said abruptly, so that he wouldn't get the wrong idea about her headlong response.

It didn't work. He was looking more smug by the minute. "You *were* lonely," he echoed.

She glared at him. "Very lonely. I couldn't help it."

"Do I look as if I feel taken advantage of?" he asked pleasantly.

She searched for words and couldn't find any.

He leaned back against the desk, watching her. "You hated intimacy with Barry, didn't you?"

She hesitated. Then she nodded. "He said things…" She couldn't bear to remember them. "He hated the way I froze when he touched me. I couldn't bear for him to touch me.

He liked to talk about what he did with other women—'' She broke off and turned away. ''Oh, God, you can't imagine what it was like!''

He moved behind her. His lean hands held her shoulders without pressure. ''I'm getting a pretty raw picture of it,'' he said curtly. ''But it's over now. You have to start putting it behind you.''

She turned in his grasp, her blue eyes wide and frightened. ''What if I can't? What if I really am cold, like he said?''

He pursed his lips and his eyes smiled at her. ''Corrie,'' he said softly, ''if I hadn't pulled back when I did, could you have stopped me?''

She felt the color whip up in her cheeks like a soufflé.

''You're not cold,'' he assured her.

''But we didn't...!''

''If we had,'' he emphasized, ''it wouldn't have been any different.'' His eyes held hers. She couldn't drag them away, and heat ran through her body like fire. ''You might draw back at first, but it would only be a momentary withdrawal. I can make you so hungry that you could take me without preliminaries at all.''

Her eyes showed the faint curiosity the remark brought forth.

''You don't understand? For a woman who was married, Corrie, you're singularly naive.'' He told her, bluntly, exactly what he meant, and her indrawn breath was audible.

''You don't know very much about your body, do you?'' he asked quietly. ''I'm sorry that you think sex is something dark and cruel. It isn't. It's a way of expressing feelings and needs that we can't put into words.''

''Have you ever done it with someone you loved?'' she asked, just as bluntly.

He hesitated. His chest rose and fell slowly. ''No,'' he said after a minute. ''I've enjoyed women and they've enjoyed me, on a no-strings basis. But I've been very careful about my liaisons. There's never been a commitment.''

''And never will be,'' she said, echoing what he'd said before. ''You've said so often enough.''

His pale eyes narrowed as he studied her face. ''You'll want to marry again,'' he said. ''You're not the sort of woman who would feel comfortable having children without a husband.''

She turned away, feeling empty as his hands left her shoulders. She wouldn't want children because they wouldn't be Ted's. How could she tell him that? ''I don't want marriage or children anymore,'' she said dully.

''Coreen, all men aren't like Barry!''

She looked back at him solemnly. ''How does a woman know before she marries a man what he'll be like as a husband? How does she know that he won't hurt her or abuse her, or be unfaithful to her?''

''If he loves her, that will all fall into place,'' he said curtly.

''Some men can't be tied down to just one woman,'' she replied. ''You ought to know. You change your women like you change your saddles,'' she added ruefully. ''Every other newspaper has you pictured with some new woman.''

''Gossip pages run on gossip,'' he said shortly. ''I enjoy the company of pretty women when I go out.''

''Of course, and why shouldn't you? You're a bachelor. You have no ties, no responsibilities.'' She looked away from his curious expression. ''But a married man should care enough to give up other women. Or at least, I used to think so. Barry never gave up anything.''

''Barry didn't love you,'' he said flatly.

''He owned me,'' she replied. ''He used to say that he bought and paid for me, and maybe he did. God knows, Dad would never have been so comfortable at the end if he hadn't intervened. And I'd have had no place at all to go.''

Ted didn't like remembering that. He'd given her no help, offered no comfort. Even if he'd wanted to, Barry made sure that he kept the two of them separated. He was jealous, Ted realized now. Barry had noticed the looks Ted was giving Coreen and it had made him want her, but only to keep her from Ted. Why hadn't he ever realized that Barry competed with him? Barry had lied to both of them, to keep them apart. And he hadn't known.

Coreen noticed Ted's angry scowl and turned away. "Sorry," she said. "I don't mean to keep dragging the past up."

"Yes, I know." His eyes were faintly sad as they searched over her. "I'm sorry that we can't change it."

She shrugged. "Everyone goes through unpleasantness. We just have to remember that there's always a light at the end of the tunnel."

"Is there?" He held her eyes with his. "You're vulnerable with me. Is it because Barry was cruel to you, or is it because we never made love and you're curious?"

She lifted her chin. "Maybe it's both."

"Maybe it's neither." He stuck his hands into his pockets and studied her mutinous face. "But the years are still wrong. You need a young man."

"So you keep saying. If you believe it, why did you send Barney away?"

He glared at her. "Don't you have something to do?"

She sighed. "I wish I did. Sandy once said you needed help in here. I can type. And I can take dictation, if you don't go too fast."

He glanced at the desk irritably, noticing its disorder and remembering how it came to be in such a mess.

"You can start with that," he said, nodding his head toward it. "And next time I lay you down, I won't stop," he added unexpectedly.

She lifted both eyebrows in what she hoped was sophisticated cynicism. "If you don't, you'll marry me," she said with equal candor.

Once, the very word marriage would have stopped him in his tracks. Now, he didn't find it so threatening. And the more he was around Coreen, the hungrier and lonelier he felt. He glared at her.

"I'd better practice more control, in that case," he said mockingly.

"Yes, perhaps you should." She wasn't going to back down ever again, she decided. Her eyes met his bravely. "I'm not taking anything these days."

His cheeks went ruddy and she noticed that his eyes began to darken as they fell suddenly, explicitly, to her waistline.

"You're too old for children, remember?" she said with pure sarcasm.

He looked back up. His eyebrows arched. "I'm not too old to make them," he said with a soft threat in his deep voice. "So don't push too hard."

She felt alive; more alive than she had since she was single and Ted had been her whole world. She didn't understand her own bravado. But she did know that she wasn't afraid of what he was threatening. She wasn't afraid of him at all.

"If we had a child," she said deliberately, "it would have blue eyes."

His jaw tautened. He didn't reply. He turned away from her to look for his hat. "I have some business to take care of. If you want to tidy the office, go ahead. But don't move anything off the desk. I'll never be able to find it again."

"Okay."

"Where's Shep?"

"Over there." She gestured at the corner, and grinned. "Mrs. Bird boiled him a drumstick but he left it, to follow me."

He smiled at her. "You and that pup."

"He's the most wonderful present I ever had. I mean it."

"I know." He paused beside her on his way out and tilted her face up to his with a tender hand so that he could search her eyes. "I like seeing you smile. You don't do it very often these days."

"I'm getting better."

He nodded. His gaze fell to her mouth and the fingers on her chin went rigid.

"Afraid to kiss me?" she whispered boldly.

He smiled faintly. "Maybe I am. You and I are explosive."

Her eyes were curious. "Isn't it always like that, for a man?"

His thumb slid over her chin and moved up to tug at her soft lower lip. "Not for me," he confessed quietly. "I only feel this fever with you, Corrie," he whispered against her mouth as he took it.

It was a mistake. He knew it the minute he felt her lips part beneath the ardent pressure of his mouth. He groaned and dropped his hat on the floor in the rush of his need to get her against him. He half lifted her into his aroused body and his tongue penetrated the soft depths of her mouth. He felt her shiver and heard her moan, and the world spun away.

Someone was knocking at the door. He heard it, as if from deep in a well. He lifted his head and found himself fighting to breathe. Coreen's eyes were half-closed with desire, her mouth swollen and red, her body arched slightly, yielded, waiting. His hand was smoothing hungrily over her undamaged breast and he felt her heart beating like mad under it.

"What is it?" His voice sounded hoarse, even when he raised it.

"That man's here about the new combine, Mr. Regan!" one of his men called through the door.

"Tell him I'll be there in ten minutes!" he yelled back.

"Yes, sir!"

Footsteps died away. Coreen hadn't moved, or protested, or tried to pull away.

"Do you want more?" he asked coolly, angered by his own weakness.

She had no pride left. "Yes," she whispered, "please."

"Corrie…!"

"Please," she whispered again, tugging at his head.

Her eyes closed as he bent helplessly to her waiting mouth. The kiss was deeper this time, slower, more achingly thorough than ever before. His powerful legs trembled as she pushed closer to his aroused body and he felt her softness and warmth against him.

His lean hands found her hips and tugged her rhythmically against him while he kissed her until he had to stop for air.

"Do you realize that I could take you right here, standing up, right now?" he asked in a rough whisper.

"Yes," she said simply.

He parted her lips with his, and pushed his tongue slowly past her teeth once, twice, deeper with each movement. "Open your mouth a little more," he whispered raggedly. "Let me touch you…more deeply…inside!"

She cried out at the imagery and her whole body vibrated as he deepened the kiss to blatant intimacy. His legs parted and he pulled her between them, raising her so that they were perfectly matched, male to female. He groaned so harshly that her nails bit into him as she tried to get even closer, to satisfy the hunger in him that she could almost taste.

Her fingers went, trembling in their haste, to the buttons on his shirt. He made a feeble attempt to stay them, knowing too well what was going to happen to him if she touched his chest. But he didn't really want to stop her. Seconds later, when he felt her fingers caressing through the thick mat of hair that covered him to the waist and below, he shuddered and cried out.

She caught her breath at the unfamiliar sound. It excited

her even more to know that she could arouse him so easily. Instinctively, her mouth moved down to his chest and pressed hungrily against it through the thick mat of hair. His heartbeat shook her for the one, long instant that he gave in to his own need.

"No," he ground out, shuddering as he finally managed to pull her away and hold her back from him with bruising hands while there was still time. "Oh, God…no, Corrie!" he said hoarsely.

She lifted her face and looked into his ravaged eyes with slowly dawning comprehension. "I'd let you," she whispered feverishly.

His eyes closed and his teeth ground together. His hands on her shoulders hurt her while he fought his own desperate need.

"Ted, I'd let you," she repeated brokenly.

He rested his damp forehead against hers and dragged in enough breath to fill his lungs. "No. I could make you pregnant," he whispered, shaken.

He sounded as if that would be the end of the world as far as he was concerned. He didn't want a child. He didn't want commitment. In the fever of their kisses, she'd forgotten. But he hadn't. He was shaken, but not enough to forget the possible consequences of making love to her.

She took a long, shaky breath. "Yes," she said a minute later, "that's right. Silly of me…not to remember."

He barely heard her. His body was in the grip of a kind of pain he hadn't experienced since adolescence. "Stand still, honey," he whispered roughly. "Don't make it worse…."

She hadn't realized that she was shifting restlessly, brushing his hard body. She stood very still while he concentrated on his breathing until the rigor of his body began to relax. She watched him unashamedly, learning things about him, about men, that she hadn't known. Her eyes were curious, running over him like hands, searching out all the signs that gave away his raging desire and its slow—very slow—containment.

He felt her rapt eyes on his face. "Stop staring," he muttered as he took one last breath and the steely fingers on her shoulders began to relax.

"I'm curious," she said simply, and her gaze was faintly self-conscious. "I've never seen you like this."

His eyes speared into hers. "Proud of yourself?" he asked curtly.

She nodded. "In a way. Nobody ever wanted me that much. Does it hurt?"

He laughed coldly. "My God…!"

"Well, does it?" she persisted. "Some books say it does and some say it doesn't, but they all agree that a man can control it if he has to. Barry said he couldn't, and that was why he hurt me. But it wasn't true, was it?"

He let out one last deep breath. "It depends on how aroused he is." His eyes narrowed. "Did you work him up the way you just worked me up, and then refuse him?"

The light went out of her. He couldn't seem to accept that it wasn't her fault. She didn't realize that it was frustration talking.

She moved back from him. "I couldn't have worked him up if I'd been a born seductress," she said with quiet pride. "He pretended that I was cold. The fact was, he didn't want me. He never wanted me, not physically. He was…" She couldn't say it. She couldn't get the word out.

He was still straining to breathe normally. "He was what?"

"It doesn't really matter, does it? He's dead." She went to the office door and opened it. "I'd like a cup of coffee. I'll start working in here after I've had it, if that's all right."

"I'll be gone in five minutes," he said flatly. "You can start when I leave."

She nodded. She didn't look back on her way to the kitchen.

Ted went out the door in a flaming rage. Twice in one day he'd let her knock his legs out from under him. She'd seen how vulnerable he was to her, and put a weapon in her hands that she could break him with if she chose. He'd never been so helpless. Did she know? Of course she knew! And she had every reason in the world to use his own weakness against him. He didn't know how he was going to protect himself.

He couldn't come straight back home, he knew that. What he needed was breathing space. That was it. He needed a business trip. He walked toward the waiting mechanic down by the garage where the combine sat, racking his brain all the way for a legitimate reason to leave the ranch.

Coreen sat down to supper with Sandy, who seemed unusually quiet and puzzled. They started without Ted, and Mrs. Bird had only set two places.

"Is something wrong?" Coreen asked Sandy.

"I don't know." She studied the younger woman with evident puzzlement. "Have you and Ted had an argument?"

Coreen quickly lowered her eyes. "Sort of," she said. "Why?"

"He phoned Mrs. Bird and said that he was going to Nassau this afternoon. Without coming home to change, without packing…"

Coreen felt the blow all the way to her knees. So his opinion of her was really that low, was it? Now he thought she'd be laying in wait for him, trying to seduce him into marriage. He already thought she'd teased Barry into suicide by denying him her body. God knew what he thought of her after this afternoon's episode.

"I see," she said when she realized that Sandy was waiting for an answer.

"And he took Lillian with him, apparently."

That was the final straw. Coreen put down her fork and burst into tears.

"That's what I thought," Sandy murmured sadly. She got up and took Coreen into her arms. "Poor baby," she sympathized soothingly. "Love doesn't die just because we want it to, does it? Even after the way he's treated you, you can't stop."

"I hate him!" She choked. "I hate him!"

"Of course you do," Sandy said, comforting her. "He's an animal."

"He thinks I drove Barry to suicide by teasing him." She whimpered. "He still thinks I killed him!"

"No, he doesn't. He's just fighting a rear-guard action. He's convinced himself that he's too old for you and he isn't going to give in. He's let our childhood warp his whole life. I'm sorry that he's hurting you like this."

Coreen cried until her throat was raw. Then she dabbed at her eyes with the hem of her blouse and took the tissue Sandy handed her and blew her nose.

"I can't stay here anymore," she told Sandy when she was calm. "It's tearing me apart."

"I know. But you're not strong enough."

"I am. If you'll let me rent the apartment, and Ted will give me the living allowance he promised, I think I'm well enough to get a job. I can type and I can take dictation. There must be somebody in Victoria who'll hire me."

Sandy grimaced. "This won't do," she said. "You can't..."

"I have to!" Coreen's eyes were tortured. "I'd go to him on my knees, begging for anything he cared to give me, if I stayed. Don't you see? I love him!"

Sandy ground her teeth. "That bad, huh?"

"Oh, yes." Coreen laughed bitterly. "That bad. And he doesn't want commitment, children, or me in that order. He said so before he left." She didn't mention what had prompted it, or the close call they'd had in Ted's study.

She didn't need to. Sandy's eyes were shrewd and she wasn't blind to the tension between her best friend and her brother.

"He'll kill me when he comes back and finds you gone," she told Coreen.

"No, he won't. He'll be relieved," came the weary reply. "Will you help me?"

Sandy sighed heavily. "I don't suppose I have a choice."

Coreen smiled. "No. Neither do I. I'll be fine," she added reassuringly. "I'm much better."

Sandy didn't argue. Heaven knew, it was going to be unbearable for Coreen if Ted was as determined as usual to keep her at arm's length. The evidence of two years ago was still disturbing.

"What about Shep?" she asked.

Coreen didn't like thinking about leaving her puppy. "He'll have to stay here," she said miserably.

"I'll bring him to visit on weekends, how about that?" Sandy asked.

Coreen smiled through her tears. "You're the best friend I have."

"And you're mine. I wish my brother was less of a trial to both of us!"

A wish that Coreen silently affirmed.

Two days later, packed and silent, she rode to Victoria ahead of Sandy with her bags in the small foreign car that Sandy had loaned her to drive. Her ribs were still a little sore, but she was more than capable of getting around by herself.

The apartment was spacious, big enough for two people to

share and not run into each other. It even had a nice view. The girls stocked the refrigerator and shelves and then it was time for Sandy to go.

"You know the number at the ranch if you need me," she told Coreen, "and I'll be up with Shep next Saturday. You're sure you'll be all right?"

"This is Victoria, not New York," she murmured with a smile. "I'm perfectly safe here."

"I do hope so. Mrs. Lowery and her husband live in the unit next door. They're sweet old people. If you get in trouble, all you have to do is knock on the door. Mr. Lowery is a retired police officer," she added with a grin.

"I'll remember. Thanks, Sandy. For everything."

Sandy glowered at her. "I should have done this sooner," she said. "I kept hoping that Ted might relent. I should have known better. He's too old to change his ways now."

"That isn't really surprising, is it?" Coreen asked sadly. "If he'd wanted to marry anyone, he'd have done it long before now. I've been living in dreams. I always thought that if you loved somebody enough, they'd have to love you back. But it isn't like that." She brushed back her thick, short hair. "Amazing, isn't it, that I'm still mooning over the same man? And he still doesn't want me."

"I think you're wrong about that," Sandy said quietly. "I think he wants you very much."

"But not for keeps" came the sad reply.

Sandy couldn't deny it. Ted had made his choice very apparent. He was willing to leave the country with one woman to make another woman leave him alone. He gave hard lessons. Coreen wouldn't forget this one very soon.

"I'll see you Saturday. Call if you need anything."

Coreen assured her that she would. When the door closed, she was truly alone for the first time in years. Once she got used to it, she told herself, she was probably going to enjoy it. It was getting used to it that was going to be hard.

She spent a lonely weekend, hoping all the time that the telephone would ring and Ted would tell her he'd made a terrible mistake. She listened for his knock at the door. But Monday came, and Ted didn't. He was in Nassau with Lillian. Presumably he'd been making his feelings clear to Coreen. And he had. This time, she got the message. By Monday, she was resigned to a future that wouldn't ever contain Ted.

Sandy had given her a couple of places to apply for work, and she went not only to those, but to four others that she found on the bulletin board in the labor office. And miracle of miracles, one of her job leads panned out the very same day. A local real estate office had an immediate opening for a receptionist, and Coreen was exactly what the woman who ran the office had in mind.

She started work Tuesday. Her typing speed suited the agency very well, and her personality proved an asset to the business. She fielded appointments for her boss and the other four agents who worked out of the small office as if she'd been born to it. She went home tired at the end of the long day, because she wasn't used to this sort of work, but she loved what she was doing and it showed. She felt safe, secure in her own ability to hold down a job and pay the rent. Her self-esteem blossomed.

By Saturday, when Sandy arrived with an excited Shep in the car with her, Coreen was beaming. She'd had her hair trimmed and was wearing new clothes. She looked bright and happy, and the dark shadows under her blue eyes were beginning to recede.

"You look so much better!" Sandy exclaimed. "I can't get over the change in you!"

"Isn't it great?" came the bubbling reply. "I never dreamed how much fun it would be to work like this, with only myself to provide for. I make a salary with my own two hands and I don't have to ask anybody for anything! I won't even need the allowance from the trust, and I can pay rent on the apartment, too!''

Sandy looked hesitant. ''Don't get too independent too soon, will you? Take it easy. You're still not completely well, and you could overextend yourself.''

''Don't be such a worrywort,'' Coreen teased. By this time, she was on the floor playing with Shep. ''He's grown, hasn't he? Oh, I miss him so!''

She missed Ted, too, and watching the trainer work out with the horses. But she had to put up a good front. She couldn't let them think that she was pining for the ranch. For him.

It was such a good front that she convinced Sandy entirely. The older woman went back home morose and quiet, so that Mrs. Bird walked around worrying for another week.

Ted came home two weeks after he'd left, and in between there hadn't been a telephone call or even a postcard. He looked haggard. His tan was the only healthy-looking thing about him. His temper certainly hadn't improved in his absence. He was out near the stable giving two of his men hell over some tasks he'd assigned that hadn't gotten finished by his return.

He stormed back in just in time for supper. He sat down at the table and frowned when he noticed that Mrs. Bird had only set two places.

Sandy helped herself to roast and mashed potatoes while Ted fought not to ask the question he dreaded putting into words.

''Don't bother looking for her,'' Sandy said after a minute. ''She's gone.''

Chapter 9

"Coreen's gone?" Ted echoed. He glowered at his sister. "Where has she gone?"

"She moved up to Victoria two weeks ago. I've let her rent the apartment there. She has a job, too. She's receptionist to a real estate agency, and she's blooming."

It took him a minute to adjust to the news. He hadn't expected her to leave. He'd stayed away, hoping to get his passion for her under control before it broke the bonds completely. The way they'd loved had been so sweet that he hadn't slept a night since. He wanted her to the point of madness, but he couldn't afford to give in. It was what was best for her, he'd told himself when he left. But two weeks of self-denial had only made him bad-tempered. All he could think about was the years of anguish she'd spent with Barry because of him. He'd wanted to spare her the ordeal of being tied to an older man and being discontent. But he'd caused her such pain, all from noble motives. And what he'd done to himself didn't bear thinking about.

Then he remembered without wanting to that he'd found a job for Barney in Victoria. Did Coreen know that was where Barney was? Was that why she'd wanted to go there? She must have thought about why Ted had left so abruptly, and put his absence down to revulsion at her abandon in his arms or fear of being seduced by her. He'd even taunted her with Barry in his fervor to keep her from seeing his weakness for her. Had his abrupt departure pushed her into another man's arms, for the second time?

"Oh, no," he said wearily. He rested his forehead on his raised fists, propped on the table by his elbows. "God, not again!"

"What are you groaning about? By the way, how's Lillian?" Sandy asked pointedly while she munched on a small piece of roast beef.

"I don't know."

"You took her to Nassau. Did you misplace her?" she taunted.

He lifted his head and glared at her. "She was on the same plane with me. We weren't together."

"You said you were. You told Mrs. Bird you were."

He groaned again.

"It's just as well. Coreen cried for two days before she went to Victoria," she said, putting the knife into his heart with venomous accuracy. She wasn't sorry when he went pale. "She left here cursing you for all she was worth. But when I saw her Saturday, she was as bright as a sunbeam. She didn't even mention you."

He glared at his sister.

She ate another piece of meat. "This is delicious. Lost your appetite?" she asked pleasantly.

He pushed the plate aside and drank his coffee black. "Yes."

"You said that you didn't want her often enough. She finally listened. Aren't you glad?" she added.

He didn't answer her. He drank some more coffee.

"You're too old for her, remember?" she persisted. "And you don't want children. She's still young. She wants to get married and have a family. I heard Barney say the same thing to his father last month, that he was ready to settle down." She brightened as Ted went pale. "Say, didn't you get him a job in Victoria? Won't it be funny if they meet up there and end up married?"

Ted got up from the table, so sick that he couldn't look at food. He walked blindly into his study and slammed the door viciously behind him. He walked to the portable bar and picked up the whiskey bottle.

"No," he told himself. "No, this isn't the answer."

He stared at the squat crystal decanter and at the glass. "On second thought," he muttered, pulling out the stopper, "why the hell not?"

He was well into his second glass when he sat down behind the desk and let his imagination run wild. Coreen had probably already found Barney or vice versa. They were probably out together tonight, at a movie or a theater. He might even have driven her up to Houston to a show. He glowered at the desk, remembering how it had felt to have her lying on her back under his aching body, giving him kiss for feverish kiss. Would she kiss Barney that way?

He doggedly refused to remember that it hadn't been Coreen who'd pulled back at all. It had been himself. She'd even offered...

"No!"

His own voice shocked him. He was letting this business go to his head. His hormones were manipulating him. He couldn't give in, now. He knew that he was wrong for Coreen. She was too young for him. Even if she'd told the truth and she hadn't been able to want Barry, maybe she'd only turned to Ted out of frustration. After all, she'd wanted him years ago and he'd pushed her away. Maybe it was curiosity.

His clouded mind raced on. Or was it that she'd just re-discovered her femininity? She'd discovered that she could want someone after all, and he was male and handy. He didn't like that thought at all. He'd come home convinced that he was never going to be cured of his passion for her. He wanted her. He needed her. His own principles weren't enough to save him from his hunger. If she'd been here when he got home, nothing would have spared her. But she was gone, and he was caught between his hunger and his conscience all over again.

Despite her bad marriage, she was still capable of passion. Would it be the same with Barney that it had been with him? If it was only desire, wouldn't she be able to feel it for someone else as well as himself? Barry had treated her badly, but she'd wanted Ted so much. His head spun remembering how much. She'd begged him...

He took another drink, trying to drown out the sight of her drowsy, soft eyes as she begged for his mouth. He couldn't bear to remember that he'd pushed her away so cruelly and left. He always left, but she went with him anyway. That didn't make sense. But then, not much did. He stared at the decanter. How many drinks had he had: one or two? Or was it three? He was beginning to lose count. He was also feeling better about the situation. If only he could remember what the situation was....

Sandy found him slumped over the desk an hour later. She clucked her tongue.

"Poor old thing," she murmured, moving the whiskey de-canter back to the bar. "You just won't give an inch, will you?"

"She left me," he drawled half-consciously.

"You left her," she corrected him. "She's in love with you."

"No," he replied. "She never loved me. Too young to love like that."

"Love doesn't have an age limit," she told him. "She loved you all those long years, and you never did anything but push her away. First it was Barry. Now it's going to be Barney. She'll ruin her life. She'll waste it with other men, when all she wants in the world is just you, gray hair and all."

"Oh, God, I'm too old!" he growled. "Too old to be her husband, to be a father! She'd get tired of me, don't you see? She'd want someone younger, and I wouldn't be able to let her go!"

She frowned and stopped in place, staring down at him incredulously. Did he realize what he was admitting?

"Ted?" she said softly.

He put his head in his hands. "Nobody else," he said dizzily. "Nobody, since the first time I saw her, standing in the feed store in that old blouse and shorts. Wanted her so much. Wanted her more...than my own life. Never anybody else, in my life, in my heart, in my bed..." He sighed heavily and slumped, his head on his forearms. Beside him, Sandy gaped at his still figure. Why...he loved Coreen!

She didn't know what to do. She couldn't betray him. On the other hand, was he going to ruin his life and Coreen's by keeping his feelings to himself? She had to do something. But what!

In the end, there was nothing she could do. She half led, half carried him to the sofa and dumped him there, with a quilt from his bed for cover.

"You're going to hate yourself," she told his unconscious figure.

It was much later before he came out of it, groaning and holding his head. He was violently ill and he had a headache that wouldn't quit. He went to bed, oblivious to Sandy's worried eyes following him, and didn't surface until the next day.

By then, he was himself again, rigidly controlled and giving away nothing at all. He sat down to breakfast looking as bright as a new penny. Without a word, he dared Sandy to mention the day before.

"I have a job in Victoria today," she informed him. "I may stay overnight with Coreen, if I'm very late."

"Suit yourself."

She didn't look up. "Any messages?"

His pale eyes met hers head-on. "No."

She leaned back in her chair with her second cup of coffee in her hand. "You've already wasted two years of your life, and hers, being noble," she said bluntly. "Barney is just like Barry, happy-go-lucky and as shallow as a fish pond. He probably wouldn't hurt her, but she'd be just as unhappy with him. Suppose she falls headlong into another bad marriage?"

He didn't react at all. "It's her life. She has to make her own mistakes."

"You're her biggest one," she said, irritated beyond discretion. She put the cup down hard. "She's never loved anyone else. I don't think she can. And she's had nothing from you except rejection and heartache and cruelty." She got up from the table, glaring at him. "I'm sorry I ever became friends with her. Maybe if I hadn't, she'd have been spared all this misery."

His pale eyes lanced into hers. "You have no right to pry into my private life. Or Coreen's."

"I'm not trying to," she returned. "I won't make any attempts to play Cupid, I promise you. In return, you might consider keeping a respectful distance while Coreen gets over the last few miserable years of her life."

He glanced down at his plate. "That's what I intended all along."

"Good. Maybe I'm wrong about Barney. Maybe he'll be the best thing that ever happened to her."

His hand clenched on his coffee cup. "Maybe he will."

She hesitated, but there was really nothing more to say. She left him sitting there, his eyes downcast and unreadable.

* * *

Coreen had, indeed, discovered Barney. Rather, he'd discovered her, at a local fast-food joint one day when they were both catching a quick bite to eat. She'd been delighted to find a familiar face, and he was already infatuated with her. It had been a short jump from there to one date, and then another.

Sandy had come up for the night while she was on a job, and she hadn't mentioned Ted at all. But Coreen had mentioned Barney. She was enjoying her life, having decided that loving Ted was going to kill her if she didn't put a stop to it.

She put on a good front. Sandy could see right through it, and she hated the pain she read in Coreen's blue eyes when she didn't think it was showing. She hoped Ted knew what he was doing. He might have just lost his last chance for happiness. But she wished Coreen well, all the same. If Barney could make her happy—well, she deserved some happiness.

But love didn't develop between the two of them. Coreen enjoyed Barney's company, and he hers. They both knew that friendship was all they could expect, and not only because of Coreen's lingering feeling for Ted. Barney had found a woman whom he adored, too, but she was married. There was no hope at the moment that anything could develop there. He was like Coreen: awash in a tempest of feelings that he could never express.

It gave them something in common, and bound them closer together. Since they enjoyed the same sort of movies, they started sharing rental costs and spending Friday evenings at the apartment, watching the latest releases over popcorn and soft drinks.

When Sandy discovered this new ritual, she was amused at the innocence of it. Occasionally she dropped in to share the popcorn, and she and Barney became friends, too.

"You're spending a lot of time in Victoria lately," Ted said one Friday afternoon. "What's the attraction?"

"I like to see Coreen. And Barney, of course."

He went very still. "Barney?"

"I go up occasionally to watch movies with them at the apartment on Friday nights," she explained innocently. "They're always together these days. Friday is movie night."

His eyes flashed. "They're sleeping together in my apartment?" he blurted out furiously.

"Do you realize what you're saying?" she asked quietly. "Think, Ted. Is that really the sort of woman you think Coreen is?"

He was insanely jealous. He couldn't begin to think through his violent emotions. Coreen, with Barney...

"Don't you even realize how cruel Barry was to her?" she persisted. "Do you seriously believe that she could lead some sort of promiscuous existence after what she suffered with him? Don't you know that she's frightened of intimacy?"

"Not with me, she isn't," he said bluntly, and before he thought.

Her eyes widened and her mouth snapped shut.

"I haven't seduced her, if that's what the disapproving look signifies," he said with a mocking smile. "I still have a few principles that I haven't sold-out."

"You might have spared her that," she said.

"She might have spared me as well," he returned.

She relented a little. "I'm sorry. I suppose you think you're doing it for her, don't you?"

He averted his face. "You remember how it was when we were kids."

"And you don't," she said curtly. "Mother didn't love him. She never loved him. She loved what he had. She didn't even want us, because we interfered with her life-style. But he insisted, because he was crazy about kids."

"She loved him when they got married," he said doggedly.

"You don't believe that. You haven't believed it for a long time. It's something you've held on to, to give you a reason to keep Coreen at arm's length."

He didn't answer her. She could see the indecision and the pain in his face.

"Spill it," she said abruptly. "Come on, let's have all of it. What's the real reason?"

It was a shot in the dark, but his face went pale. So there was something...!

"Tell me!" she demanded.

He ground his teeth together. "Barry said that what she loved was my money. When I wouldn't play ball, she settled for his."

"And you believed him."

"It made sense. Look at me," he muttered. "I'm sixteen years her senior. Barry said we looked ridiculous together, that people laughed at the age difference."

"Barry was jealous of you, and he played on your conscience," Sandy replied. "You don't really believe these things, Ted. You can't."

He pushed the coffee cup away from his restless fingers and leaned back. "It happened once before," he reminded her. "When I was twenty-six, and I thought I might marry Edie."

"And then discovered that she was already bragging to her friends about all the expensive things she was going to buy herself when she got you to the altar. I remember."

He smiled faintly. "So do I," he said. "Coreen wants me, all right. She always has. But wanting isn't enough. And right now, I can't be sure that she isn't trying to gain back the self-esteem she lost because Barry called her frigid."

"Maybe she is," she said. "If that's the case, it's Barney who's helping her get it back."

His face went hard. "He's closer to her own age."

"Yes, he is," she agreed pleasantly. "And they get on

like a house on fire. He treats her so gently. Nothing like Barry did. He takes her out and buys her flowers and even cooks supper for her when she's tired. Quite a guy, Barney.''

He felt, and looked, sick to his stomach. He hadn't thought it was serious. From the tidbits of gossip Sandy let slip, he'd convinced himself that as far as Coreen was concerned, Barney was more like a girlfriend with chest hair than a boyfriend. Now, he wasn't so sure.

''I see.''

''I'm glad you've decided to let go, Ted,'' she said gently. ''It's a kindness, if you have nothing to give her. She's finding her own way now, standing on her own feet for the first time in her life. Away from you, she's a different woman.''

''Different how?'' he asked.

''She's happy,'' she said.

He got up from the table and left the room without another word. Watching him go, Sandy regretted what she'd said. If Coreen was just putting on an act, if she did still love Ted, then what Sandy had just told him might have destroyed her last chance for happiness.

It was Sunday. Coreen had gone to church with Barney and seen him off on a two-day business trip at the Victoria airport afterward. The apartment was very quiet now, and she couldn't find anything on television that she really wanted to watch.

The buzz of the doorbell was almost welcome, except that it was probably going to be a salesman or a neighbor wanting to chat. She wasn't in the mood for either.

Jeaned and T-shirted, and barefoot, she went to the door muttering and peeped through the keyhole. Her hand froze on the chain latch. She stared, drinking in the angry face of the man she'd hoped she might forget. Her eyes closed and she leaned against the door with her heart pounding audibly in her chest. *Ted!* It was Ted, and she loved him and wanted him. And he wanted no part of her.

"Open the door, Coreen," he said shortly.

"How do you know I'm home?" she demanded angrily. "I might be out, for all you know!"

"Obviously you aren't."

She sighed. If she'd kept her big mouth shut...

She pulled aside the chain latch and unwillingly opened the door. "Come in," she said in a subdued tone. "It's your apartment after all. I'm just the tenant."

He paused to close the door behind him before he followed her into the living room and sailed his cream-colored Stetson onto the counter of the bar. He was dressed in a suit and tie and he looked formal. His eyes drifted down to her pretty bare feet and he concealed a smile. Her slender figure was very well outlined in the close-fitting jeans she had on, and the T-shirt was almost see-through, despite its colorful message that invited people to visit Texas.

"How are you?" he asked.

She sat down on the arm of the big armchair. "As you see."

His pale eyes went around the room. There was no sign of occupation. She was here, but she'd made no mark on the room at all.

"I haven't trashed the furniture," she said, misunderstanding his scrutiny.

"No wrestling matches with Barney on my sofa on Friday nights?" he chided with more venom than he knew.

She lifted her chin. "We can always watch movies at Barney's apartment if you don't like me bringing him here," she said.

His eyes flashed angrily. They pinned her, making her feel like backing away. But she didn't. She'd gained new self-confidence over the weeks since Barry's death—mainly because of Ted himself. She stood her ground, and admiration filtered through the anger in his eyes.

"I don't give a damn what you do with Barney," he said.

As if she didn't already know that. His absence from her life in recent weeks had made his lack of interest plain.

But he looked worn. There was no other word to describe it. His lean face had deep hollows in it, and there were new lines around his firm mouth and between his eyes.

"You look tired," she said with involuntary gentleness.

Her words hardened him visibly, and at once.

"Oh, I know," she said heavily, "you don't want concern from me. God forbid that I should worry about you."

He stuck his hands into the pockets of his expensive slacks and went to stand by the window. It was a hazy summer day. He watched the clouds shift on the horizon, dark and threatening clouds that carried the promise of rain.

"Why did you come, Ted?" she asked after the long silence grew tedious.

He didn't turn. "I wanted to make sure that you were all right."

She didn't read anything into that statement. She stared at his back without blinking. "I'm fine. I have a good job and I'm making friends. I'll be able to do without that allowance, in fact. If I refuse it, can you give it to charity?"

He turned, frowning. "There's no need for gestures," he said coldly.

"It isn't a gesture. I don't want Barry's money. I never did." She smiled at his expression. "Disappointed? I know you'd rather think that I married him for all that nice money."

He didn't react at all. "There's no provision if you refuse the money. The trust will remain untouched."

She shrugged. "Then do what you like about it. But I won't accept it. I wouldn't have married Barry if it hadn't been for Papa, anyway. At least one good thing came out of it—he had the medical care he needed.''

''Why didn't you ask me for help?'' he demanded.

She lifted both eyebrows, astonished. ''It never would have occurred to me,'' she stammered.

''Your father was a friend of mine, as well as a business acquaintance,'' he said curtly. ''I would have done anything I could for him.''

She averted her eyes.

He moved closer. Something about her posture disturbed him. ''You're hiding something.''

She hesitated, but he looked capable of standing there all night until he got an answer. ''Barry warned me not to ask you for any financial help. He said that you'd told him you wanted me to marry him and get out of your hair. He made sure that I knew not to ask you.''

His breath left in a violent rush. ''My God,'' he said roughly. ''So that was it.''

''I didn't really need telling, Ted,'' she added quietly. ''You'd made it clear that you wanted nothing to do with me. Even when Dad was so sick, you hardly came near the place. And when you did…''

''When I did, I had nothing kind to say to you,'' he finished for her. ''Barry kept me upset. He wouldn't let me near you, did you know that? He said that you hated me.''

Her eyes lifted to his in time to see the flash of pain those memories kindled in his face.

''But I told him no such thing,'' she said hesitantly.

''Didn't you?'' He laughed bitterly. ''He said that you'd agreed to marry him because you thought he had more money than I did.''

Chapter 10

Coreen just stared at him. She wasn't going to make any more denials. If he believed her mercenary, let him.

He smiled at her stony countenance. "Yes, I know," he murmured, "I always think the worst of you, don't I? But he made it all sound so logical. Lie after lie, for two years and more, and I swallowed every one."

She traced a tiny smear of oil on the knee of her jeans. "They weren't all lies," she said. "He told you I was frigid, and I am."

"Not with me."

She lifted her eyes to his face. "There's more to intimacy than a few kisses, and you know it. You know what I mean, too. I destroyed him in bed. I made him incapable, every time…"

His face fascinated her. It looked like an image frozen in ice. "Do you realize what you're telling me?" he asked slowly.

"Yes," she said stiffly. "I'm telling you that I wasn't woman enough…"

"No!" He knelt beside the armchair, his eyes so close to hers that they filled the world. "Did he ever make love to you completely?"

"Completely?"

He told her, explicitly.

"Ted, for God's sake…!" She exploded.

She got up, and so did he. He caught her arms before she could move away. His face was drawn, almost white. He shook her gently. "Tell me!" he demanded.

"All right! No, he…he didn't!"

He didn't react for several seconds. When he did, it changed him. All the color rushed back into his lean face. He looked at Coreen with wonder, with fascination.

"You're still a virgin," he said unsteadily.

She glared at him. "Rub it in."

He couldn't seem to accept what he'd heard. He bit off a curse and got up, moving away from her. It had been bad enough before. Now it was unbearable. Corrie had never had a man. She'd been married, abused, tormented, but she'd never been intimate with Barry. She was chaste, in every real respect.

He ran his hand over his forehead, feeling perspiration there despite the air-conditioning in the apartment.

"What difference does it make now?" she asked angrily. "He's dead!"

"You really don't know, do you?" he asked. He didn't look at her.

"Know what?"

His hands balled into fists in his pockets. His head was bowed while he fought needs and desires that almost exploded into action.

He took a long breath and stared out the window. "How do you feel about Barney?" He glanced over his shoulder at her. "And please don't, for God's sake, tell me it's none of my business."

"It isn't," she said doggedly. But she relented. "He's my friend. We enjoy the same things."

"Do you love him?"

Her eyes answered him long before she averted them. "I like him," she hedged. "I'm not ready to love anyone," she added firmly. "I've just come through a disastrous marriage."

"I know that." He let out a long breath and turned to look at her, perched on the arm of the chair, looking belligerent and pretty. "Are you happy, Corrie?"

"Who is?" she replied quietly, with a cynicism far beyond her years. She tucked a lock of hair behind one small ear. "I'm content."

"Content." What a lukewarm word. It didn't suit someone like Corrie, who had been bright and beautiful before Barry made a hell of her life. Truthfully he hadn't done much to make her happy himself. All these years, he'd been thinking about himself, about protecting his heart from being broken, about preventing Corrie from taking over his life. He hadn't given a thought to how badly he was hurting her with his indifference, his cruelty.

"There must have been times when you blamed me for a lot of your problems," he said.

"Don't flatter yourself. I can make my own mistakes and pay for them. I don't have to blame them on other people."

He traced a pattern on the bar next to him. "I used to think that I didn't, either." His eyes were faraway, wistful. "Perhaps our view of ourselves is corrupted."

"You don't need anyone." She laughed. "You're completely self-sufficient."

His head turned toward her. "All I have is Sandy," he said quietly. "No one else. When she marries, I'll be completely alone with my principles and my conscience and my noble ideals. Do you think they'll keep me warm on long winter nights, Corrie, when I'm hungry for a woman in my arms in the darkness?''

She didn't like that thought. ''You don't have any trouble getting women.''

He lifted an eyebrow. ''Getting them, no. I'm sinfully rich.''

''Everyone knows that.''

He nodded. ''That's the problem. At my age, I never know the real motive when women come on to me.''

It sounded as if he might be trying to tell her something. She didn't know what. A brief silence fell between them. ''Would you like some coffee?'' she asked finally.

He nodded.

She went into the kitchen to make it, aware at intervals of his studious gaze from the living room. But he didn't join her, not until she had everything on a tray. He met her at the kitchen door and carried the tray to the coffee table.

''I made some sugar cookies yesterday,'' she said, indicating several of them on a small platter.

''And you think I have a sweet tooth?'' he asked with a faint smile as he sat down beside her on the sofa. He'd taken off his suit jacket and tie and rolled up the sleeves of his white linen shirt. He looked rakish with the top buttons of that shirt undone. She had to stifle a memory of opening them herself and touching him, kissing him, where the hair was thickest over those warm, firm muscles.

''You used to have one,'' she said finally.

''I'm partial to lemon....'' He bit into one and chuckled. She'd used lemon flavoring. ''Were you expecting me?'' he asked.

She was outraged. ''Of course not! I like lemon myself, so don't get arrogant, if you please.''

''Oh, I've given up arrogance, Corrie. It got too damned expensive. Put cream into this coffee for me, will you? No sugar.''

She complied. He couldn't do it himself, of course. He sat there in his lordly way watching her perform these menial tasks for him with the arrogance he said he'd forsaken. Fat chance!

She handed him the china cup and watched him balance it, in its saucer, on his broad, muscular thigh. She realized that she was staring and averted her attention to her own cup.

"Did you really bake the cookies?" he asked conversationally.

She nodded. "I've been studying cookbooks lately. I haven't made desserts in a long time. Dad was a borderline diabetic, remember? He wasn't supposed to have sweets and I didn't like to eat them in front of him."

"You can make these as often as you like," he murmured, finishing off another one. "They're good."

"Thanks." She nibbled on one without tasting it. "How's Sandy?"

"Missing you. So is Shep."

"She brought him to see me," she said.

"I know. He cries at night."

Her face stiffened. "When I get a place of my own, I'll bring him home."

"There's an easier way. Why don't *you* come home?"

She dropped her eyes. "The ranch isn't my home."

He finished his coffee and put the cup and saucer down on the table. Then he leaned back and slowly undid the rest of the buttons of his shirt, his eyes holding Coreen's relentlessly while he slid the fabric back from the thick salt-and-pepper hair that covered his broad chest.

Her lips parted as she tried to breathe normally. "Would you like some more coffee?" she asked a little breathlessly.

He shook his head slowly. He tugged the fabric out of his slacks and unfastened his belt. He slipped it out of the loops and tossed it to one side. Then he leaned back again, his legs splayed, and smiled at her with cool, dark arrogance. When he spoke, his voice was like velvet.

"Come here," he said.

Her eyes widened like saucers. Her heart began to run. It wasn't fair of him to taunt her this way, to invite her to make a fool of herself twice in one lifetime. Her lower lip trembled as she clamped down hard on her passion for him.

He began to smile, because he knew how hard it was for her to resist him. He'd always known.

"Afraid of me?" he taunted gently. "We'll go at your pace. I won't make you do anything you don't want to."

Her eyes burned with sudden tears as she remembered her own weakness, and what had followed it. "Are you having fun, Ted?" she asked, her voice choked. "Why don't you hit me and see if that feels as good as mocking me does?" She got up and started to leave the room.

He was faster. She'd barely gone two feet before he had her. She was caught and turned and held, her cheek against thick hair and damp muscle, the clean scent of him in her nostrils, the warmth of his body enveloping her.

"Don't cry," he whispered at her temple. His voice wasn't quite steady, and his hands were bruising against her back. "I'm not playing. Not this time."

"It will be just like it was before," she whispered brokenly, hitting him impotently with her fist. "You've hurt me enough…!"

His chest rose heavily under her cheek. "Yes. You, and myself. Now it all seems rather futile, although I meant well, at the time." He tilted her chin up so that he could see her ravaged face. "Take a good look, honey. I'm not a young man anymore."

"Did you ever notice how much younger Abby Ballenger is than Calhoun?" she asked solemnly.

He'd tried not to. The age difference between the long-married couple was pretty much the same as that between Ted and Coreen.

He frowned down at her. "Oh, yes," he said. "I've noticed."

"They have three sons," she reminded him. "And they've been married forever. Abby would die for Calhoun."

His jaw clenched. "No doubt he would for her, too."

Her eyes fell to his jutting chin and just above it to the long, firm lines of his mouth. The warm embrace was making her weak, just as being close to him always had. She wanted to crawl into his arms and stay there forever. But she had to remember that her time with him was limited to brief kisses that he always regretted and, somehow, made her pay for.

She let her eyes fall to his chest with a long sigh. "Isn't my time about up?" she asked.

"Up?"

"And by now, you should be feeling enough guilt to say something unpleasant and chase me away."

He grimaced as he stared over her head toward the wall beyond. "Is that what I do?"

"It used to seem like it."

He smoothed a lean hand over her hair and pressed her cheek closer to his bare flesh. The contact made his body ripple with pleasure. "I'll probably always feel a little guilt," he said deeply. "I could have spared you Barry."

"How? By sacrificing yourself in his place?" she asked with soft bitterness.

"It wouldn't have been a sacrifice." His mouth eased down to her forehead and pressed there softly, moving lazily to close both her eyes in turn. His warm hand cradled her cheek while his thumb moved over her lips. "Can you hear my heartbeat?" he whispered huskily.

"It's...very fast."

His hand moved down, slowly, over her breast to cup it

tenderly. The heel of his palm pushed against her. "So is yours," he murmured. "Fast and hard."

She had no secrets from him now. Her trembling seemed to accelerate at their proximity.

"Come closer," he murmured as his mouth hovered over hers. "I want to feel your legs against mine."

"Isn't it…dangerous?" she whispered.

"Yes."

The tender amusement belied the threat. She moved forward a step and caught her breath at the feel of his body so intimately.

"Don't pull away," he said at her lips. "I don't mind if you know how aroused I am. It doesn't matter anymore."

Her hands spread out on his bare chest, and they tingled at the contact.

"Caress me," he said huskily, nibbling her lips. "Drive me mad."

She brushed her palms against him and looked up into eyes that darkened with pleasure. "Do you like it?"

"I like it." He nuzzled her nose with his, her mouth with his lips. The silence in the room was shattered by the sound of their ragged breathing. "I'd like it better if I could feel you with nothing between us."

She must be crazy. In fact, she was convinced of it when her hands went to the fastening at her back and slipped it while her mouth answered the teasing of his lips. She pushed up her T-shirt and suddenly felt her breasts starkly bare against the thick mat of hair that covered his damp skin.

"God!" he groaned, going rigid.

She stood very still, her wide eyes seeking his for reassurance.

His hands were tremulous on her face as he tilted it up to his blazing eyes. "Open your mouth." He bit off the words against her lips.

It was the last thing she understood in the turbulent

minutes that followed. His hands, his mouth, the burning fever that no amount of contact seemed to quench made her mindless. His skin dragged against hers and she wept because she couldn't get close enough. She told him so in shaky whispers against his devouring mouth.

"There's only one way you and I will ever get close enough to each other," he said roughly. "And you know exactly what it is."

"Yes," she moaned. Her arms contracted around his bare back, her hands digging into the hard muscles of his shoulders. "Ted!"

He bent suddenly and lifted her into his arms. His eyes frightened her with their glitter. He hesitated, asking a question that he didn't have to put into words.

She buried her face in his throat and clung to him, shivering. Whatever he did now, it would be all right. If she had nothing else, she'd have now.

His arms shuddered as he stood there, feverish, aching for her.

"At least…make me pregnant," she whispered, anguished. "Give me that, if I can have nothing more."

The words shocked him. He looked down at the warm burden in his arms and felt them all the way to his heart. "Corrie!" he whispered.

Her eyes opened, dazed, helpless. "Is it really so shocking a thing to ask?" she asked miserably. "I know you don't want commitment. I won't ask anything of you, in case you're worried about that."

He couldn't speak. He clasped her to his heart and rocked her, poleaxed, lost for words.

"Oh, Ted, don't you want a child?" she asked in a wobbly whisper. "I'd take ever such good care of him, or her. And you could come and visit when you wanted to…"

His eyes closed on a harsh groan, and for an instant his arms hurt her.

She bit her lower lip. He hadn't moved. Not a step. He just stood there holding her, cradling her. Probably feeling sorry for her as he realized the depths of her humiliation, she thought miserably. He didn't know what to do now.

She forced herself to breathe slowly, so that her pulse rate began to lessen a little. She didn't know how she was going to ever look him in the eye again. She'd humbled herself too far this time, gambled for stakes that suddenly seemed impossibly high. When would she ever learn?

"Please put me down now, Ted," she said with the little bit of dignity she retained.

His mouth slid over her wet eyes and closed them. He didn't put her down. He moved toward the armchair and slowly dropped down into it, cradling her like treasure.

"Ted?" she repeated.

His cheek rubbed against hers as he searched blindly for her mouth. It was wet. But she couldn't think anymore, because he was kissing her. It felt very much like desperation, so urgent that she felt the bruising pressure of his mouth and arms like a brand.

Her hand went up to his lean face and traced its line from the temple. She touched his closed eye and felt the moisture that drained from it. It took a minute to register, and then her eyes flew open and she pulled back from him.

His pale eyes were as wet as his cheek. He stared into hers without embarrassment, without subterfuge.

"Lie still," he said roughly. He dealt with the disheveled fabric that only half concealed her and tossed it carelessly onto the floor. His hand traced her bare breasts, lingering on the long scar across one, tenderly exploring her in a silence that blazed with hope.

He bent toward her and, with aching tenderness, drew his mouth over the length of the scar.

He nuzzled the hard nipple with his nose and then his mouth, testing its firmness until she gasped.

"Would it embarrass you to breast-feed a child?" he whispered then.

Hope flared through her like wildfire. "No!"

His mouth opened on her with gentle hunger. He arched her up to his ardent lips and held her there, in a bow. "I probably won't be as fertile as a young man," he said gruffly. "It may take longer."

She gasped, cradling his face to her. She trembled with joy as understanding dawned.

He buried his lips between her breasts and he kissed his way down to her waistline, where his mouth rested hungrily for a long time.

When he finally came up for air, he moved them both to the sofa, where he stretched out with an exhausted Corrie in his arms. His long legs tangled with hers intimately, casually, as if they'd lain together like this all their lives.

His head rested on a sofa pillow while hers lay over his heart and listened to its heavy, hard beat. Skin against skin, breath against breath. The intimacy was as exciting as it was unexpected.

"Why did you stop?" she asked drowsily.

His hand smoothed down her back to her waist. "We aren't going to make our first child until we're married," he said softly.

She stiffened. "But...but you said..."

He rolled her over onto her back and looked down into her wide, tender blue eyes hungrily. "I said that we could try to make a baby together," he whispered. "I didn't say that I wanted our child to be illegitimate."

"You don't want to get married."

He kissed away the quick tears, smiling with cynical self-reproach. "No, I don't," he agreed quietly. "I think you'll grow tired of me in time and wish you'd waited for a younger man to love. But I suppose I'll have to deal with that when the time comes."

She searched his beloved face with eyes that worshiped it. "You'll have a very long wait," she whispered. "I fell in love with you when I was barely twenty. I've loved you every day since. I'd give up my home, my self-respect, my honor…my very life for you."

Dark color burned along his cheekbones. "Corrie…"

"It's all right, Ted. I know that you don't feel that way about me," she continued with quiet dignity. "But maybe after the children are born and you grow to love them, you'll be happy."

He was so choked with feeling that he could hardly speak. He touched her soft mouth lightly, searching for words. "It's so damned hard for me," he began.

She put her fingers over his mouth with a soft sigh. "You don't have to say a thing."

His pale eyes slid down her body and she winced.

"I'm sorry about the scar," she said, looking at it. "Maybe it will fade."

"Do you think I care?" he ground out.

She winced again at his tone. "Ted…"

"Your breasts are perfect," he said flatly. "Scar or no scar. You're perfect to me. You always have been. Always!"

She didn't know how to answer that.

He ran a rough hand through his damp hair, looked down at her and groaned. "I can't handle any more of this without doing something about it," he said huskily, and rolled away from her.

He got to his feet, walking away to the kitchen. He came back minutes later with a fresh pot of coffee. By then, Corrie had her clothing back in its former order and was trying not to meet his eyes.

He poured coffee, aware of her shy glances at his broad, bare chest.

"Like what you see?" he chided gently.

She glared at him. "You don't have to gloat."

"Sure I do." He chuckled. "It isn't every day that a woman offers herself up like a living sacrifice. Isn't that what they used to do with virgins in primitive times—offer them to some frightening monster as a deterrent?"

"You're not a monster," she returned, lifting her coffee to her mouth. "And I'm not afraid of you."

"I noticed," he said dryly. He leaned back, sliding an affectionate arm around her shoulders to draw her to his chest again. He lifted his legs onto the coffee table and crossed them lazily. "Where do you want to be married?"

Her eyes darted up to his face. "Are you sure?"

He nodded. "Where?"

"Jacobsville, then. And Sandy can be maid of honor."

"Since you're so keen on the Ballengers, I'll ask Calhoun to be best man."

She didn't know if he was being sarcastic, but it sounded that way. She was quiet.

He tilted her chin. "You're like an open book to me," he said solemnly. "I wasn't trying to sound cynical. Did I?"

She nodded.

He sighed. "You'll get used to me. A lot of times I say things in the heat of the moment that I don't really mean. I lose my temper sometimes when I shouldn't. I'm set in my ways."

"I know."

He lifted an eyebrow. "Second thoughts, Corrie?"

She stared into her coffee cup. "I want to have your baby," she whispered. "Ted, for heaven's…sake…!"

The coffee had gone everywhere, as if his hand had suddenly developed a huge spring. He muttered apologies and started grabbing for paper napkins to mop them both up.

"Don't say things like that to me when I've got a cupful of hot coffee, for God's sake!" he raged, glaring at her from his superior height. "Don't you know that it's taking every ounce of willpower I've got to sit here calmly with you when all I want to do is get you into the nearest bed!"

Chapter 11

Coreen flushed wildly at the stark exclamation. "Well, you don't have to make it sound like some sinful orgy, do you?"

"That's what it is," he returned. "Sinful. Dangerous. Delicious. Forbidden."

"You want it, too," she accused.

"I want you," he said heavily. "You! It never stops." His eyes betrayed him, for once. "It never has and it never will."

The confession made her breathless. She sat down, ignoring the coffee stains on the sofa, and stared up at him helplessly.

"Why don't you laugh?" he demanded. "Don't you feel entitled to rub my nose in it? I've given you enough hell over the years that you should feel vengeful."

"All I feel is hungry," she whispered. "I love you so much, Ted," she added on a shaky breath. "More than you could imagine in your wildest dreams."

His face went hard. "Prove it. Marry me tomorrow."

"Tomorrow," she agreed huskily.

"No protests? No postponements?"

She shook her head.

He nodded slowly. "All right."

He left five minutes later. The next morning they were married by a nervous justice of the peace in Jacobsville, with a shocked and delighted Sandy for maid of honor and a highly amused Calhoun and Abby Ballenger for witnesses.

After the ceremony, everyone congratulated her and then Ted, and walked out arm in arm, speaking in incredulous whispers.

"Shell-shock," Ted informed Coreen when they were back at the Victoria apartment two hours later. "They think I've lost my mind."

"So do I," she agreed.

He turned, his pale eyes possessive on his new wife in her neat white suit and pale pink blouse. There had been a pillbox hat with the ensemble and a white veil over it. Ted had lifted the veil to kiss her with brief affection in the justice of the peace's office.

"I want you," he said roughly. "Right now."

She flushed. She'd thought they might have a meal, go to a movie, do something together. Apparently this was his idea of togetherness, and perhaps the only sort he wanted with her.

"All...all right," she said, taken aback.

He shepherded her into the bedroom, closed and locked the door and took the phone off the hook. It wasn't even dark, and she was intimidated by the passion in his eyes and the urgency of his hands on her clothing.

"I won't hurt you," he said unevenly as he divested her of jacket, blouse and skirt in short order. "I swear to God I won't. Just...bear with me, if you can."

"Of course," she said nervously.

He slid the rest of her clothing from her stiff body and

lifted her gently onto the bed. His pale eyes wandered over her like loving hands, lingering, possessing until a muffled groan broke from his tight lips.

He sat down and pulled off his boots. Coreen turned her head away while he undressed, dreading her own inability to respond so quickly to him.

Scant minutes later, he pulled her into his arms and she felt the impact of his nudity against her like a long, hot brand. She gasped.

He broke her mouth open under his, and his hands began to smooth over her back in long, slow caresses. She felt his arousal against her smooth belly and stiffened.

"Open your eyes," he said huskily. "Watch me while I take you."

She flushed as she complied, her embarrassment plain in the eyes that watched him lever above her.

He coaxed her legs apart and eased between them. She felt him in total intimacy and was shocked into looking down. Her eyes widened and her body went rigid.

"So that's what you think," he murmured gently, and smiled. He chuckled as he settled himself against her and relaxed. "No," he said. "Not quick. Not this time. I only want you to get used to the feel of me. But you'll beg me before you get me."

She didn't understand. Not then. But fraught minutes later, after his mouth had explored every silken inch of her and then his hands had kindled sensations that had to be sinful because of their incredible stimulation, she did understand.

She was perspiring madly, shivering all over with a throbbing ache in her lower body that was new and frightening. And he kept the intimate contact between them, but when she lifted her hips to coax him into possession, he lifted free of her tempting pressure.

By the third time it happened, she was in tears. "Oh...please," she sobbed, lifting to him in such a tense arch that her whole body shuddered with the strain. "Oh, please, it aches...so!"

"Aches," he agreed huskily. "Burns. Throbs like a wound." His lean hand slid up her thigh and caught it firmly. "Look, Corrie. Look!"

He pulled her up toward the hovering threat of his masculinity and slowly, tortuously, let his body ease into hers.

She gasped, shivering, at the feel of him. She was so aroused that the tiny hesitation her body caused him was only part of the miracle. She looked down and her eyes dilated feverishly as she saw them join.

Her rose flush mirrored his own fascination. None of his experiences had prepared him for the shock of her virginity, or its implications. He was her first lover. In spite of everything, he was the first.

His fingers dug into her soft thigh and he caught his breath. "My God," he whispered, awed.

Her own eyes sought his then, wet with tears, wide with wonder.

His teeth clenched at the hot wave of pleasure that shot through him as he felt her take him completely. He met her eyes for a second before he groaned and lost control.

She felt the impact of his weight on her as he pressed her hungrily into the mattress, his hands under her hips, his muscular body suddenly dancing with hers in a rhythm that she felt to the soles of her feet.

"Match me," he whispered urgently into her mouth. "Yes...yes! Take me...take all of me....take me, Corrie!"

She cried out as the deep, dragging pleasure suddenly spread over her like fire, throbbing, throbbing, throbbing!

He groaned harshly and his breath raked his throat as he gave in to the same madness that had her in its sweet grip. For endless, aching seconds, they shared the same soul.

His forehead was damp against her breasts. She felt her

heartbeat, like an unsprung watch, shaking him in her clasping arms.

"I couldn't have waited one more minute," he whispered harshly. "Years of waiting, years of holding you in my arms, only to wake at dawn and find you gone!" His arms tightened and his mouth moved hungrily against her body. "I've got you now. You're mine, and I'll never let you go!"

Coreen heard him, but it took a minute for the words to register. "Years?"

"Years." He nuzzled his face against her soft breast. "Corrie, I haven't had a woman in almost three years," he said heavily.

She went very still in his arms. "But…but all those photos in the gossip columns!"

"Window dressing," he murmured with a harsh laugh. "I couldn't even feel desire for anyone else. You were all I wanted. Only you, Corrie."

"But you let me marry Barry! You said…you said you didn't want me!"

His arms contracted. "I tried so hard to be noble," he said, his voice tormented. "I wanted to spare you a husband so much older than you, whom you might regret marrying one day, don't you see? I had no idea, none at all, what a hell Barry would make of your life! I have even that on my conscience." His voice went husky. "I loved you. Loved you more than honor. More than self-respect. More than my life."

Her own words. Echoed. Felt. She closed her eyes and tears slid from them, burning her cheeks. She began to sob.

Vaguely she heard him gasp, felt his mouth taking away the tears, soothing away the pain. He eased over her, his body as gentle as his mouth, loving her with motions as tender as they were stimulating. Possessing her all over again, but with such love that she wept all through it, until the contractions began deep in her body and echoed in his, until they lay as close as two souls, straining together in the soft explosion of ecstasy that formed total communion.

He didn't move away afterward. He held her to him while he rolled over onto his back, sparing her his weight. But they were still joined, completely.

He drew in a shaken breath, feeling her so much a part of him that when he breathed, her body moved with him.

"It will be like this every time, now, when we love," he said deeply, smoothing her back with lean, tender hands.

She smiled and kissed his damp chest. "When we love," she echoed shakily. Her hands clung to him. "Don't ever let go."

His arms enfolded her and he smiled with loving exhaustion. "Well…maybe just long enough to eat," he murmured dryly. "Eventually."

Sandy glowered at both of them when they told her, six weeks later, that she was going to be an aunt.

"It's positively indecent," she muttered. "You've only been married six weeks today!"

Ted managed to look proud and sheepish all at once, his hand tight around Coreen's as she looked up at him with pure adoration.

"We're in a hurry," he said.

"No kidding!" Sandy said sarcastically.

"I'm not getting any younger," he continued, but without any traces of resentment or bitterness.

"And we did have in mind a baseball team," Coreen lied, tongue-in-cheek.

Sandy burst out laughing and hugged them both. "Well, I'm very happy," she confessed. "But what are people going to say?"

Actually they said very little. Mostly they grinned at the inseparable newlyweds who were so obviously in love and offered double congratulations.

As Ted later told his beaming wife, it was mostly his pride that had kept him from proposing to her years ago. Now Regan's pride was his wife—and the child they would both welcome.

*   *   *   *   *

THAT BURKE MAN

Chapter 1

Todd Burke sank lower in the rickety chair at the steel rail of the rodeo arena, glowering around him from under the brim of his Stetson. He crossed one powerful blue-jeaned leg over the other and surveyed his dusty, cream-colored boots. He'd worn his dress ones for the occasion, but he'd forgotten how messy things got around livestock. It had been a long time since he'd worked on his father's ranch, and several months since Cherry's last rodeo.

The girl had a good seat for riding, but she had no self-confidence. His ex-wife didn't approve of Cherry's sudden passion for barrel racing. But he did. Cherry was all he had to show for eight years of marriage that had ended six years ago in a messy divorce. He had custody of Cherry because Marie and her new husband were too occupied with business to raise a child. Cherry was fourteen now, and a handful at times. Todd had his own worries, with a huge computer company to run and no free time. He should make more time for Cherry, but he couldn't turn over the reins of his company to subordinates. He was president and it was his job to run things.

But he was bored. The challenges were all behind him. He'd made his millions and now he was stagnating for lack of something to occupy his quick, analytical mind. He was taking a few weeks off, reluctantly, to get a new perspective on life and business during Cherry's school holidays. But he was tired of it already.

He hated sitting here while he waited for Cherry's turn to race. He and Cherry had moved to Victoria, Texas, just recently, where his new head offices were located. Jacobsville, the little town they were now in, attending the rodeo, was a nice, short drive from Victoria, and Cherry had pleaded to come, because a barrel-racing rodeo champion she idolized was supposed to accept an award of some sort here tonight. Cherry's entry in the competition had been perfunctory and resigned, because she didn't ride well before an audience and she knew it.

Her name was called and he sat up, watching his daughter lean over her horse's neck as she raced out into the arena, her pigtail flying from under her wide-brimmed hat. She looked like him, with gray eyes and fair hair. She was going to be tall, too, and she was a good rider. But when she took the first turn she hesitated and the horse slowed almost to a crawl. The announcer made a sympathetic sound, and then she did it again on the next turn.

Todd watched her ride out of the arena as her part in the competition was finished. He had a heavy heart. She'd been so hopeful, but as always, she was going to finish last.

"What a shame," came a quiet, feminine voice from down the aisle. "She just freezes on the turns, did you see? She'll never be any good as a competitor, I'm afraid. No nerve."

A male voice made a commiserating comment.

Todd, infuriated by the superiority in that female voice,

waited for its owner to come into view with anger building inside him. When she did, it was a surprise.

The tall beautiful blonde who'd said those things about Cherry Burke was just complimenting herself on her steady progress. For the first time in months, Jane Parker was managing without her wheelchair or her cane. Moreover, her usual betraying limp hadn't made an appearance. Of course, she was fresh because she'd rested all day, and she hadn't strained her back. She'd been very careful not to, so that she could get through the opening ceremonies of the annual Jacobsville Rodeo and wait until its end when she was going to accept a plaque on behalf of her father. Tim had raged at her for agreeing to ride today, but it hadn't done any good. After all, she was her father's daughter. Her pride wouldn't let her ride out into the arena in a buckboard.

She stopped along the way to watch the youth competition in barrel racing. That had been her event, and she'd won trophies for it in this and other rodeos around Texas since grammar school. One particular girl caught her eye, and she commented critically on the ride—a poor one—to one of the seasoned riders leaning on the iron arena rail beside her. It was a pity that the girl hadn't finished in the money, but not surprising.

The girl was afraid of the turns and it showed in the way she choked up on the reins and hindered the horse. Jane commented on it to the cowboy. The girl must be new to rodeo, Jane thought, because her name wasn't one she knew. Here in south Texas, where she'd lived all her life, Jane knew everyone on the rodeo circuit.

She smiled at the cowboy and moved on, shaking her head. She wasn't really watching where she was going. She was trying to straighten the fringe on her rhinestone-studded white fringe jacket—which matched her long riding skirt and boots—when a big, booted foot shot across the narrow space between the trailers and slammed into the bottom metal rail of the rodeo arena, effectively freezing the elegant glittery blonde in her tracks.

Shocked, she looked down into steely gray eyes in a lean face framed by thick, fair hair.

The cowboy sitting on the trailer hitch was braiding several pieces of rawhide in his strong fingers. They didn't still, even when he spoke.

"I heard what you just said to that cowboy about Cherry Burke's ride," he said coldly. "Who the hell do you think you are to criticize a cowgirl in Cherry's class?"

She lifted both eyebrows. He wasn't a regular on the Texas circuit, either. She and her father had circled it for years. "I beg your pardon?"

"What are you, anyway, a model?" he chided. "You look like one of those blond dress-up fashion dolls in that outfit," he added as his eyes punctuated the contempt of his voice. "Are you shacking up with one of the riders or are you part of the entertainment?"

She hadn't expected a verbal attack from a total stranger. She stared at him, too surprised to react.

"Are questions of more than one syllable too hard for you?" he persisted.

That got through the surprise. Her blue eyes glittered at him. "Funny, I'd have said they're the only kind you're capable of asking," she said in her soft, cultured voice. She looked at his leg, still blocking her path. "Move it or I'll break it, cowboy."

"A cream puff like you?" he scoffed.

"That's where you're wrong. I'm no cream puff." In his position on the hitch, he was precariously balanced. She reached over, grimacing because the movement hurt her back, caught his ankle and jerked it up. He went over backward with a harsh curse.

She dusted off her hands and kept walking, aware of a

wide grin from two cowboys she passed on her way to the gate.

Tim Harley, her middle-aged ranch foreman, was waiting for her by the gate with Bracket, her palomino gelding. He held the horse for her, grimacing as he watched her slow, painful ascension into the saddle.

"You shouldn't try this," he said. "It's too soon!"

"Dad would have done it," she countered. "Jacobsville was his hometown, and it's mine. I couldn't refuse the invitation to accept the plaque for Dad. Today's rodeo is dedicated to him."

"You could have accepted the plaque on foot or in a buckboard," he muttered.

She glared down at him. "Listen, I wasn't always a cripple…!"

"Oh, for God's sake!"

The sound of the band tuning up got her attention. She soothed her nervous horse, aware of angry footsteps coming along the aisle between the trailers and the arena. Fortunately, before the fair-haired cowboy got close, the other riders joined her at the gate and arranged themselves in a flanking pattern.

The youth competition marked the end of the evening's entertainment. The money for top prizes had been announced and awarded. The band began to play "The Yellow Rose of Texas." The gate opened. Jane coaxed Bracket into his elegant trot and bit down on her lower lip to contain the agony of the horse's motion. He was smooth and gaited, but even so, the jarring was painful.

She didn't know if she'd make it around that arena, but she was going to try. With a wan smile, she forced herself to look happy, to take off her white Stetson and wave to the cheering crowd. Most of these people had known her father, and a good many of them knew her. She'd been a legend in barrel racing before her forced retirement at the age of twenty-four. Her father often said that she was heaven on a horse. She tried not to think about her last sight of him. She wanted to remember him as he had been, in the time before...

"Isn't she as pretty as a picture?" Bob Harris was saying from the press booth. "Miss Jane Parker, ladies and gentlemen, two-time world's champion barrel-racer and best all around in last year's women's division. As you know, she's retired from the ring now, but she's still one magnificent sight on a horse!"

She drank in the cheers and managed not to fall off or cry out in pain when she got to the reviewing stand. It had been touch and go.

Bob Harris came out into the arena with a plaque and handed it up to her. "Don't try to get down," he said flatly, holding a hand over the microphone.

"Folks," he continued loudly, "as you know, Oren Parker was killed earlier this year in a car crash. He was best all-around four years running in this rodeo, and world's champion roper twice. I know you'll all join with me in our condolences as I dedicate this rodeo to his memory and present Jane with this plaque in honor of her father's matchless career as a top hand and a great rodeo cowboy. Miss Jane Parker, ladies and gentlemen!"

There were cheers and more applause. Jane waved the plaque and as Bob held the microphone up, she quickly thanked everyone for their kindness and for the plaque honoring her father. Then before she fell off the horse, she thanked Bob again and rode out of the arena.

She couldn't get down. That was the first real surprise of the evening. The second was to find that same angry, fairhaired cowboy standing there waiting for her to come out of the ring.

He caught her bridle and held her horse in place while he glared up at her. "Well, you sure as hell don't look the part," he said mockingly. "You ride like a raw beginner, as stiff as a board in the saddle. How did a rider as bad as you ever even get to the finals? Did you do it on *Daddy's* name?"

If she'd been hurting a little less, she was certain that she'd have put her boot right in his mouth. Sadly she was in too much pain to react.

"No spirit either, huh?" he persisted.

"Hold on, Jane, I'm coming!" came a gruff voice from behind her. "Damned fool stunt," Tim growled as he came up beside her, his gray hair and unruly beard making him look even more wizened than normal. "Can't get off, can you? Okay, Tim's here. You just come down at your own pace." He took the plaque from her.

"Does she always have to be lifted off a horse?" the stranger drawled. "I thought rodeo stars could mount and dismount all by themselves."

He didn't have a Texas accent. In fact, he didn't have much of an accent at all. She wondered where he was from.

Tim glared at him. "You won't last long on this circuit with that mouth," he told the man. "And especially not using it on Jane."

He turned back to her, holding his arms up. "Come on, pumpkin," he coaxed, in the same tone he'd used when she was only six, instead of twenty-five as she was now. "Come on. It's all right, I won't let you fall."

The new cowboy was watching with a scowl. It suddenly had occurred to him that her face was a pasty white and she was gritting her teeth as she tried to ease down. The wizened little cowboy was already straining. He was tiny, and she wasn't big, but she was tall and certainly no lightweight.

He moved forward. "Let me," he said, moving in front of Tim.

"Don't let her fall," Tim said quickly. "That back brace won't save her if you do."

"Back brace...?" It certainly explained a lot. He felt it when he took her gently by the waist, the ribbing hard under his fingers. She was sweating now with the effort, and tears escaped her eyes. She closed them, shivering.

"I can't," she whispered, in agony.

"Put your arms around my neck," he said with authority. "I'll take your weight. You can slide along and I'll catch you when you've got the other foot out of the stirrup. Take it easy. Whenever you're ready."

She knew that she couldn't stay on the animal forever, but it was tempting. She managed a wan smile at Tim's worried figure. "Don't natter, Tim," she whispered hoarsely. "I've got this far. I'll get the rest of the way." She took a deep breath, set her teeth together and pulled.

The pain was excruciating. She felt it in every cell of her body before the cowboy had her carefully in his arms, clear of the ground, but she didn't whimper. Not once. She lay there against his broad chest, shuddering with pain.

"Where do you want her?" he asked the older man.

Tim hesitated, but he knew the girl couldn't walk and he sure as hell couldn't carry her. "This way," he said after a minute, and led the tall man to a motor home several hundred yards down the line.

It was a nice little trailer, with a large sitting area. There was a sofa along one side and next to it, a wheelchair. When the cowboy saw the wheelchair, his face contorted.

"I told you," Tim was raging at her. "I told you not to do it! God knows how much you've set yourself back!"

"No...not there!" Jane protested sharply when he started to put her down in the wheelchair. "For God's sake, not there!"

"It's the best place for you, you silly woman!" Tim snapped.

"On the sofa, please," she whispered, fighting back a sharp moan as he lowered her gently to the cushions.

"I'll get your pain capsules and something to drink," Tim said, moving into the small kitchen.

"Thank you," Jane told the tall cowboy. It was a grudging thank-you, because he'd said some harsh things and she was angry.

"No need," he replied quietly. "You might have stopped me before I made a complete fool of myself. I suppose you've forgotten more about racing than Cherry will ever learn. Cherry's my daughter," he added.

That explained a lot. She grimaced as she shifted. "I'm sorry you took the criticism the wrong way, but I won't apologize for it," she said stiffly. "She's got the talent, but she's afraid of the turns. Someone needs to help her…get better control of her fears and her horse."

"I can ride, but that's about it. I don't know enough about rodeo to do her any good," he said flatly, "even though we're as crazy about rodeo in Wyoming as you Texans are."

"You're from Wyoming?" she asked, curious.

"Yes. We moved to Texas a few weeks ago, so that…" He stopped, strangely reluctant to tell her it was because he'd moved his company headquarters there to deal with an expanded market in Texas. "So that we could be closer to Cherry's mother," he amended. In fact, that hadn't influenced his decision to move to Victoria. Marie was no one's idea of a mother, and she'd been overly critical of Cherry for some time. It was a coincidence that Marie and her husband moved to Victoria from Houston about the same time Todd had moved his company headquarters there. Or so Marie said. "She and her second husband live in Victoria."

She let her eyes slide over his lean, hard face. "Does her mother ride? Couldn't she help her?"

His eyes seemed to darken. "Her mother hates horses. She didn't want Cherry in rodeo at all, but I put my foot down. Rodeo is the most important thing in Cherry's life."

"Then she should be allowed to do it," she agreed, and she was thinking how sad it was that he and his wife were divorced. His poor little girl. She knew what it was like to grow up without a mother. Her mother had died of pneumonia when she was barely in school.

She glanced back at the man. He'd said they were from Wyoming. That explained the lack of a Texas accent. She lay back, and the pain bit into her slender body like teeth. Hot tears wet her eyes as she struggled with the anguish it caused her just to move.

Tim came back and handed her two capsules and a cola. She swallowed the medicine and sipped the cold liquid, savoring the nip of it against her tongue. If only the pain would stop.

"That's sweet," she said with a sigh.

The tall man stood looking down at her with a frown. "Are you all right?"

"Sure," she said. "I'm just dandy. Thanks for your help."

She wasn't forthcoming, and he had no right to expect it. He nodded and moved out of the trailer.

Tim came after him. "Thanks for your help, stranger," he said. "I'd never have got her here by myself."

They shook hands. "My pleasure." He paused. "What happened to her?" he added abruptly.

"Her daddy wrecked the car," he said simply. "He was killed instantly, but Jane was pinned in there with him for three hours or more. They thought she'd broken her back," he concluded.

There was a harsh intake of breath.

"Oh, it was a herniated disk instead. It's painful and slow to heal, and she'll most always have some pain with it. But they can work miracles these days. She couldn't walk right away, though, and we weren't sure if she'd be paralyzed. But she got up out of that bed and started working on herself. Stayed in physical therapy until even the doctors grinned. Never knew a girl like her," he mused. "This thing has taken some of the fight out of her, of course, but she's no quitter.

Her dad would have been proud. Sad about her career, though. She'll never ride in competition again.''

"What in hell was she doing on that horse this morning?''

"Showing everybody that nothing short of death will ever keep her down," Tim said simply. "Never did catch your name, stranger.''

"Burke. Todd Burke.''

"I'm Tim Harley. I'm proud to meet you.''

"Same here.'' He hesitated for just a minute before he turned and went back along the aisles. He felt odd. He'd never felt so odd in his life before. Perhaps, he thought, it was that he wasn't used to proud women. She'd surprised him with the extent of her grit and stubbornness. She wasn't a quitter, in spite of impossible circumstances. He didn't doubt that she'd ride again, either, even if she didn't get back into competition. God, she was game! He was sorry he'd managed to get off on the wrong foot with her. He'd been irritated by the remarks she'd made about his daughter. Now he realized that she was trying to help, and he'd taken it the wrong way.

He was sensitive about Cherry. His daughter had taken more vicious criticism from her own mother than she was ever likely to get from a stranger. He'd overreacted. Now he was left with a case of badly bruised pride and a wounded ego. He smiled a little bitterly at his own embarrassment. He deserved it, being so cruel to a woman in that condition. It had been a long time since he'd made a mistake of such magnitude.

He wandered back down the lane to join his daughter, who was excitedly talking to one of the rodeo clowns.

"Dad, did you see her, that blond lady who accepted the plaque?'' she asked when he was within earshot. "That was Jane Parker herself!''

"I saw her.'' He glanced at the young cowboy, who

flushed and grinned at Cherry, and then quickly made himself scarce.

"I wish you wouldn't do that," Cherry said on a sigh. "Honestly, Dad, I'm fourteen!"

"And I'm an old bear. I know." He threw an affectionate arm around her. "You did fine, partner. I'm proud of you."

"Thanks! Where did you disappear to?"

"I helped your idol into her motor home," he said.

"My idol…Miss Parker?"

"The very same. She's got a bad back, that's why she doesn't ride anymore. She's game, though."

"She's the best barrel racer I ever saw," Cherry said. "I have a video of last year's rodeo and she's on it. The reason I begged to come to this rodeo was so that I could meet her, but she isn't riding this time. Gosh, I was disappointed when they said she'd retired. I didn't know she had a bad back."

"Neither did I," he murmured. He put an arm around her and hugged her close. She was precious to him, but he tended to busy himself too deeply in his work, especially in the years since her mother had walked out on them. "We haven't had much time together, have we? I'll make it up to you while we're on vacation."

"How about right now?" She grinned at him. "You could introduce me to Miss Parker."

He cleared his throat. How was he going to tell her that her idol thought he was about as low as a snake?

"She's so pretty," Cherry added without waiting for his answer. "Mother's pretty, too, but not like that." She grimaced. "Mother doesn't want me to come up next week, did she tell you?"

"Yes." He didn't add that they'd argued about it. Marie didn't spend any more time with Cherry than she had to. She'd walked out on the two of them for another man six years ago, declaring that Cherry was just too much for her to handle. It had devastated the young girl and left Todd

Burke in the odd position of having to forego board meetings of his corporation to take care of his daughter. He hadn't minded, though. He was proud of the girl, and he'd encouraged her in everything she wanted to do, including rodeo. Marie had a fit over that. She didn't approve of her daughter riding rodeo, but Todd had put his foot down.

"What does she see in him?" Cherry asked, her gray eyes flashing and her blond pigtail swinging as she threw up her hands in a temper. "He's so picky about everything, especially his clothes. He doesn't like pets and he doesn't like children."

"He's brilliant. He has a national bestseller. It's number one on the *New York Times* list. It's been there for weeks," Todd replied.

"You're smart, too. And you're rich," she argued.

"Yes, but I'm not in his class. I'm a self-made man. I don't have a Harvard degree."

"Neither does he," Cherry said with a giggle. "He hasn't graduated. I heard Mama say so—not so that he could hear her, though."

He chuckled. "Never you mind. If she's happy, that's fine."

"Don't you love her anymore?" she asked.

His arm contracted. "Not the way I should to be married to her," he said honestly. "Marriage takes two people working to make each other happy. Your mother got tired of the long hours I had to spend at work."

"She got tired of me, too."

"She loves you, in her way," he replied. "Don't ever doubt that. But she and I found less in common the longer we lived together. Eventually we didn't have enough to sustain a marriage."

"You need someone to look after you," she told him. "I'll get married one day, you know, and then where will you be?"

He chuckled. "Alone."

"Sure," she agreed, "except for those women you never bring home."

He cleared his throat. "Cherry…"

"Never mind, I'm not stupid." She looked around at the dwindling crowd. "But you need someone to come home to, besides me. You work late at the office and go on business trips all over the place, and you're never home. So I can't go home, either. I want to go to school in Victoria in the fall. I hate boarding school."

"You never told me that," he said, surprised.

"I didn't want to," she admitted reluctantly. "But it's just awful lately. I'm glad I'm out for the summer." She looked up at him with gray eyes so similar to his own. "I'm glad you took this vacation. We can do some things together, just you and me."

"I've been thinking about it for a long time," he confessed. "I'm looking forward to having a few weeks off," he lied convincingly, and wondered how he was going to survive the lack of anything challenging to do.

She grinned. "Good! You can help me work on those turns in barrel racing. I don't guess you noticed, but I'm having a real hard time with them."

He recalled what Jane Parker had said about Cherry, and he allowed himself to wonder if it might not do both women good to spend a little time talking together.

"You know," he mused aloud, "I think I may have some ideas about that."

"Really? What are they?"

"Wait and see." He led her toward their car. "Let's get something to eat. I don't know about you, but I'm starved!"

"Me, too. How about Chinese?"

"My favorite."

He put her into the old Ford he'd borrowed while his Ferrari was being serviced, and drove her back into Jacobsville.

* * *

They had lunch at the single Chinese restaurant that was nestled among half a dozen barbecue, steak and fast-food restaurants. When they finished, they went back out to the arena to watch the rest of the afternoon's competition. Cherry was only in one other event. She did poorly again, though, trying to go around the barrels. When she rode out of the arena, she was in tears.

"Now, now." Todd comforted her. "Rome wasn't built in a day."

"They didn't have barrel racing in Rome!" she wailed.

"Probably not, but the sentiment is the same." He hugged her gently. "Perk up, now. This is only the first rodeo in a whole string of them. You'll get better."

"It's a waste of time," she said, wiping her tears. "I might as well quit right now."

"Nobody ever got anywhere by quitting after one loss," he chided. "Where would I be if I'd given up when my first computer program didn't sell?"

"Not where you are today, that's for sure," she admitted. "Nobody does software like you do, Dad. That newest word processor is just radical! Everyone at school loves it. It makes term papers so easy!"

"I'm glad to hear that all those late hours we put into developing it were worth the effort," he said. He grinned at her. "We're working on a new accounting package right now."

"Oh, accounting," she muttered. "Who wants any boring old stuff like that?"

"Plenty of small businesses," he said on a chuckle. "And thank your lucky stars or we'd be in the hole."

Cherry was looking around while he spoke. Her face lit up and her eyes began to sparkle. "It's Miss Parker!" The smile faded. "Oh, my..."

He turned and the somber expression on his daughter's

face was mirrored in his own. Jane was in the wheelchair, wearing jeans and a beige T-shirt and sneakers, looking fragile and depressed as Tim pushed her toward the motor home with the horse trailer hitched behind it.

Unless he missed his guess, they were about to leave. He couldn't let her get away, not before he had a chance to ask her about working with Cherry. It had occurred to him that they might kill two birds with one stone—give Miss Parker a new interest, and Cherry some badly needed help.

Chapter 2

"Miss Parker!" Todd called.

She glanced in his direction, aware that he and a young girl with fair hair in a pigtail were moving toward her. The wheelchair made her feel vulnerable and she bit down hard on her lip. She was in a bad temper because she didn't want that rude, unpleasant man to see her this way.

"Yes?" she asked through her teeth.

"This is my daughter, Cherry," he said, pulling the young girl forward. "She wanted to meet you."

Regardless, apparently, of whether Jane wanted the meeting or not. "How do you do," she said through numb lips.

"What happened to you?" Cherry spluttered.

Jane's face contorted.

"She was in a wreck," her father said shortly, "and it was rude of you to ask."

Cherry flushed. "I'm sorry, really I am." She went to the wheelchair, totally uninhibited, and squatted beside it. "I've watched all the videos you were on. You were just the best in the world," she said enthusiastically. "I couldn't get to the rodeos, but I had Dad buy me the videos from people who taped the events. I'm having a lot of trouble on the turns. Dad can ride, but he's just hopeless on rodeo, aren't you, Dad?" She put a gentle hand over Jane's arm. "Will you be able to ride again?"

"Cherry!" Todd raged.

"It's all right," Jane said quietly. She looked into the girl's clear, gray eyes, seeing no pity there, only honest concern and curiosity. The rigidity in her began to subside. She smiled. "No," she said honestly. "I don't think I'll be able to ride again. Not in competition, at least."

"I wish I could help you," Cherry said. "I'm going to be a surgeon when I grow up. I make straight *A*'s in science and math, and Dad's already said I could go to Johns Hopkins when I'm old enough. That's the best school of medicine anywhere!"

"A surgeon," Jane echoed, surprised. She smiled. "I've never known anyone who wanted to be a surgeon before."

Cherry beamed. "Now you do. I wish you didn't have to leave so soon," she said wistfully. "I was going to pick your brain for ways to get over this fear of turns. Silly, isn't it, when the sight of blood doesn't bother me at all."

Jane was aware of an emptiness in herself as she stared into the young face. It was like seeing herself at that age. She lowered her eyes. "Yes, well, I'm sorry, but it's been a long day and I'm in a good deal of pain. And we're interviewing today."

"Interviewing?" Cherry asked with open curiosity.

"For a business manager," Jane said sadly, glancing at Tim, who winced. "Tim can't manage the books. He's willing to keep on as foreman, but we're losing money hand over fist since Dad's death because neither one of us can handle the books."

"Gosh, my dad would be perfect for that," Cherry said

innocently. "He's a wizard with money. He keeps the books for his compu—"

"For the small computer company I work for in Victoria," Todd said quickly, with a speaking glance that his intelligent daughter interpreted immediately. She shut up, grinning.

Tim stepped forward. "Can you balance books?"

"Sure."

Tim looked at Jane. "There's the foreman's cabin empty, since Meg and I are living in the house with you," he remarked. "They could live there. And you could help the girl with her turns. It would give you something to do besides brooding around the house all day."

"Tim!" Jane burst out angrily. She glanced apprehensively at Todd Burke, who was watching her with unconcealed amusement. "I'm sure he has a job already."

"I do. Keeping books for my...the computer company," he lied. "But it doesn't take up all my time. In fact, I think I'd enjoy doing something different for a while." He pursed his lips. "If you're interested, that is," he added with practiced indifference.

Jane's eyes fell to her lap.

"I'd love to learn how to win at barrel racing," Cherry said with a sigh. "I guess I'll have to give it up, though. I mean, I'm so bad that it's a waste of Dad's money to keep paying my entrance fees and all."

Jane glowered at her. She glowered at him, too, standing there like a movie cowboy with his firm lips pursed and his steely gray eyes twinkling with amusement. Laughing at her.

"She won't hire you," Tim said with a glare at her. "She's too proud to admit that you're just what she needs. She'd rather let the ranch go under while she sits on the porch and feels sorry for herself."

"Damn you!" She spat the words at Tim.

He chuckled. "See them eyes?" he asked Todd. "Like wet sapphires. She may look like a fashion doll, but she's all fur and claws when things get next to her, and she's no quitter."

Todd was looking at her with evident appreciation. He grinned. "Two week trial?" he asked. "While we see how well we all get along? I can't do you much damage in that short a time, and I might do you a lot of good. I have a way with balance sheets."

"We couldn't be much worse off," Tim reminded his boss.

Jane was silently weighing pros and cons. He had a daughter, so he had to be settled and fairly dependable, if Cherry was any indication. If she hired anyone else, she'd have no idea if she was giving succor to a thief or even a murderer. This man looked trustworthy and his daughter apparently adored him.

"We could try, I suppose," she said finally. "If you're willing. But the ranch isn't successful enough that I can offer you much of a salary." She named a figure. "You'll get meals and board free, but I'll understand if that isn't enough—"

"If I can keep on doing my present job, in the evenings, we'll manage," Todd said without daring to look at his daughter. If he did, he knew he'd give the show away.

"Your boss won't mind?" Jane asked.

He cleared his throat. "He's very understanding. After all, I'm a single parent."

She nodded, convinced. "All right, then. Would you like to follow us out to the ranch, if you're through for the day?"

"We're through, all right," Cherry said on a sigh. "I'm dejected, demoralized and thoroughly depressed."

"Don't be silly," Jane said gently, and with a smile. "You've got an excellent seat, and you're good with horses. You just need to get over that irrational fear that you're going to go down on the turns."

"How did you know?" Cherry gasped.

"Because I was exactly the same when I started out. Stop worrying. I'll work with you. When we're through, you'll be taking home trophies."

"Really?"

Jane chuckled. "Really. Let's go, Tim."

He wheeled her to the cab of the motor home and opened the door. "I guess bringing this thing ten miles looks odd," Tim murmured to Todd, "but we had to have a place where Jane could rest. We've carried this old thing to many a rodeo over the years. She takes a little coaxing sometimes, but she always goes."

"Like Bracket," Jane mused, glancing back to the trailer where her palomino gelding rode.

"Like Bracket," Tim agreed. He reached down. "Let's get you inside, now, Jane."

Before he could lift her, Todd moved forward. "Here," he volunteered. "I'll do the honors."

Tim grinned, his relief all too obvious. Jane wasn't heavy, but Tim was feeling his age a bit.

Todd lifted Jane gently out of the wheelchair and into the cab of the big vehicle, positioning her on the seat with a minimum of discomfort. She eased her arms from around his neck a little self-consciously and smiled. "Thanks."

He shrugged powerful shoulders and smiled back. "No problem. Where does the chair go, Tim?"

He folded it and the older man climbed up into the motor home and stowed it away. He got behind the wheel and paused long enough to give directions to Todd about where in Jacobsville the ranch was located before he and Jane waved goodbye and drove away.

"Dad!" Cherry laughed. "Are we really going to do it? What will she say when she finds out?"

"We'll worry about that when the time comes. The ranch budget sounds like a challenge, and you could use some pointers with your riding,'' he added. ''I think it may work out very well.''

''But what about your company?'' Cherry asked.

''I've got good people working for me and I'm on holiday.'' He ruffled her hair. ''We'll think of it as summer vacation,'' he assured her. ''It will give us some time together.''

''I'd like that,'' she said solemnly. ''After all, in four years I'll be in school, and you probably won't get to see me twice a year. I'll have to study very hard.''

''You're smart. You'll do fine.''

''Yes, I will,'' she assured him with a grin. ''And you can have all your medical care free.''

''I can hardly wait.''

''Don't be sarcastic,'' she chided. ''And you have to be nice to Miss Parker, too.''

''She doesn't like me very much.''

''You don't like her, either, do you?'' she asked curiously.

He stuck his hands into his pockets and frowned. ''She's all right.''

''If you don't like her, why are you going to help her?''

He couldn't answer that. He didn't know why. She was a woman in a wheelchair, who looked as if in her heyday she'd been nothing more than a fashion doll on a horse. But she was crippled and in bad financial circumstances, and all alone, apparently. He felt sorry for her. Funny, that, because since his failed marriage, he didn't like women very much except when he had an overwhelming desire for someone female in his arms. Loving and leaving wouldn't be possible with Jane Parker. So why was he going out of his way to help her? He didn't know.

''Maybe I feel sorry for her,'' he told Cherry finally.

''Yes, so do I, but we mustn't let her know it,'' she said firmly. ''She's very proud, did you notice?''

He nodded. ''Proud and hot tempered.''

''What familiar traits.''

He glowered at her, but she just grinned.

At the luxurious house Todd had bought in Victoria, they packed up what gear they'd need for a few days, explained their forthcoming absence to their puzzled housekeeper, Rosa, promised to be back soon and drove in the borrowed Ford down to Jacobsville to the Parker ranch.

It wasn't much to look at from the road. There was a rickety gray wood and barbed-wire fence that had been mended just enough to hold in the mixed-breed steers in the pasture. The barn was still standing, but barely. The dirt road that led past a windmill to the house had potholes with water standing in them from the last rain. It had no gravel on it, and it looked as if it hadn't been graded in years. The yard was bare except for a few rosebushes and a handful of flowers around the long porch of the white clapboard house. It was two stories high, and needed painting. One of the steps had broken through and hadn't been replaced. There was a rickety ramp, presumably constructed hastily for the wheelchair, on the end of the porch. There was the motor home and horse trailer in the yard, next to a building that might be used as a garage by an optimist. A small cabin was nestled in high grass that needed cutting; the foreman's cabin, Todd thought, hoping that it was more than one room. Nearby was a bigger structure, a small one-story house. It was in better condition and it had rocking chairs on the porch. The bunkhouse?

''Welcome!'' Tim called, coming out to meet them.

They got out and Todd shook hands with him. ''Thanks. If you'll tell me where to put our stuff…?'' He was looking toward the cabin.

''Oh, that's where old man Hughes lives.'' Tim chuckled. ''He helps me look after the livestock. He can't do a lot, but he's worked here since he was a boy. We can't pension him off until he's sixty-five, two more years yet." He turned. "Here's where you and the girl will bunk down." He led them toward the small house and Todd heaved a sigh of relief.

"It needs some work, like everything else, but maybe you can manage. You can have meals with us in the house. There are three other hands who mend fences and look after the tanks and the machinery, do the planting and so forth. They're mostly part-time these days, but we hire on extra men when we need them, seasonally, you know."

The house wasn't bad. It had three big bedrooms and a small living room. There was a kitchen, too, but it didn't look used. There was a coffeepot and a small stove and refrigerator.

"I could learn to cook," Cherry began.

"No, you couldn't," Todd said shortly. "Time enough for that later."

"My wife Meg'll teach you if you want to learn," Tim said, volunteering his wife with a grin. "She likes young people. Never had any kids of our own, so she takes up with other people's. When you've settled, come on over to the house. We'll have sandwiches and something to drink."

"How's Miss Parker?" Cherry asked.

Tim grimaced. "Lying down. She's not well. I've called the doctor." He shook his head. "I told her not to get on that horse, but she wouldn't listen to me. Never could do anything with her, even when she was a youngster. It took her papa to hold her back, but he's gone now."

"She had no business on that horse," Todd said, pointedly.

"That was a bad attack of pride," Tim told him. "Some newspaperman wrote a column about the rodeo and mentioned that poor Jane Parker would probably come out to accept the plaque for her father in a wheelchair, because she was crippled now."

Todd's face hardened. "Which paper was it in?"

"That little weekly they publish in Jacobsville," he said with a grimace. "She took it to heart. I told her it was probably that Sikes kid who just started doing sports. He's fresh out of journalism school and fancies himself winning a Pulitzer for covering barrel racing. Huh!" he scoffed.

Todd mentally stored the name for future reference. "Will the doctor come out?"

"Sure!" the wizened little man assured him. "His dad was Jane's godfather. They're great friends. He has an assistant now, though—a female doctor named Lou. She might come instead." He chuckled. "They don't see eye to eye on anything. Amazing how they manage a practice between them."

"The doctor isn't married?"

He shook his head. "He was sweet on Jane, but after the accident, she cut him dead if he so much as smiled at her. That was just before Lou went into practice with him. Jane doesn't want to get involved, she says."

"She won't always be in that chair," Todd murmured as they walked toward the house.

"No. But she'll always have pain when she overdoes things, and she won't ride well enough for competition again."

"That's what she told Cherry."

Tim gave him a wary glance. "You won't hurt her?" he asked bluntly.

Todd smiled. "She's very attractive, and I like her spirit, but I've had a bad marriage and I don't want to risk another failure. I don't get serious about women anymore. And I'm not coldhearted enough to play around with Jane."

Tim sighed. "Thanks. I needed to hear that. She's more vulnerable than she realizes right now. I'm not related to her, but in a lot of ways, I'm the only family she's got—well, Meg and me."

"She's a lucky woman," Todd replied.

He shrugged. "Not so lucky, or she wouldn't be in that chair, would she?"

They walked up onto the porch, avoiding the broken step. "Meant to fix that, but I never get time," Tim murmured. "Now that you're here to tear your hair out over the books, maybe I'll be able to get a few odds and ends done."

"I can help, if you need me," he volunteered. "I do woodwork for a hobby."

"Do you!" Tim's face brightened. "There's a woodworking shop in the back of the barn. We built it years ago for her dad. He made all the furniture in the house. She'll like having it in use again."

"Are you sure?" he asked doubtfully.

"You can always ask her."

They walked into the living room. Jane was lying on the sofa, putting up a brave front even though her face was stark white with the effort. Cherry was curled up in an armchair beside the sofa, her cheek on her folded arms, listening raptly to her idol.

"Doctor should be here soon," Tim told Jane. He paused to pat her gently on the shoulder. "Hang on, kid."

She smiled at him, and laid her hand briefly over the one on her shoulder. "Thanks, Tim. What would I do without you?"

"Let's agree never to find out," he returned dryly.

"Okay." She glanced toward Todd Burke. The expression on his lean face made her angry. "I'm not a cripple," she said belligerently.

He knelt by the sofa and pushed back a strand of her hair. It was wet, not with sweat, but with tears she'd shed involuntarily as the pain bit into her. He felt more protective about her than he could understand.

"Don't you have something to take?"

"Yes," she said, shaken by his concern. "But it isn't working."

He tucked the strand of hair behind her small, pretty ear and smiled. "Guess why?"

She made a face. "I wouldn't have tried to ride out into the arena if it hadn't been for that damned reporter," she said gruffly. "He called me a cripple!"

"Cherry and I will rush right in to town and beat the stuffing out of him for you."

That brought a pained smile to her face. "Cover him in ink and wrap him up in his newspaper and hang him from a printing press."

"They don't have printing presses anymore," Cherry said knowledgeably. "Everything's cold type now…offset printing."

Jane's blue eyes widened. "My, my, you are a wellspring of information!" she said, impressed.

Cherry grinned smugly. "One of my new teachers used to work for a newspaper. Now he teaches English."

"She knows everything," Todd said with a resigned air. "Just ask her."

"Not *everything*, Dad." She chuckled. "I don't know how to do barrel-racing turns."

"I hear a car," Tim said, glancing out the window. "It's him."

Todd frowned at the way Jane's eyes fell when he looked into them. Did she have mixed feelings about the doctor and was trying to hide it? Maybe Tim had been wrong and Jane had been sweet on the doctor, not the other way around.

Todd got to his feet as a tall man with red hair came into the room, carrying a black bag. He was dressed in a nice gray Western-cut suit with a white shirt and a black string tie. Boots, too. He removed a pearl gray Stetson from his head, and tossed it onto the counter. Pale blue eyes swept the room, lingering on Todd Burke, who stared back, unsmiling.

"This is Dr. Jebediah Coltrain," Tim introduced the tall,

slim man. "When he was younger, everybody used to call him Copper."

"They don't anymore. Not without a head start," the doctor said. He didn't smile, either.

"This is Todd Burke and his daughter Cherry," Tim said, introducing them. "Todd's going to take over the book work for us."

Coltrain didn't say much. He gave Todd a piercing stare that all but impaled him before he nodded curtly, without offering a hand in greeting. He was less reserved with Cherry, if that faint upturn of his thin lips was actually a smile.

"Well, what fool thing have you done this time?" Coltrain asked Jane irritably. "Gone riding, I guess?"

She glared at him through waves of pain. "I wasn't going to let them push me out into that arena in a wheelchair," she said furiously. "Not after what that weasel of a sports reporter wrote about me!"

He made a sound deep in his throat that could have meant anything. He set about examining her with steely hands that looked menacing until they touched and probed with a tenderness that set Todd's teeth on edge.

"Muscle strain," Coltrain pronounced at last. "You'll need a few days in bed on muscle relaxers. Did you rent that traction rig I told you to get?"

"Yes, we did, under protest," Tim said with a chuckle.

"Well, get started, then."

He lifted her as if she were a feather and carried her off to her bedroom. Todd, incensed out of all reason, followed them with an audible tread.

Coltrain glanced over his shoulder at the other man with a faintly mocking smile. He didn't need a road map to find a marked trail, and he knew jealousy when he saw it.

He put Jane down gently on the double bed with its carved posts with the traction apparatus poised over it.

"Need to make a pit stop before I hook you up?" Coltrain asked her without a trace of embarrassment.

"No, I'm fine," she said through clenched teeth. "Go ahead."

He adjusted the brace that lifted her right leg, putting a pleasant pressure on the damaged hip that even surgery hadn't put completely back to rights. "This won't work any miracles, but it will help," Coltrain told her. "You put too much stock in articles written by idiots."

"He didn't write it about you!"

He lifted an eyebrow. "He wouldn't dare," he said simply.

She knew that. It irritated her. She closed her eyes. "It hurts."

"I can do something for that." Coltrain reached in his bag and drew out a small bottle and a syringe. He handed a package to Todd. "Open that and swab the top of the bottle with it."

He had the sort of voice that expects obedience. Todd, who never took orders, actually did it with only a lopsided grin. He liked the doctor, against his will.

Coltrain upended the bottle when Todd had finished, inserted the needle into the bottle and then drew up the correct amount of painkiller.

He handed Todd another package containing an alcohol-soaked gauze. "Swab her arm, here."

He indicated a vein in her right arm and Todd looked at him.

"It's not addictive," the doctor said gently. "I know what I'm doing."

Todd made a rough murmur and complied. It embarrassed him to show concern for a woman he barely knew. Coltrain's knowing look made it worse.

He swabbed her arm and Coltrain shot the needle in, efficiently and with a minimum of pain.

"Thanks, Copper," Jane told him quietly.

He shrugged. "What are friends for?" He took a few sample packages out of the bag and gave them to Todd. "Two every six hours for severe pain. They're stronger than the others I gave you," he told Jane. "You can push this to five hours if you can't bear it, but no sooner." Coltrain fastened his bag and gave Jane a reassuring smile. "Stay put. I'll check on you tomorrow."

"Okay." Her eyes were already closing.

"I'll sit with you until you go to sleep," Cherry volunteered, and Jane smiled her agreement.

Coltrain jerked his head toward the living room. Tim and Todd followed. He closed the bedroom door behind them.

"I want her X-rayed," he told them without preamble. "I think it's muscular, but I'm not going to stake my life on it. The last thing she needed was to get on a horse."

"I tried to stop her," Tim told him.

"I realize that. I'm not blaming you. She's a handful." He eyed Todd openly. "Can you keep her off horses?"

Todd smiled slowly. "Watch me."

"That's what I thought. She isn't safe to be let out alone these days, always trying to prove herself." He grabbed his Stetson and started toward the door. "She's in too much pain to be moved today. I'll send an ambulance for her in the morning and make all the necessary arrangements at Jacobsville Memorial. She won't like it," he added wryly.

"But she'll do it," Todd replied easily.

For the first time, Coltrain chuckled. "I'd like to be a fly on the wall tomorrow when that ambulance gets here."

The telephone rang and Tim answered it. He grimaced, holding it out to Coltrain.

The other man picked it up with a rough sigh. "Coltrain," he said as if he knew who was calling.

His face grew harder by the second. "Yes. No. I don't give a damn, it's my practice and that's how I do things. If you don't like it, get out. Damn the contract!" He glanced at the wide-eyed faces near him and shifted his posture. "We'll talk about this when I get back. Yes, you do that." He put the receiver down with a savagely controlled jerk of his lean hand. His eyes glittered like blue water on a snake's back. "Call me if you need me."

After he was gone, and was driving away in a cloud of dust, Tim whistled through his teeth. "It won't last."

"What won't?" Todd replied.

"Him and Lou," he said, shaking his head. "They'll kill each other one day, him with his old-fashioned way of practicing and her with all this newfangled technology."

Todd found himself vaguely relieved that the doctor had someone besides Jane to occupy his mind. He wasn't sure why, but he didn't like the tenderness Coltrain had shown Jane.

Chapter 3

Jane was restless all through the night. When Cherry went to bed, Todd sat with Jane. Tim had handed over the books earlier, so he took the heavy ledger with him. He looked through it while Jane slept, his reading glasses perched on his straight nose and a scowl between his eyes as he saw the inefficiency and waste there on the paper.

The ranch had almost gone under, all right, and there was no need. In addition to the beef cattle, Jane had four thoroughbred stallions, two of whom had won ribbons in competition, and on the racetrack before her father's death. She wasn't even putting them at stud, which could certainly have added to the coffers. The equipment she was using was obsolete. No maintenance had been done recently, either, and that would have made a handsome tax deduction. From what he'd seen, there was plenty of room for improvement in the equipment shed, the outbuildings, the barn and even the house itself. The ranch had great potential, but it wasn't being efficiently used.

He scowled, faintly aware of a tingling sensation, as if he were being watched. He lifted his head and looked into curious blue eyes.

"I didn't know you wore glasses," Jane said drowsily.

"I'm farsighted," he said with a chuckle. "It's irritating when people think I'm over forty because of these." He touched the glasses.

She studied his lean, hard face quietly. "How old are you?"

"Thirty-five," he said. "You?"

She grinned. "Twenty-five. A mere child, compared to you."

He lifted an eyebrow. "You must be feeling better."

"A little." She took a slow breath. "I hate being helpless."

"You won't always be," he reminded her. "One day, you won't have to worry about traction and pills. Try to think of this as a temporary setback."

"I'll bet you've never been helpless in your whole life."

"I had pneumonia once," he recalled. His face hardened with memory. He'd been violently ill, because he hadn't realized how serious his chest cold had become until his fever shot up and he couldn't walk for pain and lack of breath. The doctor had reluctantly allowed him to stay at home during treatment, with the proviso that he had to be carefully watched. But Marie had left him alone to go to a cocktail party with his best friend, smiling as she swept out the door. After all, it was just a little cough and he'd be fine, she'd said carelessly. Besides, this party was important to her. She was going to meet several society matrons who were potential clients for her new interior-design business. She couldn't pass that up. It wasn't as if pneumonia was even serious, she'd laughed lightly on her way out the door.

"Come back," Jane said softly.

His head jerked as he realized his thoughts had drifted away. "Sorry."

"What happened?" she persisted.

He shrugged. "Nothing much. I had pneumonia and my wife left me at home to go to a cocktail party."

"And?" she persisted.

"You're as stubborn as a bulldog, aren't you?" he asked irritably. "You're prying."

"Of course I am," she said easily. "Tell me."

"She went on to an all-night club after the cocktail party and didn't come home until late the next morning. She'd put my antibiotics away and hadn't told me where, and I was too sick to get up and look for them. By the time she got home, I was delirious with fever. She had to get an ambulance and rush me to the hospital. I very nearly died. That was the year Cherry was born."

"Why, the witch!" Jane said bluntly. "And you stayed with her?"

"Cherry was on the way," he said starkly. "I knew that if we got divorced, she wouldn't have the baby. I wanted Cherry," he said stiffly.

He said it as if it embarrassed him, and that made her smile. "I've noticed that you take fatherhood seriously."

"I always wanted kids," he said. "I was an only child. It's a lonely life for a kid on a big ranch. I wanted more than one, but…" He shrugged. "I'm glad I've got Cherry."

"Her mother didn't want her?"

He glowered. "Marie likes her when she's having guests, so that she can show the world what a sweet, devoted mother she is. It wins her brownie points in her business affairs. She's an interior designer and most of her work comes from very wealthy, very conservative, Texans. You know, the sort who like settled family men and women on the job?"

"Does Cherry know?"

"It's hard to miss, and Cherry's bright. Marie and I get

along, most of the time, but I won't let her dictate Cherry's life for her." He intercepted a curious glance. "Rodeo," he said, answering the unspoken question. "Marie disapproves."

"But Cherry still rides."

He nodded. "I have custody," he said pointedly.

"And Cherry adores you," she agreed. She smiled, still drowsy from the pain medication. "I feel as if I'm flying. I don't know what Copper gave me, but it's very potent."

"Coltrain strikes me as something of a hell-raiser," he said.

"He was, and still is. I like him very much."

One gray eye narrowed. "Like?"

"Like." She was fighting sleep. Her slender hands smoothed over the light sheet that covered her. "I wanted to care about him, at first, but I couldn't feel like that with him. I think I'm cold, you see," she murmured sleepily. "I don't...feel those things...that women are supposed to feel...with men..."

Her voice drifted away and she was asleep.

Todd sat watching her with a faint frown, puzzled by that odd statement. She was a beauty. Surely there had been men over the years who attracted her, and at least one lover; perhaps Coltrain, for whom she hadn't felt anything. The thought was uncomfortable.

After a minute, he forced himself to concentrate more on the figures in the ledger and less on the lovely, sleeping woman in the bed. Jane's sex life was none of his business.

The ambulance came promptly at ten o'clock the next morning, and Jane's blue eyes snapped and sparkled when Todd told her that Coltrain had insisted on an X ray.

"I won't go!" she raged. "Do you hear me? I won't go to the hospital...!"

"He only wants you X-rayed to be sure that you haven't

broken anything,'' Todd said. He was alone in the bedroom
with Jane. Tim had prudently found something to do several
miles away from the house, and Meg had gone shopping,
taking Cherry with her. Only now did Todd realize why.

''I haven't broken anything!'' she said hotly. She'd already
had the traction apparatus removed so that she could go to
the bathroom. Now she was sitting on the side of the bed in
her pale blue cotton pajamas, her blond hair disheveled
around her shoulders while she glared at the men who
brought in the trolley.

''I won't go!'' she continued.

The ambulance attendants looked doubtful.

Jane waved a hand at them. ''Take that thing away!''

''Stay right where you are,'' Todd said quietly. He moved
toward Jane. ''Coltrain said you go. So you go.''

She verbally lashed out at him, furious that she was being
coerced into doing this. ''I tell you, I won't...!''

He ignored her words and simply picked her up, cradling
her gently against his broad chest as he turned toward the
stretcher. She felt her breasts flatten against that warm
strength and something incredible happened to her senses.
She gasped audibly at the sensations that rippled through her
slender body at the unfamiliar contact. Until now, the only
man who'd ever seen her so scantily clad had been Coltrain,
in a professional capacity only. And now here she was in
arms that made a weakling of her, that made her whole body
tingle and tremble with odd, empty longings.

All too soon, Todd put her on the stretcher and the ambulance attendants covered her with a white sheet. They were
quick and professional, towing her right out toward the ambulance, which had backed up to the porch and was waiting
for her.

''I'll follow you in the car,'' Todd told her. The way she
was watching him made him uneasy. He couldn't help feeling
her violent reaction to his touch. It had been in her whole

body, even as it lay in her eyes right now, surprised and vulnerable eyes that made him very uncomfortable. "What, no more harsh words? No more fury?" he taunted, hoping to stop those soft eyes from eating his face.

Her teeth clenched, as much from physical discomfort as temper. "You're fired!" she yelled at him.

"Oh, you can't fire me," he assured her.

"Why can't I?"

"Because you'll lose the ranch if you do," he said, meeting her angry eyes levelly. "I can save it."

She wavered. "How?"

"We'll discuss that. After you're X-rayed," he added. He moved back and the ambulance attendant closed the double doors on Jane and her confused expression.

"I told you I was all right!" Jane raged at Coltrain when he'd read the X rays and assured her that nothing was broken, chipped or fractured.

"I didn't say you were all right," he returned, his hands deep in the pockets of his white lab coat. He looked very professional with the stethoscope draped loosely around his neck. "I said you hadn't broken anything. You were lucky," he added irritably. "My God, woman, do you want to break your back? Do you want to spend the rest of your life lying in bed, unable to move!"

She bit her lower lip hard. "No," she said gruffly.

"Then stop trying to prove yourself," he said shortly. "The only opinion that ever matters is your own! Damn the reporter. If he's too stupid to report the truth, he'll dig his own grave one day. If he hasn't already," he added.

"What do you mean?"

"I mean that the local rodeo association has banned him from the arena," he told her.

Her eyebrows shot up. "But rodeo is the biggest local sport going, especially this time of year!"

"I know." He smiled smugly. "I sit on the board of directors."

"You did it," she said.

"I had a lot of help," he replied. "It was a unanimous decision. I wish you could have seen Craig Fox's face when he was told he couldn't send his new reporter to cover any more rodeos." He fingered his tie. "As a matter of fact, the hardware store and the auto parts place pulled their ads this week. Their owners have sons who compete in the rodeo."

She whistled through her teeth. "Oh, boy."

"I understand that the reporter is making a public apology, in print, in this week's edition," he added. "You, uh, might take a look on the editorial page when your copy comes." He patted her shoulder absently. "He eats crow very well."

She laughed, her bad temper gone. "You devil!"

"You're my friend," he said with a smile—something rare in that taciturn face.

"And you're mine." She reached out and held his lean hand. "Thanks, Copper."

He nodded.

Todd Burke, coming into the treatment room with Dr. Lou Blakely, stopped and glared at the tableau they made. The lovely blond woman beside him didn't give away anything in her expression, but her eyelids flickered.

"When you're through here, I'd like to speak to you, Dr. Coltrain," Lou said quietly. "I had Ned Rogers come in for some lab work. It isn't good, I'm afraid. I let him go home, but we'll have to have him back to give him the results."

He let go of Jane's hand, reluctantly it seemed to Todd, and turned to his partner. "Was it so urgent that you couldn't tell me after I'd done my rounds here?" he asked shortly. "Who's minding the office?"

Her cheeks flushed. "I've just finished doing my own rounds," she said, furious that he thought she was chasing him here. "And it *is* noon," she said pointedly. "I'm on my lunch hour. Betty's had her lunch. She's minding the phone."

"Noon?" He checked his watch. "So it is." He turned toward Jane and started to speak.

"I'll drive Jane back home, if she's through here," Todd interjected, joining them. "I have some questions about the book work. I can't do anything more until they're answered."

Lou studied the newcomer curiously and with a nice smile. "I'm Dr. Louise Blakely," she said, holding a hand out to be shaken. "Dr. Coltrain's partner."

"Assistant," Coltrain said carelessly, and with a pointed glare. There was no interest in his eyes, no curiosity, nothing except a faint glitter of hostility.

"Todd Burke," Todd introduced himself, and smiled. "Nice to meet you, Dr. Blakely."

Lou glanced at Coltrain. "The contract I signed says that we're partners, Dr. Coltrain," she persisted. "For a year."

He didn't reply. His pale eyes went back to Jane and he smiled. "I'll be around if you need me. Take it easy, okay?"

Jane smiled back. "Okay."

He patted her shoulder reassuringly and started for the door. "All right," he told Lou curtly. "Let's have a look at Mr. Rogers's test results."

Todd watched them go before he helped Jane into the wheelchair the nurse had brought into the room. She was wheeled out to the exit and Todd loaded her into his Ford. They were underway before he spoke.

"Are you jealous of Lou?" he asked abruptly, because he'd seen the way she watched Coltrain and Lou Blakely.

"Because of Copper? No," she said easily. "I was wondering about Lou. She's…I don't know…fragile around him. It's odd, because she's such a strong, independent woman most of the time."

"Maybe she's sweet on him," he suggested.

"For her sake, I hope not," she replied. "Copper is a

confirmed bachelor. His work is his whole life, and he likes women but only in numbers."

Todd smiled faintly.

She glanced at him with twinkling eyes. "I see that you understand the way he feels. That's the way you are, too, isn't it?"

He nodded. "A man who's been burned doesn't go around looking for fires," he said pointedly. He braked for a traffic light and then pulled out into the road that led out of Jacobsville toward the Parker ranch.

She stared out at the summer landscape as they left town, smiling at the beauty of flowers and crops in the field. "I can understand why you might feel that way," she said absently.

"I'm glad," he replied curtly, "because there was a look in your eyes that worried me when I lifted you onto the stretcher back at the house."

Her eyebrows raised. "You're blunt," she said.

"Yes, I am. I've found that it's easier to be honest than to prevaricate." His hands tightened on the steering wheel. "You're easy on the eyes and I think I'll enjoy working for you. But I'm not in the market for a love affair. It's the challenge of getting your ranch out of hock that appeals to me—not seducing you."

She didn't react visibly. She folded her arms over her breasts lazily and leaned back against the seat. It didn't show that she felt cold and empty and wounded inside. "I see."

"And now you're offended," he said with a cutting edge to his voice, "and you'll pout for the rest of the day."

She laughed. "I'm impressed that you know me so well already, Mr. Burke," she returned. "And your modesty is refreshing!"

His brows collided. He hadn't expected that mocking reply. "I beg your pardon?"

"You feel that I'm so overcome with panting passion for

you that I have to be warned off. I never realized I was that dangerous. And in a wheelchair, too.'' She wiggled her eyebrows at him. "Since you're *sooooo* attractive, Mr. Burke, aren't you afraid to be alone in the car with me? I might leap on you!''

He was disconcerted. He glanced at her and the car swerved. He muttered under his breath as he righted it in his lane.

Jane began to enjoy herself. He didn't seem the sort of man who was easily rattled. She'd managed that quite nicely. She couldn't wait to do it again. Two could play at his game.

"You're making me sound conceited," he began.

"Really? Well, you do seem to think that no normal woman can resist you.''

He sighed angrily. "You're twisting my words.''

"I do find you attractive," she said. "You're everything I've ever wanted in a man. I think you're handsome and intelligent and sexy. Shall we just have sex right now or wait until you stop the car?''

The car swerved again and he braked to avoid going into the ditch. "Miss Parker!''

She was enjoying herself. For the first time since the wreck, she could laugh. She had to fight to get herself under control at all.

"Oh, I'm sorry," she said when she got a glimpse at his hard features. "Really, I am.''

He pulled onto the ranch road, his teeth clenched. She made him out to be an utter fool, and he didn't like it. He wasn't used to women who were that good at verbal repartee. Marie was sarcastic and biting at times, but she was never condescending. Jane Parker was another kettle of fish. He had to remember that her body was fragile, even if her ego wasn't.

"I haven't laughed like that in months," she said, calmer

when he pulled up at the front door. "I do apologize, but it felt good to laugh."

He cut off the ignition and turned in the seat to face her. His eyes glittered, as they had at their first meeting. He was trying to control emotions he'd never felt to such an extent.

"I don't like being the butt of anyone's joke," he said curtly. "We'll get along very well if you remember that."

Her eyes iced over. "We'll get along better if you remember that I don't like men who talk to me as if I were a giddy adolescent on a hero-worshiping tangent."

His jaw clenched. "Miss Parker, I'm no boy. And I do know how a woman reacts—"

"No doubt you do, with your wide experience of them." She cut him off. "I've been alone for some time now," she added, "and I'm not used to being touched. So before you read too much into my reactions, you might consider that any man would have produced the same reaction."

He didn't like that. His expression went from surprise to cold courtesy. "I'll get you into the house."

"No, you won't," she said pleasantly. The look in her eyes wasn't pleasant at all. "Please ask Tim to bring the wheelchair. I find that I prefer it to you."

His face registered the insult. He knew already how she hated the stigma of the chair. But he didn't react. He should have kept his mouth shut.

"I'll get it," he said.

He left her in the car and went into the house, fuming. Tim came out of the kitchen where he'd been talking to Meg.

"How is she?" he asked at once.

"Out of humor, but physically undamaged," Todd said. He grimaced. "I made her mad."

"That's a step in the right direction," the older man said, smiling. "She needs shaking up. Pity she doesn't like Copper," he added on a sigh. "He'd be perfect for her."

"Because he's a doctor?" Todd asked impatiently.

"Because they grew up together and he knows ranching," came the reply. "He'd never have let the place get in this mess." He eyed Todd narrowly. "Do you think you can get us out of the financial tangle I landed us in?"

Todd reached for the wheelchair. "I think so," he said. "It's not as bad as you think. Mainly it's a matter of improving the operation and utilizing some resources. It will take time, though," he added as he pushed the chair toward the porch. "Don't expect instant answers."

"I don't," Tim assured him. "Why can't you just carry her inside?" he asked as an afterthought.

"Never mind." Todd bit off the words.

Tim's eyes twinkled. He followed the younger man out to the car and watched the byplay as Todd eased Jane into the chair and pushed her up onto the porch. She was stifling hot words, and he was controlling a temper that almost slipped its bonds. Tim took a longer look and liked what he saw. She wasn't brooding anymore, that was obvious. If anything, she was seething.

"Will you call Cherry and tell her I'm putting lunch on the table, Todd?" Meg called from the kitchen.

"Sure."

He put the car away and went to find his daughter, who was riding in the fenced arena, going around the barrels very slowly.

"Hi, Dad," she called, waving her hand.

"How's it going?" he yelled.

"Fine! I'm working slowly, like Jane told me to. How is she?"

"She's all right," he replied. "Meg's got lunch ready. Put your horse up and come on in."

"Okay, Dad!"

He stuck his hands into the pockets of his slacks and went back to the house. Meg had coffee and sandwiches on the long dining-room table, where Jane and Tim were sitting. He washed up and then they waited for Cherry, who came to join them a few minutes later.

"You'll need some food before you start on those books again." Tim chuckled, watching Todd raid the sandwich platter before he passed it along to his daughter. She helped herself, talking animatedly to Meg and Tim.

"I love to see a man with a healthy appetite," Jane murmured, to needle him. She was sitting next to him and nibbling delicately on her own sandwich.

Todd glared at her. She finished her sandwich and leaned toward him, sniffing.

"Umm," she murmured huskily, so that only he could hear while Tim and Meg were talking. "What *is* that cologne you're wearing? It's very sexy."

He didn't reply, reaching for his coffee cup instead with an expression as hard as steel.

"Jane, Todd said that he thinks he can get us operating in the black," Tim said to Jane.

"Really?" Jane smiled at him. "Can we afford it?"

He sipped his coffee and put a sandwich on his plate. "It's going to require some belt tightening, if that's what you mean," he said, refusing to rise to the bait. He looked directly at her. "And you're going to have to borrow enough to make some improvements."

She let out a long breath. "I was afraid you'd say that. I don't think we can borrow any more."

"Yes, you can," he said, without telling her why he was sure of it. His name would convince any banker to let her have the loan, if he was willing to stand behind it. And he was. He dealt in amounts that would make her mind boggle. The amount she needed to get the ranch on its feet was paltry indeed compared to his annual budget. His backing would give her a good start, and it was an investment that would pay dividends one day. Not that he expected to capitalize on it. He'd be in the guise of a guardian angel, not a working partner.

She gnawed her lower lip, all signs of humor gone. "What would we have to do?"

He outlined the changes he had in mind, including the improvements to buildings, putting the stallions out to stud, building a breeding herd, leasing out unused land and applying for land development funds through government agencies.

Jane caught her breath mentally at the picture he painted of what could become a successful ranch, with horses for its foundation instead of cattle. It had been her father's dream to make the ranch self-supporting. Jane had tried, but she had no real knowledge of finance. All she knew was horses.

"Besides these changes," Todd added, "you have a name with commercial potential. It's a hell of a shame not to capitalize on it. Have you considered endorsing a line of Western clothing? Other rodeo stars have gone into such licensing. Why not you?"

"I...couldn't do that," she said hesitantly.

"Why?"

"I'm not going to be photographed in a wheelchair!"

"You wouldn't have to be," he said curtly. "The wheelchair is only temporary. Didn't the doctor tell you so?"

She rubbed her temples. She was on the way to a king-size headache. Todd Burke headache number one, she thought whimsically, and had to bite back a grin.

"I can't think that anyone would be interested in a line of clothing advertised by a has-been."

"You aren't a has-been," Cherry said quietly. "You're a legend. My gosh, at the riding school I went to they had posters of you all over the place!"

She knew the poster had been made, but she didn't realize that anybody had actually paid money for one. She looked blankly at Cherry.

"You've forgotten, haven't you?" Tim asked. "I told you that they had to reprint the posters because of the demand. But it was right after the wreck. I guess you weren't listening."

"No," she agreed. "I was in shock." She looked at Todd. "If there's a chance that we can make the ranch into a paying operation, I want to take it. If I lose, okay. But I'm not going under without a fight. Do whatever you like about the loan and the financing, and then just point me in the right direction. I'll do whatever you want me to."

"All right," Todd said. "We'll give it a shot."

Chapter 4

Todd insisted on going to the Jacobsville bank alone when he went to apply for the loan. It wouldn't do for Jane to find out how he was going to manage financing for his improvement program.

The bank manager was sworn to silence and he had received Todd's written backing for the loan. A few phone calls and it was all arranged. He had the necessary amount credited to Jane's account and then he set about replacing old equipment and hiring contractors to make improvements to existing buildings on the ranch.

When Jane saw the first bill, she almost called for a shot of whiskey.

"I can't afford this," she gasped.

"Yes, you can," Todd assured her. He sat across from her at the desk in the study. "You certainly can't afford to let things go further downhill. In the long run, maintenance is much less expensive than replacing everything you own."

She groaned. "But the electric fence...!"

"Less expensive than replacing a wood and barbed wire one, and less damaging to livestock," he said. "I've also contacted the Soil Conservation Service about assistance with a pond for water impoundment."

"A tank," she said absently. "We call them tanks here in Texas."

He raised an eyebrow but he made no further comment. "Another thing," he added, "I've arranged for some roof repairs on the house. You've got pots and pans all over the place to catch the water from leaks. If you don't fix the roof, you'll have to replace it. The wood will eventually rot."

"How will I pay for it all?" she asked the ceiling.

"I'm glad you asked," he said with a smile. He leaned back, propping one big booted foot against the lower rung of a nearby chair. In the pose, he looked lean and fit and very masculine. Jane had to control a sigh, and hide the surge of attraction she felt.

"Well?" she prompted.

"I'm advertising two of the stallions for stud purposes," he said. "They're champions with well-known bloodlines and they'll command a high price. I'm also going to purchase two or three good brood mares. We're going to breed them to other champions. Their offspring will add to our own blood stock, and the ones we don't add to the stud, we'll sell."

"We'll need a better barn," she began.

"We're going to build one," he said. "I've already hired a contractor."

"You take my breath away," she said, leaning back. "But all this will take time, and the ranch is on the edge of bankruptcy as it is," she added worriedly.

"That's where you come in," he said quietly. "I've approached a clothing manufacturer in Houston. They're interested in having you promote a line of women's Western wear, primarily leisure wear, such as jeans."

"Do they know…?"

He nodded. "They won't photograph you in a wheelchair." He told her the sum they were offering and she flushed.

"You're kidding!" she bellowed.

He shook his head. "Not at all. You'll want to see the manufacturer, of course. I wouldn't expect you to endorse clothing you haven't seen."

She was excited at the prospect of having her name on a line of clothes, but she was afraid to become overenthusiastic. No deal was final until contracts were signed. And there might be a reason to keep her from signing. "I won't endorse something cheap or sloppy," she agreed.

"I'm fairly sure that this is a reputable clothier," he told her, "and not a fly-by-night enterprise. We'll see. They'd like to come down and talk to you next Friday."

She smiled. "Okay."

He watched her with interest. Her face was animated, her blue eyes twinkling. She looked like a different woman. Her hair was in its usual long braid, held in place with a rubber band, a few wisps of it escaping down into her face. She brushed it away impatiently and his eyes fell reluctantly to the soft thrust of her breasts against the knit fabric of her blue pullover shirt.

"Stop that," she said at once, lifting her chin. "If I can't ogle you, you can't ogle me."

His eyebrows arched. "I don't remember saying you couldn't ogle me."

"Yes, you did. Quite emphatically. This is a business relationship now. Let's keep it that way."

He chuckled softly, then pursed his lips. "Are you sure you want to?" he asked with a honeyed drawl.

She was already out of her league, and she knew it, but she wasn't going to let *him* gain the upper hand. She simply smiled. "Yes, I'm sure," she told him. "Now what time next Friday do these people want to see me?"

By the next Thursday morning, all the arrangements were finalized for the meeting with the clothing manufacturers and the public relations people. The improvements on the house were underway, and noise had become a part of everyday life.

Jane escaped to the corral with Cherry after breakfast to get away from the carpenters. Todd was holed up in the study with the telephone, and the door was firmly closed. Jane wondered how he could hear above the chaos.

"Noise, noise," she groaned, holding her head. "I'm going to shoot those men just to get the hammers stopped!"

"It will be better to get the leaks stopped," Cherry told her with a cheeky grin.

"Ha!"

Cherry finished saddling the nice little quarter horse mare her father had bought her. "I named her Feather. Isn't she pretty?" she asked.

"She's very pretty, and she can do those turns blindfolded," Jane assured her. "You have to trust her, Cherry. You have to sit loose in the saddle and not pull on the reins. If you can do that, she'll make those turns as tight as a drum."

Cherry slumped a little. "I can't," she said miserably. She sat down on a bale of hay beside Jane, holding the reins in one hand while Feather nibbled at the hay. "I do try, Jane, but when she goes so fast around those turns..."

"You're afraid you'll fall off," Jane finished for her.

"Well, there's that, too," Cherry said. She picked at a piece of straw and snapped it between her fingers. "But it's the horse I'm most afraid for. My first time on the barrel-racing circuit, a rider went down and so did the horse. The fall broke the horse's leg." She threw away the straw. "They were going to put her down, but I begged and begged, and Dad bought her for me. She lives with a relative back in Wyoming, and she's doing fine, but I've had a hard time racing ever since that day.''

Todd hadn't told Jane that. She slid an affectionate arm around the girl and hugged her warmly.

''That's very rare, you know,'' she said gently. ''People in rodeo, people who ride, love their horses. Nobody ever uses an animal in a way that will harm it—not if they want to stay in rodeo. Cherry, I've been riding for twenty years, since I was five, and I've never had a horse go down under me when I was barrel racing. Never. I've fallen off,'' she added humorously. ''And once I had a rib broken when a horse kicked as I fell. But when I was racing, there wasn't a single mishap.''

''Really?'' Cherry asked, brightening.

''Really. Riding skill is largely a matter of having a well-trained horse and then not trying to exert too much control over the horse. Haven't you watched riders put quarter horses through their paces?''

''Sure. They're wonderful to watch. All a good rider has to do is just sit and the horse does all the work of cutting a steer out of a herd.''

''That's right. The horse knows his job, and does it. Where the problem begins is when the rider thinks he knows more than the horse and tries to take control.''

Cherry's gray eyes widened. ''Oh. Oh!''

Jane grinned. ''You're getting the picture, aren't you?''

''Wow! Am I ever!''

''Now let that sink in while you're putting Feather through her paces,'' she suggested. ''And don't rush. Just go slow and easy.''

''Slow and easy,'' Cherry echoed.

''What is this, a conference?'' Todd asked from the doorway.

"Cowgirl talk." His daughter chuckled. "Hi, Dad! Want to come and watch me?"

"Sure, in just a minute. I have to talk to the boss."

"I always thought *you* were the boss," she murmured as she went past, sharing a private joke with him.

He chuckled. "So did I," he agreed.

"See you later, Jane!" Cherry called. She led Feather out into the sunlight and climbed aboard with ease.

"She looks happy," Todd remarked.

He was looking very Western in his jeans and boots and blue patterned shirt with the gray Stetson pulled low over his eyes. He had a rodeo rider's physique, square shouldered and lean hipped, with long, powerful legs. Jane tried not to notice and failed miserably. It was a good thing there was so much shadow in the barn.

"We were talking about barrel racing. She told me about the injured horse you bought for her, back in Wyoming. That was kind of you."

"Kind." He shrugged. "I didn't stand a chance once she started crying. Tears wear me down."

"I'll have to remember that."

He cocked an eyebrow. "*Cherry's* tears," he said emphatically. "I'm immune to any others."

She snapped her fingers. "Darn the luck!"

His pale eyes swept over her slender body. She hadn't come down here in the wheelchair. She had her crutches instead. "That's dangerous," he said pointedly. "You could take a bad fall trying to maneuver through the gravel."

"No pain, no gain," she told him. "I can manage or I wouldn't have tried. I don't enjoy spending weeks in bed."

He decided that it might be best to ignore the remark. "I've been talking to Cherry's mother. She does want her this weekend after all," he said. "She's going to take Cherry shopping, so I'll drive her up about ten tomorrow morning. With any luck, I'll be back before those clothing representatives arrive. But in any case you need to have your attorney read the contract before you sign it.''

"I know that,'' she said.

"Good.''

She got up from the bale slowly and held on to her crutches, easing them under her arms. It was hard going, balancing on them, but she was doing better at it every day.

"Do Cherry and her mother get along?'' she asked as they left the barn and went toward the corral where Cherry was practicing.

"Yes, most of the time. Cherry doesn't like her stepfather.''

"I don't imagine she does. Many children of divorced parents live with a hope that their real parents will get together again, or so I've heard.''

"Cherry knows better. She hated the way it was before the divorce. Too many arguments can make home life hell for a young girl.''

"I suppose so.''

"Didn't your parents ever argue?'' he asked her.

"I don't know. My mother died when I was barely old enough to start school. My dad raised me. Well, my dad and Tim and Meg,'' Jane amended.

"It must have hit you hard to lose him.''

She nodded. "At least I still had Tim and Meg. That made it easier. In an odd way, the injury helped, too. It gave me a challenge, kept me going. If I'd had time to sit and brood, I think I might have gone crazy. I miss him so.''

Her voice was husky with feeling. He glanced down at her with mingled emotions. "I lost my mother nine years ago,'' he said. "My dad followed her two years later. I remember how it felt. We were a close-knit family.''

"I'm sorry.''

His broad shoulders rose and fell. "People die. It's the way of things.''

"That doesn't make it easy."

"No."

They stopped at the corral fence. Cherry was leaning over Feather's neck, talking softly to her. She glanced at Todd and Jane, grinned and suddenly urged Feather into a gallop.

As they watched, she bent low over Feather's mane, her hands not clinging to the reins, closed her eyes and let nature take its course. Feather took the first barrel so low that she seemed to slither around it, easily regaining her balance and heading for the barrel at the other end of the corral at the same feverish pace. She circled that one with the same ease, and kept going until an elated Cherry whooped loudly and gently reined her in on the side of the corral where the surprised, delighted adults were standing.

"Did you see?" Cherry burst out, red-faced and laughing so hard that tears ran down her dusty cheeks. "Oh, did you see! I did it!"

"I saw," Jane said with a smile. "Cherry, you're just great!"

"You're the great one," the girl said shyly. "After all, you told me how to do it. I won't be afraid anymore. Feather knows just what to do. All I have to do is let her."

"That's right. Slow and easy. You're doing fine now."

"I am, aren't I?" Cherry asked.

"You're a champ," Todd said as he found his voice, his eyes sparkling with pleasure. "I'm proud of you."

"Thanks, Dad!" She laughed again, and gave Feather her head.

"Don't overdo!" he yelled after her.

"No way!" came floating back over the sound of hoof-beats.

"So much for slow and easy," Jane murmured, watching the young girl.

Todd had a booted foot propped on the lowest fence rail. He glanced down at Jane with hooded eyes, unsmiling. She looked frail, but her slender body had a nice curve to it, and her breasts were firm and pert under that open-neck knit shirt. Her hair was loose around her shoulders for a change, faintly wavy and very pretty. Like Jane herself.

"Slow and easy," he said half under his breath, thinking of another exercise, one that made his heart begin to race.

Jane heard the deep note in his voice and looked up. Her eyes were trapped in the gray glitter under his hat brim. His lean hand came up to her face, cupping her cheek in its warmth while his thumb slowly traced the line of her upper lip until he made it tremble.

She couldn't get a breath of air into her starving lungs. She swallowed, and her lips parted helplessly while she struggled to find a teasing remark to break the tension.

Todd's own lips opened as he watched hers. His thumb slid down to the edge of her white teeth and caressed it lazily. Her mouth was as soft as a petal, warm, full.

Then suddenly, somehow, she was closer to him. She could see the pulse in his neck throbbing, feel the heat off his body. That cologne he wore was in her nostrils as the wind picked up and blew at his back.

He hadn't moved. His body was open and she was at an angle to that propped leg, so that they were standing in an intimacy that was respectable and tantalizing at the same time. She could almost feel the hard pressure of his legs against hers, the threat of his body so close to hers. Her heart was beating madly in her throat. Her eyes fell to his hard mouth, where it parted, and for an endless space of seconds, she saw it in her mind's eye, pressed ruthlessly, demandingly, against her own.

His breath was warm and unsteady. She could taste the coffee on it. He breathed and she felt his breath against her parted lips where his thumb was exploring. She felt it, felt him, felt the hunger that had been a stranger all her life until now.

She moved closer, as if he willed her to, moved jerkily on her crutches until she was standing right in the fork of his body and she could feel him just barely touching her—his long legs, his chest, his flat stomach, his hips—barely, barely touching, teasing, intimidating.

She made a husky, whimpering little sound in her throat and suddenly pressed herself to him.

Tim whistled loudly, Feather snorted, the roar of a car's engine all exploded into the tension and Jane actually moaned.

She jerked away from Todd so fast that she fell against the fence. His arm shot out to spare her the impact of a fall, righting her and the crutches, all without looking directly into her eyes. He was as shaken as she seemed to be, and angry that she'd gotten to him at all.

"Damn you." He bit off the words furiously.

She hit his broad chest with a flat hand. "You started that!" she accused hotly. "Damn you, too!"

"Todd! That building contractor's coming up the driveway!" Tim called before he went back to meet the man.

"I told you," Todd continued, ignoring the interruption, "that I'm not in the mood for an affair!"

"I'm the one on crutches," she snapped back. "It isn't as if I threw myself at you!"

"Isn't it? I didn't come to you!"

"Todd!" Tim called again.

He released Jane from his furious glare long enough to look toward Tim. "I'll be right there!"

Tim made a thumbs-up gesture and greeted the newcomer.

Todd looked back at Jane, who was pale but not backing down an inch. Her chin was thrust out and she was looking at him with eyes as angry as his own.

"You know what you do to a man with those bedroom eyes," he accused curtly. "You've probably had more lovers than I have."

"And just think, *I* didn't have to *pay* them!"

His breath inverted and he seemed to grow taller and more threatening in the space of a few seconds. "You...!" he began in a thunderous undertone.

She pulled herself up as tall as she could with the crutches and her hand slipped, grabbing at the crosspiece for support. She managed it, barely.

The pathetic little movement brought Todd back to his senses. Disabled she might be, but she had spirit. She wouldn't back down, or give up, no matter how formidable the opposition. He was furious, but even through his anger he felt admiration for her spunk.

"When you get back on your feet properly," he said deeply, "we'll have this out."

"What's the matter, big man, afraid to try your boxing gloves on a woman with crutches?" she taunted.

He chuckled despite his bad temper. "Not when the woman's got a switchblade in her tongue," he retorted. "Hellcat!"

"Pig!"

His eyebrows lifted. "Who, me?"

"Oink, oink!"

He searched her flushed face, her tousled hair, her wide angry blue eyes for a long moment, aware of faint regret. He wasn't going to let himself be seduced into another dead-end relationship. But, oh, he was tempted. This woman wasn't like anyone he'd ever known.

"And don't drool over me," she snapped.

"Optimist," he countered lazily.

She made a rough sound under her breath and turned unsteadily on her crutches. "I want to be there when you talk to the contractor. It's my ranch he'll be working on."

"I planned for you to meet him," he assured her. "That's why he's here."

"You might have given me a little advance notice," she said angrily.

"That's why I came down to the barn in the first place," he told her. "We got sidetracked."

"*You* got sidetracked," she accused with a harsh glare. "You started it."

"I had help," he returned. He stared her down. "How many men did it take to perfect that simpering, hungry look of yours?"

She glared and turned away. She didn't answer him, hobbling along on her crutches as fast as she could.

"If I could balance on one leg, I'd crack one of these crutches over your head," she said icily.

"You must have given the good doctor fits," he mused. "He still drools over you."

"He's a good man," she said shortly. "And he knows me."

"I don't doubt it," he drawled meaningfully.

She flushed. The going was rough on that gravel. She blew a strand of hair out of her face as she soldiered on.

The contractor was leaning against the hood of a nice green Mercedes, waiting for them. He was lean and elegant looking, darkly tanned, with black eyes in a swarthy face topped by straight, long black hair in a ponytail.

"This is Sloan Hayes," Todd introduced them. The Native American builder shook hands with Jane and then with Tim.

"We haven't met, but I've certainly heard of you," Jane said with a polite smile. Most people had. He was very famous and she was surprised that Todd knew him. "This is a small job..."

"We're glad to get it," Hayes replied suavely. "It's been slow lately," he hedged. "Your, uh, manager here has gone over the plans with me, but he wanted you to see them before we finalize the work. I brought the blueprints along so that you could inspect them."

"That's very nice of you," Jane said with a smile.

He cocked an eyebrow and smiled back. "I should have mentioned that I've been a rodeo fan all my life. I've seen you ride." He shook his head. "Hell of a shame about the accident. I'm sorry."

She was surprised, but not offended, by his openness. "I'm sorry, too, but life has these pitfalls. We have to adapt."

"Any idea what you'll substitute for rodeo in your life?" he continued.

She smiled. "How about raising champion horses?"

He chuckled. "Sounds like a winner. That's one of my own hobbies." His eyes narrowed appreciatively on her slender body.

Todd's face went stiff. "The plans?" he prompted.

Sloan gave him a deep look. "I'll get them."

"We can look them over in the study," Jane said. "Tim, will you have Meg get some coffee and cake and bring it on a tray when she's ready?"

"Sure thing!" Tim said, grinning.

Jane smiled at Todd as they waited for Sloan Hayes to get his blueprints. "He's very nice," she said with a deliberate sweetness. "I think this project is going to be a lot of fun."

"Just don't get too wound up in the project director," he cautioned. "He isn't marriage material, but he likes women...."

"Is *that* why you hired him? Thanks!" she said under her breath and smiled broadly when Sloan joined them on the porch.

"Here, let me help you with those crutches," the builder offered as they went into the house.

"Why, how very kind of you!" Jane said enthusiastically.

Todd followed them inside, the gnashing of his teeth all but audible. Complications were breaking out all over. First the redheaded doctor, now the builder. Well, he wasn't joining any queues and he didn't want her in the first place.

Having settled that in the privacy of his own mind, he forced himself to concentrate on the business at hand.

They went over the blueprints. Jane had several questions, but all in all, she was very satisfied with what the builder had drawn up.

"Do we need so much space in the barn?" she asked finally, when they were drinking coffee and eating slices of Meg's wonderful lemon pound cake.

"You do if you're serious about turning this place into a stud ranch," Sloan said quietly. "You have to have immaculate facilities for the livestock. That sort of thing doesn't go unnoticed by customers. There will be a certain amount of socializing necessary, also. And you'll have to do some renovation to the house to make it fit in with the overall look of the ranch."

She bit her lower lip and glanced at Todd worriedly.

"You can do it," he said simply. "The money's there. It's all arranged."

"I didn't think that far ahead," she said, troubled.

"You'll have to," Sloan said. "This change is going to foster others. It's a commitment."

She stared down into her lap. She wasn't sure she wanted such a change.

"We'll talk about it later," Todd said. "Meanwhile, sleep on it before you decide. Sloan's got a few other jobs to finish first."

"That's right," the builder said with a nice smile. "You don't have to jump into anything. Weigh the consequences. Then decide what you want to do."

"I will. Thank you for being patient," she said gently.

He smiled at her. "Oh, I'm known for my patience," he said, tongue-in-cheek. "Ask Todd."

Todd lifted an eyebrow. "I won't lie for you."

"I would for you," the other man said with hidden intent. "In fact, I have." Which was true, because Sloan had put up a warehouse for Todd's computer company, and now he was keeping mum about Todd's real background.

"Have some more coffee and shut up," Todd murmured with a grin.

"Point taken. Now about these outbuildings," he told Jane. "This is what I'd suggest..."

By the time he left, Jane had a picture of what the ranch would look like once it had been transformed. The cost was enormous, but the profit could be enormous as well.

Now, it all rested on her ability to sell her name for that endorsement, so that she could afford the improvements. But she wasn't going to say yes unless she felt she was doing the right thing. And she wouldn't know that until she met the manufacturer. She was going to reserve judgment until the next day, when they conferred.

Chapter 5

Jane barely slept that night, wondering what would come of her meeting with the clothier and the company's public relations representative. It didn't help that Todd left early the next morning with Cherry for Victoria.

"I'll be back before they get here," he assured Jane. "Stop brooding."

"I'll try. It's a big decision. I just hope that they'll ask me to endorse a line I can feel comfortable putting my name on." She hugged Cherry, and the girl returned the embrace with genuine fondness. In a short time, they'd become close. "Have a good time with your mother, and have fun shopping."

"Sure. You take care of yourself. No dancing," she teased, nodding toward the crutches.

Jane laughed softly. "Okay."

"I'll see you Monday."

Jane nodded, and waved them off. Todd looked glad to go. Perhaps, like her, he needed some breathing space. She wondered if he planned to spend the weekend at the ranch or go off on his own. Probably, she thought bitterly, he had plenty of women just waiting for the chance to go out with him. As good-looking as he was, she didn't doubt his attraction for the opposite sex. In a way, she was glad that she was exempt from his attentions. The very brief glimpse she'd had of his ardor the day before at the corral made her knees weak in retrospect. He wasn't the sort of man to play games with inexperienced women. He didn't know that she was inexperienced, either, and she had no intention of giving herself away.

She went back inside, glad of the time she was getting to distance herself from Todd's disturbing presence. She went over the books, amazed at what he'd accomplished in so short a time. He really was a wizard with figures. How, she wondered, could a man with such superb business sense spend his life working for someone else? He could have made a fortune by putting his analytical mind to work in his own interests. Perhaps he had no ambition, she decided finally.

She might have changed her mind if she could have seen him later that morning, sitting behind the desk in the president's office at Burke-Hathaway Business Systems. He'd long since bought out the Hathaway who was the old head of the company, but he left the name. It was known in south Texas, as Burke wasn't, and that made it good for business.

He made several pressing telephone calls, dictated letters and made arrangements to have leftover business sent down by fax. He'd installed a machine in the study, and he told his secretary that he'd telephone her with instructions as to when he wanted business documents sent. It wouldn't do for Jane to be in the study when he was working. He felt a twinge of guilt at keeping this from her, but after all, he *had* told her that he would be keeping his job and working for her on the side. In effect, he was.

That might bother him one day, but there was no reason
for her to know the truth about his private life. She was just
a temporarily disabled woman whom he felt sorry for. On a
whim he'd decided to help her. It was a diversion, a challenge. Life had gone sour for him lately, with his business
prospering and orders coming in faster than he could fill
them. He'd been stagnating with nothing to challenge his
quick mind. He had good people, subordinates, who did all
the really interesting work—inventing new software, balancing books, marketing. All he did was public relations work,
making contacts, conducting high-level meetings, signing
contracts and talking to bankers and stockholders. The thing
that had made the company fun in the first place was the risk.
He'd left any real risk behind when the company became one
of the Fortune 500. These days, he was the chief executive
officer and president of Burke-Hathaway.

He was a figurehead.

But not on the Parker ranch. No, sir. There, he was necessary. He was the one thing standing between Jane and
bankruptcy, and it made him feel good to know that he could
make such a difference in her life. There was the challenge
he needed to put the color back into his life. And it was
helping Cherry, too. She and Jane were already friends. The
girl hadn't had much fun in her life, but she really loved
rodeo and Jane was the perfect person to help her learn the
ropes. In fact, it had helped Jane already. She was less broody
and more determined than ever to get her broken body back
into some semblance of normalcy. All around, to sign on as
Jane's business manager was one of the better decisions of
Todd's life.

Then if it was such a great move, why, he asked himself
as he signed letters on the mahogany desk, did he feel so
morose and out of humor? He and Jane should have been
friends, but they weren't. Jane fought him at every turn, and
all at once, yesterday, he'd precipitated a physical awareness

in her that he regretted. She was vulnerable now, and he should have known better than to start something he couldn't finish.

She was so lovely, he thought angrily. Under different circumstances, he'd have made a dead set at her. But although she was old enough to have had lovers, he wondered about that side of her life. The doctor was interested in her, but there was no hint of real intimacy between the two of them. Old lovers would show it. They couldn't help but show it.

"Mr. Burke, you have to initial this contract as well," his secretary reminded him gently, pointing to two circles in the margin.

"Sorry." He initialed all three copies in the appropriate places and pushed them toward her. "Anything else pressing?"

"No, sir, not until next week."

He got up from the desk. "I'll be in and out," he said. "Mostly out. But I've left a number where I can be reached in case of an emergency." His steely gray eyes met hers. "Notice that I said *emergency*."

"Yes, sir." Miss Emory was in her early fifties and unflappable. She smiled. "Are you in disguise, sir?"

He chuckled. "In a manner of speaking, yes, so take care."

"Yes, sir."

"I'll check with you periodically. If anything urgent crops up, fax me. You don't need to explain anything, just state that I need to phone you. Sign your first name, not your last, to the fax. That way if anyone sees it, they'll just think I'm getting messages from a girlfriend."

Miss Emory chuckled. "Yes, sir."

He stacked the paperwork on the edge of the desk and left Miss Emory to deal with it. He had a feeling that she was going to earn more than her regular check for the next few weeks. He hoped he wasn't going to regret the decision that had taken him to Jacobsville.

The executive vice president from SlimTogs leisure wear was a young woman named Micki Lane. She had a nice smile and a firm handshake. Jane liked her at once. Her companion, however, was another sort altogether. Rick Wardell was a high-powered promoter with a fixed smile and determination in every line of his body. He verbally pushed Micki to one side and began to outline what would be expected of Jane if the company decided to use her.

Micki started to protest, but she was no match for Rick's verbal onslaught. Jane, however, was.

She held up a firm hand when the man was in full spate. "Wait a minute," she said pleasantly. "I haven't said that I want or need to do this endorsement. Furthermore, I'm not endorsing anything that I haven't seen."

"But we're very well-known," Rick said, sounding less confident than before.

"Of course you're well-known to most people," Jane replied. "But not to me," she said emphatically. "I'm rodeo from the boots up. I come from a long line of rodeo people. That means that if I endorse a product, a lot of fans will buy it. I want to be sure that I'm putting my name on something that's attractive, fairly priced and durable."

Rick's face tautened. "Listen, honey, you don't seem to understand that we're doing you a favor—" he began angrily.

"Nobody calls me *honey* unless I say they can," Jane interrupted. "I'm no wallpaper girl." Jane's blue eyes were flashing like lightning, and the man's mouth closed abruptly as he realized that he'd overstepped the mark and the situation was deteriorating rapidly.

Before Jane could say anything more, the borrowed car Todd was driving pulled up behind Rick's flashy little red sports car. He got out and joined the small group, taking in the situation with one long look.

"Burke! Glad you're here. I don't think Miss Parker understands what a favor we'd be doing her to put her name on this new line," Rick began, smiling as if he were certain that another man would surely side with him. "Maybe you can talk some sense into her."

"Surely the 'favor' extends in both directions?" Todd interrupted suavely. "Or hasn't your sales manager told you that several boutiques are queueing up already to place orders for any merchandise endorsed by Jane Parker?"

Rick laughed nervously. "Well, certainly, but..." He laughed again. "Perhaps we could start over?"

Micki was standing near Jane, looking irritated.

"Ms. Lane, isn't it?" Todd asked, and moved forward to shake hands with her. His eyes narrowed. "Excuse me, but I thought you were sent here to negotiate with Miss Parker?" He glanced pointedly toward Rick Wardell as he spoke.

"I was," Micki replied. "Mr. Wardell is in charge of sales and promotion."

Jane smiled at Rick. It wasn't a nice smile. She hadn't liked his condescending tone. "In order to have something to promote, I have to sign a contract. Frankly I don't think there's a chance in hell that it's going to happen. But it was nice of you to come out, Mr. Wardell. You, too, Miss Lane."

Micki stepped in front of Rick. "I'd like to show you our new line of jeans," she said quietly, "along with some of the new T-shirts we've adapted to imitate rodeo styling—with fringe and sequins and beads. They're machine-washable and guaranteed not to shrink or fade. I think you might like them."

Jane was impressed. She smiled. "Well..."

Micki glanced toward a very defensive-looking Rick, and the buried steel in her makeup began to show itself in her cool smile. "Mr. Wardell wanted to come along so that he could meet you. Now that he has, I'm sure that he won't mind leaving the contractual discussion in my hands. Will you, Mr. Wardell?'' she added pointedly.

He smiled uncertainly, then cleared his throat. ''As you say, that might be best.'' He grinned, showing all his teeth. ''Nice to have met you, Miss Parker, and I hope we'll be doing business. Burke.'' He nodded, still grinning, and turned to stride quickly back toward his sports car.

''If I sign anything, it had better have a clause that that man isn't to come within shooting range of me,'' Jane said bluntly, glaring after him. ''I hate being talked down to!''

''Rick has his drawbacks, but he could sell ice to Eskimos. We're slowly drawing him into the twentieth century,'' Micki said with a grin. ''I'll have a few words with the division boss about it when I get back. Meanwhile, couldn't I show you these samples, now that I'm here?''

''Well…I guess so,'' Jane agreed.

Micki smiled and went to get the case from her own car, a neat little tan sedan.

''It seems as though I arrived in the nick of time,'' Todd said quietly.

Jane looked up at him, still defensive. ''Just in time to save that man's life, for a fact. The condescending, stuck-up son of a—''

''He's a super salesman,'' he said pointedly. ''He's a master at sucking up to people when he feels he has to.''

''He'll think he's found lemon heaven if he tries it on me!''

Todd chuckled. He liked the way she looked when she was animated. ''You've got a temper.''

''No kidding!''

''Calm down,'' he advised. ''I won't try to force you to sign with them, but it would be to your advantage. The money for these repairs has to come from somewhere. This would almost pay for it. And if the line is as good as Micki says it is, you won't have a reason to refuse.''

''I can give you a good one, and it drives a red sports car!''

''You won't even have to talk to him again. I promise.''

She eased up a little. ''Well, if you promise.''

''That's the spirit.''

Micki came back, the sun shining on her sleek black hair. She was a pretty woman, slight and sedate looking, with dark eyes and an olive complexion. She smiled, and her eyes sparkled.

''Can we sit down?'' she asked. ''I've been on my feet all day and I'm tired.''

Probably, Jane thought sagely, because the woman could see that Jane was tiring as she leaned heavily on the crutches. Business sense and diplomacy were a nice mixture, and Jane knew even before she saw and approved of the clothing samples that she was going to sign that contract.

She gave the contract to her attorney to look over, but she sent Micki off with her assurances that she would do the endorsement. Micki was relieved and elated when she shook hands with both of them and left. Todd watched her out the door, his lips pursed thoughtfully.

''She isn't married,'' Jane remarked, aware of a faint twinge of jealousy that she was going to smother at once. ''And she's very pretty.''

He turned, his hands deep in the pockets of his tan slacks. Muscles rippled in his long arms, emphasized by the clinging knit of his yellow sports shirt. ''So she is,'' he agreed. ''But she's off limits.''

''Why?''

''I don't seduce business contacts,'' he said frankly. ''It's bad for my image.''

Her eyebrows lifted. "I didn't know accountants worried about things like that."

Business executives did. But he couldn't say it. He'd almost made a serious blunder. He laughed off his own remark. "I might work for her one day," he explained. "It's better if I don't get involved with potential bosses."

"Or current ones?" She was fishing and grinning. "Thank God!"

He glowered at her. "There's no need to look so relieved."

"Sorry. It slipped out. Erase it from your memory." She leaned back on the sofa and stifled a yawn. "It's been a long day. I'm sleepy."

"Why don't you stretch out there and take a nap?" he asked. "I've got some figures to catch up and Meg and Tim have gone grocery shopping. You've got nothing to do, have you?"

"Not right now, anyway." She stretched back onto the cushions, stifling a grimace. She was sore from the walking she'd done for the past two days on the crutches. "I suppose I'm a little less fit than I thought," she said with a self-conscious smile. She tucked a pillow under her head. "The crutches are hard going." Her eyes closed. "But I hate the wheelchair."

"Go to sleep," he said gruffly. He stood there watching her, his eyes narrow on her pale face in its frame of long, silky blond hair. She did look like a fashion doll, all the way up and down, from her pretty face to her slender, curvaceious body and long, elegant legs. He liked the way she looked. But he couldn't afford to pay too much attention to it. This was a very temporary job, and soon he was going to be back in the fast lane. He had to be objective and remote.

He turned and went into the study, closing the door gently. He had enough paperwork of his own to occupy him until supper, much less the additional burden of Jane's. It was a shame that things in his company had become complicated at just the wrong time. But he'd manage. The challenge was refreshing. He couldn't remember when he'd enjoyed himself so much.

In the weeks that followed, a bond developed between Jane and Cherry. They were all but inseparable, especially out at the corral where Cherry worked on perfecting her technique on horseback. She was better. She had self-confidence and the turns weren't making her hesitate. She gave Feather her head and watched the little mare incredulously as she sailed through her paces.

Jane was proud of her pupil, and that showed, too. She spent less time brooding about her slow progress and began to show marked improvement as her therapy sessions became fewer and farther between.

Todd, on the other hand, was finding his job harder by the day. The paperwork and the building work were easy, but being close to Jane all the time was wearing him down. An accidental touch of their fingers sent his heart racing. A look that lingered too long made him tingle down to his toes. He found himself watching her for no reason at all, except that he liked to look at her. And his vulnerability made him bad-tempered. He was spending a lot of time with Micki Lane, going over the contracts with the attorneys before Jane signed them. She was pretty and interested in him, and he needed a diversion. So without counting the cost, he called her up and invited her to a dance.

The dance at the Jacobsville Civic Center was one of the monthly events that passed for socializing in Jacobsville. Jane had gone to them frequently before her accident, often with Copper Coltrain. But she'd given up dancing because of her injury. When Cherry mentioned casually that her dad was taking that pretty leisure wear executive to it, Jane was unprepared for the surge of jealousy she felt. She liked Micki, but it was hard to think of her with Todd. At least, she thought miserably, she'd have Cherry for company.

Only it didn't work out that way. Cherry accepted a last-minute invitation to spend the weekend with her mother and caught an early bus to Victoria. Then Tim and Meg announced that they'd be gone, too. Jane felt miserable and tried desperately not to show it. It seemed that everyone was going to desert her.

Todd thought that Jane seemed pale when he was ready to leave to pick Micki up that evening. He paused with the car keys jingling in his pocket. "You don't mind being here alone?" he asked. He looked very attractive in tan slacks, cream-colored boots and a patterned Western shirt and black string tie.

"Of course not," Jane said proudly. "I'm used to being by myself when Tim and Meg go to visit their daughter. They go at least one Saturday a month and they don't get in until late," she added.

He looked concerned. He didn't like having her on her own so far from any neighbors.

"This isn't a big city," she said, exasperated. "For heaven's sake, nobody's going to break in and kill me! I've got a shotgun over there behind the door, and I know how to use it!"

"If you have time to load it," he muttered. "Do you know where the shells are?"

She made a face. "I can find them if I have to."

He threw up his hands. "Oh, that's very reassuring! I hope any potential intruders are polite enough to wait while you do that!"

"I'm almost twenty-six years old!" she raged at him. "I can take care of myself without any tall, blond nursemaids!

You just go on and mind your own business. I'm looking forward to a quiet evening with a good book!''

"I can see how that will benefit you," he said sarcastically. He picked up the book on the table beside the end of the sofa where she was lounging in jeans and a loose green shirt. "A source book on the battle of the Alamo. How enlightening."

"I like to read history," she said.

"Romance novels might do you more good," he returned. "A little vicarious pleasure would be better than nothing, surely."

Her blue eyes flashed. "If I want romance, I know where to go looking for it!"

"I'm flattered," he said, deliberately provocative.

"Not *you*," she said angrily. "Never you! That's wishful thinking on your part. You're not that attractive to me!"

"Really?" He bent toward her. She averted her face, but he reached behind her head with a steely hand and turned her face up to his. She had one quick glimpse of flint-hard gray eyes before his hard mouth came down on hers.

She reached up instinctively to push at him, but his teeth were nibbling her shocked, set lips apart. He tasted of mint and smelled of sexy cologne. The clean scents seduced her as much as the sharp, teasing movements of his mouth.

Her fingers clenched on his shirtfront in token protest. She made a sound, but his free hand came to her throat and he began to smooth it in gentle caresses. She felt her breath catch as the lazy pressure of his mouth touched something hidden and secret, deep inside her body. She felt like a coiled spring that was suddenly loosened. Her quick intake of breath was echoed by the faint groan that pushed past his hard mouth into her parting lips.

He caught her grasping fingers and spread them against the front of his soft shirt, moving them sensually from side to side over the hard, warm muscles. His breathing quickened, as did hers, and his hand moved to press her mouth closer into the demanding contact with his.

Her faint whimper excited him. He gave in to the red-hot waves of pleasure, hardly aware that he'd moved until he felt her body under his as he eased down on the sofa with her.

She felt the cushions at her back, his lean strength touching her from shoulders to thigh, his arms around her, his mouth touching and lifting, seducing, demanding in a silence so fraught with emotion that she could hear the sound of her own heartbeat.

His hands were under her blouse, against the skin of her back, exploring her as if she belonged to him. One long leg was insinuating itself between both of hers, gently so as not to jar her, seductively slow.

She managed to get a fraction of an inch between her mouth and his, and she struggled for breath and presence of mind.

"No…" she whispered jerkily.

His left hand tangled in her long hair while the right one roughly unsnapped the pearly studs of his shirt. He was wearing nothing underneath the fabric, and without hesitation, he gently pushed her face against thick hair and clean, cologne-scented bare skin, coaxing her mouth to touch him just below his collarbone.

She hadn't experienced that sort of intimacy. She fought it, trying to remember that he was on his way to another woman.

He shifted, so that her lips were touching the hard, tight thrust of a male nipple. His hand, behind her head, guided her, insisted, without a single word.

She was curious and attracted, so she did what he wanted her to do. She wasn't prepared for the ripple of muscle under her mouth or the soft, tortured moan that sounded above her head.

She hesitated, but his hand contracted in her hair and he

moaned again, shifting. She gave in, suckling him, tasting him in a heated interlude that made her lower body seem to swell with new sensations.

Both his hands were in her hair now, guiding her mouth around the fascinating territory of his chest. It expanded violently as she kissed him, and he groaned even as he laughed at the delight her touch gave him.

He moved to lie on his back, his mouth swollen, his eyes glittering with emotion, his chest bare and throbbing when she finally lifted her head to look down at him.

He smiled with a kind of secret fever, stretching so that the shirt fell away. He arched, holding her eyes.

She pressed both hands to the wall of his broad chest, testing the wiry silkiness of the hair that covered him, watching him watch her while she touched him exploringly.

His hands pressed down over hers, holding them where his heart beat roughly, quickly, at his rib cage.

"You don't even know what to do," he said half angrily. "Do you need an instruction manual?"

She blinked, feeling sanity come back with a rush. Her hands jerked back and she gasped. She moved away from him and sat up, grimacing as the movement caught her painfully. She could only imagine how she must look with her hair disheveled and her mouth swollen and her face flushed. Her eyes were like saucers.

He stared at her as if, for a moment, he didn't even recognize her. In fact, she hardly resembled the pale, composed woman he saw every day. He remembered her stinging comment and bending to kiss her in anger. Then the whole situation had gotten out of hand. How could he have forgotten himself so completely?

With a muffled curse, he got to his feet and fastened his shirt, straining to breathe normally. Of all the harebrained, stupid things he'd ever done…!

Jane was feeling equally addled. After that last sarcastic

remark he'd made, he was going to be lucky if she ever spoke to him again! She picked up her book and opened it in her lap, refusing to even look at him. She was embarrassed, nervous and defensive because she'd been so vulnerable.

He finished snapping his shirt and tucked it back into his slacks. His hands were faintly unsteady, which made him furious. She got to him without even trying. He seemed to have no control whatsoever once he touched her. That had never happened with Marie, even in the early days of their romance. And she just sat there, so cool that butter wouldn't melt in her mouth, looking unaffected when he could barely breathe. That alone made him furious.

"Nothing to say?" he asked, glancing at her with steely gray eyes. "Would you like to repeat that bit about not finding me attractive?" he mocked.

She wouldn't look up. Her face reddened a little more, but otherwise, no expression showed in it. She didn't say a word.

He moved to the door. "I'll lock this behind me."

She nodded, but he wasn't looking.

He went out without another comment. His heart was still racing and he wasn't sure that his knees wouldn't buckle on the way to his car. Whatever Jane did to him, he hated it. He only wished he knew how to handle it. He had nothing to give her. It wasn't fair to lead her on when he felt that way. If she could be led on, that is. She'd been responsive enough until the last, when she'd seemed shocked and outraged. But she hadn't said a word. Not a word. He wondered what was going on in her mind.

He cursed as he fumbled the key into the ignition of his car and started it. Well, it didn't really matter what she thought, because that wasn't going to happen again. He'd have a good time with Micki and forget that Jane even existed.

Chapter 6

Only it didn't quite work out that way. Micki was a delightful companion, but when Todd held her while they were dancing, he felt nothing beyond a comfortable pleasure. The wild excitement that Jane engendered just by looking at him with her big blue eyes was totally missing.

"It was nice of you to invite me," Micki said with a smile. "But won't Jane mind?"

He scowled. "Jane is my employer," he said stiffly.

"Oh. Sorry. It was just that the way she looked..."

He pounced on that at once. "The way she looked...?" he prompted, and tried not to appear as interested as he was in her answer.

She laughed apologetically. "I thought she was in love with you," she explained.

His face was shot through with color. He stopped dancing. "That's absurd," he said slowly.

"Not really. You've obviously been kind to her," Micki continued, "and she was badly hurt in the wreck, wasn't she?

I suppose it's inevitable that a woman will feel something for a man who helps her when she's in trouble. Mr. Kemble, her attorney, said that you've literally pulled her out of bankruptcy in a few short weeks and helped her get the ranch back on its feet.''

He looked troubled. "Perhaps. The ranch had plenty of potential. It just needed a few modifications.''

"Which you've accomplished. Jane is lovely, isn't she? Our advertising people are ecstatic about building a television campaign around her because she's so photogenic.''

"She's easy enough on the eyes,'' he said noncommittally.

"And surprisingly modest about it. I've known of her for years, of course, since I grew up in Jacobsville. I'd heard that Dr. Coltrain gave up when you came to the Parker place. He's been going around with Jane for a long time. He's not a man I'd find easy to think of romantically, not with his temper, but Jane was fiery enough to stand up to him. Everyone thought they'd make a match of it eventually.''

His face tautened. "Did they? Well, he only comes out to the place once in a while to check on her.''

Micki hid a smile. "Oh, I see.''

His broad shoulders shifted. "I'm certain that she could have gotten married long before this if she'd wanted to.''

"I don't know. Most men seem to think a woman as lovely as Jane has more admirers than she can sort out, and a lot of pretty women don't even get asked out because of that perception. Actually I don't remember Jane dating anyone seriously. Except Dr. Coltrain, of course.''

He was getting tired of hearing about Coltrain. "At her age, she's bound to have had a serious love affair.''

"Do you think so?'' Micki asked with studied carelessness. "If she has, it's been very discreet. Her reputation is impeccable.''

He swung her around to the music. "What do you think of the band?'' he asked with a pleasant smile.

She chuckled to herself. ''It's nice, isn't it? I do enjoy a good two-step.''

Todd was out of sorts by the time he drove Micki home, leaving her at the door with a chaste kiss before he sped back toward the ranch. It had been a pleasant evening, but he hadn't been able to get Jane's hungry kisses out of his mind. Then there was Micki's careless comment that she thought Jane was in love with him. That had set his mind spinning so that he took Micki back long before he normally would have.

When he drove away from her apartment house, it was barely eleven o'clock, and he was damned if he was going home that early. He stopped by a small bar out in the country and had a couple of beers before he drove the rest of the way out. By then it was almost one, and a more respectable hour for a man who'd enjoyed himself to be getting in.

He'd planned to go straight to the little house where he and Cherry were staying, but the lights were still on in the ranch house and he didn't see Tim's car out by the garage.

Frowning, and a little concerned, he went up to the front door and tried it. It was unlocked. Really worried now, he opened it and went in, closing it with a quiet snap and then working his way cautiously past the empty living room and study, down to the bedrooms.

There was light under only one door. He opened it and Jane gaped at him. She was sitting up in bed reading, wearing a low-cut blue satin gown with spaghetti straps. Her hair was loose around her shoulders and the firm, silky slopes of her breasts were bare almost to the nipples in her relaxed pose.

Lamplight became her, he thought helplessly. She was the most beautiful woman he'd ever seen. His whole body clenched at the thought of what lay under that silky fabric.

''Why the hell is the front door unlocked?'' he asked shortly.

"It isn't," she faltered. "I locked it and left the lights on in case Meg needed to come in…"

"It wasn't locked. I walked right in. And they haven't come back. Did you check the answering machine?"

She frowned. "No. I took a couple of aspirin because my back was hurting, and then I lay down," she began.

He averted his eyes from her body. "I'll check for any messages." He went out, grateful for something besides the sight of her to occupy his mind. He went to the telephone in the living room and pressed the Play button on the answering machine. Sure enough, Tim had phoned to say that he and Meg would be spending the night with their daughter so that they could go to church with her the next morning. A distant relative was visiting and they wanted to get reacquainted.

He listened dimly as the machine reset itself and beeped. His heart was beating furiously in his chest. Two beers didn't usually affect him, but he hadn't eaten in a while and his head was reeling with the sight of Jane in that gown and what Micki had said about Jane being in love with him. What if he went into her bedroom and slid that silky gown off her breasts? Would she welcome him? If she loved him…

He muttered a curse and ran a hand through his damp hair. He should get out, right now, before he did something really stupid.

He got as far as the front door. He couldn't force himself to go through it. After a brief struggle with his conscience, he gave in to the pulsating need that was making him ache from head to toe. She could always say no, he told himself. But he knew that she wouldn't. Couldn't. He put on the locks, turned out the outside light and then the living room and study lights.

Jane had put down her book. When he walked back into her bedroom, she was sitting just where he'd left her, looking more vulnerable than ever.

"Did they…call?" she asked, her voice as choked as her

body. She, too, was remembering the heated lovemaking of earlier in the evening and hungry for more of it. From the look on his hard face, so was he. She loved him so much that all thoughts of self-preservation had gone right out of her head in the hours since he'd left for his date. She had no pride left. Loneliness and love had eaten it away.

"They won't be home until morning," he said stiffly.

She looked at him with wide, helpless eyes, a little frightened and a little hungry. Everything she felt lay open to his searching eyes.

With a smile that was part self-contempt and part helpless need, he slowly closed and locked the bedroom door. He held her eyes while his hand went to snap off the main switch that controlled the bedside lamps.

The room went dark. She sat, breathing unsteadily, waiting. She saw the outline of him, big and threatening, as he came around the bed and slowly sat down beside her. Then she felt his lean, strong hands, warm on her arms as he slid the straps down and let the gown drop to her waist.

She felt herself shiver. Her breath caught. She felt the air on her body and the need for him was suddenly the most important thing in her life. She arched back with a faint moan, imploring, coaxing.

"I should be shot," he breathed. And then his warm mouth was on her soft, bare breasts, his hands gentle on her body as he eased her down on the bed.

She'd never known a man, but her responses were so acutely hungry that Todd didn't realize it at first. Her headlong acceptance of his deep kisses, of the caresses that grew more intimate as he eased her out of the gown and the faint briefs under it, made him too reckless to notice her shy hands on his chest.

She smelled of flowers and her body was the sweetest kind of warm silk under his mouth. He smoothed his lips over her from head to toe, enjoying her in a silence that trembled with sensation and sensuality.

When he was near the end of his patience, he divested himself of his clothing and drew her gently against the length of him. She caught her breath and tried to pull away, but his mouth on hers stilled the feeble protest.

''Are you using something?'' he asked feverishly against her mouth.

''Wh...what?'' she managed shakily.

''Are you on the Pill?'' he persisted.

''N-no.''

He groaned and reached down for his billfold. Thank God he was prepared. He'd never felt the blind need she kindled in his tall, fit body.

His question had almost brought Jane back to sanity as she realized the enormity of what she was doing, but his mouth found hers again, gently, while he did what was necessary. And the tender, passionate kisses and caresses weakened her so that all she felt was an aching emptiness that cried out to be filled.

''I'll be careful, baby,'' he whispered as he drew her to him, on his side, so that he wouldn't jar or injure her back. His long leg slid between hers and his hands positioned her gently so that he could ease into intimacy with her. ''Easy, now.''

Her nails bit into his shoulders. She wanted him, but it stung. She buried her mouth against his collarbone and whimpered, but even then she didn't fight.

He wasn't so far gone that he didn't realize what was wrong. He stilled, breathing roughly, his hands like steel clamps on her slender hips. ''Jane...?'' he whispered, shocked.

She was struggling to breathe. She moaned.

His powerful body shivered with the effort to hold back, even for a space of seconds. ''God, baby, I didn't know...!''

He groaned harshly. "I have to! Forgive me, I can't stop! I can't!"

He surged against her, blind with a need as old as time, as unstoppable as an avalanche.

There was a fierce flash of pain. She cried out. He heard her in the back of his mind, and hated himself for what was happening, but he was totally at the mercy of the white-hot need in his loins. Tormented seconds later, the painful tension in his body snapped and blinding, furious pleasure lifted him to heights he'd never known in his life. Then, he fell again to cold reality and felt the guilt and anguish of the trembling body containing his.

He kissed away the tears, his hands as gentle now as they had been demanding only minutes before. "Forgive me," he whispered piteously. "Oh, Lord, I'm sorry! It was too late by the time I realized."

She lay her cheek against his cool, damp chest and closed her wet eyes. It had been painful and uncomfortable, and now her back was hurting again.

"You're twenty-five years old," he groaned, smoothing her hair. "What were you doing, saving it for marriage?"

"That isn't funny." She choked.

He drew in a sharp breath. "I suppose you were. You're so damned traditional."

She bit her lower lip. "Will you leave, please?"

He kissed her closed eyes. "No. Not until I give you what I had."

"I won't let you do that again!" she said hotly, hitting at him. "It hurt!"

His lips brushed against hers. He drew her hand to his mouth and kissed it, too. "The first time usually does, or so I'm told," he said gently. "But I can give you tenderness now."

"I don't want...!"

His mouth covered hers softly, slowly. He coaxed it to

open to the lazy thrust of his tongue. His hands slid over her tense body, soothing her even as they began to incite her to passion. She didn't understand how it could happen. He'd hurt her. But she was moving closer to him. Her arms were lifting to enclose him. Her breasts were swelling under his hands and then his mouth, and she felt a tension building inside her that made her legs start to tremble.

He was gentle. He lay on his back and smoothed her body completely over him, deftly joining their bodies while he whispered soft, tender commands at her ear. His steely hands on her hips pulled and pushed and shifted her, so that she felt the fullness of him inside her building into an ache that blinded her with its promise.

She sobbed helplessly, clinging to him. "Oh...no," she whispered breathlessly as she felt her senses begin to climb some unbelievable peak.

"Don't fight it," he whispered at her temple. His voice was soft, but his breathing was quick and sharp, like the tug of his hard fingers and the thrust of his hips.

She whimpered as the pleasure caught her unaware and she stiffened on his body.

"Yes, that's it," he whispered feverishly. "That's it! Give in to me. Give in, Jane, give in! Let it happen!"

She heard her voice rising in sharp little cries as he increased the rhythm. Then, all at once, she went over an edge she hadn't expected, into realms of hot, black pleasure that took control of her body away from her brain and made her oblivious to everything except the hard heat of him filling her.

She pushed down as hard as she could and shuddered endlessly, frozen in pleasure, deaf and blind to the joyous laughter of the man holding her. Only when she was completely satisfied did he allow himself the exquisite pleasure of release.

He smoothed her long, damp hair over her spine and lay

dreaming of the ecstasy he'd shared with her for a long time, until her faint weeping ceased and she lay still, trembling a little, on his spent body.

Her breasts were as soft as down. He shifted a little, so that he could feel them rubbing against his chest. His hands slid down to her hips, where they were still joined, and he pressed her closer into him.

She gasped. The touch of him was unbearably pleasurable, even now.

He mistook the gasp. "It's all right," he said gently. "You were protected, both times. I don't take that sort of risk, ever."

She was too embarrassed to know what to say. Her fingers clenched against him and she lay still, uncertain and hesitant in the aftermath.

He stretched stiffly and laughed. "But it was a near thing, I'll tell you that," he confessed. "Is your back all right?"

She bit her lip. "Yes."

He eased her onto her side and pulled away. Her teeth went deeper into her lip as reality fell on her like a cold brick.

He felt on the floor for her gown and briefs and laid them on her breasts. He bent and kissed her tenderly. "You'd better get your things back on," he whispered. "It's chilly."

She fumbled into them, listening to the rustle of fabric as he dressed by the side of the bed. She felt tears sting her eyes and hated herself for the one lapse of a lifetime. She hadn't even had the presence of mind to protect herself. Thank God he'd thought of it. And now there was the future to think of. How could she ever face him again, after this? He'd know how she felt about him. But whatever he felt was well concealed. He hadn't said a word while he was making love to her, except for soft commands and endearments. But there hadn't been one confession of love.

While she was worrying, he tucked her under the sheet and pushed her hair away from her face. "Sleep well," he

said, trying not to betray how awkward he felt. Her cheek
was wet. Did she hate him? Was she sorry? She'd tried to
stop him, but he couldn't stop. Did she understand? Then,
afterward, he'd wanted to make amends in the only way possible. He knew he'd given her pleasure, but would it be
enough to make up for what he'd taken?

She turned her face away with a faint sigh and he left her.
There would be time enough in the morning for talking, for
explanations and apologies.

Jane was stiff and sore when she woke up. She opened her
eyes and blinked from the brightness, and then she remembered. She sat up in bed, flushing with memories that made
her feel hot all over.

She moved the top sheet away and grimaced at the betraying faint stains on the bottom one. She got out of bed
and stripped away the sheet, throwing it on the floor, and her
gown and briefs along with it. She went into the bathroom
and showered herself from head to toe before she dressed in
jeans and a round-neck yellow T-shirt and sneakers. Then
she bundled up the laundry and put it into the washing machine, starting the load before Meg came in.

"Hey, that's my job," Meg complained gaily when she
got home and found the drier running and another load of
clothes going through the spin cycle in the washer.

"I didn't have anything to do," Jane said with a poker
face and a smile. "Everyone's gone for the weekend except
Todd. He was late getting in last night. He took Micki Lane
to a dance."

"She's pretty," Meg said, frowning. "I thought maybe
you liked him."

She shrugged. "He's very nice. I think he's a great accountant."

Nice. Meg sighed mentally at her dashed dreams of a romance between the two of them, and shooed her charge out of the kitchen while she saw to lunch.

But when Meg put it on the table, Todd still hadn't come to the house. Jane had been dreading it since dawn, uncertain of how she was going to face him. She was ashamed and embarrassed and a little afraid of having him taunt her with her helplessness.

"Where's Todd?" Meg asked when she had the salad and bread on the table.

"I don't know. I haven't seen him today," Jane said.

"It isn't like him to miss lunch." She went to the window and looked out. "His car's gone."

"Maybe he had a date with Micki today," Jane ventured, not looking up.

"Wouldn't he have said?"

Jane smiled. "He doesn't have to report to us."

"I guess not. Well, I'll call Tim and we'll eat."

It was a brief, pleasant lunch. Meg talked about their daughter and the distant cousin who'd come to visit. And if Jane was unusually silent, it went unremarked if not unnoticed.

Just before dark, Todd drove up with Cherry. Obviously, Jane thought, he'd gone up to Victoria to get her even though she'd said she was going to take the bus. Perhaps he was as uncomfortable as Jane now, only wanting to forget what had happened and needful of putting some space between them.

She was sitting on the sofa watching the news when they came in.

"How was your weekend?" Jane asked Cherry.

"Not very pleasant," Cherry said, without saying why. She smiled at Jane. "You look pale. Are you okay?"

She had to fight not to look at Todd. "I'm fine. I've had a lazy day."

"I need to check some figures. I'll take the books back

over to the house with me, if you don't mind," he said, addressing Jane for the first time, his tone formal and remote.

"Of course," she said to his chin and even smiled. "Have you both eaten?"

"We had supper on the way," Todd said shortly. He went to get the books and came back with them tucked under one arm. "Say good-night, Cherry."

"Good night," the girl said obediently, aware of a new tension between the two adults in her life. She was too sensitive to mention it, though. And anyway, her dad had been quiet and unapproachable. Probably, she thought sadly, there had been another argument. It saddened her that her father and her new friend couldn't get along.

Jane called good-night and went back to her television program. She hadn't looked directly at Todd, or he at her. She wondered if things would ever be the same again.

The builders worked diligently at the repairs and finished right on schedule. Inspecting the new barn, Jane was amazed at their progress. It was a good job, too, not a slipshod effort.

The next step was to buy brood mares. Jane and Cherry went with Todd to an auction at a well-known horse ranch outside Corpus Christi. Todd and Jane looked at the catalog, not at each other, and Cherry enthused over each horse as it was led into the rink.

Jane had an excellent eye for horseflesh. Before her father's death, even he had deferred to her on buying trips. Todd quickly realized her ability, and he followed her father's example. They bought three good brood mares and a colt with excellent bloodlines. Todd arranged for them to be transported to the ranch and rejoined Cherry and Jane.

"Can we stop and get an ice cream on the way back?" Cherry asked, wiping away sweat. "It's awfully hot!"

"If Jane isn't too tired," he said stiffly.

"I'm fine," she said carelessly, putting an affectionate arm around Cherry. She was walking without her crutches now, although not as quickly as before. Two or three times, she'd had to fight the impulse to get on her horse and ride like the wind. Perhaps that was a realizable dream, but not just yet.

"Then we'll stop down the road a bit," Todd replied.

There was a small ice cream shop in a stand of mesquite trees, just off the main road. Although it was a bit isolated, there were plenty of cars surrounding it, and the small picnic area was full.

"We can sit under the trees," Cherry said. "Jane and I will grab the seats while you get the ice cream, Dad. I want a chocolate shake."

His head turned and he looked at Jane. "What would you like?" he asked politely.

"I'll have the same, thanks," she said, avoiding his eyes. She turned and walked away with Cherry.

Todd watched her hungrily. He'd handled the whole situation badly, and now he didn't know what to do. His conscience had tortured him over the past few days. He didn't sleep at night for it. He hadn't exactly forced her to do something she didn't want to, but she'd wanted him to stop and he couldn't. He'd taken away her right to give her chastity to a man she married. She might have loved him once, but he no longer thought she cared at all. She wouldn't look at him. If he came into a room, she found an excuse to leave it. She was subdued and withdrawn except when Cherry was around. And it was his fault. If only he hadn't touched her in the first place.

The man asked him again for his order and he snapped back to the present long enough to give it. He took the paper tray of milkshakes when the man came back and paid for them.

Minutes later, the three of them were sitting under the tree with the breeze playing in Jane's hair, sipping the cold, refreshing shakes.

"Don't you love chocolate?" Cherry said enthusiastically.

Jane smiled at her. "Yes, but it doesn't love me. Sometimes it gives me migraines."

"Why the hell didn't you say so?" Todd demanded angrily.

She glanced at him, startled by the venom in his tone. "I love chocolate."

"Which is no reason to deliberately bring on a headache."

She glared back at him. "I'll eat what I like. You're not my keeper!"

"Uh, what do you think of the colt, Jane?" Cherry interrupted quickly.

"What?" She was staring into Todd's furious eyes and he was staring back. The anger slowly began to fade, to be replaced by something equally violent, simmering, smoldering hot.

Cherry hid a smile. "I'll get some more napkins," she said.

Neither of them seemed to notice her leaving. Jane's face was getting redder by the second, and Todd's eyes narrowed until they were gray slits, full of heat and possession.

His hand reached out and caught hers hungrily. "Shall we stop pretending that nothing happened?" he asked roughly.

Chapter 7

Jane felt his fingers contracting, intimately interlacing themselves with her own. She couldn't quite breathe normally, and her eyes were giving her feelings away.

"We've been dancing around it for days," he said huskily. He held her eyes searchingly. "I still want you," he added heavily. "More than ever."

She tore her gaze from his and looked down at their hands. "It shouldn't have happened."

"I know," he said surprisingly. "But it did. I've never had it that good, Jane. I think you and I could have a very satisfying relationship."

She looked up, but that wasn't love in his eyes. It was hunger, certainly. But it was an empty hunger. "You mean, we could have an affair," she said quietly.

He nodded, dashing her faint hopes of something more. "I've tried marriage," he said bitterly. "I don't believe in it anymore. But you can't deny that we go up like fireworks when we're together. There won't be any consequences, any repercussions."

"What about Cherry?" she asked stiffly.

"Cherry's fourteen," he replied. "She knows that I'm no monk. She doesn't expect fairy-tale endings."

Her sad eyes searched his. "Doesn't she? I'm afraid that I do." She withdrew her hands from his.

His eyebrows arched. "You aren't serious, surely? You don't expect to marry a man and stay married for life, do you?" he added with a mocking laugh.

"Yes, I do, despite what…what happened the other night," she replied, her chin lifted proudly. "I'll be honest with him about it. But I do believe in love and I think people can stay together if they have common interests and they're willing to work at it."

He sat up straight, his mouth tightened into a thin line. "You don't think Marie and I worked at it?" he asked in a dangerously soft voice.

"It takes two people, committed…"

"Committed is the right word," he said on a harsh laugh. "People who get married should be committed!"

She saw then that his mind was closed on the subject, and all her hopes fell away. She smiled sadly. "I'm sorry. I don't have a bad marriage behind me, and I still believe in fairy tales. I don't want to have an affair with you, Todd."

His eyes glittered narrowly. "You loved what I did to you."

She shrugged, although it took her last bit of courage, and she smiled. "Sure I did. It was wonderful. Thanks."

He looked positively outraged. His high cheekbones flushed angrily and he opened his mouth to speak as Cherry came back with a handful of napkins.

"Here you go," she said, putting them down. "Isn't it nice here in the shade?"

Todd bit off what he was going to say. He finished his milkshake and got up. "We'd better get back," he said curtly. "I've got a lot of paperwork to catch up."

"But, Dad…" Cherry protested. She grimaced at the look he shot her. "Okay, okay, sorry!" She finished her milkshake with a wistful smile at Jane, and they all went back to the car.

The next few days were strained. Jane watched Cherry work with Feather and she conferred with Micki Lane about the plans for the advertising campaign.

"We'll need some publicity shots," Micki told her. "When can you come up to Victoria to do them?"

Jane picked a day and Micki offered to come and get her. "No, thanks," Jane said, "I'll have one of the hands run me up." She couldn't bear to see Micki with Todd.

"Oh. Well, okay," Micki said sadly. "How's Todd? I haven't heard from him lately."

"He's fine. Working hard, of course," she added matter-of-factly. "They're just finished putting up our new barn and he's been working closely with the contractor."

"I see," Micki said. She sounded happier. "I guess it takes up a lot of time, hmm?"

"A lot." More than he gave any other project, she thought, and probably it was just an excuse to keep out of Jane's way. Even Cherry was complaining about the fervor with which her father had approached the barn building and repairs.

"Then I'll see you Friday, yes?" Micki asked.

"Friday at nine," Jane agreed.

She didn't mention her trip to Todd or Cherry. She could ask Tim to drive her up, she was sure.

Meanwhile, she had to go to Dr. Coltrain for her checkup. He tested her reflexes, listened to her heart and lungs, checked her blood pressure and asked a dozen questions before he pronounced her blooming.

"Except for those bags under your eyes," he added, his piercing blue eyes on her drawn face. "Burke getting you down?"

She glared at him. "Todd Burke is none of your business."

He grinned at her. "I'm not blind, even if you are."

"What do you mean?"

"Oh, you'll find out one day." He leaned back in his chair and swiveled around. "Don't take it too fast, but I think you could start walking more."

"How about riding?"

He hesitated. "Slowly," he said. "For brief periods, and not on any of your usual mounts. That palomino gelding is gentle enough, I suppose. But don't overdo it."

"Bracket is gentle," she assured him. "He'd never toss me."

"Any horse will toss you under the right circumstances, and you know it."

She'd forgotten that he practically grew up on horseback. He rode as well as she did—better. He'd done some rodeo to help put himself through medical school.

"I'll be careful," she promised him.

"What's this I hear about you selling clothes?" he asked suddenly.

She grinned. "Meg told your mother, didn't she?" she asked. "I thought she would. I'm going to endorse a line of women's Western wear. It's very well made and I'll be on television and in magazines promoting it. In fact," she added, "I'm going up to Victoria on Friday to do the publicity photos for the magazines."

"How are you going to get there?"

"I thought I'd ask Tim…"

"Ask me," he said with a slash of a grin. "I'm driving up to confer on a leukemia case at the hospital there. The patient is one of mine who moved away. You can ride with me."

"I may be there all day," she warned.

He shrugged. "I'll find something to keep me busy."

She smiled broadly. "Then I'd love to. Thanks."

"I'll pick you up at the ranch about eight-thirty. We can stop for coffee on the way."

"Okay. I'll look forward to it."

"How did you get here?"

"Meg dropped me off on her way to the grocery store. She'll be waiting in the parking lot. She only had a few things to get."

"Why didn't Burke bring you?" he asked.

She flushed. "Because I didn't ask him to!"

He pursed his lips. "I see."

She stood up. "No, you don't. Thanks for the ride. I'll see you in the morning."

"Jane."

She paused at the doorway, turning to meet his level gaze. "Do you need to ask me anything?"

She went scarlet, because she knew exactly what he meant. "No," she whispered huskily, "I do not!"

"Okay. No need to color up," he said gently, and smiled with affection. "But I'm here if you need me, and I'm not judgmental."

She drew in a slow breath. "Oh, Copper, I know that," she said miserably. "I wish…" she said huskily.

"No, you don't," he mused, smiling. "I had a case on you a few years ago, but our time passed. A blind man could see how you feel about Burke. Just be careful, will you? You're as green as spring grass, and that man knows his way around women."

"I'll be careful," she replied. "It's good to have a friend like you."

"That works both ways," he said.

There was a perfunctory knock on the door and Lou Blakely looked in. "Excuse me," she said with a glance at Jane, "Mr. Harris won't talk to me about his hemorrhoids. Could you…?"

"I'll be with you in a minute," he said shortly.

She closed the door quickly.

"You're very rude to her, aren't you?" Jane remarked quietly. "She's a sweet woman. It hurts her when you snap, haven't you noticed?"

"Oh, yes," he said, and for a minute he didn't look like the man she knew. "I've noticed."

She let it drop, saying goodbye and pausing only to pay the receptionist before she went out to find Meg. Copper had been the kindest of boys when they were young, even though he was five years her senior. But he was different with Lou. He seemed to dislike her. Odd that he'd accepted her into his practice if he found her so irritating.

Meg drove Jane back to the ranch. She found Cherry waiting on the porch for her, beaming.

"I did it!" she told Jane excitedly. "I beat my old time! I wasn't even afraid! Oh, Jane, I've done it, I've overcome the fear! I can hardly wait for the next rodeo."

"I'm happy for you," Jane said with soft affection. "You're a great little rider. You're going to go far."

"I'll settle for being half as good as you," she said with worshiping eyes.

Jane laughed. "That won't be hard these days."

"Don't be silly. You'll always be Jane Parker. You've made your mark in rodeo already. You're famous! And you're going to be even more famous when you make those commercials."

"Well, we'll see. I'm not counting my chickens before they hatch!"

The photo session was the main topic of conversation at supper.

"I'll run you up to Victoria in the morning," Tim volunteered. "Or Todd might, if he can spare the time from that barn," he added, teasing the younger man, who was taciturn over his chicken and mashed potatoes and beans.

Todd looked up at Jane without any emotion. "If she wants me to, I don't mind," he said.

"Thank you both, but I have a ride," Jane said. She smiled. "Copper's got to go up there on a case, so he said I could go with him."

Todd didn't say a word, but the hand holding his fork stiffened. "The good doctor gets around, doesn't he?" he asked.

"Yes, he does. He's quite well-known in these parts. He graduated in the top ten percent of his class," she added. "He's very intelligent."

Todd, who'd never had the advantage of a college education, was touchy about it. He'd made millions and he was well-known in business circles, but there were still times when he felt uncomfortable around more educated businessmen.

"Dad's smart, too," Cherry said, as if she sensed her father's discomfort. "Even if he isn't a doctor, he's made lots of—"

"Cherry," her father said, cutting off the rest of her sentence.

"He's made lots of friends," Cherry amended, grinning cheekily at her parent. "And he's very handsome."

Jane wouldn't have touched that line with a pole. She finished her chicken and reached for her glass of milk.

"The chicken was great, Meg," she commented.

"It's nice to see everyone hungry again," Meg muttered. "I get tired of cooking for myself and Tim and Cherry."

"I guess the pain takes away your appetite sometimes, doesn't it, Jane?" Cherry asked innocently.

"Sometimes," she agreed, and couldn't look at Todd.

He tilted his coffee cup and drained it. "I'd better get back on the books."

"A couple of faxes came in for you today," Meg remarked. "One's from someone named Julia," she added with a twinkle in her eyes.

"Who's Julia?" Cherry asked, then her eyebrows lifted. "Oh. *Julia!*"

Her father's glance silenced her.

"I guess she's missing you, huh?" Cherry asked, grinning secretively.

"I don't doubt it," Todd agreed, thinking of the thousand and one daily headaches that Julia Emory was intercepting on his behalf while he lazed around in Jacobsville working for Jane. He put down his napkin. "I'd better get in touch with her. I'll, uh, reverse the charges," he assured Jane. "I wouldn't want to impose on my position here."

Jane only nodded. So he had other women. It shouldn't have come as a surprise. He was very handsome and fit, and she knew now why any woman would find him irresistible in bed. She flushed at her intimate memories of him and covered it by taking a large swallow of milk.

When Todd was gone, the conversation became more spontaneous and relaxed, but the room seemed empty.

"Did you ever think about marrying Dr. Coltrain?" Cherry asked Jane when Tim left and Meg started clearing away the supper things.

"Well, yes, I did, once," Jane confessed. "He's very attractive and we have a lot in common. But I never felt, well, the sort of attraction I'd need to feel to marry a man."

"You didn't want him in bed, in other words," Cherry said matter-of-factly.

"Cherry!"

"I don't live in a glass bottle," the young girl said. "I hear things at school and Dad's amazingly open about what I can watch on television. But I don't want to jump into any sort of intimacy at my age," she added, sounding very mature. "It's dangerous, you know. Besides, I have this romantic idea that it would be lovely to wait for marriage. Jane, did you know that some boys even feel that way?'' she added with a giggle. ''There's Mark, who goes to school with me, and he's very conservative. He says he'd rather wait and only do it with the girl he marries, so that they don't ever have to worry about STDs.''

''About what?''

''Sexually transmitted diseases,'' she said. ''Honestly, Jane, don't you watch television?''

Jane cleared her throat. ''Well, obviously I haven't been watching the right programs, have I?''

''I'll have to educate you,'' the girl said firmly. ''Didn't your parents tell you anything?''

''Sure, but since I never liked a boy enough...'' She hesitated, thinking about how it had been with Todd, and her face colored.

''Oh, I see. Not even Dr. Coltrain?'' she asked.

Jane shook her head.

''That's really sad.''

''I'll find someone, one of these days,'' Jane assured her, and looked up, right into Todd's quiet, interested eyes.

''Hi, Dad! I've been explaining sex to Jane.'' She shook her head as she got up. ''Boy, and I thought I was backward! See you later, Jane, I'm going to saddle up Feather!''

She ran out the door, leaving Todd alone with Jane, because Meg was in the kitchen rattling dishes as she loaded the dishwasher.

''Do you need a fourteen-year-old to explain sex to you?'' he asked quietly. ''I thought you learned all you needed to know from me.''

She bit her lower lip. ''Don't.''

He moved closer, a sheaf of papers in one lean hand, and stood beside her chair. ''Why deny us both the kind of pleasure we shared?'' he asked. ''You want me. I want you. What's wrong with it?''

She looked up into his eyes. "I want more than a physical relationship," she said.

He reached down and touched her cheek lightly. "Are you certain?" he said softly.

She grimaced and tried to look away, but he caught her chin and held her flushed face up to his eyes.

"So beautiful," he murmured. "And so naive. You want the moon, Jane. I can't give it to you. But I can give you pleasure so stark that you bite me and cry out with it."

She put her fingers against his hard mouth. "You mustn't!" she whispered frantically, looking toward the kitchen.

He caught her wrist and pulled her gently up out of the chair and against him, so that they were touching all the way up and down. "Meg wouldn't be embarrassed if she saw us kissing. No one would, except you." His hand tightened, steely around her fingers as he used his grip to force her even closer. Something untamed touched his face, glittered in his eyes as he looked down at her. His mouth hovered just above her lips. "You can deny it all you like, but when I hold out my arms, you'll walk into them. If I offer you my mouth, you'll take it. You're a puppet on a string, baby," he whispered seductively, letting the word arouse explosive memories in her mind.

She meant to protest. She wanted to. It was just that his hard mouth was so close. She could feel its warmth, taste the minty scent of it on her parted lips. Of course she wanted to deny what he was saying. What *was* he saying?

He bent a fraction of an inch closer. "It's all right," he whispered, moving his hips lazily against her, so that she trembled with kindling fevers. "Take what you want," he challenged.

She was sure that she hated him. The arrogant swine...

But all she wanted to do was kiss him, and it was a shame to waste the opportunity. It was so easy to reach up to him, to pull his hard mouth onto hers and feel its warm, slow pressure. It was so sweet to press her slender body into his and feel his swift, unashamed arousal.

He wasn't even holding her. His free hand was in her hair, savoring its silky length while she kissed him hungrily, passionately. He tasted of coffee and he smelled of spicy cologne. He was clean and hard and warm and she loved the feel of his powerful body against hers. Her legs began to tremble from the contact and she wondered if they were going to support her for much longer.

It was a moot point. Her nearness was as potent to him as his was to her. Seconds later, he put the papers on the table and wrapped her up in his arms, so that not a breath separated them. His mouth opened, taking hers with it, and his tongue pushed deep inside her mouth in a slow, aching parody of what his body had done to hers that long night together.

She moaned with the onslaught of the pleasure, trembling in his arms as the kiss went on and on.

His hands slid up and down her sides until they eased between and his thumbs worked lazy circles around her taut breasts. He remembered the taste of them in his mouth, the warm envelope of her body encircling him in the darkness. One hand went to her hips and gathered her against him roughly, and she cried out at the stab of discomfort in her hip.

The sound shocked him into lifting his head. His eyes were blank with aroused ardor, but all at once they focused on her drawn face.

"Did I hurt your back?" he asked huskily.

"A little," she whispered.

"I'm sorry." He brushed the hair away from her face. "I'm sorry, baby. I wouldn't hurt you for all the world, don't you know that?"

"You did..." she blurted.

His eyes glittered. "Yes. God, yes!" He actually shivered.

"I didn't know until I'd torn you, there..." His eyes closed and he shivered again with the memory. "I thought I might die of the pleasure, and the shame, because you asked me to stop and I couldn't." His mouth smoothed softly over hers. "You don't know what it's like, do you, to want someone past reason, past honor? I wanted you like that. I would have killed to have you, in those few blind seconds that robbed me of reason. I was ashamed, Jane," he breathed into her mouth, "but I was too excited to pull away. I'm sorry."

She closed her eyes, drinking in the feel of him. "It's all right. Afterward—" she hesitated, and her body clenched at the memory of afterward "—I...I think I understood."

His mouth was hot on her eyelids, her cheeks, her chin. "I thought you were never going to stop convulsing," he whispered. "I remember laughing with the pure joy of it, knowing that I'd given you so much pleasure."

"So that was why...!"

"Yes." His hands framed her face and he looked deep into her eyes. "Come to bed with me tonight. I'll give you that pleasure again, and again. I'll make love to you until you fall asleep in my arms."

She wanted to. Her eyes told him that she wanted to. But despite the pleasure she remembered, she also remembered his easy rejection of her when his passion was spent. He'd left her as soon as he was finished, with no tenderness, no explanations, no apologies. He wanted her now, desperately. But when he was satisfied, it would be the same as it had been before, because he only wanted her. He didn't love her. He was offering her an empty heart.

She closed her eyes against the terrible temptation he offered. That way lay self-destruction, no matter how much temporary relief he gave her.

"No," she said finally. "No, Todd. It isn't enough."

He scowled. She was trembling against him. Her mouth was swollen and still hungry for his, her arms still held him.

"You don't mean that," he accused gently.

She opened her eyes and looked up at him. "Yes, I do," she said quietly. She pulled away from him, slowly, and stepped back. "You're handsome and sexy, and I love kissing you. But it's a dead end."

"You want promises," he said shortly.

"Oh, no," she corrected. "Promises are just words. I want years of togetherness and children." Her face softened as she thought of a little girl like Cherry, or perhaps a baby boy. "Lots of children."

His face went rigid. "I have a child."

She searched his eyes. "Yes, I know. She's a wonderful girl. But I want one of my own, and a husband to go with them."

He was seething with unsatisfied passion and anger. "Wouldn't it be a great world if we all got exactly what we wanted?"

"It certainly would." She moved away from him, concentrating on each breath. She held on to the back of her chair. "And maybe I never will. But my dreams are sweet," she added, lifting her eyes. "Much sweeter than a few weeks of lust that end with you walking right out of my life."

His face went even harder. "Lust?"

"Without love, that's all sex is."

"You little hypocrite," he accused flatly, and reached for her. He was kissing her blindly, ardently, when the door opened and a shocked Cherry stopped dead in the doorway.

Chapter 8

Todd lifted his head, freezing in place, while Jane gently pushed away from him, red-faced.

"Sorry," Cherry murmured, and then grinned. "I was looking for Meg. Don't let me interrupt anything."

She darted past them into the kitchen and closed the door pointedly.

"I'm sorry," Todd said curtly, pushing his hair off his forehead. "That was a stupid thing to do."

Jane didn't know what stupid thing he meant, so she didn't reply. She moved away from him and sat down, her back aching from the unfamiliar exercise. He hesitated for a few seconds, but he couldn't think of a single defense for his uncharacteristic behavior.

"Excuse me," he said, picking up the papers from the table. "I'd better get to work."

He left her sitting there, and he didn't look back on the way out. Cherry came in a few minutes later, and grimaced when she saw that Jane was alone.

"I didn't mean to burst in," Cherry told her. "I didn't expect... Gosh, I never saw Dad kiss anyone like that! Not even my mother, when I was little!"

Jane flushed. "It was just a...mistake," she faltered.

"Some mistake. Wow!" She chuckled. Her whole face lit up. "Do you like him?"

"Don't start building dreams on me and your father," Jane said somberly. "There's no future in it. He doesn't want marriage and I don't want anything else," she added flatly.

Cherry's face fell. "Oh."

"You're still my friend, Cherry," she said with a smile. "Okay?"

Cherry's mouth curled down but after a minute she smiled back. "Okay."

Jane went up to Victoria with Copper and spent most of the day posing in various articles of SlimTogs for the photographer. He was nice, and very helpful, and considerate of Jane's back problem. It was worse today because of Todd's ardor the night before, but Jane wasn't about to mention that to anybody. It was only a twinge, anyway.

"That should wrap it up," Micki said a few minutes later, after she'd talked to the photographer. "Jack said that he got some great shots. We'll make our selection for the layout and then we'll be in touch with you. There may be a couple of promotional appearances, by the way, at a rodeo and maybe for the opening of one of our new stores. We'll let you know."

"It was fun," Jane said. "I enjoyed it. And I really do like the clothes."

"We like you," Micki said with a nice smile. "You're a good sport. Uh, Todd didn't come up with you, did he?"

She shook her head. "He's still up to his neck with projects on the ranch. My own men answer to him, now, not to me. I'm going to have a hard time getting control back when he leaves.''

"Is he leaving?''

"Not anytime soon, I don't think,'' Jane replied. She hated Micki's probing questions, but she couldn't afford to say so and reveal her own feelings for the man.

"He's very attractive,'' Micki said, her smile wistful and a little sad. "I guess he's got plenty of girlfriends.''

"I don't doubt it,'' Jane replied. "They even fax him letters,'' she said absently.

Micki chuckled. "Well, that lets me out of the running, I suppose. You're not sweet on him yourself, are you?'' she added curiously.

"I'd have to get in line,'' Jane said. "And I'd be a long way back.''

"Just our luck, isn't it? A dreamy man like that doesn't come along every day, but there's always a woman in possession, I guess.'' She shook her head. "I think I'm destined to be an old maid.''

"Marriage isn't everything,'' Jane said. "You might become the head of your corporation.''

"Anything's possible. But I have a secret, sinful hunger for dirty dishes and ironing a man's shirts and having babies. Shameful, isn't it? Don't tell anyone.''

"You closet housewife, you!''

Micki chuckled. "I love what I do, and I make a lot of money. I can't complain. It's just that once in a while I don't want to live alone.''

"Who does?'' Jane asked. "But sometimes we don't have a choice.''

"So they say. I'll be in touch soon, okay? Have a nice trip home.''

"Thanks.''

Jane went downstairs and phoned the hospital. Copper

drove over to pick her up. But instead of heading home, he took her to Victoria's nicest restaurant for supper.

"But I'm not dressed properly," she protested, gesturing toward her chambray blouse and matching long skirt.

"Neither am I." He was wearing a sport jacket and a knit shirt with his slacks. "They can stare if they like. Can't they?"

She laughed. "All right, then. I'd be delighted to have dinner with you, if you don't mind the casual clothes."

"I never minded."

He took her inside the swanky restaurant, where he ordered her meal—lobster and steak and salad, topped off with an ice-cream-covered brownie.

"I'll have sweet dreams about that dessert for years," she murmured on the way home.

"So will I."

She turned her head toward him. He was single-minded when he drove. Probably he was like that when he operated, too. He specialized in diseases of the lung, and he was a surgeon of some note. He occasionally was called in to operate in the big city hospitals. But in recent years, he stayed close to home. He was mysterious in many ways. An enigma.

"Do you want children?" she asked suddenly.

He chuckled. "Sure. Are you offering?"

She flushed. "Don't be silly."

He glanced at her. "Say the word. I'm willing if you are. I like kids and I wouldn't balk at marriage. We've got more in common than a lot of people."

"Yes, we have. But there's just one thing missing."

He smiled ruefully. "And I know what it is."

"Two out of three isn't bad."

"No," he agreed. "But I couldn't live with a woman who suffered me in bed, Jane. That would be impossible."

"I know." She reached across the seat and slid her hand into his where it rested on the gearshift. "I'm sorry. I wish I felt that way."

His fingers contracted. "You do. But with Burke, not me."

She didn't deny it. She leaned her head against the h⌐

rest. "He wants to have a blazing affair and then go back to Victoria."

"What do you want?"

"Marriage. Children. Forever after."

"He might want those things, too, after he got used to you."

"He might get tired of me."

"Life doesn't come with guarantees," he said gently. He glanced at her drawn, unhappy face. "You have a history of migraine. I wouldn't dare prescribe birth control pills for you, because of that. But there are other tried-and-true methods."

"Copper!"

He held on to her hand. "Grow up. We don't always get the brass ring. That doesn't mean we can't get some pleasure out of the ride. At least you'd have some sweet memories."

"I'm surprised at you," she said.

He glanced at her. "No, you're not. And I'm not surprised or disappointed in you for being human. Sex is a natural, beautiful part of life. It's very rare that two people love each other enough to experience its heights. Burke may not want to marry you, honey, but he loves you."

"What!"

"I think you know it, too, deep down. He's pretty readable to another man. He was jealous of me the first time he saw me."

"That could be sexual jealousy."

"It could have been. But it wasn't. He's too protective of you." He patted her hand gently. "He had a bad marriage, didn't he, and he's probably afraid to take another chance. But if he cares enough, eventually he'll give in. Isn't it worth fighting for?"

"Fighting for." She grimaced. "I can't. I just can't. That…belongs in marriage."

"couldn't agree more. It does. But, then, from my point
    marriage is just a matter of time. He loves you. You
    nd he strikes me as a pretty conventional fellow.
    hter to think of, too."

"He says he'll never marry again."

"The president said he wouldn't raise taxes."

She looked at him and burst out laughing. "Don't compromise your principles," he advised. "But you can keep him interested without tearing your clothes off for him."

"I suppose so."

"Now, tell me about this ad promotion."

She did, glad to talk about some subject less complicated than Todd Burke.

When they got home it was well after dark and Todd was in the house with Meg, pacing the floor.

He went out to meet Jane as she came up the steps, having thanked Copper and waved goodbye.

"Where have you been?" he demanded.

She lifted both eyebrows. "Having lobster and steak."

"And then?" he challenged angrily.

"And then," she whispered, leaning close, "we got into the back seat and made love so violently that all four tires went flat!"

He stared at her long and hard and then suddenly laughed. "Damn you!"

She went close to him, putting both hands against his shirt-front. "I couldn't make love with anyone except you," she said, living up to her new resolve to tell him nothing but the truth, always. "I love you."

His heart ran away. She was the very picture of femininity, and the sight of her long hair made him ache to feel it against his bare chest, as he had the night they loved each other. He gathered up a handful of it and drew it to his cheek.

"I love you, too," he said unexpectedly. His breath sighed out at her temple while she stood still against him, unbelieving. "I loved you the night I took you." He kissed her eyelids closed. "People can't satisfy each other that completely unless they love, didn't you know?"

"No," she whispered, stunned by the revelation.

His mouth moved gently down to her soft lips and traced them. "Won't you change your mind?" he asked huskily.

Her hands clenched on his shirtfront. "Copper won't give me the Pill because I have a history of migraines," she said bluntly.

His body froze in position. "You talked to that cowboy doctor about the Pill?"

"No, he talked to me about it! He knows that I love you."

He didn't know how to take it. For a moment, anger overshadowed what she was saying. And then, all at once, understanding pushed its way into his mind.

He moved back, frowning. "You can't take the Pill?"

"That's right. So the risk of a child would always be there. I couldn't...do anything about it, if I got pregnant," she added firmly. "And since I feel so strongly about it, I don't want to take any more chances with you. I didn't...that is, nothing happened last time."

"I took precautions," he said stiffly.

"Yes, I know. But accidents happen."

His hands stilled on her shoulders. He was quiet, thoughtful. A child with Jane would be a disaster. He couldn't walk away from a child. He could picture a little girl with long blond hair and big blue eyes in a taffeta dress. He could take her to birthday parties, as he'd taken Cherry when she was little. Or there might be a little boy, whom he and Jane could teach to ride. A son.

"You're very quiet," she remarked.

"Yes."

"I'm sorry," she said, lifting her eyes to his. "But it's better not to start things we can't finish. And I'd be the last person in the world who'd want to trap you."

He searched her sad eyes. His fingers touched her lower lip, testing its softness. "Marie didn't want to make a baby with me," he said roughly. "We were both drunk and I knew she was on the Pill. But she'd forgotten to take it a few times. That's the only reason Cherry was conceived."

"For heaven's sake!"

"Are you shocked?" he asked lazily. "Jane, she didn't want a child. Some people don't."

"Yes, I know, but now she loves Cherry."

"So do I. With all my heart. And the day she was born, when they put her into my arms, I cried like a boy. It was unbelievable to have a child of my own."

The awe and wonder of the experience touched his eyes just briefly, before he banished it. He looked down at Jane and his hands cradled her hips. "Even if I were...willing— which I'm not," he added curtly, "you won't be able to carry a child, not for a long time." He grimaced. "And as you say, the risk would always be there, if you couldn't take the Pill. But you were willing to take any risk with me that night," he reminded her.

"Yes, but it didn't happen," she said curtly. "Nothing happened afterward!"

Her tone startled him. She sounded disappointed.

He didn't speak for a minute. His eyes searched her downcast face. "Jane...you wanted to get pregnant, didn't you?"

She bit her lower lip almost through and pulled away from him. "What I wanted is nobody's business except my own, and it's a good thing that you aren't forced into doing something you'd hate."

"Maybe so. But..."

She laughed. "Don't look so somber. Everything's all right. You'll go back to your job in Victoria and I'll make a fortune selling clothes with my name on them. We'll both do fine."

"Will you marry Coltrain?" he asked bluntly.

"I don't love him," she said sadly. "If I did, I'd marry him in a minute."

"Marriages have succeeded on less."

"And ended on more."

He couldn't debate that. He touched her lips with his. "I won't stop wanting you. If you change your mind, you only have to say so."

"I can't. I can't, Todd." She moved away and left him standing there. He wanted her, that was obvious, but he'd hate her if anything happened. He'd marry her, certainly, if there was a child. But it would be a hateful relationship. She didn't want him that way.

The next Friday, Todd drove Cherry up to Victoria to spend another weekend with her mother. He stayed in town, too, to get some of his own impending paperwork out of the way and to keep his mind off Jane. The hunger he felt for her was becoming a real problem.

Cherry waved goodbye to him from her mother's elegant front porch. The house Marie shared with William, her second husband, was a startling white restored Victorian, with gingerbread woodwork and a gazebo on a spotless manicured lawn. It had all the warmth of a photograph, but it suited a woman who was trying to build an interior design business in south Texas.

"Your father seemed very out of sorts," Marie remarked as she and Cherry went inside.

"I think it's because of Jane," the girl replied with a grin. "I caught them kissing, and I mean kissing!" she added, shaking her hand with appropriate facial expressions.

Marie made a curt movement. "Todd has said repeatedly that he doesn't want to marry again," she said.

"Never say never," Cherry murmured and grinned. "Jane's been helping me with my turns. She says I'm just the picture of elegance on horseback. I wish I could be more like her," she said, without realizing how dreamy she sounded. "She's so beautiful, and everyone knows who she is in rodeo. She's going to endorse some women's Western wear. They'll have her on TV and in magazines... Gosh, it's so exciting!"

Marie wasn't jealous of Todd anymore. Their marriage was history. But she was jealous of her only daughter, who now seemed to be transferring all her loyalties to a disabled rodeo star with a reputation that was already fading. She didn't like it one bit.

"I thought we might go shopping again tomorrow," Marie ventured.

Cherry started to speak and ended in a sigh. "All right."

"You should love pretty clothes, at your age," Marie said, clinging desperately to the only real common desire they still shared, a love of clothes.

"I do, I guess," Cherry said. "Rodeo clothes, at least. But I'd love some new books on horses and medicine."

"Books! What a waste of time!"

Cherry's eyebrows arched. "Mother, I'm going to be a surgeon."

Marie patted her shoulder gently. "Darling, you're very young. You'll change your mind."

"That isn't what Jane says, when I tell her about wanting to practice medicine," Cherry said sharply.

Marie glared at her. "And that's quite enough about Jane," she said sarcastically. "I'm your mother. You don't talk back to me."

Cherry's mouth pulled down. "Yes, ma'am."

Marie smoothed over her perfect coiffure. "Let's have tea. I've had a very hectic morning."

Doing what, arranging the flowers? Cherry thought irritably, but she only smiled and didn't say another word. Compared to Jane, who was always doing something or reading about ranching or genetics, Marie was very dull stuff indeed. Her life seemed to be composed of clothes and society, and she had no interests past them.

Her father, like Jane, had an active mind and he fed it constantly with books and educational television. Cherry remembered her parents being together very rarely during her childhood, because Marie didn't like horses or riding, or reading, or computers. Cherry and her father shared those interests and that had formed an early bond between them. Now Jane, also, shared the same interests. Cherry wondered if her father ever noticed. He seemed very attracted to Jane physically, but he paid little attention to her leisure pursuits. She'd have to get them together long enough to push them into really talking.

Remembering the pleasure in Jane's face when she'd said she was going to Victoria with Dr. Coltrain brought Cherry up short. The doctor would be formidable competition for her father. She'd have to see if she couldn't do something to help. The more she thought about having Jane for a step-mother, the happier she became.

Marie and William had an engagement Saturday night, so she decided to run Cherry back to the ranch early that after-noon. She phoned Todd at the office to tell him that she'd drop the girl off, but he was involved in a business meeting so Miss Emory took the message and promised to relay it.

Marie smiled to herself as she and Cherry got into her silver Mercedes. Somehow she was going to throw a spanner into Todd's spokes and prevent her daughter from becoming lost to the competition. She already had a good idea of how to do it, too.

"Does Jane know that your father is rich?" she asked Cherry.

"Heavens, no," Cherry said, defending her idol. "She doesn't even know that he owns a computer company. All Dad has told her is that he keeps the books for a company in Victoria."

"My, my. Why the subterfuge?"

"Well, Dad felt sorry for Jane," she said without thinking that she might be betraying her father to her mother. "She hurt her back in a wreck and she could barely walk. The ranch was in trouble. She didn't have anyone who could manage money to help her. So on an impulse, Dad offered to take over the manager's job. You wouldn't believe what he's done for her. He's improved the property, bought live-stock, got her into a licensing venture with that clothing man-ufacturer—all in a few weeks. I heard him say that the ranch is going to start paying back the investment any day now."

"Where did she get the money to do all that? Has she got money of her own?" Marie asked with studied carelessness.

"Oh, no, she was flat broke, Dad said. He went to the bank and stood good for a loan to make the improvements. She doesn't know."

Ammunition, Marie was thinking. "Tell me about Jane," Marie coaxed.

It didn't take much to get Cherry talking about the woman she worshiped. In the drive to Jacobsville, she told Marie everything she knew. By the time they reached the Parker ranch, Marie had enough to put the skids under the former rodeo queen and get back her daughter's loyalty.

"I do wish you'd consider spending the rest of the summer with me," Marie said as they pulled up at the front door. "We could go to Nassau or down to Jamaica. Even to Martinique."

"I'd love to, but I have to practice for the rodeo in August," Cherry explained. "I really need to work on my turns."

"Oh...horses!" Marie muttered. "Such a filthy hobby."

"They're very clean, actually. There's Jane!"

Marie got out of the car and studied the woman approaching them. Jane was wearing jeans and a pink T-shirt. Her blond hair was in a braid down her back and she wasn't wearing any makeup, but that didn't lessen her beauty. If anything, it enhanced it. She was slender and elegant to look at, and she had grace of carriage despite her injury. She was twice as pretty as Marie. The other woman, at least ten years Jane's senior, had no difficulty understanding Todd's interest and Cherry's devotion to the woman. Marie hated her on sight.

"Jane, this is my mother. Mom, this is Jane," Cherry introduced them, beaming.

"I've heard so much about you," Marie said with reserved friendliness. "How nice to meet you at last, Miss Parker."

"Call me Jane, please," the other woman said kindly. She slid a welcoming arm around Cherry, who smiled up at her with the kind of affection she used to show her mother. It made Marie go cold inside. "I've missed you," she told Cherry.

"I've missed you, too," Cherry said warmly.

"Would you like tea, Mrs...."

"Oh, call me Marie. Yes, I'd love a cup," Marie said formally.

Jane grimaced. "I meant a glass of iced tea, actually."

"That would be fine."

"Come in, then."

Jane led the way into the spacious living room. Marie's keen eye could see dozens of ways to improve it and make it elegant, but she bit down on her comments. She wanted to worm her way into Jane's confidence and criticizing the decor wasn't going to accomplish that.

"Could you ask Meg to fix some tea and cookies on a tray?" Jane asked Cherry.

"Sure! I'll be right back!"

She was gone and Marie accepted Jane's offer of a seat on the wide, comfortably upholstered sofa.

"Well, you're not at all what I expected," Marie began with a kind smile. "When my husband—excuse me, my *ex*-husband," she amended sweetly, "told me that he'd taken a little job down in Jacobsville to help a poor crippled woman, I had someone older in mind!"

Chapter 9

At first Jane thought that she might have misheard the other woman. But when she leaned forward and looked into Marie's cold eyes, she knew that she hadn't.

"I'm not crippled," Jane said proudly. "Temporarily slowed down, but not permanently disabled."

"Oh. I'm sorry. I must have misunderstood. It doesn't matter. Whatever your problem is, Todd felt sorry for you. He's a sucker for a hard-luck story. Amazing, isn't it," she added, watching Jane as she played her trump card, "that a multimillionaire, the head of an international corporation, would sacrifice his vacation to get an insignificant little horse ranch out of the red."

Jane didn't move, didn't breathe, didn't flinch. She stared at the older woman blankly. "I beg your pardon?"

Marie's pencil-thin brows rose. "You didn't know?" She laughed pleasantly. "Well, how incredible! He's been featured in God knows how many business magazines. Although, I don't suppose you read that sort of thing, do you?"

she added, allowing her eyes to pause meaningfully on the latest issue of a magazine on horsemanship.

"I don't read business magazines, no," Jane said. She touched her throat lightly, as if she felt choked.

"Todd must have found it all so amusing, pretending to be a simple accountant," Marie said, leaning back on the sofa elegantly. "I mean, what a comedown for him! Living like this—" she waved a careless arm "—and driving that pitiful old sedan he borrowed. Honestly, he had to have the chauffeur drive the Ferrari and the Rolls twice a week just to keep them from getting carbon on the valves."

Rolls. Ferrari. Multimillionaire. Jane felt as if she were strangling. "But he keeps the books," she argued, trying desperately to come to grips with what she was being told.

"He's a wizard with figures, all right," Marie said. "He's an utter genius at math, and without a college education, too. He has a gift, they say."

"But, why?" she groaned. "Why didn't he tell me the truth?"

"I suppose he was afraid that you might fall in love with his bank account," Marie said with a calculating glance. "So many women have, and you were a poverty case. Not only that, a crippled poverty case. You might have thought he was the end of the rainbow."

Jane's face went rigid. She got to her feet slowly. "I make my own way," she said coldly. "I don't need any handouts, or anybody's pity."

"Well, of course you don't," Marie said. "I'm sure Todd would have told you the truth, eventually."

Jane's hands clenched by her side. She was white.

The sound of running footsteps distracted Marie.

"Meg says she'll bring the— Jane! What is it?" Cherry asked as she entered the room, concerned. "You look like you've seen a ghost!"

"Yes, you are very pale," Marie said. She glanced worriedly at her daughter. She hadn't counted the cost until now. Cherry was looking at her with eyes that grew steadily colder.

"What did you say, Mother?" she asked her parent.

Marie got up and clasped her hands in front of her. "I only told her the truth," she said defensively. "She'd have found out anyway."

"About Dad?" Cherry persisted. When Marie nodded, Cherry's face contorted. She looked at Jane and felt the older woman's pain and shock all the way to her feet.

Marie was feeling less confident by the second. Cherry's eyes were hostile and so were Jane's. "I should go, I suppose," Marie began.

"That might be a very good idea, Mother," Cherry said icily. "Before Dad comes home."

Another complication Marie hadn't considered. She gnawed her lower lip. "I never meant to…"

"Just go," Jane snapped.

"And the sooner the better," Cherry added.

"Don't you talk to me that way! I'm your mother!" Marie reminded her hotly.

"I'm ashamed of that," Cherry said harshly. "I've never been so ashamed of it in all my life!"

Marie's indrawn breath was audible. Her pale eyes filled with sudden tears. "I only wanted…" she began plaintively.

Cherry turned her back. Marie hesitated only for a moment before she scooped up her purse and went quickly to the front door. The tears were raining down her cheeks by the time she reached the Mercedes.

Inside the house, Jane was still trying to subdue her rage. She sat down again, aware of Cherry's worried gaze.

"Is what she said true? That your father owns a computer company, that he has a Ferrari and a Rolls and he's spending his vacation getting my ranch out of debt because he feels sorry for me?" Jane asked the girl.

Cherry groaned. "Oh, it's true, but it's not like that!

Mother's just jealous because I talk about you so much. I guess I upset her when I made her realize how little we had in common. It's all my fault. Oh, Jane…!''

Jane took another steadying breath and folded her hands in her lap. "I wondered," she said absently. "I mean, with a brain like that, why would he still be working for somebody else, at his age. I've been a fool! He played me like a radio!"

"He didn't do it to hurt you," Cherry argued. "Jane, he just wanted to help. And then, after we'd been here for a while, he didn't know how to tell you. I'm sure that's why he hasn't said anything. He cares for you."

Cares. He'd said that he loved her. *But you don't keep secrets from people you love,* she was thinking. He'd lied by omission. He'd let her fall in love with him, and he had to know that there was no future for them. If he'd been a simple accountant, perhaps it would have worked out. But he was a multimillionaire, a powerful businessman. What would he want with a little country girl from south Texas who only had a high school education and no social skills? She wouldn't know what to do with herself at a society party. She wouldn't even know what utensils to use. And she was a rancher. Her eyes closed as the reality closed in on her.

"Talk to me," Cherry pleaded.

Jane couldn't. She gripped her legs hard as she fought with her demons. Todd was coming back today. She'd have to face him. How would she be able to face him, with what she knew?

Then the solution occurred to her. *Copper.* She could invite Copper over for supper, and play up to him—if she warned Copper first that she was going to—and she could put on a good act. It had all been a mistake, she hadn't meant what she said about loving him, she was lying…

"I don't want your father to know that your mother told me the truth," Jane said after a minute. Her blue eyes met Cherry's gray ones evenly. "I'll talk to him later."

"Mother's not vindictive, really," Cherry said in her mother's defense. "She's just shallow, and jealous. It's funny, really, because she doesn't even know how to talk to me. Not like you do. Please don't hate me because of this, Jane."

"Cherry!" Jane was genuinely shocked. "As if I could hate you!"

The young face softened. Cherry smiled. "We're still friends?"

"Certainly we are. None of this has anything to do with you and me."

"Oh, thank goodness," she said heavily.

"It's just as well, really," Jane continued without looking directly at Cherry, "because I'd decided that things wouldn't work out with your father and me, anyway. He isn't really the rancher type."

Cherry frowned. "But he comes from ranching people in Wyoming. He grew up around horses and cattle."

"Still, he doesn't spend much time with them now," Jane insisted. "If he's the president of a company, then he lives in the fast lane. I don't. I can't."

Cherry saw all her dreams coming apart. "You could get to know him better before you decide that you can't."

Jane smiled and shook her head. "No. You see, Dr. Coltrain and I were talking the other day. Copper's like me, he's from Jacobsville and his family has lived here as long as mine has. We're suited to each other. In fact," she lied, "I've invited him for supper tonight."

"You didn't tell me," Cherry protested.

"I didn't know you'd be here, did I?" she asked, and sounded so reasonable that Cherry was totally fooled. "For all I knew, your father was going to drive up to Victoria to get you tomorrow."

"Yes, that's so," Cherry admitted.

"You're welcome to have your supper with us," Jane offered, hoping against hope that Cherry would refuse and trying not to look too relieved when she did. She was also hoping that Copper would come to supper when she invited him, or she was going to get caught lying to save face.

"I expect Dad and I will go out and get something, when he gets home, like we do most nights," Cherry said uncomfortably.

"That will be nice."

"Jane, don't you care about him at all?" Cherry asked plaintively.

"I like him very much," Jane said at once. "He's a very nice man, and I owe him a lot."

Cherry felt sick. She managed a wan smile and made an excuse to go over to the small house where she and her father were staying.

When she was gone, Jane let go of the tears she'd been holding back and was just mopping herself up when Meg walked in with a tray of cookies and cake and tea, smiling.

The smile faded at once when she saw Jane's ravaged face. "Is she gone already? What in the world happened?"

Jane wiped savagely at the traces of tears. "Everything!" she raged. "That pirate! That cold-blooded, blond-headed snake!"

"Todd? Why are you mad at our accountant?"

"He's no accountant," Jane said viciously. "He's the head of a computer company and he's worth millions!"

Meg started, and then burst out laughing. "Oh, for heaven's sake, pull the other one!"

"It's true! He's got a Rolls at home!"

Meg set the tray down. "There, there, they were putting you on. Why, Todd's no millionaire!"

"He is," Jane insisted. "Cherry didn't want to agree with what her mother told me, but she did. Her mother might lie to me. Cherry never would."

Meg was less certain now. She frowned. "If he's a millionaire, why's he down here keeping your books?"

"Because I'm a poor cripple," Jane said huskily. "And he felt sorry for me. He's spending his vacation getting me out of the hole." She put her face in her hands and shook her head. "Now I don't have to wonder why the bank let me have the loan, either. I'm sure he stood good for it. I'll owe him my soul!"

Meg wiped her hands on her apron, hovering nervously. "Jane, you mustn't get upset like this. Wait until Todd gets back and talk to him about it."

"What will I tell him?"

"That you didn't know…"

"And now that I do?" she asked openly. "I'll tell him I know he's rich, and then he'll never be sure if I care for him or his wallet, will he? He might think I knew all along. His ex-wife said that he's been featured in all the business magazines. I don't read them, but he doesn't know that."

"I see what you mean."

Jane got up from the sofa. "Well, I'm going to set his mind at ease, with a little help."

"From whom?"

"Copper, of course," Jane said. "He's already said that Copper and I seemed to be an item. Why shouldn't we be? Copper said he'd marry me in a minute if I was willing."

"That's no reason to get married! Copper deserves better!"

Jane stared at her housekeeper. "Of course he does, and it won't be for real. I'm going to ask an old friend for a favor, that's all."

Meg relaxed. "As long as he doesn't get hurt."

"He won't." She didn't add that she would. She'd already been hurt. But Todd wasn't going to know. She was going to turn the tables on him and save her pride. It was the only thing she had left to protect herself with now.

* * *

As she'd guessed, Copper was willing to help her out by coming over to supper. He was on call, though, so he brought his beeper with him. They sat down to an early supper of fried chicken and vegetables. Jane was wearing a white dress and her hair was immaculately brushed back and secured with white combs. She looked elegant and very beautiful, except for the hollow expression in her eyes.

"Does it matter so much that he's got money?" Copper asked her over coffee.

"It would to him, if he thought it was the reason I was attracted to him," she said.

"He'll know better."

"How?"

"He loves you, you idiot," Copper said curtly. "He'll be furious, and not at you. I don't doubt he'll have some choice words for his ex-wife."

"Maybe he'll thank her," she returned lightly. "After all, he was in a bit of a muddle here. He'd backed himself into a corner playing the part of a working man with no prospects."

"It probably meant more to him that you loved him in his disguise."

"How would he know that I hadn't been in on the secret all along?"

Copper nodded; it was a logical question. But he was smiling when he put down his napkin. "Because Cherry will tell him how shocked you were."

"Maybe I'm a good actress. Cherry's mother said that plenty of women had wanted him for his bank account."

"And don't you think he'd know the difference between a woman who wanted money and a woman who wanted him?"

"I don't know," Jane said honestly.

"Listen…"

The front door opened without even a knock and Todd stalked into the dining room. He was wearing a gray business suit with a spotless white shirt and a silk tie. His boots were hand-tooled leather. He was wearing a Rolex watch on his left wrist and a signet ring with a diamond that would have blinded a horse. For the first time, Jane saw him as he really was: an authority figure bristling with money and power.

He didn't smile as he stared at her, and his gaze didn't waver. "When Miss Emory finally got to me with Marie's message, I canceled a meeting. I was waiting for Marie when she got back home. I've had her version of what she said. Let's have yours."

Copper cleared his throat, to make sure that Todd knew he was sitting there.

Todd glanced at him with cold gray eyes. "I haven't missed the cozy supper scenario," he told the doctor. "But I know why it's being played out. Do you?"

"Oh, I have a dandy idea," Copper replied. "Wouldn't it have been easier all around to just tell the truth in the first place? Or were you having fun at Jane's expense?"

Todd laughed without mirth. He stuck his hands into his slacks pockets and stared at Jane from his superior, elegant height. "Fun. I've got merger negotiations stacked one on another, international contracts waiting for consideration, stockholders telephoning twice a day... No, I haven't been having fun. I've put my life on hold trying to get this horse ranch out of bankruptcy so that Jane would at least have a roof over her head. It was an impulse. Once I started the charade, I couldn't find a way to stop it."

"You could have told me the truth," Jane said stiffly.

"What truth?" he asked pleasantly. "That I felt sorry for you, because you were hurt and such a fighter despite your injuries? And that you stood to lose everything you owned just for lack of an accountant? I couldn't walk away."

"Well, thanks for all you did," Jane replied, averting her

eyes. "But now that you've got me on my feet, I can stay there all by myself."

"Sure you can," he agreed. "You've got a licensing contract and some decent stock to breed. You'll make it. You would have anyway, if Tim had been a little sharper in the math department. This is a first-class operation. All I did was pull the loose ends together. You're a born rancher. You've got what it takes to make this place pay, with a little help from Tim and Meg."

The praise unsettled her, even as it thrilled her. At least he didn't think she was an idiot. That was something. But the distance between them was more apparent than ever now that she knew the truth about him.

She clasped her hands tightly out of sight in her lap. "And you?"

"I've got a business of my own to run," he said. "Cherry will start back to school soon. We'd have had to leave anyway, a little later than this, perhaps. Cherry owes you a lot for what you've taught her. She has a chance in rodeo now."

"Cherry is my friend. I hope she always will be."

"Cherry. But not me?"

She looked up into his eyes. "I'm grateful for what you did. But you must surely see that we live in different worlds." She sighed wearily. "I'm not cut out for yours, any more than you're cut out for mine. It's just as well that it worked out this way."

"You haven't tried," he said angrily.

"I'm not going to," was the quiet reply. "I like my life as it is. Exactly as it is. I'm very grateful for the help you gave me. I'll repay the loan."

His face hardened. "I never doubted that you would. I backed it. I didn't fund it."

She nodded. "Thank you."

His chest rose and fell heavily. He glared at Copper, because he could say none of what he wanted to say with the unwanted audience.

"Shall I leave?" Copper offered.

"Not on your life," Jane said shortly.

"Afraid of me?" Todd murmured with a mocking smile.

"There's nothing more to say," she replied. "Except goodbye."

"Cherry will be devastated," he said.

She drew in a breath. "Yes, I know. I'm sorry. I don't want to hurt her. But, it's the only thing to do."

He looked unapproachable. "Perhaps we see different things. If you'll have Tim phone me Monday morning, I'll explain to him what I've done. You need a business manager, unless you want to end up in the same financial tangle you started in."

"I know that. I'll take care of it."

"Then I'll say good night."

"I'm grateful for everything," Jane added stiffly.

He looked at her for a long moment. "Everything?" he said in a sensuous tone.

She colored. It seemed to be the reaction he'd wanted, because he laughed coldly, nodded to Coltrain and stalked out, closing the door behind him.

Copper stared at her. "You fool. Is pride worth more than he is to you?"

"At the moment, yes," she said icily. She was fighting tears and trying not to show it. "He's a pompous, hateful…"

"You shouldn't have forced this discussion on him before you had a couple of days to think about what you wanted to do," he said gently. "Impulses are very often regretted."

"Is that a professional opinion?" she asked angrily.

"Personal, professional, there isn't much difference," he replied. "You're going to be sorry that you didn't give him a chance to talk."

"I did," she said with wide, innocent eyes. "And he did."

"He defended himself. That's all he had time to do. With me sitting here, he hardly had the opportunity to do any real discussing."

"It's all for the best," she told him quietly.

"If you want to spend the rest of your life alone, maybe it is. But money isn't everything."

"When you don't have any, it is."

He glowered at her. "Listen to me, this might be the last chance you get. He's proud, too, you know. He won't come crawling back, any more than I would in his place. He's not the sort."

She knew that, too. She put her napkin on the table and stood up. "Thanks for coming over tonight. I don't think I'd have had the nerve to face him if you hadn't been here."

"What are friends for?" he asked. He stood up, too, and took her gently by the shoulders. "There's still time to stop him. You could go over to the cabin and have it out."

"We had it out," she argued.

"No, you didn't. You sat there like a polite hostess, but you sure as hell didn't do any discussing."

"I can take care of my own life, thank you."

"If that's true, what am I doing here?"

She searched his eyes. "Moral support."

He smiled. "I asked for that."

"I'm sorry. I really do appreciate your coming over so quickly when I asked."

"You're welcome. I hope you'll do the same for me if I'm ever in a comparable situation. But all you did was postpone the problem, you know. You didn't solve anything."

"I saved face," she replied. "He'll go back to Victoria and run his company, and I'll stay down here and breed horses and make money selling clothes."

"You'll be lonely."

She looked up. "That's nothing new. I was lonely before he came here. But people learn every day how to live with being lonely. I have a roof over my head, my books are in great shape, my body's healing nicely and I'm going to get this ranch back on its feet. It's what Dad would have wanted.''

"Your dad would have wanted to see you happy.''

She smiled. "Yes, but he was a realist. Todd wouldn't have married me," she said quietly. "You know it, too. I'm not the sort of woman rich men marry. I've got rustic manners and I don't know how to dress or use six forks for one meal.''

"You could learn those things. You're beautiful, and elegant, and you have charm and grace. No woman born with a silver spoon could do better.''

She grinned through her heartbreak. "You're a prince.''

He sighed and checked his watch. "I'm done talking. I have to make rounds at the hospital. Call if you need me. But I wish you'd reconsider. You're not perfect. Why expect it of other people?''

"I never lied to him," she said pointedly. "In fact, I don't think I've ever really lied at all.''

"You let him think we were romantically involved. That's lying.''

"Implying," she corrected. "The rules don't say you can't imply things.''

"I'll keep that in mind. I'll be in touch." He bent and kissed her cheek gently. "Try not to brood too much.''

"I will.''

She watched him go. The house was suddenly emptier than ever, and when she heard a car door slam minutes later, the whole world seemed that way. She peered through the curtains just in time to watch Todd and Cherry go down the driveway for the last time. The house they'd occupied was closed up and dark, like the cold space under her own heart.

Chapter 10

Life became boring and tedious without Todd and Cherry, but the ranch prospered. Jane was a natural organizer. She discovered talents she hadn't ever realized she possessed, because her father had always taken care of the business end of the ranch. Now, she called breeders, made contacts, put ads in horse magazines and newspapers, faxed messages back and forth on sales and hired people to create sales catalogs for her. It was becoming second nature to handle things. Even Tim stood in awe of her.

The clothes licensing was also moving right along. The first of the television commercials had aired, and she was told that sales had shot up overnight. The commercials helped get her name in front of a larger segment of the public and helped in the stud operation. She was suddenly a household word. Despite the fact that she didn't like looking at herself on television and in print media ads, she had to admit that it was getting business.

But it was a lonely sort of life. She couldn't ride, although she'd tried once and ended up in bed for several days with a stiff and painful back. She could keep books, though, by using Todd's figures and backtracking to see how he'd arrived at them. While she was by no means his equal, she had a good head for figures and she picked up what was necessary very quickly. Life was good, but it was a lonely life. She wondered if Todd was glad to be gone out of her life.

In fact, some of Todd's employees wished that he would go out of their lives! Since his return to Victoria, nothing had been done right in any department he visited. The desks in the secretarial pool were sloppy. The new products division wasn't designing anything he liked. Furthermore, people weren't taking proper care of their floppy disks—he found one lying next to a cup of coffee on a desk. The marketing department wasn't out in the field enough selling new programs. And even Todd's secretary, the highly prized Miss Emory, was admonished about the state of her filing system when he went looking for a file and couldn't find it where he thought it should be.

It was no better at home. Cherry came in for criticism about the clothes she chose to wear to begin the next school year, her lack of attention to educational programming, and the certainty that she would end up in prison because she watched episodes of a popular adult cartoon on a music network. In fact, the first time he saw an episode of the cartoon, he called the cable company and had the channel that carried it taken out of his cable package.

Cherry was willing to go along with the understandable reaction—after all there was a generation gap. But when he canceled Cherry's horsemanship magazine after it featured an article on Jane, she felt that he was carrying things a bit too far.

"Dad," she ventured the week of the Victoria rodeo in

which she was to compete, "don't you think you're getting just a little loopy lately?"

He glared at her over the top of his *Wall Street Journal.* "Loopy?"

"Overreacting. You know—canceling stuff." She cleared her throat at the unblinking glower she received. "Honestly, Dad, Miss Emory used a word I'll bet she never even thought until this week, after you grumbled about a letter she typed. And that's nothing to what Chris said when you threw his new computer program at him."

He put down the newspaper. "Is it my fault that people around me have suddenly forgotten how to do anything?" he asked curtly. "I have every right to expect good work from my employees. And you know why I canceled that garbage on television, not to mention that magazine..."

"Jane was in the magazine in two places," she said. "In a feature article, with color photos, and in a full-page ad. Didn't she look great?"

He averted his eyes. "I didn't notice."

"Really?" she asked. "Then why did you have the magazine open on your desk, where the photo was?"

He flapped the pages of his financial paper noisily. "Don't you have homework to do?"

"Dad, school hasn't started back yet."

He frowned. "Hasn't it?"

She got up out of her chair. "You could call her, you know."

"Call her!" He threw the paper down. His gray eyes flashed fire. "Call her, hell! She wouldn't even listen! She gave me all this *toro excretio* about different worlds and how...what are you laughing at?"

"*Toro excretio?*" she emphasized, giggling as she realized what the slang meant.

"I heard it from the wife of a concrete magnate," he said.

"We sat on a committee together. Best description I ever heard. Anyway, don't change the subject."

"You could have tried to change Jane's mind."

"What would be the point?" he muttered. "She wanted to get married, until she found out who I was."

Cherry smiled. "That sounds nice. She'd certainly look lovely in high fashion, and I can't think of anyone who'd make a better stepmother."

"You've got a mother," he said harshly.

"We don't speak, haven't you noticed?" she asked coldly. "She hurt Jane."

He avoided her gaze. "Yes. Don't think I didn't give her my two cents' worth as well about that, but she's pregnant, I understand. She was emotional when she carried you."

"Maybe a new baby will make her happier."

"Ha!"

"Well, it will keep her occupied," Cherry continued. "What about Jane?"

"She's going to marry the cowboy doctor from hell and have little doctors, I guess," he muttered.

Cherry grinned. "Fat chance, when she's crazy about you. You're crazy about her, too. You just won't admit it. You'd rather roar around up here and drive everybody who works for you to using strong language or getting drunk on weekends."

"They don't do that!"

"Chris did, after you threw his program at him," Cherry informed him. "And he said that he was going to move out to California and help develop a virtual reality program for disgruntled employees so that they could turn their bosses into mud puddles and drop rocks in them."

"Vicious boy." He sighed. "I guess I'll have to give him a raise. God knows, he'd set virtual reality back twenty years."

She laughed. "And what about Jane?"

"Stop asking me that!"

"I'll bet she cries herself to sleep every night, thinking she's not good enough for you."

His face went very still. "What?"

"Well, that's what she thought. When Mom told her you were the head of a company and filthy rich, she went as white as a sheet. Mom made her feel bad about being a rancher and not reading intellectual magazines and not being upper crust."

"How dare she!" Todd said icily. "Jane's every bit as upper crust as your mother is!"

"Nobody told Jane that. She has a very low self-image."

"Stop talking like a psychologist."

"Merry's going to be one. She says I have a very good self-image."

"Nice of her."

"Anyway, Jane only has a high school education…"

"So do I, for God's sake!"

"…and she doesn't feel comfortable around high society people…"

"You know how I hate parties," he muttered.

"…and she thought you'd probably not want to have somebody like her in your life in a serious way."

"Of all the harebrained, idiotic, half-baked ideas! She's beautiful, doesn't she know that? Beautiful and kind and warm and loving." His voice grew husky with memory, and his body tingled with sweet memories. "She's everything a woman should be."

"The doctor sure thinks so," Cherry said with a calculating glance. "In fact, it wouldn't surprise me one bit if she didn't marry him on the rebound. He'd be over the moon. He's crazy about her."

His eyes narrowed. "She doesn't love him."

"Lots of people get married when they don't love each other. He's a good doctor. He can give her everything she wants, and they've always been good friends. I'll bet they'd make a wonderful marriage.''

''Cherry...!''

''Well, Dad, that shouldn't bother you,'' she said pointedly. ''After all, you don't want to marry her.''

''The hell I don't!''

Cherry's eyebrows shot up. ''You do?''

He hesitated, started to deny the impulsive outburst, and then settled into the chair with a heavy sigh. ''Of course I do,'' he said harshly. ''But it's too late. I wasn't honest with her at the beginning. I've made so many mistakes that I doubt she'd even talk to me now.''

''If she loves you, she would.''

''Sure,'' he scoffed. ''The minute I call her up, she'll hang up. If she knows I'm coming to the ranch, she'll leave. I didn't spend several weeks there without learning something about her reactions.''

Cherry puzzled over that. He was right. Jane would be like a whipped pup, eager to avoid any more blows.

Then she had a thought. ''The rodeo,'' she said. ''I'm going to compete in the rodeo, and Jane knows about it. Do you really think she'd miss watching me through my paces after all the time she put in on me?''

He pursed his lips, deep in thought. ''No. But she'll disguise herself.''

''Probably.''

''And she'll sit as far away as possible.''

''That, too.'' She grinned. ''You could ask Chris to sit in the audience up on the top of the stands and watch out for her.''

''Chris would sell me down the river...''

''Not if you give him that raise.''

He groaned. ''The things I don't do for you!''

''We'll all live happily ever after,'' Cherry said smugly.

"After you grovel enough to Jane and convince her that you can make her happy."

"I'm not groveling."

She grinned. "Have it your way."

"I'm not!"

She left him protesting and went over to Merry's house to watch television.

Tim and Meg had a light supper with Jane the afternoon of the Victoria rodeo. She sat there deep in thought, picking at her food, as usual, and not talking, also as usual.

"Are you going up to Victoria to watch Cherry compete?" Tim asked her.

She glowered at him. "No. *He'll* be there."

"Of course he will, he's her father."

She stabbed a piece of carrot. "I'd like to watch her. But I don't want to run into him."

"You could wear a scarf and dark glasses," Meg advised. "And a dress. You never wear dresses. He wouldn't recognize you. Especially if you sat way up in the stands. He'll be right down front where Cherry is."

Jane thought about that. Meg was right. That's exactly where he'd be. She dropped the piece of carrot into her mouth and chewed it. "I guess I could do that. There'll be a huge crowd. Anyway, I doubt if he'll even look for me."

"Well, of course he would…" Tim argued.

Meg kicked him under the table and he winced.

"I mean, of course he wouldn't," Tim amended.

Jane glanced at him and then at Meg. "Are you two up to something?"

"My goodness, no," Meg said easily and smiled. "But it would be nice to know how Cherry did in the competition. We watched her practice, day after day."

That would explain their interest. "I guess I might go up for the barrel racing, if Tim can drive me," Jane said.

"Sure I can. Meg can come, too."

"I'd love to," Meg agreed. Jane missed the relief on Meg's features that was quickly erased.

"We'd better get a move on, then," Jane said after a glance at her watch. "It will take us a little while to get there, and there's sure to be a crowd."

She pulled on a simple green-and-white cotton sundress, with sandals and a white cardigan. She put up her long blond hair and tied a scarf over it and then secured a pair of dark glasses over her eyes.

Meg walked past the door and looked in.

"Will it do?" Jane asked, turning toward her.

"It's perfect," Meg assured her, and went on down the hall.

Jane nodded at her reflection. Nobody would recognize her in this getup, she concluded.

She might not have been so confident if she'd heard Meg on the telephone in her quarters a couple of minutes later, telling Cherry every detail of Jane's disguise, as they'd already conspired.

"I feel guilty," Meg said.

"Never you mind," Cherry replied. "It's all for a good cause. Think how miserable Jane and Dad are going to be if we don't do something!"

"Jane's lost weight."

"Dad's lost weight *and* employees," Cherry murmured dryly. "If he keeps on like this, some of the people in his software development department are going to stuff him into a computer and ship him overseas. This has just got to work. I'll see you both tonight."

"Good luck, honey," Meg said with genuine affection. "We'll all be rooting for you."

"Thanks. I think I'm going to need all the help I can get.

But knowing that Jane is in the stands will do me more good than anything.''

''She'll be there. Don't you worry.''

Meg hung up and went to meet Jane in the hall. ''Goodness, you certainly do look different!'' she said.

''I feel different. Now all I have to do is sit far enough away so that nobody recognizes me.''

''Your own dad, God rest his soul, wouldn't recognize you like that,'' Meg said dryly.

''Well, hopefully Todd won't,'' Jane murmured, adjusting the scarf. ''I have no wish whatsoever to get into any more arguments with him. But I can't miss seeing Cherry ride. I hope she wins.''

''So do we,'' Tim agreed.

They drove up to Victoria in the truck. Riding was much easier for Jane since the pain in her back had eased. The damage was repairing itself and the pain only came now when she did stupid things—like trying to gallop on horseback.

It had been a bitter blow to realize that her rodeo days were over, but she was dealing with that. If only she could deal half as well with the sorrow that losing Todd had caused her. Not a day went by when she didn't long for him.

He wouldn't feel that way about her, she was certain. A man with so much wealth and status wouldn't want an ordinary rancher from south Texas. Not when he could have movie actresses or top models or high-powered business executives. Having seen Marie, so poised and capable and able to run her own business, she had some idea of the sort of woman who appealed to Todd. And Jane was not that type.

It was more than likely that Marie had told the truth: Todd had only taken the job on an impulse because he felt sorry for Jane. He'd been kind, in his way, but she didn't need his pity. The best thing she could do now was to stay out of his way and not spoil Cherry's big night.

Cherry would be the one to suffer, if they had another argument, and Jane thought the girl had been hurt enough already.

Cherry wrote to her, though, and she wrote back. It wasn't as if they'd parted in anger. But Todd complicated that tenuous friendship. Jane was fairly certain that he didn't approve of his daughter's friendship with Jane, and it was a fair bet that Marie didn't.

When they arrived at the arena the parking lot was almost full. The floodlights were silhouetted against the dark sky and the opening ceremonies had already begun.

They got their tickets and then Jane made her way very carefully to the top rung of the spectator section, leaving Meg and Tim down front. She sat apart from the other few people, but she noticed a young man giving her covert looks. If he was a masher, she mused, he had a long way to fall. He'd better keep his distance.

She settled into her seat. The light cardigan felt good, because there was a slight nip in the summer night air. She sighed and worked to keep her mind on the people in the arena. But all it really wanted to do was think about Todd. Her heart raced at the thought that he was here, somewhere, in this very place. She was close to him again, even if he didn't know it. How wonderful it felt to know that.

There was competition after competition. She sat through bareback bronc riding, steer riding, steer wrestling and calf roping. The competitors were narrowed down as man after man failed to meet the time limit. Prizes were awarded. And then, finally, the barrel-racing competition was announced and the first rider was out of the gate.

Cherry was fourth. An excited Jane sat on the edge of her seat. Part of her mourned because she would never compete again. But her heart raced, her blood surged as she watched Cherry go through her paces, watched the girl match the best time Jane had ever done. There were cheers when Cherry

rode out of the arena. Jane felt the sting of tears in her eyes
as she knew, deep inside, that nobody was going to beat
Cherry tonight. All the hard work and practice and patience
had paid off. She felt as if she were in the saddle with her
protégé. It was a wonderful feeling—the sort a parent might
have, pride in a child.

It was no surprise at all when the winner was announced,
and it was Cherry. Jane watched her accept her trophy as
flashbulbs went off, and her proud father gave her a warm
hug from the sidelines.

Todd! Jane watched him with an ache that went all the
way to her toes. She'd been in his arms, too. She knew how
it felt, but in a different way than a daughter would. She was
empty inside, an outsider looking into a warm family circle
that she could never share.

It was time to go. She got up from her seat and carefully
made her way down to the seats where she'd left Tim and
Meg, but they were nowhere in sight. Perhaps they'd gone
to congratulate Cherry, something Jane would love to have
done, but she didn't dare. Not with Todd so close.

With a sigh of pure longing, she went toward the place
where they'd left the truck, but she must have forgotten its
exact position. She couldn't seem to find it.

While she was standing among the dark vehicles, searching, there was a sound nearby and she was suddenly picked
up in hard, warm arms that felt all too familiar.

Her eyes met gray ones in a set face as she was carried
toward a waiting black Ferrari.

"Take off those damn glasses," Todd said curtly.

She fumbled them away from her wide, shocked blue eyes.
"How did you...?"

"Cherry conspired with Tim and Meg," he replied, turning toward his car.

"Where are they?"

"At the house, waiting for us." He met her eyes as he

reached the car. "They're going to have a long wait," he added sensuously. "We have some lost time to make up."

"Now, you just wait a minute," she began.

"I've waited too damn long already," he breathed as his mouth lowered onto hers and stilled every word in her mouth and every thought in her whirling brain.

She faltered, trying to decide how to save her pride.

"Give up," he whispered. "Kiss me."

"I can't... We don't... It wouldn't—" she murmured dizzily.

"You can, we do, and it *will* work," he said on a husky laugh. "We're going to get married and raise several more cowgirls and maybe even a cowboy or two."

"You don't want to marry someone like me," she said sadly.

"Yes," he told her, his loving eyes on her face. "I want to marry someone exactly like you, a woman who has a heart as beautiful as her face and body, a woman who loves me and my daughter fiercely. I want you, Jane. Now and forever."

She couldn't believe it was really happening. She looked into his eyes and sailed among the stars.

"I see dreams in your eyes," he said softly. "Marry me, and I'll make them all come true, every one."

"I'm not educated..."

"Neither am I." He kissed her hungrily before he opened the door.

"I'm not sophisticated," she persisted.

"Neither am I." He put her into the passenger seat and carefully belted her in.

"I can't stand high society parties..."

"Neither can I." He closed her door and got in beside her.

"Todd..."

He cranked the powerful engine, reversed the car, eased it out of the parking lot and headed for open country. His hand found hers after he'd shifted into the final gear, and he held on tight.

"I've been lonely. Have you?" he asked.

"Lonelier than I ever knew I could be," she said, capitulating.

"I wanted to telephone you, or come to see you, but I knew you wouldn't listen. You're as proud as I am."

"Sadly, yes."

"But we'll manage to get along, most of the time. And after we argue, we'll make up."

She smiled, leaning her head on his shoulder. "Oh, yes."

"And Cherry will be the happiest girl in her class when school starts in Jacobsville."

"Are we going to live in Jacobsville?" she asked with a start.

"Of course. I haven't finished saving the ranch yet," he said dryly.

"Oh, I see. So that's it. You want my ranch, you black-hearted villain," she accused and ruined it with a giggle.

"Yes, I do," he said fervently. "Because without me, you'll end up right back in the red again. You'll forget to use purchasing orders for supplies, you'll get the figures in the wrong columns, you'll forget to keep proper receipts for taxes..."

"Actually," she said sheepishly, "I've already done all those things."

"God help me!"

"Now, now. I'm sure you'll get us in the black again in no time," she said, making a mental note to mess up her accounts before he took a look at them. "After all, you did start a computer company all by yourself."

He glowered at her. "It was easier than trying to run a ranch, all things considered. At my business, people do what I tell them to."

"I'll do what you tell me to. Some of the time," she replied.

"That's what I was afraid of."

She closed her eyes. "I'll make you like it."

He chuckled and drew her close. "Of course you will."

Halfway home, he found a small dirt track and pulled the car onto it, under some trees. He turned off the engine and turned to Jane. He held his arms out and she went into them.

Turbulent minutes later, he lifted his head. Her eyes in the dim light were sparkling with emotion like blue sapphires and she was clinging to him, trembling faintly as his lean hand smoothed softly over her bare breasts.

"We have to go home," he whispered reluctantly.

"Are you sure?" She reached up and kissed him hungrily.

He groaned, but he pulled back just a fraction of an inch. "Not really. But this isn't wise."

"Why not?"

He glanced in the rearview mirror with a rueful smile and quickly rearranged her disheveled clothing. "Because the local sheriff's department has deputies with no romance in their souls."

"How do you..." The flashing lights behind them caught her eye, and she made a shocked sound as a tall man came up to the driver's side of the car and knocked.

A resigned Todd let the window down and grinned at the unsmiling uniformed man. "I know, this is the wrong place for what we were doing. But our daughter and several other people are congregated in our living room at home, and there's no privacy anywhere!"

The uniformed man looked from Jane to Todd and made an amused sound deep in his throat. "I know what you mean. My wife and I have four kids and they never leave the house. Lot of garbage, that talk about teenagers always being on the go. All mine want to do is play video games and eat pizza."

"I know just what you mean."

"All the same," the deputy said wryly, "this really isn't..."

"The best place. I get the idea." Todd grinned again. "Okay. We'll go home."

"Rent them a movie," he suggested. "Works for my brood. You put on one of those new thrillers and they won't even know if you're still in the house."

"That's the best idea yet. Thanks!"

He smiled. "My wife and I have been married twenty-six years," he said with a chuckle. "You wouldn't believe some of the diversions we've come up with to keep them busy. Have a nice evening." He touched the brim of his hat and went back to his car.

"You let him think we were married," she accused gently.

"Why not, when we will be by the end of the week," he said warmly. "I can't wait."

She slid her hand into his when he cranked the car and started to reverse it. "Neither can I."

They were married a few days later, with Tim and Meg as witnesses and Cherry as maid of honor. It was a quiet ceremony in Jacobsville, with no one except the four of them. Afterward, they all went out to eat at Jacobsville's best restaurant and then Todd and Jane flew down to Jamaica for a very brief honeymoon before school started.

Despite their need for each other, they'd been very circumspect until the vows were spoken. But no sooner were they installed in their room overlooking the bay in their luxurious Montego Bay hotel suite when Todd picked her up and tossed her onto the king-size bed, following her down before she had time to get her breath.

"Oh, but we really should...go and look...at the ocean," she teased as he brushed lazy, sensuous kisses on her parted lips.

"Indeed we should." His lean hand smoothed down her

body, kindling sharp desires, awakening nerves. She gasped and shivered when he trespassed under the thin elastic of her briefs. "Do you want to go now?" he whispered into her mouth as his hand moved exploringly.

She moaned.

He laughed softly, moving his mouth to the soft curve of her breasts under the scoop-neck knit top. "That's what I thought."

In no time at all, they were both nude, twisting against each other in a fever of deprived need. He urgently drew her into the taut curve of his body, but even then he was tender, fitting her to him in a silence punctuated with the soft gasps of pleasure that he drew from her mouth with each glorious lunge of his body as it worked its way hungrily into hers.

He nibbled at her mouth while his hand, curved over her upper thigh, drew her insistently to meet the rhythm of his powerful body.

He lifted his head to watch her reactions from time to time, and despite the glitter of his eyes and the sharp drag of his breathing, he seemed totally in control. On the other hand, she was sobbing and shivering, clinging desperately to him as the sensations, which were still so new to her, flung her body to and fro against his in waves of hot pleasure.

She arched into him violently, and his hand contracted. "Gently," he whispered. "We have to be careful of your back."

"Gen...tly?" she groaned. "Oh, Todd...I'm...dying!" She pushed against him again, following the trail of the pleasure that had grasped her so viciously just seconds before.

"Here, then." He guided her, watching until he saw her response quicken. He smiled through his own tension as he gave her the ecstasy she pleaded for. Her eyes widened and went black with shock as she stiffened and then convulsed under his delighted gaze.

She felt the tears slide from her eyes as oblivion carried

her to heights she'd never dreamed of scaling. And then, just when she was returning to her body, she saw him laugh and then groan as he pushed against her and shuddered with his own satisfaction.

He fell heavily against her, his heartbeat shaking him, and rolled to his side with her clasped against him. One long leg wrapped around her, drawing her even closer while he worked to breathe.

"If it keeps getting better," she whispered into his throat, "I think it may kill me."

He chuckled. "Both of us."

"You laughed," she accused softly.

He lifted his damp head and looked into her eyes, smiling. "Oh, yes." He traced her mouth. "With shock and pleasure and the glory of loving and being loved while I made love. I've never felt so complete before."

She smiled shyly. "Neither have I. Even though it was good the first time."

He kissed her softly. "We'll have years and years of this, and children, and challenges to keep us fit. And I'll love you until I die," he added fervently.

She pressed closer. "I'll love you just as long!" She closed her eyes. "Even longer."

He made a contented sound and bent to kiss her soft mouth. But very quickly the tenderness grew stormy and hungry, and she rolled into his arms again, as hungry as he.

Later, lying in Todd's arms as the morning sun silvered the bed, she thought that she'd never been happier or more fulfilled in her whole life. Or more weary.

"Exhausted already?" he exclaimed when she shifted in his arms and groaned as her sore muscles protested. "I'll have to feed you more oysters!"

"I'll feed you to the oysters if you don't let me sleep," she teased, nuzzling closer. "I know we agreed that it would be nice to start our family right away, but I'll die of fatigue before we get to the first one at this rate!''

He chuckled and kissed her forehead softly. ''We'll sleep a bit longer, then. Happy?'' he murmured drowsily.

''Happier than I ever dreamed I could be.''

''And your back...is it all right?''

''It's fine. Actually, I think this is therapeutic for it.''

''All the more reason to exercise it twice a day.''

She kissed his bare shoulder. ''Later. I've had no sleep in two days. I kept thinking that your ex-wife would find some way to sabotage the ceremony.''

''That wasn't likely,'' he said with a weary grin. ''Cherry had made several threats. I think she's going to be a very formidable surgeon when she gets out of medical school. Anyone who can buffalo Marie shouldn't have any trouble with hospital staff.''

Jane smiled. ''She and her mother do get along better now, at least.''

''Oh, Marie learned her lesson the hard way. If she isn't nice to you, she'll lose her daughter. That's the one thing that made her apologize to you, and it's kept her pleasant.'' He stretched lazily. ''She even offered to redecorate the ranch house for you free after she has the baby.''

''I'll think about that.''

''I had a feeling that's what you'd say. She means well.''

''I know. I love you.''

He smiled. ''I love you.''

He drew her close and pulled the sheet up over them. In the distance, the crash of the surf was like a watery serenade. Jane closed her eyes and turned her face into Todd's chest. And her dreams were sweet.

* * * * *

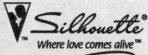